D0191938

the dark

THE GUARDIANS OF TIME TRILOGY

by

Marianne Curley

the named

the dark

the key

BOOK TWO IN THE GUARDIANS OF TIME TRILOGY

the dark

marianne
curley

BLOOMSBURY

Copyright © 2003 by Marianne Curley
First published by Bloomsbury Publishing 2003
This edition published 2005

All rights reserved. No part of this book may be used or reproduced
in any manner whatsoever without written permission from the publisher,
except in the case of brief quotations embodied in critical articles or reviews.

Published by Bloomsbury Publishing, New York, London, and Berlin
Distributed to the trade by Holtzbrinck Publishers

Library of Congress Cataloging-in-Publication Data
Curley, Marianne.
The dark / by Marianne Curley.
p. cm.
Series: Guardians of time; 2.
Summary: When their 600-year-old mentor Arkarian is captured
by the evil Marduke and banished to the underworld, sixteen-year-old
Ethan and his apprentice Isabel risk everything to save him.
ISBN-10: 1-58234-853-7 • ISBN-13: 978-1-58234-853-7 (hardcover)
ISBN-10: 1-58234-664-X • ISBN-13: 978-1-58234-664-9 (paperback)
[1. Space and time—Fiction. 2. Fantasy.] I. Title.
PZ7.C9295 Dar 2003   [Fic]—dc21   2002028335

Printed in the U.S.A.
3 5 7 9 10 8 6 4

Bloomsbury Publishing, Children's Books, U.S.A.
175 Fifth Avenue, New York, NY 10010

All papers used by Bloomsbury Publishing are natural, recyclable products
made from wood grown in well-managed forests. The manufacturing processes
conform to the environmental regulations of the country of origin.

Dedicated to the memory of the late Tony Williams,
my agent for six years,
who never stopped believing in me

Before the world can be free
A bloom of murdered innocence shall be seen
In the woods above the ancient city of Veridian
Where nine identities shall be revealed

It will come to pass that a king shall rule
But not before a leader pure of heart awakens
And an ageless warrior with an ancient soul
Shall guide with grace and providence

Beware, nine shall see a traitor come and go
From whence a long and bitter war will follow
And the Named shall join in unity
Yet suspicion will cause disharmony

A jester shall protect, a doubter cast a shadow
And a brave young warrior will lose his heart to death
Yet none shall be victorious until a lost warrior returns
And the fearless one emerges from a journey led by light and strength

Take heed, two last warriors shall cause grief as much as good
From the midst of suspicion one shall come forth
The other seeded of evil
Yet one shall be victorious while the other victorious in death

Prologue

She screams. And her scream is heard from one end of the universe to the other. The words, 'They will suffer,' are wrenched from between purple lips. Lathenia, the Goddess of Chaos, stares through her sphere to the past. A sphere she uses to create enough chaos to alter the present and produce a future that will have the world at her feet.

As she watches, a young soldier of the Guard pierces her lover's throat with his dagger for the second time. She screams again. How can her soldiers stand by and allow the only man she has ever loved to die? *'How!'*

Lathenia claws at the crystal with unnaturally-long fingers, leaving permanent indents. Finally, her body shudders, in time with her love's last breath.

Silence fills the chamber. In slow motion her head lifts and scours the marble walls. Her silver eyes flash the colour of fire. *'They will suffer!'*

A shrunken man, elderly, with eyes that have seen far, and for too long, approaches carefully from behind. 'Your Highness, might I have a word?'

Lathenia turns. Even in the midst of grief, her ethereal

beauty cannot be concealed. 'What is it, Keziah? Can't you see what's happening down there? They have killed him. Such a cunning ploy, to tempt him with the image of his own daughter! It is Arkarian's plot. He is the mastermind of everything they do. He has tormented me for six hundred years too long!'

Keziah has seen his mistress angry before – many times – but this ... this seeming loss of control is new to him. He shivers. Grief and passion make a volatile mix.

'Tell me, Keziah, did Marduke not worship me? Why should the image of his daughter, a child he hasn't seen for twelve years, distract him? It was a trick! What caused his blindness?' Her eyes lower and she mutters, 'Perhaps he still loved the woman who bore her.'

Keziah shrugs and tilts his head, snow-white hair drapes across one elevated, bony shoulder. 'I know not, Highness, but now is not the time to doubt Marduke's loyalty. He proved many times in the twelve years that he was your most adoring servant. You must return his mortal body, and do it quickly. Remember, he is in the past.'

She nods. Red hair, like silk woven straight from a caterpillar's cocoon, drifts across her flawless. skin. As she straightens to her full height, towering almost half a body length over Keziah's ageing limbs, her fingers clench into tight fists. Returning to the sphere, she summons Marduke.

Even before his lifeless body completely forms before her, the Goddess moves to the crystal table and throws herself across his massive chest. Blood, still oozing from the knife wound to his throat, touches her hand. She wails, her grief a tangible entity in the circular chamber.

Once again Keziah approaches, and having known the

Goddess his entire lifetime, a mere fraction of hers, he timidly touches her shoulder.

'What is it!'

Keziah clears his dry and withered throat, 'The others, Highness.'

Lathenia pierces him with blazing eyes. Keziah's heart misses two beats in a row. 'The injured, Mistress. We can't let them die in the past, for they could all be healed in our chambers and be of use to you again. They are your soldiers and loyal to the cause.'

She nods, and Keziah's lungs exhale. Returning to the sphere, she waves her hand over the crystal. The room fills with the sound of moaning, the heat of mortal flesh, the scent of sweat and blood as the Goddess's soldiers materialise. One of them, a young man, approaches. He stops mid stride at the look in his Goddess's eyes. It is a look of such distress, he feels that to continue holding her gaze would be a physical intrusion. He bows his head deeply, 'Your Highness, what should we do with the injured?'

She flicks her hand at him. 'Have you no sense, Bastian? Organise those still standing to carry the injured to the healing chambers.'

Bastian flicks an uncomfortable glance at the two lifeless bodies amongst them. 'What about the dead?' he whispers.

'Leave them. Their souls are already wandering the middle realm.'

Bastian cringes at the thought. Though he knows little of this place called the middle realm, he knows it is another world entirely. Once, he thought there was only earth. He has learned a lot in his time with the Order. More than he could ever have learned if he had chosen to remain unenlightened.

As Bastian organises the removal of the injured, he realises one soldier is missing.

'She has turned traitor.' Lathenia verbalises his suspicions. 'She will die.'

'I'll find her.'

'Forget her for now. The Guard will protect her and keep her hidden for a long time. But your chance will come.'

With the last of the injured removed, Bastian makes for the door, but Lathenia calls him back. 'Stay, I must talk with you.'

Bastian inhales a deep breath, his hands clasped tightly before him. They're shaking and he doesn't want his Goddess to see this weakness. He has never seen her so distraught before. Losing Marduke appears to have destabilised her. Although familiar with her usual violent temper, her added distress brings a stab of terror to his heart. But what could he have done to stop that blade from repeatedly slashing the master's throat? It was as ugly as it was incisive. It was also skilful. 'Yes, Highness?'

'Tell me what happened.'

Green eyes widen for an instant, then flick briefly around the smooth white walls, and he swallows. Surely she must already know, having seen everything through her sphere, or why would Marduke's body be lying before her now on that narrow crystal table?

At his hesitation Lathenia screams her words from across the room, 'Tell me how the best of my soldiers can be defeated by so few of theirs! Tell me, Bastian, the name of the one who's hand held the lethal dagger!'

'He ... he appeared young, Highness.'

'You are forgetting that while in the past, all are disguised.'

'Yes, but … his eyes. There was something about his eyes. And well, as you know, eyes don't change—'

She cuts him off with a wave of her hand. Of course she knows how it works. Wasn't she the one who started it all? Conceived first, she should have been born first! Sharing the womb with Lorian had been difficult from the start. He continually manipulated her position until her life-cord became wrapped around her neck. But even this inconvenience couldn't stop her from claiming her rightful first position. Except Lorian shoved her to the rear at the very moment of birth, forcing his way past her into the loving arms of a very proud father. So she'd had to find a way to overcome the obstacle of being born second. She spent centuries figuring out a way to cause enough chaos to disrupt her brother's ministrations. She learned that chaos gave her power. She found it by tampering with the past. And the stronger she became, the more she understood anything was possible, including total domination of all the worlds.

She started gathering an army of similar-minded followers, and built a time-shift labyrinth with bricks that could not be seen by human eyes. She called her army the Order. Others called it the Order of Chaos. But as her powers surged, so did that of her opponents. Assembling a Tribunal with Lorian at its head, they formed a guard against her. Whenever her soldiers used the labyrinth to venture into the past, so did the soldiers of the Guard, causing her to fail many times. Needing a sanctuary that could be safe from both mortal and immortal hands, she started constructing a city. But Lorian revealed hidden powers to usurp her. He stole her ideas, her designs. The construction became the Citadel. Today, her soldiers only use the adjoining labyrinth, where time travellers from both alliances are endowed with the special knowledge needed before venturing on their journeys. Lorian controls the Citadel, but she wants it back! And this time she will fortify it so that no one, not even her power-hungry brother, will steal it from her. And at last she will rule over all!

Lathenia's eyes linger on Bastian. She remembers how he came to be a part of her Order – a lonely child, living in poverty with parents constantly feuding. How he wanted to scream at *them* for a change, instead of cowering beneath his makeshift bed or inside a narrow closet with his hands thrust tightly over both ears. Why couldn't he have a home like the other children at school? Why couldn't his parents stop screaming at each other? Why did they both drink so much? But most of all he wanted to control his world, and he wanted the pleasures that he sensed the world could give him.

He also had power. So she waited and watched. The day he ran off into the woods, tears of pain and hurt and frustration streaming down his face, she found him. It was his eighth birthday, the day his parents decided to separate. She offered him everything he dreamed of. And he accepted greedily. She gave him a new name and taught him many skills. And while he continued to live with his father, the man remained a drunkard and oblivious to his son's otherworldly life. And her victory was sweet, for here was one soldier her brother would not get his hands on.

As her thoughts return to the present, she notices Bastian's hands shaking, and wonders if she made a mistake. But no, he has been true to the Order from the day of his

Initiation, eight years ago. It is why he is so highly ranked among her elite. But today … *today,* he let her down. Without any warning she slaps his face. The force of it sends Bastian to the floor. 'You should have done more!'

He gets up. 'There was nothing—'

'There is never nothing—!'

Bastian thinks quickly. He glimpses Keziah. 'I think there was a wizard amongst them.'

This suggestion seizes her attention. 'What did you say?'

'A wizard, your Highness.'

'Explain.'

'The boy worked some sort of magic. He created an image of a girl. It distracted—'

She cuts him off with a wave of her hand, but her eyes narrow as she contemplates Bastian's theory. She soon dismisses it with a shake of her head. 'The closest the Guard have to a wizard today is a man called Arkarian. Watch out for him, Bastian, for he is their jewel. Without him, they are nothing. And while he is highly skilled, even *he* cannot perform magic. Keziah is the last of a dying breed. There was another who could perform magic once, but, threatened, Lorian disposed of him.'

'How will I know this "jewel", Highness?'

One finely arched eyebrow lifts. 'You will know Arkarian by his blue hair and violet eyes. Both are impossible to miss in the mortal world, should he have reason to surface. He lives in the Citadel now, but his working chambers are somewhere around Veridian.'

'What would you have me do to him when I find him?'

She laughs, a mocking sound, causing Bastian's hands

to start shaking again. 'Do you think Arkarian will come knocking on your door? He has lived for six hundred years and gained many skills in that time, so do not underestimate his abilities. And do not be fooled by the number of years he has lived. He stopped ageing when he turned eighteen. Know this, Bastian, time has not affected Arkarian in any way except to change the colour of his hair and eyes. Even if he did reveal himself to you, you would fail miserably, just as you failed to save—' She stops abruptly, caught by an idea that lifts her spirits as a plan for retaliation begins to form. 'Wait.' She stares at Bastian with the directness that makes his eyes flutter to the side. 'Perhaps you *can* be of use, after all your miserable mistakes today.'

He bows his head deeply. 'I'm at your mercy, Highness. Tell me what to do.'

She looks directly into the boy's eyes: his whole body shudders. 'Without revealing your allegiance, I want you to bring me the identity of one of the Named.'

'The *Named*, Highness?'

'Yes, and don't look at me so blankly. The Named are the select group of nine members of the Guard. The elite branch of the Guardians of Time. An army originally formed to protect the earth from … well, *me*.' She gives a mocking laugh. 'The Named, according to the Prophecy, are the soldiers who will go into battle against me. In the meantime it is their task to protect Veridian. One day they will have a king, but for now they have Arkarian.'

Lathenia gives Bastian a thoughtful look. 'There are many branches of the Guardians of Time, each one headed by a member of their Tribunal. It is these Tribunal members who govern a sector of the earth using

16

their own soldiers. Combined, they work as a council. But they are fools, Bastian, for Lorian makes all the decisions.'

He nods, understanding, and she says, 'Why do you think so many of my soldiers and theirs come from that small town called Angel Falls?'

Bastian's head shakes. 'I don't know.'

'Because Angel Falls shelters Veridian, and Veridian is everything! It has power, Bastian. It was for a time the most powerful city in all the worlds, and so far advanced your earthly technology comes nowhere near it, not even today.'

With difficulty Bastian meets his Goddess's eyes. 'Where is this city? Can I see it?'

'The city is under the lake at Angel Falls. It is one more thing that Lorian keeps hidden from me. But one day – soon – I will find the way in, and its secrets will be mine.'

'Is there something in particular you want from this city, Highness?'

Lathenia's eyes flash at the young man. He is more astute than she realised. Perhaps his other power is finally starting to reveal itself. 'There is a key, in the shape of an eight-sided pyramid. If you find it, Bastian, I would make you a king, and your realm would be immense. But heed my warning – the key has the power to kill any mortal that touches it.'

Bastian swallows deeply, his mind focused on the concept of becoming royalty. The idea of his own realm sparks visions of grandeur. And now that Marduke is … well, gone, maybe his own talents will be more noticed. 'It must be an important key, Highness. Does it open a chest of treasures?'

She scoffs at the boy's naivety. 'Perhaps one could call it that. But it's not the sort of treasure that will bring you wealth, Bastian. It is a treasury of weapons. The finest and most powerful to be found in all the worlds.'

In the ensuing silence Lathenia's eyes wander back across the room to the still body of her loved one. Bastian watches as the Goddess's hand, with her unusual fingers, splays across the blood-stained chest of the Order's highest-ranked master. 'You must forget the key for now, Bastian. And forget Arkarian too. I will deal with him. You don't have the power. Not yet at least. And he is much more highly skilled than the average Guard. I have a plan for him that I will spin into action very soon. But I do have a mission for you. An important one.'

'I am nothing but your humble servant.'

'Bring me the name of the one who's hand held the dagger that stole Marduke's breath.' Spinning her head, Lathenia pins Bastian with ice-cold eyes, 'He may even attend your earthly school! Find him! Do you understand, Bastian?'

Bastian nods and takes a deep breath. 'Yes, Highness. I am to bring you the name of Marduke's murderer.'

Somewhat comforted by the very thought of revenge, Lathenia's attention returns to Marduke's slain body before her. A wave of grief grips her as she gently runs her fingers over the disfigured half of his face, the empty eye socket, the vacant side of his mouth, old scars from a previous battle with one of the Named. She kisses the cavities softly. 'The world will pay for this death. They will feel my grief. They will see my rage.'

'And so they should, Highness,' Keziah makes himself known once more.

She stares at the shrunken old man, seeing he has

more to say.

'But perhaps, Mistress, for a small price …' He makes a money motion with the fingers of his left hand, 'something can be done to ease your pain.'

Her shoulders lift, her chin rises. 'Speak, Keziah. For your life it had better be worth the words that flow from your shrivelled lips.'

He coughs into his cupped hand, his chest rattling and whistling. Catching his breath again he says, 'If you are prepared to make a journey in search of your beloved's soul—'

'I would do anything to save him. Explain yourself. And quickly, my patience is sorely tested this day.'

'The middle realm, Highness. The place Marduke's soul wanders, looking for a white bridge that will lead him to his final destiny.'

'Of course! He died within a mortal body while still in the past! If we reach him in time, Keziah, before he crosses that bridge …' Her words drift away, but her meaning remains clear – there is a chance Marduke will live again. The very thought makes her immortal heart lurch.

'We will need your assistance to venture there, Highness. And perhaps your hounds could be of use to find him quickly.'

'I won't need my hounds to find him,' she dismisses. 'I would know him in any world.'

'There's just one more thing,' Keziah says, hesitating.

'Go on, old man! Hurry!'

'Your voice must be the one of his soul-mate, or he will not return.'

She smiles, and without answering, transports them into a grey and twisted forest, Bastian included for the experience.

With the sudden drop in temperature, Bastian shivers. 'Are you sure Marduke's soul is in this place, Keziah?'

Keziah snorts as the Goddess moves on ahead, as if she were one of her own hounds drawn to the scent of an injured rabbit. 'Do you doubt me, Bastian?' Keziah replies.

'I just don't like it here. It's all so …'

'Dull?'

'I was going to say colourless.' His eyes shift up and around. 'How far to the—' He doesn't finish his thought. Instead his eyes grow into huge orbs as they become fixed and staring. Suddenly he screams and throws both hands up to protect his face.

Keziah notices the boy's distress. 'Clear your thoughts!' he instructs him. 'Your fears will manifest into solid forms in this world.'

Slowly Bastian's hands lower. When he looks this time, the snakes are gone, and he sighs with relief.

Keziah gives Bastian a closer examination. 'You had better stay close. When we find Marduke, our return will be swift. You wouldn't want to be left behind. I doubt the Goddess will come back for *you*.'

Bastian's eyes widen and he rubs his arms to try and warm them. 'I just hope we find Marduke soon.' He pulls down a twisted silver vine blocking his path, and finds he has to run to catch up. Even ancient Keziah, with his rattling chest, is way ahead of him already.

It seems like hours and many kilometres later before they stop. Though how this is possible Bastian cannot fathom. Just up ahead he sees the broad back of a large, hunchbacked creature, but doesn't take much notice as he has seen many odd-looking creatures these past few hours. Some were terrifying, others simply piteous. Blowing on his half-frozen fingertips in an attempt to stop frost bite from setting in, Bastian tries to take in his surroundings. A broad river flows alongside him. Grey, of course. A vast valley sprawls seemingly forever beyond its shores. He suddenly wonders why they have stopped, when he hears his Goddess call out the one word he has been waiting these past hours to hear, *'Marduke!'*

The hunchbacked creature up ahead stops and slowly turns. Bastian realises with a sudden thump deep in his chest, that this creature – this *beast* – is in fact Marduke, changed beyond recognition. The hideous sight makes him step backwards, losing his balance against a grey boulder. 'Your Highness,' he hisses, attempting to regain his composure. He tries to speak again, but finds he must first moisten his lips with a tongue turned dry. 'Your Highness, are you … are you sure you wish to return … *that?*'

She doesn't answer, and Bastian watches as she gulps deep in her throat and moisture fills her eyes. He gasps softly, his heart thundering even more loudly against his rib cage. The distraught look on his Goddess's face – *the tears!* – something he has never seen on her before, never thought her capable of, shocks him.

Finally she breathes, 'They will pay dearly for this. They will pay with blood, with fear, and with many lives.'

Chapter One

Isabel

Nowhere is safe any more. Every few weeks we change training grounds. Today we're on the mountain, on an open field over the top of Arkarian's chambers. Not that you can see Arkarian's chambers, they're hidden within the mountain. There is a secret entrance that can't be seen from the outside. It opens on command – usually only Arkarian's. The Guard has to maintain a high level of secrecy, our lives are constantly in danger. And since Marduke's death, nothing is the same. He died a year ago today.

Marduke thought he could use my brother Matt as bait. His plan for revenge ended up dragging Matt into the Guard before he was ready. Marduke had already killed Ethan's sister Sera, as part of his payback plan for losing half his face in an earlier conflict with Ethan's father Shaun. It was this fight that turned Marduke from being one of the Guard's trusted members, to a traitor.

A cold shiver runs through me. It's the memory of how close we came to losing so much. My brother for one. He didn't know anything about the Guard then. Now he's a member. Well, at least he's trying to be.

Ethan is his Trainer, and I think Matt is proving to be a frustrating Apprentice.

I don't usually come up and watch Matt's sessions, unless I'm training too. But today Ethan asked me to assess Matt's progress. It's dangerous for all three of us to disappear after school together on a regular basis. Our history teacher Mr Carter, who is also one of the Named, is always warning us. 'It could attract attention,' he often says. 'You just never know who's watching.'

Our identities, though revealed to each other, have to remain concealed from any member of the Order who might be hanging around. There could be some-one at school, one of our own 'friends' for all we know. The very thought sends another wave of shivers all over me. I rub my arms to get rid of the goose bumps under my jumper. It's not snowing up here yet, but the weather is turning colder now that winter is approaching. I just wish this day would hurry up and pass. I can't seem to get rid of the creepy feeling that something's going to go wrong.

'Hey, Isabel, are you OK over there? I've got a jacket in my bag. Why don't you put it on?'

I groan softly under my breath. That's Matt of course, overly concerned as ever. When will he under-stand I'm only one year younger than him and able to look after myself? Haven't I spent most of my life prov-ing just that? 'I'm not cold!'

He gives me a long, frustrated, when-will-she-grow-up kind of look, which sets my blood boiling. I take a deep breath, reminding myself it's just the way he is. And he's not just protective of me. He takes what he perceives to be his responsibilities very seriously. Like watching over Mum, for instance. That's why he resents her boyfriend Jimmy so much, even though he's also a member of the Guard. (Mum's not, and she's never to find out.)

Maybe that's why Matt's the chosen one. Chosen by the Prophecy, that is, to be our leader. Arkarian explained it all. But I'm not so sure telling Matt was such a good idea. I wasn't shown the Prophecy until I was ready to handle it.

Ethan nudges Matt with an elbow. 'Come on, we've got a lot to get through today.'

Air hisses out between Matt's teeth and he rolls his eyes, totally frustrated. He knows that while he's picking up some good fighting techniques with all this training, it's his skills – his *powers* – that are going to be his real strengths. But so far there has been no sign of any paranormal abilities whatsoever. I know my brother like the skin on my own hands. He's been drawn into the Guard before his time – a situation that couldn't be avoided. But now here he is, unprepared, his powers nowhere in sight, even after a whole year! No wonder he feels inadequate.

Mostly I understand what he's going through. So far only one of my powers has revealed itself – that of healing. I have another one, or perhaps even two, and don't know what they are yet. But since my healing skills have been useful, I feel a certain contentment, as if I'm pulling my weight within the Guard.

Now Ethan's powers are legendary. He's the illusionist. He can move things, too, with just his mind. And luckily for him, he has a third skill, his instinctive trust in the Prophecy. Last year, as a reward for his loyalty, a Tribunal gathering in Athens saw Lorian honour him with the power of flight. I don't mean that Ethan can suddenly fly like a bird. It's an ability to transport him-self from one spot, almost instantly, to another. Even though it's been a year, Ethan hasn't quite mastered using his wings yet. The other day he transported him-self into a cow paddock, both feet firmly lodged in freshly dropped and steaming cow dung. When Matt and I got to the scene we couldn't stop laughing for at least an hour.

And to make matters worse, while Matt is physically fit, he's never been the sporty type, and hasn't a clue when it comes to self-defence. While I was into every-thing outdoorsy growing up, he was into protecting me. And now he just can't seem to slow his mind down long enough to find his central focus.

'Don't sweat it, Matt,' Ethan tries to reassure him. 'Your powers will reveal themselves when you're ready.'

Matt throws down his sword, point first into the soft, grass-covered earth. 'That's easy for you to say. Since I haven't developed any powers yet, Arkarian won't let me go on a mission. Do you know what that feels like?' He doesn't wait for Ethan to answer. 'No, you wouldn't. You've been going on missions since you were, what? Two years old?'

Ethan can't help a soft smile. He's proud of his ser-vice. But he's not going to rub it in. They have prob-lems, these two. Only since Matt became Ethan's Apprentice have they started to trust each other. But it's a slow process. I don't know if they'll ever get back the friendship they had when they were kids. It all changed when Rochelle came to our school. Matt fell in love with her on first sight. Trouble was, so did Ethan. But Rochelle chose Matt and they were together for one-and-a-half years. Ethan was pushed aside. But it turns out Rochelle was only pretending to love Matt. She worked for the Order. Marduke was her master. And it was part of his plan for revenge on Ethan's father, that Rochelle blow Matt and Ethan's friendship to pieces. She played her part well, but at the battle last year in France, she defied Marduke and saved Matt's life. Despite that, Matt can't seem to let go of his resentment. And it hasn't helped that Rochelle's been away in hiding all this time. She's not a member of the Order any more. She defected and has chosen to join the Guard. The two of them need to talk. Otherwise he's not going to move on.

'Four,' Ethan begins explaining. 'I was four when Arkarian introduced me to this other world. But I was five before I was allowed to go on any missions – a whole year.'

Matt snorts, then tries another tack to prove his point. 'Isabel went on a mission after only three weeks of training.'

'But she already had one of her powers.'

'Yeah, healing! That would hardly protect her in a dangerous situation.'

'She's also very able, physically,' Ethan adds.

Matt kind of grunts an acceptance. His eyes shift sideways to where I'm sitting on a blanket hugging my knees. 'I know Isabel's different. She's kind of ...'

Ethan looks at me too. 'A freak of nature.'

He doesn't mean it literally. He's wearing a grin from ear to ear. Once I would have misread that look as flirting. It's hard not to. Ethan and I spend a lot of time together, and well, I really like him. Have for most of my life. But Ethan's made it pretty clear he's not interested in me romantically. We're just friends. Really good friends. And I'm OK with that. There's someone else I find myself thinking about. But, well, that relationship seems to be going nowhere too.

'Yeah,' Matt says, agreeing with Ethan about me. 'Even so, she gets allocated missions.'

'But not on my own,' I sing out. It's the one thing that really bugs me. OK, other than healing, I don't have any physical powers, but how many times do I have to prove to the Tribunal I'm physically capable? Sure, I don't look strong, being small and all, but if they would just give me a chance …

'I just don't get how it's possible for anyone to be so physically driven.' I tune in to what Ethan is saying. 'Is there nothing your sister can't do to perfection, or die trying?'

I'm about to say, 'very funny', but the thought doesn't make it into words. A sudden explosion of pain rocks the inside of my head. Grabbing both sides of my face I hit the ground in front of me. I would call for help, but the pain is so intense the only sound possible is a gasping groan from deep in my throat.

'Isabel?'

I think that's Matt's voice, but something strange, something powerful, is happening inside my head. I open my eyes but only see white blinding light. It terrifies me and I shut them again. 'Oh hell!'

'Isabel!'

Matt and Ethan run to either side of me, trying to help me sit up, but the light and the pain are too strong for me to move very much. 'Something … something is wrong.'

'What is it?' Matt screams, then yells at Ethan, 'Go for help!'

Ethan puts his arms around my shoulders and starts rocking me gently. 'Can you tell us what's happening?'

'White light. Pain. Something wrong.'

'What are you doing?' Matt screams at Ethan. 'Can't you see she's in agony? What good will that do?'

'Give us a second, Matt,' he says. Then to me, 'Try to relax.'

I struggle to do as Ethan says, but the pain in my head is too intense. 'Can't.'

'Try again. Don't fight whatever it is.'

Somehow the pain eases and I sense a change. The light shifts, softening from bright white to grey, and finally an image starts to form.

'What the hell is happening?' Matt yells, sounding frantic.

'Wait,' I manage to whisper, holding my hand up to allay some of Matt's fears. 'I'm OK.'

As I sit back on my heels the images trying to form in my head become clearer. They roll in front of my eyes like a movie for a few seconds. A movie that I can both see and feel. Unconsciously I clutch at my chest. The images bring with them a disturbing sense of horror and despair.

At last they disappear, and my heart rate starts to slow. But I'm shaking all over and can't seem to stop. I look straight up to the sky. It's blue, only a few cirrus clouds forming on the horizon to the north. Nothing serious. For a second I think I see something up there, like a flash of zigzag lightning of the most amazing colour, but that's impossible. Yet the dark images I just experienced have left me with a weird sense of impending catastrophe – a catastrophe that will come from the sky!

Digging my fingers into Ethan and Matt's arms for leverage, I stagger quickly to my feet. 'We have to get out of here!'

'What?' Matt glances around with a dumbfounded expression on his face. 'What's going on with you? You scared me half to death just then.'

I drag on their arms. There's no way I can explain the feeling I have right now, or the sense of disaster that has engulfed me with the passing of those strange images. 'Just come. Quickly.' I glance at the sky again, that urgent feeling growing unbelievably stronger, an urgency to get the hell out of this vast open field. 'We have to find shelter.'

Matt straightens his shoulders and puts his hands on his hips. 'What are you talking about? A minute ago I was ready to call an ambulance, now you look as if you're about to run a marathon.'

Ethan is easier to convince. He starts thinking straight away, pointing in a northerly direction. 'There's a cave. It's only a few minutes into the woods that way.'

'What's going on?' Matt asks, not understanding and growing more frustrated by the second. 'Someone explain.'

Ethan flicks him an impatient look. 'There's no time for an explanation. Just do what we say.'

I yank on Ethan's arm, but just as I'm about to start running, a chill sweeps through me. It feels as if the blood in my veins is turning to ice. Every hair on my body suddenly stands on end, including the ones on top of my head!

'What's happening?' Ethan cries out as his hair, and Matt's too, also stands on end. 'The air is alive.' Quickly he starts collecting our things – a rug and backpacks, some mugs we were drinking out of.

I grab his arm. 'We don't have time to collect our things. We'll get them later, OK?'

He drops what he's collected and starts to run, making sure to keep Matt in front of him. But we don't get far before a sudden screeching sound makes us stop dead and stare in the direction it came – the sky overhead. Then it happens again, this time with such force we have to cover our ears. It sounds like a piece of silk ripping into a thousand strings.

'What on earth . . .?' Matt mutters, staring up at the sky.

Somewhere in my mind I know we should be running for shelter, but the sky has the three of us mesmerised. It's still blue, but in one place, almost directly overhead, something strange is happening. Something has started falling.

'Take cover!' Ethan calls out.

We hit the ground.

But whatever it is, it doesn't drop all the way. And when we dare to look up, we see something resembling a deep, dark hole in the sky.

'What could that be?' Ethan asks.

Before our eyes, the hole in the sky contracts as if sucking in a breath. Then from within it, clouds – if that's what they are – thick and black and shiny like oil fresh from the bowels of the earth, propel outwards. Again we fall to the ground, but there's no safety here, so we hurry to our feet.

Within seconds these black clouds roll across the hillside, darkening the area around us. Lightning, in amazing colours of purple, green, yellow and brilliant red, streaks across the sky, spreading its tendrils in all different directions.

Ethan shakes me, and has to scream to be heard over a sudden burst of strong wind. 'Move!'

We start running again, as fast as we can without falling over, but that cave Ethan was talking about is still far away. We're not going to make it. Thunder, like I've never heard before, shatters the ground, making us stumble over wide-opening cracks. The air thickens, and hail starts to fall. But this is no ordinary hail. Besides the fact that it's freezing cold, this hail is jagged and heavy, like large, sharply-angled rocks. And when it hits something solid, it explodes, burning a hole in its wake. It's as if the ice itself is composed of an unstable element. At least unstable in this world.

'Here!' Matt screams out. He whips his shirt off and throws it over my head. I squirm around until it covers the both of us, glancing up to see Ethan doing something similar with his own. So now I have two layers of fabric protecting me. I doubt it will have much effect, but it's worth a try. Anything would be, to protect us from this strange exploding hail.

'Look at that!' Matt calls out, keeping his head low. 'The hail's causing fires.'

'Unbelievable!' Ethan sounds stunned. 'Look at the holes in the ground.'

We keep running, leaping over the increasing number of holes. But it gets harder with every step as the sky grows even darker, so much that it would be easy to believe it were closer to midnight than four in the afternoon. As the hail and deafening thunder intensify, I notice the shirts being held over my head start turning red. The guys are using their arms to protect me! They're covering me, while taking most of the hits from the hail themselves. I scream and tug at their shirts, trying to find their arms. 'Pull them down! Stop, you idiots! I can look after myself!' They ignore me and continue to hold their arms purposefully out of reach.

Up ahead the tree-line draws closer, and the prospect of finding shelter under the canopy of the forest has us push our weary legs to their physical limits. But just as we get there a streak of purple lightning screeches over our heads, striking the tree directly before us. The power of the hit tosses us metres into the air. The three of us scramble around on all fours, momentarily disoriented. And if the other two are like me, dazed and deafened as well. Somehow we crawl to the forest edge, skirting around the tree, now nothing more than cracked and burning timber. Slowly the ringing in my ear decreases and my hearing returns.

Once inside the canopy of the forest the hail eases, but the storm intensifies, ripping trees from their roots and overturning boulders that twenty-ton cranes would have trouble shifting. It feels as if this storm has a purpose, and that purpose is to gobble us up!

'Here!' Ethan yanks on my arm. 'This way, I think.'

I see where he's heading, even though he can't see it yet himself. It's so dark in here, both Ethan and Matt would only be able to see a few feet in front of them. But thanks to my skill of sight, a gift from Lady Arabella last year at my Initiation in Athens, I can see much further. I take over the lead, and in a matter of minutes find shelter beneath an overhanging ledge forming the entrance to Ethan's cave.

At last the three of us try to catch our breath. Ethan and Matt both collapse in a huddle on the rocky floor.

Hail has left horrid cuts on their upper bodies, faces and arms and heads. They're both bleeding from the wounds, but their burns are worse. And the way Ethan is holding his head, he could even have a mild concussion.

I try to get my breathing back to normal quickly and start working on healing them straight away. I take Ethan's arm, but he pushes me away. 'Do Matt first.'

Matt protests, but I snap at him, 'You're only making Ethan wait longer by arguing, so shut up, Matt, and let me do my work.'

It seems to take for ever, the stench of their burning flesh overwhelming me for a minute so that I find it difficult to start visualising what needs to be done. I force myself to concentrate. Finally they're both healed and the three of us sit under the protective rocky ledge staring out at the strange storm that's now settled into a heavy rain depression. Drenched to the bone, we huddle together for warmth. The temperature has fallen to somewhere near freezing point.

'What the hell was that?' Matt asks.

I feel Ethan's shoulders lift, unable to answer. Slowly he turns his head in my direction, his eyebrows rising. I can almost see his thoughts ticking over. He's remembering the strange phenomenon I experienced earlier, giving me a warning of what was to come. He's figuring it out, thinking I had some sort of 'vision'. But I'm not sure he's on the right path. I'm also not sure I want to hear his theory. My mind's in a mess right now, a headache beginning to take shape.

If I did receive some sort of 'vision' or warning, who's to say it will happen again? It was hardly a warning at all really. That storm erupted too quickly. It

33

would be a useless skill to have in that sense.

'Isabel? You got any ideas?' Ethan's hand does a wide sweep of the devastation surrounding us, and I notice a slight tremor he can't conceal. 'Is this what you saw? This ... this hurricane?'

But how can I tell him this storm was not exactly what I saw, but more the tail end of what I *felt*? What I saw is unexplainable. A place of darkness, pain and suffering, where fear and despair lock around your heart like a cage from which there is no escape.

I shudder suddenly and Matt tries to warm my arms with his hands. 'I'm OK!' I say these words with more force than I mean. Instantly I'm regretful and start to say so, but he gets up and moves away, leaning against the edge of the cave opening.

'Isabel?' Ethan reminds me that I haven't answered his question.

I keep my voice soft enough so Matt doesn't hear. 'I'm not exactly sure what I saw, Ethan. That "vision" was very strange. And this storm, it's just so unreal. I can't be certain the two are connected.'

We're silent for a moment, and the rain begins to ease. And if I'm not mistaken, patches of blue sky start breaking through where trees have been uprooted. 'Who would have thought this beautiful sunny day would have ended this way?'

'Exactly,' Ethan says. 'What I want to know is why we weren't warned.'

I gaze at him in a puzzled way. 'What are you talking about?'

'Aren't hurricanes usually tracked for days before they hit land? I heard the weather report this morning. There was no mention of a hurricane.'

'We don't get hurricanes, Ethan. These are the highlands, not the tropics. And it's not even summer!'

'So what did we get?'

My eyes drift to where Ethan has picked up a small stick and started poking at a rock between his feet. 'Look, I don't really know, but it had a lot of power. Did you ever see hail like that? Ice that ignites when it hits something solid?'

He stares at me. 'What are you saying?'

I don't want to scare Ethan or anything, but he is asking for my opinion. And I know he wouldn't want to hear a watered down version just because it isn't pleasant. He's not like that. 'There's something else.'

'Go on.'

'It felt to me as if the storm came *through* the sky. As if it came from another world.'

Chapter Two

Arkarian

They're coming to see me, and they're looking for answers. Ethan, in particular, seems anxious. Whatever he's seen has shaken him badly. He'll want an explanation. And while I've lived for six hundred years, accredited master in the hierarchy of the Guard for many of those, I certainly don't know everything, as Ethan often likes to tell me. Even the Tribunal are experiencing surprises lately with Lathenia in such a rage.

Of course Isabel is coming too. I glance down at my clothes – black pants, blue jumper. I pull the elastic out of my hair, it falls loose around my shoulders. What will Isabel think? I stop myself and take a steadying breath. What does it matter? It's not as if she will notice. She once believed herself in love with Ethan. Perhaps she still is.

'Arkarian!'

It's Ethan, calling from just inside my chamber's secret door. As usual when he's overwrought, he can't screen his thoughts from me, no matter how hard I train him. One day it could prove dangerous. There are plenty of Truthseers out there in the world and they're hardly going to announce it to anyone. Marduke was one while he lived, as well as all nine members of the Tribunal. And of course truthseeing is one of Rochelle's skills.

'Did you see that thing?' Ethan storms into my work station with Isabel trailing behind.

'Hey,' Isabel says with a small smile.

'Hello, Isabel.' Total blank. She's masking her thoughts well.

'Did you see what happened up there?' Ethan asks, trying to look calm. 'What was that? What does it mean?'

Holding out my hands, I produce three wooden stools. The same three I made as a young boy. The only items I managed to salvage from one of my childhood lodgings.

The three of us sit in a triangle, and I'm glad to see they haven't brought Matt with them. Even though he's been in training for quite a while now, he's still not comfortable in my chambers. The equipment startles him – soundless technology, centuries ahead of its time. I remember when he first peered into my 3-D holographic sphere, and realised he was looking into the past, he wanted to get out so fast, he would have gone through a wall if it wasn't made of solid rock.

Ethan's fingers close around one of my arms. 'Arkarian! What was it?'

'I'll explain what I know. But you have to tell me what you saw first.'

His hands fly into the air. 'It was incredible. Something falling. Black clouds like ... like ... nothing I've seen before.'

'There was this sound,' Isabel says.

Isabel's words, more than Ethan's, send a chill up my spine. That unusual storm this afternoon has aroused my suspicions. I have to keep assuring myself that even the Goddess, consumed with grief for this whole past year, would not want a rift to form between our mortal world and any other. 'A sound, Isabel? What sort of sound?'

'A shredding sound. Ear piercing.'

Her words make my heart beat hard and loud. 'Tell me about those first moments. Did you notice anything unusual? A strange light? A smell or odour? A glimpse of darkness?'

'Yes, yes,' Ethan replies in a rush. 'All of those things, I think.'

Isabel frowns. 'I don't remember an odour, only the smell of your skin burning with that hail, Ethan.'

'You have to believe us, Arkarian. It was ... eerie. Our hair stood on end!'

'I believe you, Ethan.' I just don't want to create panic, I add silently. Even in the depths of her despair at losing Marduke, or her anger that a member of the Guard could eliminate her highest-ranking soldier, why would Lathenia take such a risk? Has she lost control of her objectivity, even her sanity?

Ethan sits, and using his training, attempts to calm down. It's unusual seeing him like this. He's experienced a lot of strange happenings in his time with the Guard. It's usually hard to faze him.

'Where do you think that storm came from?' he asks.

Isabel is already making her own assumptions. 'That storm was unearthly, that's all I'm going to say.' She looks straight into my eyes. Suddenly my thoughts are

38

hurled into confusion and I find I have to look away. I try to think why. I know that I'm on edge. Everyone is at this time. Our spies say Lathenia is close to discovering Ethan's identity. And she knows I was the one who planned our strategy the day Marduke was killed, so she wants to take her revenge on me too. But as I don't circulate in the mortal world any more, Ethan is more at risk.

It could be because Isabel's words are so near the possible truth.

I force myself to return a steady gaze and choose the words that won't increase their fears. They have to remain calm to keep doing their good work. And while Isabel's powers still haven't completely emerged, her healing skill is unequalled in the Guard's history so far. 'Lathenia is simply in a rage at losing Marduke. It's the first anniversary of his death today. Try not to concern yourselves too much.'

Isabel says softly, 'She has a very dark rage, Arkarian.'

Ethan jumps in, 'I'll say. Isabel knows all about it. Just before the storm hit—'

She whacks him with the back of her hand. He almost falls off his stool.

So, there's something else. Something that happened before the storm hit that Isabel doesn't want me to know about. I focus on Ethan for a second, but he's trying hard to conceal his thoughts. And while he's not succeeding very well, he has managed to scramble them enough so that I can't make any sense of them. Well, if Isabel wants to keep something from me, that's her choice. I won't intrude. My only concern is that what she keeps from me has something to do with what she saw up on that ridge today. I don't want either of these two getting involved in something they can't handle.

An awkward silence follows. Ethan finds himself suddenly fascinated by each hairline crack in the rock walls, while Isabel, whose face has turned the colour of blood, studies the tips of her brown boots. I decide I'd better put them out of their misery before they both bolt for the door. I have other things to tell them, but first I have to ask, 'How is Matt's training progressing?'

The two of them glance at each other, their eyes opening wide. Isabel's shoulders lift, but not in a negative way, more a defeatist one. The look exchanged concerns me deeply. 'Ethan, explain.'

He flicks Isabel a strangely apologetic glance first. 'Matt's hopeless, Arkarian. Totally uncoordinated. Are you sure the Prophecy is talking about him? I mean, could the Tribunal have got it wrong? Maybe Matt's not the one. Maybe he's not even supposed to be a member of the Guard, let alone, you know, supposed to lead the Named.'

'Matt was *Named* before his own birth. Before yours too, Ethan,' I tell him simply.

'Well, he's not doing so well.'

'Then you'll have to work harder.'

Ethan makes a scoffing sound as if the idea is outrageous. 'I don't know what else I can do. I mean, we train every day. And he's stressing about not having any powers yet.'

To me the answer lies there. 'Ease up on trying to evolve his paranormal skills. He's probably putting too much pressure on himself. That would only cause a mental block. But keep working on his physical skills.

He'll need those to defend himself. They'll be a backup until his powers emerge and he has time to work on them.'

Ethan sees my point. 'OK, I'll try.'

Silence descends again, and I can't put it off any longer. I have to tell Isabel about her forthcoming mission. It's the moment I've been dreading. This mission has been rushed, with orders coming straight from the Tribunal, specifically from Lorian, none other than our own Immortal. Normally I wouldn't be worried about sending Isabel on a mission, especially paired up with Ethan, but this mission has come with orders that refer specifically to me.

I clear my throat a couple of times, buying myself some time. It has the opposite effect of making Ethan and Isabel stare straight at me.

'Well now, there's something I have to tell you ...'

Isabel leans forward and her aura embraces mine for a fleeting moment. It takes my breath away and I find I have to start my explanation all over again. 'It's like this you see ... the next mission is to be yours, Isabel. But the details are sketchy. I'm not the one monitoring this time period, or the portal that's starting to open as we speak.' My eyes drift to the holographic sphere, then flick away.

Ethan frowns. 'So what's the problem? When do we leave?'

'This is what I'm trying to tell you: you're not going with her, Ethan.'

Isabel's head snaps back as a smile takes form. She thinks she's figured out what I'm saying. She throws a hand into the air, her voice brimming with excitement. 'Yes! I get to do this one on my own. About time you

41

lot started trusting me.'

But she hasn't understood. I tell her quickly, 'It's not what you think. You're not going on your own.'

She slumps back on to her stool, her mouth pulling into an irritated smirk. 'Great. How can I show that I'm capable of working alone, if you don't give me the chance? I may not have powers of physical strength, but I can take care of myself. I can dispense with a soldier as easily as the other more experienced members of the Named – Shaun or Jimmy, or Mr Carter.'

'It's not that we think you can't complete a solo mission, Isabel. Quite simply, it's too dangerous to send anyone out alone at this time. Normally it would be Ethan going with you. The two of you work well together. But my orders are a directive from the Tribunal, with no explanation offered or forthcoming.'

'What are you trying to say, Arkarian?' she asks.

I don't answer for a minute, wondering why Lorian would do this to me. Finally I just spit it out, 'Isabel, *I* am going to be your partner.'

She doesn't say a word, but her mouth drops open and colour drains from her face. After a minute she collects herself and sits upright, taking a big breath.

I think about her strange reaction, trying to interpret what it means, but draw a blank.

She licks her lips. My eyes are drawn there.

She notices and swallows deeply. 'Right,' she says, her voice strangely hoarse. She coughs into her hand and my eyes fly up to hers. Her mouth moves, but words seem to escape her.

Ethan starts to laugh, breaking the tension that seems to crackle in the room. I look at him and he covers his mouth with his hand and shakes his head.

'What's with you?' Isabel snaps at him.

'Oh nothing,' he says, looking like a cat with a bowl of cream between his paws. 'So when do you two leave?'

'Tonight,' I say.

'You'd better get to bed early then, Isabel. And remember, you have to act as normal as possible, or your mother will suspect something strange is going on. And don't forget you have to be asleep for transportation to take place.'

'Why are you telling me all this? I know how it works. I've been before. Remember? A hundred times.'

'Yeah, but your brain's not working real good right now,' Ethan says.

She kicks him. Hard. Her foot connecting with his shin. It must hurt. He winces, grimacing at her.

Isabel slowly regains her composure. 'Where are ...?' She stops and starts again. 'I mean, where are we going? And ... ah, how long will we be away – *together*?'

'We go back to France, to a year somewhere around the middle of the Hundred Years War, to protect the life of a six-year-old child. And as for how long we'll be there – *together* – I really don't know.'

Chapter Three

Isabel

I'm going on a mission with Arkarian. *Arkarian!* And it could take days. Maybe months. Who knows? And all this time Arkarian and I will be together. *Together!*

As I lie in bed goose bumps break out on my arms and I pull the blanket up tightly around my shoulders. But I'm not cold really. It's just the thought of my upcoming mission, the thought of spending so much time with Arkarian. *Alone!* I remember the last time I was this excited. It was my first mission. I was with Ethan and we went to England. We were in John of Gaunt's bedroom, when suddenly Ethan kissed me. But that kiss was only an excuse to get us out of a sticky situation. Arkarian wouldn't use that tactic no matter how awkward the situation we might find ourselves in. Or would he? If the situation were desperate?

I roll on to my side. If I don't get to sleep soon I won't be going at all. Of course, my physical body won't be going anywhere. It will stay here in my bed and appear as if I'm only sleeping. The body is, after all, merely a vessel for the soul. So when I shift to the Citadel, I'll have a new one that's kind of on loan. Only my eyes will remain the same. They can't change, 'cause they're connected to the soul. The Citadel controls all this. It's a wondrous place. And most importantly, this new identity will protect me from being recognised in the past.

I close my eyes, willing them to stay that way, but can't stop the thousands of thoughts racing around inside my head.

The moon makes an appearance outside my window and I get up to close the curtains. It won't make much difference, though. Lady Arabella's gift of seeing through all forms of light still keeps me awake at night sometimes. Like tonight, when I'm finding it hard to slow down, it takes a greater effort to control the gift.

While at the window I take a deep breath, drawing in some of the cool breeze that's blowing. It's then I notice a silver flash over the mountain. It creeps me out. I shut my window and hop back into bed, hoping that strange bright flash is not the beginning of another eerie storm.

This time when I close my eyes my mind drifts towards sleep. I sigh deeply, relaxing further, and at last my body is succumbing to the peaceful state needed to make the transition. I lie in this drowsy state of half-sleep, half-wakefulness for a few moments, when images start to form inside my head, and I wonder what's going on. Am I dreaming?

I see a beautiful lake with a family of ducks wading in the shallows, surrounded by water lilies. There's a wooden deck jutting part way into this lake, with a boat moored to a pole by a looped rope. It's small and painted red with blue writing on its side. A woman is sitting on the deck to the right of this boat, her legs dangling in the water, shoulders hunched forward. Her hands are folded over each other in her lap. She's looking down at her hands as if she's holding something precious there. Even though I can't see myself in this dream, I sense that I'm walking on the deck towards this woman, every step taking me nearer to knowing her identity and discovering the secret she is guarding in her palms.

The dream intensifies. I can hear the click-clack sounds my shoes make as they strike the boards beneath my feet. For a second I think the woman hears me too. She looks to her left, but remains silent. It's enough time for me to recognise her though. She's Laura Roberts, Ethan's mother.

'Mrs Roberts?' I ask in my dream.

She doesn't respond, just appears to look through me.

'Laura? What are you doing?' I peer over her shoulder. 'What have you got there?'

I see her hands clearly, and the sight of that much blood has me gasping and stepping backwards. My own hands come up to cover my mouth as I take a closer look. Trying not to retch at the sight, I study her carefully. She is bleeding from vertical slits to her arms that stretch from her wrists to half way towards her elbows. Blood has soaked through her skirt, through the timber decking, to the water below. A long-bladed knife slips through her weakening fingers to splash softly into the lake.

I try to scream, but find myself sitting up in my dark bedroom, the dream very much still with me. I shake my head to rid myself of the image, but it doesn't disappear. It's as if there is more to this dream that I must

46

see. Gathering my thoughts, I try to reach out to Laura, but some invisible force holds me back, as if my role is to watch and not interfere. Shocked, and unable to get rid of the image of Laura Roberts attempting to kill herself, I scream out.

My scream brings Matt, with my mother behind him, bursting through my bedroom door.

'What's going on?' Mum pushes past Matt in her hurry to get to me. 'Did you have a nightmare?'

Matt comes over to the other side of my bed and switches on my bedside lamp. The room fills with light that hurts my eyes. I squint and try to cover them; that dream still causing my heart to pound like a horse at full pelt.

Mum pushes the hair off my forehead with tender stroking fingers. 'Are you OK?'

'She's all right, Mum,' Matt says. 'I'll look after her.'

Mum looks at me and I try to reassure her. 'He's right. There's nothing to worry about. It was just a dream. You can go back to bed. Really.'

She hesitates. 'Are you sure, darling? Can I make you a warm cocoa first?'

I force a smile to my face. 'No, I'm fine, really. I don't need anything.'

She finally relents. 'All right, but if you want to talk you know I'm just across the hallway.'

'I'll call out if I need you, but Mum, I'm OK.'

'Jimmy will be back soon. You can talk to him too, you know.'

Matt's jaw drops open. 'She doesn't need Jimmy. I'm here!'

'Of course you are,' Mum says. 'I didn't mean—'

I grab her hand. 'It's all right, Mum. Don't worry

about Matt. I like Jimmy. I really do. I don't mind at all that he lives here now.'

Mum smiles and looks more relaxed. And once she's sure I'm all right, she goes back to bed.

Matt makes himself comfortable in my green inflatable lounge. 'What was all that screaming about?'

'I had a bad dream. And I thought I only screamed once.'

He shrugs. 'You didn't have another of those weird visions, did you?'

As soon as he says this, my heart, which is only just starting to slow down, leaps half-way up my throat. Could it have been a *vision*? Everyone knows how depressed Laura is. She never got over losing her daughter, Sera, thirteen years ago. And didn't Ethan say something only the other day about how she isn't getting any better, even though his father's been so supportive? And that even the doctors think she should be making a recovery by now, but can't understand why she isn't?

'Oh hell!'

'What did you see?' Matt asks.

Matt's question has me shifting straight into denial. I mean, it was a *dream*, not a *vision*, like that other one when my head felt as if it was going to explode. There was none of that pain or light this time. My concern for Ethan and his mother brought it on, that's all. If I tell Ethan it will only make him more worried, and he worries like hell as it is.

'Isabel?'

But if I don't tell Ethan, and it *was* a vision ...? Maybe there was no pain 'cause I was in that relaxed state of near sleep, and wasn't in a position to fight or tense up.

'Isabel! What the hell is going on? Speak to me.'

I hold my hand up to stop Matt's questions from interrupting my thoughts. I need a couple more seconds to figure this out. The last time I experienced a vision, the reality occurred only seconds later. This notion has me scooting out of bed and stumbling through a dark hallway towards the phone.

Matt follows and switches on a light. 'When are you going to realise that you don't have to solve every problem on your own?'

I bring the phone half-way to my ear. 'What did you say?'

'You're not alone in this world, Isabel. You don't have to prove you can do everything by yourself. It's about time you realised he's not coming back.'

My mouth forms a soundless gasp. He never talks about Dad! 'You're out of line.'

'Am I? Then why do you resent my help so much?' He turns away.

'Look,' I call out. 'I didn't mean to ignore you before. My dream has nothing to do with … whatever crazy place your thoughts are right now. And just for the record, I'm used to doing things for myself. I like it that way. That's all there is to it.' I can see he doesn't believe me. 'Your idea of helping me is more like total suffocation.'

My words sting, but I don't have time for this right now. 'I have to ring Ethan, OK?'

He glances around the hallway as if searching for a clock on the wall. 'Isn't it a bit late to be making phone calls?'

I brush him away with a wave of my hand, covering the mouthpiece for a second. 'I have to make this one.'

He groans. 'Don't tell me you're still fantasising over Ethan. Were you dreaming about him again?'

Now why does he have to bring my past infatuation into the conversation? 'Go away,' I hiss at him. 'I told you I'm over Ethan.'

'Well I don't believe you,' he says, but wanders back to his room anyway.

On the seventh ring Ethan answers in a groggy voice, 'Yeah?'

'Ethan, it's me.'

'Huh? Isabel? What's up? Aren't you supposed to be sleeping so you can be transported to the Citadel?'

'Yes, but …'

He reads my silence correctly. 'Oh no, did you have a vision or something?'

'Or something is right.'

'What did you see?'

Suddenly ringing Ethan feels like a really bad idea. 'I don't know how to tell you. It probably wasn't a vision at all. It was probably just a dream, really.'

'Stop babbling, Isabel. Just tell me.'

I take a deep breath, releasing it slowly. 'I saw your mother.'

'And?'

'I think she was … Ethan, she was killing herself.'

Silence. Except for his breathing, strongly, in and out.

'Ethan? Are you OK?'

'Tell me everything you saw,' he says with words carefully spaced.

I tell him about the lake and the timber decking. I tell him about the family of ducks and the water lilies. He remains silent as I explain, just listening. But when

I mention the boat, and particularly the part about it being red in colour, he jumps at me. 'Did you see a name on the boat?'

I think hard, my eyes squinting at the memory. Then I see the words painted in blue script, obviously done by a fluent and artistic hand. 'It was called the *Lillie-Arie*, or something like that.'

He moans. My hand grips the phone tightly. 'What is it, Ethan?'

'You've just described perfectly the sanatorium Mum goes to sometimes. There's a boat there they take out on to the lake. It's called the *Lillie-Marie*.' He sucks in an audible breath, as if his body needs an added burst of oxygen to verbalise his next thoughts. 'So it had to be a vision, Isabel. It wasn't a dream. You see, Mum's booked into this place.'

'Oh no, when?'

He pauses and I can almost hear him thinking, working it out. 'A week from Friday she'll be going there for a five-day stay.'

'What are we going to do, Ethan?'

'The first step will be to stop her from going.' He sighs, a weary sound. 'After that, I'm not so sure.'

My heart goes out to him. How hard must it be to cope with a mother who is continually on the edge? And Ethan's done so for thirteen years. 'You sound exhausted.'

It's the cue he needs to unload some of what he's going through. 'If only there were something I could do that would make a difference. She's not getting any better, and well, sometimes I get tired, you know?'

I make a small acknowledging sound and he goes on, 'Isabel, this is going to sound terrible, but sometimes I think Mum's being selfish. I understand that she can't help how she is. She tries, you know. She goes to the sanatorium, and she's right into meditation and group counselling. You name it, she's given it a go. It's just, inside sometimes, I get this frantic, desperate feeling that I'm going to lose her. It scares me. It scares me to know how fragile she is. And that's when I get mad. Why can't she be like other mothers? Why can't *she* be the supportive one for a change?'

'I wish I could help.'

Ethan takes a deep breath. 'It's not that bad, really. I don't mind being strong for her, especially when she's going through a rough patch – like Sera's birthday, the anniversary of her death, Mother's Day. They're the worst. Lately there's been a string of days like that, one after another. It feels like there's a crisis every day. That's why I'm tired. And now your vision.'

'Yeah, and we've got so little time to think of a solution.' I don't want to scare Ethan any more than he is already, but I can't see how his idea to simply stop Laura from going to the sanatorium is going to work. 'If we stop your mother from going, who's to say that will be enough to stop her from doing this somewhere else?'

He's silent for a long moment. 'I don't know, Isabel. All I know is that we have exactly ten days to figure out a way to save my mother's life.'

Chapter Four

Arkarian

Isabel is late. Something is keeping her. I hope Marcus Carter hasn't run into any problems co-ordinating this mission. Even though he's worked in the Citadel for a long time (as well as teaching at the local high school), tonight he's filling in for me, and he's not used to working the equipment in my chambers. Maybe I should give him a brief visit. I could use my wings and be back here in a few minutes. It would be a relief to get out of this room. This room in particular. Why is the Citadel doing this? Choosing such a room for our first mission together?

Suddenly Isabel arrives, landing squarely on her feet, her back to me. But the room gets her attention before she notices I'm here. Of course it would.

She whistles, softly, then turns and sees me. 'Wow. This is really something.'

'Well yes, though I do find the bed a bit over the top. Don't you?'

She giggles at the heart-shaped structure covered with pink and white heart-shaped cushions. Her laughter eases the tension of being thrown together in a room that could only be described as a lovers' paradise.

'It could be a honeymoon suite at a really posh – no, tacky, hotel,' she remarks. 'Why do you think …?'

Her words drift away, while her face changes colour to a deeper shade of pink than the half dozen cushions sprinkled across the double bed. But it's plain what she's asking. I shrug my shoulders and smile. 'Hmm, who knows the mind of the Citadel, or its keepers? I have no idea.'

And I really don't. The Citadel is an enigma. Even while I live here I can still be amazed. It's as if the building has a mind of its own. I've seen the high-tech machinery that lines the walls of its central work station, but sometimes it reacts as if it is working on instinct, or emotions. Though I suspect Lorian, and of course the others that live here, may have something to do with this aspect of its functioning.

I try to switch Isabel's thoughts away from this replica of Cupid's own bedroom. 'I think we'd better get going. You're late. Did you know that?'

'Sort of,' she answers ambiguously.

In another room, this one decorated more appropriately, we find ourselves clothed in period dress fitting our destination. Isabel ends up wearing a long green gown, with flowing sleeves, belted slightly above the waist. Her hair is now black, falling in an array of wild ringlets.

I stare at her for ages, completely speechless. She notices, and her hand slips to touch the bottom few curls, twirling one round and round her finger. She twirls it so tightly I think it's about to cut off her circulation. Especially when her finger starts turning purple.

I go over and unwind it. At first she doesn't get what I'm doing and stares up at me.

'Your finger's about to drop off,' I explain.

'Oh?' she says in a voice that sounds detached. Then she looks at her fingers and gasps, 'Oh!'

She spins away from me and shakes her hand a few times. After a minute she turns back. 'Well, I guess we should be going. But … I don't know who I am yet.'

'Hold on.'

Just as I say this a sprinkling of shimmering dust comes down on top of us, filling us with the knowledge and language skills we're going to need on our journey.

'Ah, so I'm a governess.'

'Phillipa Monterey,' I confirm with a bow.

'And you, who are not quite so elegantly dressed?'

I glance down at my woollen hose and coarse over-shirt secured roughly at the waist with a plaited cord, and take my cap off to reveal a mess of light brown hair. 'It appears that I am going to be a stable hand, I believe, by the name of Gascon.'

'Well, Gascon, I'm going to miss your long blue hair. How on earth will I find you in a crowd now?'

Her humour makes me laugh, easing any lingering tension between us. Lately she's been so mysterious. I'm concerned she's keeping something from me that might affect our mission. I think I know what it is anyway. Perhaps she doesn't want to mention it yet because it frightens her. As we step into our departure room, I can't help asking, 'Has your second skill emerged, Isabel?'

She stops. 'Don't tell me Ethan's right when he says there's nothing you don't know?'

'There's a lot I don't know, such as what exactly your new power is.'

She sighs wistfully. 'I think I'm experiencing psychic visions, or something like that.'

'Are these visions of the future? Or of the past?'

She seems surprised by my questions. 'So both are possible, huh?'

'Yes. And when you've evolved this skill, you'll be surprised what you can do with it.'

'How do you mean?' she asks.

'You may be able to project your own images and issue warnings; one day, perhaps even heal.'

'Wow. Well right now I have to admit these visions are a little scary. I don't know how to control them, and they can be painful like you wouldn't believe. They hit without warning – anywhere, anytime.'

'So how many have you had?'

An opening appears in the wall before us, and as we near it, ready to leap into the past, she turns just slightly. 'I think I've had two. The first was that powerful storm only seconds before it happened. And last night I saw Ethan's mother trying to kill herself.'

She goes to leap, but I grab her arm. 'Show me.'

'What?'

'Recall the vision and don't try to block your thoughts.'

She closes her eyes and the vision unfolds for my viewing. When it is over, she leaves me with my thoughts and silently leaps.

I drop behind her on to a well-worn dirt road, outside a stone wall with high wooden gates. The time appears to be early dawn. And even while I've made many time-journeys before, I still experience a moment of intense excitement and relief, when the leap is successful.

While we straighten our clothes and gather our bearings, I can't get Isabel's graphic vision out of my mind. Ethan, my Apprentice since he was a child of four years, has seen so much in his life. Ever since his sister was murdered by Marduke, he's lived with a seriously depressed mother. While his father was unable to help, he took on the huge responsibility of caring for her. Ethan has had an uneasy life, full of fear and sadness and feelings of utter helplessness. He coped. And coped well. But he's only human. How much more can he take?

Before we go any further I lay my hand on Isabel's arm. 'All those years as Ethan's Trainer I've watched him suffer, but couldn't do anything to help.'

She glances into my face. Time and motion cease to exist.

Then she says, 'No one could, Arkarian. Does anybody know why Laura's depression has gone on for so long? Or why she isn't getting any better?'

'Losing a child, no matter how long ago, can't be easy. But the fact that Laura is getting worse, has me thinking there's something else stopping her from moving past her grief. Something that's keeping her constantly on edge.'

'Like what?'

'I don't know. It's just a theory. But what does worry me is how Ethan will cope. Does he know about your vision?' We push through the gates and make our way past several small wattle-and-daub cottages to the castle up ahead.

'He does, and he's really worried.'

'Try to reassure him, Isabel, that everything will be all right.'

'He thinks saving his mother will be as simple as stopping her from going to the sanatorium.'

Is it possible to avert a tragedy by simply stopping a person from being in the place at the time they've been seen to take their own life? 'I think we need to find the cause of Laura's continuing anxiety.'

'But how?'

'Don't worry, I'm not going to stop working on this problem until I've figured out what's wrong. I promise.'

'You have to hurry, Arkarian. There are only ten days until Laura goes to this place.'

'Yes. And a lot can happen in ten days.'

Chapter Five

Isabel

Arkarian doesn't know who this six-year-old French girl is in relation to history, or where the danger is going to come from. And he doesn't know why this girl's life is so important that the Immortal commanded Arkarian be part of this mission right at the last minute. All we know is that this child won't live past her sixteenth year. The year she falls pregnant and gives birth. Arkarian can't find anything on the child she bears either. It's as if the baby is raised by the pixies.

Well, I never did fully believe what Ethan takes as sacred — that Arkarian knows everything. And thankfully I've learned to mask my thoughts from him, even though sometimes it's a struggle. If I didn't, I would be in a fine mess. My thoughts have been anything but decent. And when our eyes meet, I swear, it's like there's no oxygen in the room. But something else is happening that I can't quite figure out. It's really weird. A seed has taken root in my stomach. A seed of fear. It's like there's a clock counting down the time we have together.

I put these thoughts aside while I concentrate on how best to protect this child. Her name is Charlotte, and she's the only daughter (the only child in fact) of a Duke and Duchess. Unfortunately, last year the Duchess passed away with a wasting disease, and now the child is lonely and depressed. She has an aunt, her mother's sister, Lady Eleanor, who greets me at the entrance to the keep. She takes a good look at me from head to toe, and then at Arkarian, who remains a little way behind me. With a tight nod, she invites me inside, shutting the door in Arkarian's face.

'What happened to your carriage? Why did you arrive on foot, with only that stable-hand for company?' she snaps.

Behind us, the Duke himself appears. He makes a sarcastic scoffing sound. From what I learned earlier, the Duke spends a lot of time at court in the King's company. Or on the battlefield leading the royal troops. And from the look Lady Eleanor gives him, I'm guessing it's not just the Duke's daughter who finds his absences lengthy.

'Why do you have to be suspicious of everyone who wears a skirt in my company?'

I have to be careful not to laugh outright at the Duke's words. Apparently I'm not the only one who's aware of Lady Eleanor's longings.

'My carriage was set upon by thieves,' I explain. 'Everything except the clothes on my back was stolen or destroyed. That stable-hand helped me find my way. His name is Gascon.'

The Duke's hand gestures towards me. 'There you are, Eleanor. Are you satisfied?'

He's bitter, but his attitude is not my concern. It's the

girl I'm here to worry about. 'When shall I meet the young lady?' I ask.

The Duke raises his eyebrows at Lady Eleanor, who runs up a nearby flight of stairs. Her departure fills the spacious hall with the most awkward silence, as the Duke stares out of a window to the courtyard beyond, content to say nothing.

'Excuse me, my lord, may I ask where I shall be staying?'

He taps his finger repeatedly on the stone ledge before him. I wonder if he's going to bother replying. Eventually he turns his head, 'No doubt Eleanor will have organised a chamber for you.' He waves dismissively at Arkarian outside. 'The boy can go to the stables. Old François will show him where he can stay.'

He looks away, discouraging further conversation. Lady Eleanor returns with the Duke's daughter and my attention quickly re-focuses. Charlotte seems small for her age, and thin, with pale skin, huge blue eyes, and a mop of blonde ringlets. I fall in love with her on sight, feeling drawn to this beautiful child with the sorrowful eyes and small down-turned mouth. I get on my knees to be at her height. 'Hello, Miss Charlotte.'

She answers me with nothing but a drooping head and silence, her thumb tucked into her mouth. She rocks on her heels and looks to the stairway.

Take it slowly, I tell myself, and try again. 'My name is Phillipa, and I'm going to be your—' I don't finish my words as my attention is seized by a series of thumping sounds coming from behind her. I look across and find myself staring straight into the eyes of a large dog, a Great Dane, easily the largest I've ever seen.

I jump up, my first instinct to run. But Charlotte calls to it excitedly, and the animal prances over, tail wagging. Charlotte then folds her body across the dog's broad back, giving it a loving embrace and muttering sweet nothings into one of its rigid, upright ears. The dog turns its massive head and begins enthusiastically licking the girl's face and arm.

'Oh for pity's sake, do something, Adrian,' Lady Eleanor moans dramatically.

The Duke drags himself from the window, takes one look at the dog and his daughter embracing, then turns his palms outwards. 'The animal makes her happy. God knows nothing else around here does.'

The Duke smiles at me sadly. 'The beast accompanies my daughter everywhere. You'll have to win him over before you get close to Charlotte.'

Minutes later Lady Eleanor shows me to my room upstairs, Charlotte and her dog trailing behind us. 'I'm sure you'll be comfortable in here, the likes of this chamber I doubt you've ever seen before.'

My eyes do a broad take of the room. It certainly is spacious and elegantly furnished, with beautiful oak panelling. Two sets of mullioned windows overlook a courtyard below, an exquisitely hand-carved desk separating them. A door leads to Charlotte's bedchamber, while a painted bench adorns the wall to the right. A king-size bed, with four posts that are fixed to the ceiling, sits on a raised platform jutting out from the opposite wall. A beautiful tapestry hangs above it. I go over for a closer look.

'Mama made it,' a little voice informs me from behind. 'She loved to stitch.'

When I turn around Lady Eleanor is walking out of

the door, leaving me alone with Charlotte. I point to the dog. 'What's his name?'

'Papa says it should be Horse.'

'Hmm, I wonder why?' I mutter beneath my breath.

Charlotte drops to her knees and gives the dog another of her trusting embraces. She rests her head on its massive chest. 'But I call him King Charles, in honour of our king. Don't you think he looks like a monarch?'

'He does indeed.' But thoughts of King Charles, or any king, soon disappear as Arkarian – or I should say, Gascon – walks in and stands by the door. He addresses me politely.

'Pardon, my lady. Lady Eleanor says it is time for your ride.' Charlotte nods happily and begins looking for her gloves and riding whip. The dog follows her like a shadow.

'What do you think we should do with him?' I whisper.

'Well, his instincts would be to protect the girl. That can't be bad.' Arkarian walks over to the dog, bends down and strokes it behind one of its pointy ears. 'He seems friendly enough.'

'The Duke says I'll need permission from him to get close to Charlotte.'

Charlotte hears and giggles, giving Arkarian a sideways glance. I introduce him as Gascon. The dog suddenly moves and, instinctively, I step back.

Arkarian laughs. 'You don't look comfortable. Is your sixth sense telling you something?' he adds in a whisper. 'Or are you just not good with animals?'

I think about this for a minute. At my Initiation last year I was endowed with many gifts from the Lords and Ladies of the Tribunal. But it was the head of the Tribunal – Lorian – who gave me the gift of enlightenment of my sixth sense. I shrug, because sometimes it's not clear whether it's my sixth sense, or simply fear. 'The only thing I'm sure of, is that I'm not good with animals with sharp teeth.'

Arkarian looks around the room. 'Is that her bedroom over there?' he says softly.

I nod and Arkarian frowns thoughtfully. 'We're going to have to take shifts watching her,' he explains, but his attention is soon drawn to King Charles, who is now sitting up with Charlotte on his back. She clasps her hands about his neck, and starts rocking backwards and forwards. Suddenly Charlotte slides off the dog's back, runs round and kisses it between its eyes, accidentally poking her finger in one of them.

'Oh sorry, Charlie,' the girl says affectionately, then gives Charlie's ears a stroke as she takes off with a giggle.

When Charlotte has finished playing with the dog, she comes over to Arkarian. Surprising me, she takes his hand without any sign of shyness. 'Will you lead my pony, Gascon?'

We go to the stableyard, where François has the pony saddled and ready. We are given instructions to take Charlotte to her favourite place – a waterfall near a bend in the river that runs through the Duke's lands. As we walk, we keep an eye out for anything that looks suspicious.

'We're going to have to be very careful,' Arkarian says softly. 'I've been talking with a few servants. Apparently there have been no new members to the household recently, or for the last few months, so the

Order hasn't made an appearance yet. And I'm starting to get the feeling they're waiting for a specific reason before showing themselves – like *our* arrival.'

'Do you think they're after *us*, and not the child?'

'If they're not after the child, then you know what this is, don't you?'

It hits me, and a shiver passes from my head straight down to my toes. *'A trap?'*

'It's possible.'

'Oh great!' Words fail me for a moment, giving my brain time to think. I drop my voice to a whisper. 'You were only switched with Ethan at the last minute. So if the Order have finally figured out who Ethan is, they're probably expecting him to be on this mission instead of you.'

'Well – '

'This is a trap to kill Ethan!'

'Look, we can't jump to conclusions. Not yet. There could be other reasons Lorian substituted me in Ethan's place. But I have to wonder why not Shaun or Marcus?'

To me the answer is easy: Lorian has a great belief in Arkarian's ability. But I don't air my thoughts. Arkarian would only deny it. While he is by far the most talented, powerful member of the Guard, he would never acknowledge it. 'So do you think Charlotte is safe after all?'

'We can't take anything for granted. Who knows the mind of an immortal?'

'Well, it's been a year since Marduke's murder. The Goddess's patience must be exhausted by now.'

'Yes, which means she may act out of character. That's why we must be prepared for anything.'

Chapter Six

Arkarian

By the end of the ride Isabel has formed a strong bond with the child. It's an easy thing to do. I feel myself doing the same. And that's something I've managed to avoid for almost six hundred years. It's just that Charlotte is well mannered and kind and so trusting. Many times she is close to tears.

After dinner with the Duke and Lady Eleanor, Charlotte insists that I must tell her another story. It's unheard of for a mere stable-hand to be invited inside, but the Duke finally agrees. I think he is relieved to see his daughter smiling again.

With King Charles beside them, Isabel and Charlotte curl up by the hearth. As Charlotte cuddles the dog, Isabel whispers, 'You know, it wouldn't hurt for her aunt to be a bit kinder. That woman doesn't come across as the loving mother type.'

I have to agree, and while I can't find much in history on Charlotte, I did discover that Lady Eleanor will one day become the mistress of this very castle, marrying the Duke and taking the title of Duchess. But I'm reluctant to let Isabel know. She would hate the thought of Lady Eleanor becoming Charlotte's step-mother. Forming attachments to those we help is strictly forbidden. This is an essential rule. It's quite easy to develop friendships, and difficulties in letting go have caused serious situations for members of the Guard before. That was the catalyst for all our problems with Marduke. Thirteen years ago he changed the past by trying to stop the woman he fell in love with from catching the plague. His partner was Ethan's father Shaun. Shaun tried to stop him. They fought and Marduke suffered severe facial injuries.

'The only reason that woman would want a child for herself would be to secure an inheritance,' Isabel concludes.

Charlotte stirs, murmuring for another story, and Isabel lets the matter drop. She strokes the girl's forehead. 'Patience, Charlotte. Here, wait.' Isabel moves around on the rug, positioning Charlotte's head in her lap. 'Is that comfortable?'

Charlotte nods, then looks up at me. 'Hurry, Gascon. You must tell me a story before I fall asleep. You have so many! And my eyes are getting heavy.'

Even with heavy eyes, it takes the telling of three long stories – myths from ancient Greece and Macedonia – before Charlotte's soulful blue eyes finally close in sleep.

Isabel continues stroking the girl's forehead. 'Should we carry her to bed?'

Through the connecting doorway, I glance into her room, and wonder what the Order have in mind regarding this child. Has the portal to this time period been opened solely to draw Ethan out? It can only open for a short period, and only ever once. No one can return to the exact time twice. Or is there a genuine threat to Charlotte's well-being? It would be a mistake to underestimate the enemy. And from what I saw earlier of the child's own bedroom – narrow windows with heavy drapes, closet doors, wardrobes and wooden chests – there are plenty of hiding places should someone suddenly appear. 'Why don't we leave Charlotte here where we can keep a close eye on her? It's warm by the fire.'

Agreeing, Isabel makes Charlotte comfortable with some pillows. King Charles nestles in beside her, his head on his paws, his eyes slowly closing.

The two of us go and sit against the foot of the four-poster bed, and after a while Isabel sighs and yawns. Without realising it, she sags against my shoulder. After this long day, she's completely exhausted. Looking across at Charlotte, she comments softly, 'She looks so innocent.'

'As only a child can.'

'Why would anyone want to harm her?' She shivers suddenly.

Instinctively, and against my better judgement, I pull her closer to me. She rests her head on my shoulder as if it is the most natural thing in all the worlds to do.

But it's a mistake. I become aware of her heart beating, her lungs expanding with every breath, her skin beneath my touch.

She moves, and her head slides to my chest. Shifting into sleep, she wraps her arm around my waist. Now I'm aware of *my* heart beating too, slowly, in sync with hers. I know I should push her away. But if my life depended on it, right now, that would be impossible.

She mumbles something; her breathing slow and

rhythmic. Unable to stop myself, I kiss the top of her head.

She shifts and wakes, quietly becoming aware of how her arm lies around my chest. Withdrawing it in jerking movements, she sucks in a deep breath, sitting up straighter. 'I must have fallen asleep.'

'Only for a minute or two.'

Her head turns to me. 'Did I miss anything?'

I recall my kiss to the top of her head, and can't help a secret smile. 'Nothing. Nothing at all.'

'Oh good. I wouldn't want to miss anything important, like maybe the Goddess herself dropping in to say hello.'

Her comment has me scoffing. 'I've lived six hundred years, and I haven't met the woman yet.'

She seems surprised.

'Lathenia only shows herself on exceptional occasions.'

A sudden sound from the hearth, a moan from King Charles, seizes our attention. The dog is waking, slowly stretching out his limbs and arching his back.

Charlotte starts to stir and reaches for her pet. But something about the dog seems strange, abnormal. Its eyes are changing, losing their animal shape. It's as if they are no longer the eyes of a dog but that of … 'Grab the girl!' I yell.

'What's wrong?' Isabel asks, sounding confused.

'I think your desire to meet the Goddess is about to come true.'

She runs to Charlotte. '*What!* No way! But how?'

'I think Lathenia has been using one of her hounds to get close to Charlotte and trick us into thinking the Order had not arrived yet. It gave her time to study us.'

'Do you think she's worked out—'

An ear-piercing squeal cuts off anything else she has to say. Grabbing Charlotte with a gentle but firm hold, Isabel pulls her to the side, turning the child's face into her skirts.

'Don't turn around, whatever you hear,' I tell her.

The sight of Charlotte's 'pet' standing on its hind paws and stretching into the air while howling as if in agonising pain, would terrify little Charlotte. Especially as the dog has started changing shape as well, right before our eyes! Its long limbs stretch out and grow longer, losing their dog form, and transforming into slender arms and legs – human ones.

Only seconds later a fully-formed woman stands before us. A woman who would stand taller than most men, with ankle-length, bright red hair and eerie silver eyes.

The Goddess of Chaos straightens her shoulders and points in my direction with one of her incredibly long fingers. 'You're not the one.'

Isabel glances at me, while still hanging on to Charlotte, who keeps trying to peep out of Isabel's skirts.

Lathenia's eyes narrow in concentration. Soon she'll figure out exactly who I am. And while it's Ethan she planned to eliminate today, she won't be too disappointed to find me here instead.

And yet how surprising to find Lathenia on this mission. Lorian must have suspected. So now I understand the reason for the late switch. In the years since my Initiation into the Guard, I've been taught the skills necessary to deal with an immortal. They can't be killed – except by another immortal – but they can be temporarily harmed, and tricked, and ultimately they could be trapped and locked away somewhere secure. Fire is Lathenia's main enemy; it's why she lives in a world of crystal, marble and ice.

So fire is what I have to focus on. I'll have to do it by using one of my skills. But Isabel and Charlotte have to be safe first. 'Get the girl downstairs.'

Isabel's eyes shift to the doorway, but this is not going to be easy. Lathenia is in the way, and Isabel doesn't know I have the skills – although untried – to deal with this immortal. She will want to stay and help. 'Phillipa, you have to get Charlotte to safety.' I try to enforce this message with my eyes.

She makes for the doorway, but Lathenia shuts it in their faces. Isabel yanks on it, but now it's stuck fast. And Charlotte is starting to whimper. 'Where's Charlie? Who is that awful woman? She's scaring me. Make her go away, Gascon.'

Isabel tells her to be calm, and all will be well. 'Trust in Gascon, my pet.'

She nods, but tears are starting, and her whimpers grow louder.

Lathenia raises her hands and I know the power these hands hold – a power so strong it can't be matched by any mortal. Her fingertips begin turning blue, and streaks of vivid light start sizzling within them, ready to dart towards me. Quickly I hold out my own hands and concentrate. Streaks of powerful current flash across the room into my open palms.

Lathenia's energy hits me and I feel my hands burn, but somehow I'm able to tolerate it. Soon my hands start glowing as her energy starts to gather in them. Concentrating hard, I split this power, thrusting half of it back at the Goddess, and half into the fireplace. Two things happen: the fire erupts with so much force the whole room glows orange and fills with intense heat; and Lathenia shrieks, a hideous, ear-piercing sound, probably from surprise rather than pain, when her own energy blasts back through her.

Collecting herself, Lathenia straightens, but her skin is charred red. I've burnt her with her own power. And now she's furious. Staring at me, she spreads one arm in a wide arc. Creaking sounds are the first indication of what she plans. My eyes shift to the furniture that's already starting to move. 'Try the door again!' I call out to Isabel.

But it doesn't budge.

The furniture starts shifting in a circular motion, picking up speed quickly.

'Hang on to anything secured to the floor or the ceiling!' I warn Isabel. 'Try the window ledge. But don't lean out too far. It's a long drop.'

Locking Charlotte between her own body and the wall, Isabel latches on to the ledge.

'Protect the child with everything you've got!'

As I say these words, Lathenia spins around on the spot, her hand raised high in the air. It becomes impossible to make out any part of her body, as she spins faster and faster. And with her spinning, the furniture takes flight. There's a bed post beside me. I give it a quick yank to see if it will hold. It seems solid enough, and I grip it with the inside corner of my elbow. I would use my hands, but they're still hot and glowing with Lathenia's energy.

Soon the furniture is moving so fast the room is a chaotic blur.

I glance at Isabel. The whirlwind has caught her

clothing. She's hanging on with only her fingers, as the forces in the room threaten to take her and the girl with them. I don't know how long she can hold on. I have to act, and do it quickly. But I'm having a hard enough time hanging on myself. And I can't see the fire through the blur of swirling furniture, which only narrowly misses us.

The whirlwind increases and Isabel screams, her body almost horizontal, with Charlotte hanging on around her waist. I have to get my bearings so that I can locate that fireplace. Then I see Lathenia slow down and stop spinning. Her face has returned to its normal, luminescent hue. She catches my eye and stares at me with a smug smile on her face. Without words I understand: she has figured out my identity.

As she stops I notice the orange glow of the fire to her right. I focus on it with everything I've been taught, drawing on the remains of her energy still pulsing in my hands. The fire erupts again, and a wave of flames sweep into the room, slowing the whirlwind. Furniture begins to drop as the winds recede, crashing to the ground and splintering into dangerous pieces. Isabel crouches with the girl buried within her skirts.

A pounding on the door can now be heard. The Duke and other voices demand to know what's going on. They want the door opened. Isabel casts me a concerned look. But a deeper concern is Lathenia, and what she might do next. I jump down and focus all my power on the fire. If I have to burn the room down to get the Goddess out of this time period, then I will take that risk.

Lathenia sees what I have in mind. One of her long fingers points into the fireplace and instantly the fire extinguishes. Then, looking satisfied, she raises her hand to me. I ignore her as best I can, and focus on the fireplace, believing that somewhere in those remains, a single spark still burns.

'You are not that good … *Arkarian!*'

Trying hard not to be distracted, I concentrate on finding that spark. I hear her laugh, a mocking sound, a gleeful sound. But it is soon cut off, as the spark I have finally found, turns into a raging fire. A fire that cannot be contained in the small fireplace. It explodes, and waves of dancing orange flames leap into the room.

She screams this time from frustration. And as the flames unfold to fill almost the entire room, she lifts above it and stares at me with flashing silver eyes. 'Don't think you've won, Arkarian. We will meet again. We will meet very soon. And the place will be of my choosing.' With these words she disappears.

I release the flames and they withdraw into the fireplace. The door bursts open and the Duke, Lady Eleanor and many servants pile into the room. At first they're beaten back by the heat and the smell of scorched furniture. But then they see the destruction in the room and can only stare.

The sound of Charlotte whimpering breaks the spell.

'What on earth is going on here?' the Duke demands.

'The lady took my dog,' Charlotte cries, and breaks into sobs.

'Um,' Isabel tries to come up with a plausible explanation. 'The dog. Well, he … he . . .'

'Yes? Get on with it!' the Duke commands.

'He slept too close to the fire,' I add, helping Isabel out.

She takes up the story. 'Yes. He was so close a spark scorched him. He went crazy, my lord. And as he ran, the flames grew larger. He tore around the room with his coat burning, spreading the flames everywhere he touched, and knocking furniture down. We tried to catch him, but it only made things worse.'

Lady Eleanor looks horrified. 'Why didn't you open the door?'

Isabel glances at the door. Beside it, scorched and turned on its side, lies a solid piece of furniture. 'The desk,' she says. 'It ended up against the back of the door. And we were so concerned with trying to contain the fire and stop the dog, that we had no time to move it out of the way.'

The Duke's eyes fall on his daughter, still crying, but unharmed. 'Well, it appears you have protected my daughter, and for that I am grateful. But what was Charlotte saying about a lady?'

'When the fire broke out, she was asleep, my lord. The "lady" she speaks of must have been in her dreams.'

'Where is the dog now?'

I glance at the open window and Isabel says, 'It leaped, my lord. Out through that window. Gascon saw it disappear into the woods.'

The Duke, appearing satisfied with our story, orders his servants to clean up the room and to take out any furniture that has been burned beyond repair. Lady Eleanor orders another room be prepared for Charlotte. 'And hurry, so that the child can quickly be put to sleep.'

Isabel finds it hard to ignore Lady Eleanor's poor choice of words. I give her a warning look and she squats down to comfort Charlotte, who is still upset over losing her beloved pet.

'I told you, Adrian, that dog was no good,' Lady Eleanor snaps at the Duke. 'You should have destroyed it the minute it turned up on our estate. I warned you it was going to be trouble.'

Charlotte's cries grow louder, and Isabel groans at Lady Eleanor's callous, unthinking words. And while I feel for Charlotte too, there is nothing Isabel or I can do about the dog. It obviously doesn't belong in this time period. Lathenia sent it for her own purposes, and now, of course, it can't return. This time portal will close as soon as Isabel and I can find a quiet space to call Marcus. We only have to call his name – loudly and with passion – and he will hear and return us to the Citadel instantly.

I tug on her arm and whisper, 'Our work is done here.'

She gives an almost imperceptible nod, then says to Lady Eleanor, 'If Charlotte's chamber is ready, I'll settle her into her bed.'

The Duke comes over and lifts Charlotte into his arms, holding her tightly. 'Thank you for your kindness towards my daughter, but I'll put Charlotte to bed myself tonight.'

Lady Eleanor comes rushing over and tugs on the Duke's elbow. 'I'll come with you. And when the child sleeps, I'll organise some mead to soothe our nerves.'

With the Duke and Lady Eleanor gone, it's not long before the servants finish removing the worst of the damaged furniture, and Isabel and I finally find ourselves alone.

'How did you do that?' she asks.

I close the door behind the last departing servant and turn around. 'Hmm?'

She makes a movement with her hands, similar to what I did when reflecting Lathenia's energy earlier. 'The hand thing.' She comes over, takes my hands in hers, then gives a little shriek. 'They're so hot! Do they hurt?'

I tug my hands out from hers. They're still a little uncomfortable, but I'm sure the feeling will soon pass. 'They're fine. Don't concern yourself.'

'I thought they were going to burst into flames, like that small fire did when you made it explode.'

She wants me to explain. 'It was just a skill I was taught to use when confronting an immortal. That's all.'

She peers at me with narrowed eyes, her curiosity thoroughly aroused. 'Really?' Her mouth twitches at one end, then the other. And while she's keeping her thoughts well screened, it's clear she's come to some fascinating conclusion about me. 'All those years ago you must have been an Apprentice. Who was your Trainer?'

For some reason Isabel makes it sound as if the answer to this question will solve the mystery about my unusual display of powers tonight. I don't want to give her information that might make her leap to any wrong conclusions. I don't know who my parents were. I was raised in many houses, by both peasants and soldiers. In some of those houses I was a slave. It wasn't until I turned eighteen, and became indentured into the Guard, that I found a form of peace. I have no last name. The only real family I have ever known is that provided by the Guard. 'Look, Charlotte is safe.

We've done our job. We really have to leave now.'

She tries to grab one of my slightly glowing hands, but I turn away.

'Not until you tell me who your Trainer was.'

'What difference does it make?'

She lifts one shoulder. 'Then why not tell me?'

'Because you'll only jump to conclusions. Crazy ones.'

'Yeah, well, why don't you let me be the judge of that?'

'We have to go, Isabel. There's so much to do when we get back.'

'I understand, but I'm not leaving until you tell me who your Trainer was.'

I groan and shake my head at her persistence. Standing with her hands on her hips, staring at me, she's not going to change her mind. That is apparent. 'All right. I was Lorian's Apprentice. Does that satisfy your curiosity?'

'Aha! I thought so.' Anyone would think this news is the most momentous she's heard in all her life. And then another thought hits her. She gets excited, like a child with a brightly coloured parcel in front of her. 'Tell me one more thing and I'll never bother you again.'

Now this I doubt, but I relent all the same. There's a feeling I can't get rid of that we have to hurry back to our time. 'This is the last question you get to ask about my past. We have to return to the Citadel now; time is passing too quickly.'

'Tell me how long.'

'I don't follow.'

'How long were you Lorian's Apprentice?'

Her question is intriguing. I honestly don't know why my apprenticeship took so long. Maybe I was just a slow student.

'Well?' she repeats.

'I don't know why you're so interested, but for what it's worth, I was Lorian's Apprentice for two hundred years.'

Chapter Seven

Isabel

Two hundred years! Arkarian was trained by the Immortal, an apprenticeship that took two hundred years! There's so much to Arkarian I don't know. So much I want to learn. Strange how the girl, Charlotte, felt drawn to him. Why? And finding out he was trained by Lorian is staggering to say the least.

And then there was that moment. That moment in his arms.

But he's right about having to return to our time quickly. It's dangerous to delay. Lathenia's warning keeps ringing in my ears. And we still have to find out how to stop Laura from taking her own life.

We shift to the Citadel and neither of us takes the landing well. We end up rolling across the floor in a room that seems to be moving. Arkarian helps me up. 'Something's wrong.'

'I feel it too. Look at this room.'

A doorway appears that has a warped look, as if it's struggling to stay open. Arkarian's eyes widen. 'Let's go!'

The doorway isn't fully formed; we have to push

through it to get out. Running down a corridor, Arkari-an leads the way down several flights of disappearing stairways.

'Where are we going?' I call out.

'To get my body back!'

A door opens to our right. It has the same warped look. We struggle through it. Once inside, Arkarian disappears. I spin around, beginning to panic, when I see him across the room. He's getting off a chair, and his blue hair and violet eyes are a welcome sight.

'We can't stay here,' he says. 'We have to get *you* back now. I don't know what's taking Marcus so long. He's controlling your transportation from my chambers, or I'd do it myself. But something must have gone wrong because you're still here. I might have to go and help him.' He sees the look on my face. 'I'll find a safe room for you first.'

'I thought all the rooms in the Citadel were safe.'

'Well they are, normally. But a "safe room" is lined with a special element. It can't be penetrated by any form.'

We look for the doorway, but there's no sign of it anywhere. 'Come on,' Arkarian mumbles at the wall, running his hands over where we first walked in. 'Open!'

I blink a few times and rub my eyes as the light in the room suddenly changes. 'Arkarian?' He's still searching for an opening and hasn't noticed. I tap his shoulder and point to the centre of the room. It's there the strangest thing is happening. All the light in the room is moving, spiralling towards this single point.

'Isabel! Quickly!' Arkarian's voice sounds desperate. He grabs my hand, gripping it tightly. Within seconds the light completely disappears. 'Whatever happens, don't let go of my hand.'

'What's going on? I can't see a thing!'

'The light's been sucked out. Marcus! Get us out of here!'

But nothing happens. Then the room is rocked by an explosion. It fills with bright blue and purple light. For a second I see Arkarian, his gentle face filled with fear, his blue hair in wild disarray as if charged by electricity. I reach out to him, but the force of the explosion has us both soaring through the air in opposite directions. My back hits a wall and I crash to the floor, banging my head very hard.

When my eyes open again, my head feels like cement, my vision blurry. But not so blurry that I can't see a giant of a man standing over me. He has hunched shoulders, so stooped, it looks as if he might drop to all fours at any moment. He's wearing a wide crimson cloak, his face hidden inside the hood. His head tilts and he grunts at me. It's an animal sound. Spittle sprays over me, and I jerk back against the wall. What the hell is going on!

The man turns from me, and with a rough voice, bellows orders across the room. My eyes follow and see an old man, stooped and very frail. But the orders are not for this strange man. Around him are four – *creatures*, unlike anything I've seen walk this earth before. At first they appear to be floating. It looks as if they have wings. One drops, and lands with a heavy thump on strangely human-looking feet.

'Enough!' the tall man screams at them. 'Hand me the key and let's be gone from this house of sickening righteousness.'

I get to my feet, looking about for Arkarian. One creature moves, and I see its wings now, awkwardly attached to its back. They flap, and hands appear from beneath them. Another shoves the first creature aside, snorting. It stumbles to the ground, and the sight of its small, round red eyes startle me.

The man in the billowing cloak grabs one of its wings with a gloved hand. 'Get up!'

As it staggers to its feet with a squawk, I get a glimpse of something on the floor. It's Arkarian! But something's wrong. He's lying in a heap and not moving. Then I see the chains at his feet and wrists secured with a lock. They're taking him somewhere. My heart leaps into my throat, especially as the old man starts throwing some sort of ash over the top of him. I take a step towards the old man to stop him but a wave of dizziness has me stumbling blindly.

'Fix the cage around him. And hurry!' the man in the crimson cloak orders.

Finding some sort of balance I stagger across the room and yank on the huge man's arm. 'What do you think you're doing? Leave him be!'

The man glares at me, and a single flash of red flares out from within his hood, as if his eyes are glowing fire. He does not answer.

I can't believe this is happening! Outrage fills me, giving me the added impetus I need. I leap up with the intention of clawing this man's eyes out, but he's so tall I end up thumping my fists into his rock-like chest. He pushes me away and I hit the floor. I get up again and ram my shoulder into his stomach.

He throws me across the room. I start to get up, and he points his hand in my direction. His fingers light up in streaks. In that same instant I'm hit by a jolt of power, like an electric current thundering through my body. I try to get up, but can't. My limbs are weak. 'Where are you taking him?'

He remains silent. As he stares at me, I try hard to glimpse inside his hood. Finally he says, 'To a place where it is midnight every day, and flowers bloom beneath a bleeding moon.'

His words have a familiar ring to them. 'Where is this place?'

He ignores my question, distracted by the walls that have started to vibrate. Alarmed, he beats the creature nearest him with the back of his hand. It squawks and flaps its wings. 'Hurry, you worthless beast.' And he asks the old man if he is finished.

'It is done,' the old man replies, bursting into a coughing fit.

The vibrating increases. It's as if the room is revolting against the happenings inside its walls. Rumbling thunder ruptures the air, while cracks appear in jagged streaks, and blinding light floods in from all directions. A deep crack opens under one of my feet. I have to leap to get over it. The man yells at his 'beasts' again. 'The Citadel has found a way to break through Keziah's enchantment. We have to leave – now!'

With these words a golden cage is wrapped around Arkarian's body and locked into place.

'Quickly!'

They're going to disappear. I can't believe this! I have to stop them. But the room is fading in and out of my vision. I force my eyes to stay open, and claw across the floor towards them. A bright flash of light blinds me momentarily. When it clears, and I can see again, every sign of the two men, the four strange helpers, and Arkarian, are gone.

Chapter Eight

Isabel

I run as fast as my legs can manage. But where to go? The Citadel is a mystery to me. On each of my visits here the corridors and stairways have been different. A room never looks the same twice. It's as if this place has a life-force of its own, always changing. Doors appear around me, opening into hundreds of different rooms; corridors lead me to stairwells that disappear beneath my feet. But after a series of these eerie connections, I find myself balanced on a moving platform with nothing under me as far as I can see. Standing still for the first time since Arkarian's abduction, I try to restore my breathing to something resembling normal, making sure I don't rock the platform in any way.

A door opens ahead invitingly and I jump into a wide hallway, which could easily be a leap into another world. Here the walls are mostly white and made of some sort of rock, like marble. And the stairwells don't disappear, but glide effortlessly instead.

I stumble into a large room that is filled with strange light and crowned by the most amazing ceiling I have ever seen. It is made of eight intricately carved panels that tower upwards to a single point. Each panel is made of etched glass or crystal or something similar in a myriad of amazing colours.

Dragging my eyes away, I move across the room towards another strong light source, a wall made entirely of clear glass. I'm a long way from the ground, at least a hundred floors. For a moment, the height makes me dizzy. But then I see that down there, in a courtyard filled with exotic flowers and shrubs, people are gathered. They look strange to me. Even their clothes are unusual. Nothing like you see on the streets in Angel Falls, that's for sure. All but a few of these people are standing around in small groups, some pointing in different directions, others shaking their heads, several crying in open distress. The sight of them is unsettling. Who are they? Why are they so distressed? Do they know what's happened to Arkarian?

If only I could find a way down to that courtyard, surely someone there will be able to help me.

I spin around, my movements frantic, as this sense of urgency evolves into sheer panic. I start to run, opening doors, trying different directions. I'm reluctant to admit, even to myself, that I'm totally lost.

Then I run straight into a man who grabs my upper arms and gives me a strong shake. 'Stand still!' he bellows in a familiar voice.

It's Mr Carter. He's my history teacher at school, and he's also the one who co-ordinates our missions. But this time, in place of Arkarian, he was supposed to be organising our return. I always thought that was done from Arkarian's chambers, but Mr Carter is here, in the

Citadel, right in front of me.

Mr Carter doesn't give me a second to ask the questions going round in my head, or even to explain what I'm doing in this part of the Citadel. He just screams at me, 'You shouldn't be here! So much time is passing. Keep still, Isabel, so I can get you back.'

'But Mr Carter—'

He makes me sit down on the spot, forcing me with strong hands. 'I know, Isabel. I know about Arkarian.'

I look up into his face, and I feel incredibly weary suddenly. 'Tell me what I can do to get him back.'

'Right now I have to get *you* back – to your time, to your bed, into your own body.'

'But—'

'And when you're returned,' he goes on explaining, 'I want you to gather the others together. We'll meet in Arkarian's chambers. It's safe there. And we'll try to figure this out.'

'Tell me first: who are those people I saw down there in that courtyard?'

His eyes bore into mine and his mouth moves once, soundlessly. He's not going to answer. Something is holding him back. Maybe he has to keep quiet while in the Citadel. Regardless, I have to know more. 'At least tell me why those people look so distressed?'

He glances away briefly. 'They're distressed at losing Arkarian.'

I sense that's not the whole story. My eyebrows lift, encouraging him.

'There's also a very real possibility that a traitor resides amongst us.'

Before I have a chance to absorb these words, or the enormity of them, his hand comes up before my face, forcing my eyes closed. 'No more questions, Isabel. Not here.'

When I open my eyes again I find myself waking up in my own bedroom. Bright sunlight blinds me for an instant, then a movement near my bed startles me into sitting up and squealing out loud. But it's only Matt squirming around in my blow-up lounge, trying to make his long body comfortable.

He hears that I'm awake and snaps, 'At last you're back. You're so lucky Mum had to go to work early this morning.'

His words send my pulse scampering. How can we waste time on trivial issues when Arkarian has been abducted? In a mad rush I scramble across the bed and grab Matt's shoulders, ripping his shirt collar in the process. 'Something terrible has happened!'

Colour disappears from his face. He takes my hands and peels them off his shirt, briefly examining the ripped collar. 'What's going on?'

Pushing him out of the way, I raid my wardrobe, quickly changing into jeans and a T-shirt. 'Arkarian's been kidnapped.'

'What?'

'Get the others. We have to make a rescue plan.' He continues to stare at me, his mouth gaping.

'Hurry!'

'What do you want me to do?'

I stop and try to calm my racing thoughts. 'OK, remember how there are nine of us?'

He nods and starts counting off his fingers. 'You, me and Ethan. Ethan's father. Mr Carter. And of course, Jimmy, who I'd rather forget.'

I try to ignore Matt's dislike of Jimmy. He hasn't

allowed himself to get to know Jimmy as I have these past twelve months. 'And don't forget Rochelle. She's with the Guard now too.' The second these words are out I could kick myself. Hearing the name of his ex-girlfriend probably still upsets him. 'Sorry, Matt. As if you could.'

He looks at me blankly and I say, 'Forget her, I mean.'

His left shoulder lifts slightly. He's trying to give me the impression thinking about Rochelle doesn't hurt any more. He's lying of course. 'I am over her. It's just … hard to forget, that's all.'

We're silent for a moment; I go hunting for my brown boots. I know they're here somewhere. Finally I spot one poking out from under my bed.

'That's only seven,' Matt says in a voice devoid of energy. I try to ignore the pull his soft, drained tone has on my emotions. They're chaotic enough right now.

'Arkarian,' I tell him. 'And the girl.'

His eyes light up for a second and he stares off in a dreamlike state. 'I think I remember her now. Wasn't it her image Ethan created in that illusion he used to defeat Marduke?'

'Yes, but she was real for the time that she was in Ethan's illusion. And her name is Neriah. She's Marduke's daughter, and when he turned traitor she had to go into hiding. These things are important. You really should remember them.'

'Right,' he says, cupping a hand around his chin, and looking embarrassed.

I smile encouragingly. Matt will get this Guard thing together one day. He has to. Arkarian believes in him.

'So let me get this right,' he says. 'You want me to gather all these people together?'

I bite back my frustration. 'Obviously you're not going to be able to find Rochelle. She's being de-briefed somewhere safe.' He nods and I go on, as that sense of urgency keeps growing stronger every second. 'Neriah hasn't been interned into the Guard yet. Her time is still to come. So you can't find her either. We might have to split up to get the others organised. Ethan's probably at school already.'

'I haven't seen Jimmy for a few days. Not that I've been looking,' he adds with sarcasm.

'That's because he's working in Veridian, making the city more secure. But you should be able to find Shaun.'

It takes what feels like an incredible amount of time, but is probably less than an hour before Ethan and Shaun arrive at Arkarian's chambers to find us waiting impatiently.

As soon as I see Ethan I can't help but run to him. He holds me for a minute, then pushes me back to peer into my face. 'Something terrible's happened, hasn't it? What is it?'

'He's been abducted.'

'Who?' Shaun asks, pulling slightly at my arm. Creases around his eyes intensify as he reads the terror in mine.

My voice, in the end, turns into a whisper, *'Arkarian.'*

Shaun goes still, his eyes staring into mine with incomprehension. Ethan's fingers dig deeply into my arms. 'How did this happen?'

I have to yank my arms free of his grip. 'We were in

the Citadel on our return from a mission to France when we were ambushed by two men – one old, the other huge. And four creatures I can hardly describe. They were hideous.'

'Did they say where they were taking him?' Shaun asks.

'The huge man said …' I stop. Sudddenly it hits me where I heard those words before – from Marduke himself. The same words Ethan hears in his night-mares sometimes, when he re-lives his sister's murder.

When I finish telling them, Matt has to find Ethan a seat. 'Where is this place where the flowers bloom under a bleeding … what did you say?'

Ethan stares up at Matt, his eyes red. 'The place Mar-duke said he was taking my sister moments before he placed his over-sized hand on her head and used his power to kill her.'

'Hell,' Matt exclaims, flicking a nervous look across to Shaun. 'What does this mean? Is Arkarian … dead?'

Shaun visibly tries to collect himself, shaking his shoulders and rubbing his arms. 'Don't assume the worst. Who knows the Goddess's purpose? She is, after all, driven by the very act of chaos.'

'Our mission tonight was a trap.'

This gets their attention.

'What do you mean?' Ethan asks.

'Lathenia turned up. She was expecting *you* to be there.'

Silence. And then they all start talking at the same time. But words are the last thing I need right now. 'I'm going to rescue him.'

Shaun touches my arm. 'Let's think this over.'

I move away from his touch. 'There's nothing

to think about. All I need is a plan.'

'And some information,' a voice from the doorway calls.

It's Mr Carter – at last!

'So where have *you* been?' Ethan asks in a suspicious tone. These two have never got along. And over the years that I've known Mr Carter as a teacher at school, he's been particularly hard on Ethan. Sometimes I can't see the sense in it, sometimes I think it's because Mr Carter sees a potential in Ethan that he believes could benefit from discipline and hard work.

'Mr Carter co-ordinated the mission last night. We met in the corridors of the Citadel not long ago.'

'So,' Ethan is quick to accuse, 'you were there when Arkarian was abducted.'

Shaun shakes his head at his son. 'Be quiet, Ethan. You assume too much.'

But Ethan isn't easily quieted. 'Maybe I do, but Carter has an odd habit of being in the wrong place at the right time. As I recall, he was the one who brought us the news last year that Marduke had Matt.'

'Ethan, it would take more than Marcus's talents to arrange something like this.'

All this debate won't bring Arkarian back; and right now that's all I can think of. 'Shut up, Ethan! Let Mr Carter tell us what he knows!'

Ethan does as he's told, and Mr Carter starts to explain, 'Arkarian has been taken to a holding place.'

'Where? What place is this?'

He looks at me, and his eyes are sad. 'A very dark place, Isabel. A place that no mortal should enter, not without protection. It's called the underworld.'

Stepping up close to his face, I tell him simply, 'I

93

would go there, protected or otherwise. Mr Carter, the dark doesn't frighten me. I have Lady Arabella's gift.'

'This darkness is profound.'

'I'll take a torch.'

'And if the torch fails?'

'In total darkness, Isabel,' Ethan reminds me, 'even you wouldn't be able to see.'

Mr Carter brings us back to the point he's trying to make. 'You have to understand, the underworld is impossible to enter or exit.'

'Arkarian's kidnappers managed, why can't we?'

'It takes immortal power to force an opening. This is Lathenia's work.'

'Then we'll get Lorian's help.'

'Lorian is … reluctant.'

'Why?' I find myself screaming.

'It's too dangerous. Getting in, finding a way out, surviving in that world – these things are practically impossible. We need as many members of the Guard that we can right now. And then there's the risk of the worlds joining – of an intermixing of species, of...' He shudders. 'Isabel, you don't understand, the creatures that live in the underworld have no souls.' He falls silent and his glance drifts away.

As I watch his face and absorb the meaning of his words, a thought comes to me. 'There's more, isn't there?'

He nods, then says, 'Lathenia is planning to eliminate Arkarian from our world.' He rubs both temples with open palms as if a headache has started to throb there. 'She is trying to force a portal to open to the time of Arkarian's birth.'

'She wants to kill Arkarian as a baby?' I ask.

'Before or after, but near enough.' While the rest of us look on wordlessly he explains, 'She will keep him secured in the underworld while her people attempt to eliminate him – body, and perhaps even soul, from the earth.'

Matt stares at the three of us in turn. 'What do we do? How do we stop this from happening?'

I explain what I think. 'Firstly we have to go back in time to stop the Goddess and her soldiers from murdering Arkarian at his birth. Then, no matter what arguments you throw at me, I'm going to find a way into this … this underworld, and I'm going to get Arkarian back.'

Ethan lays a hand on my shoulder. 'I'm going too.'

Matt adds, 'And me.'

Everyone starts talking simultaneously; our message couldn't be clearer. No one thinks Matt should go.

'You couldn't handle it,' Ethan says without malice. To him, rescuing Arkarian takes precedence over hurting anyone's feelings. But I see how Matt's face drops, and Ethan does too. 'It's just your inexperience, that's all I meant. When your powers start coming through—'

Matt shuts him up with a sharp wave of his hand. 'Cut it, Ethan. We all know my powers may never come through, so let's just get back to working out how to save Arkarian.'

A memory of the Goddess's incredible power as she raised her hands to Arkarian flashes across my eyes. Ethan, as skilled as he is, couldn't possibly fight that. Let alone Matt. 'No one's coming with me,' I say.

My words cause a riot, all of them letting me know what they think of my idea to go on my own.

Mr Carter claps his hands loudly in the air. 'Everyone be quiet! You're not listening! First things first. If we don't save Arkarian at birth, there will be no Arkarian ever in existence!'

We all stop and stare at him. 'The Tribunal has already decided how it's going to happen. Firstly, Isabel, you're not going anywhere on your own. Ethan will join you. I will co-ordinate the mission to France from Arkarian's chamber. You, Shaun, are to go and retrieve Jimmy from the city.'

'And what am I supposed to do?' Matt's strained voice breaks into the sudden silence. 'Sit in a corner and suck my thumb, while you lot go out risking your lives?'

For a long moment no one answers him. There's nothing any of us can do to make him feel better about it.

Mr Carter's eyes drop to the floor, making it obvious the Tribunal has no role set aside for Matt.

Finally it's Shaun who steps in. 'Let me put it this way, Matt. You're not being included because we can't risk anything happening to you. Whether your powers are developed or not has nothing to do with the Tribunal's decision. You're simply too important.'

Chapter Nine

Arkarian

It's the cold that wakes me. There's a numbness in my fingers. My feet feel like stones pulled straight from a frozen earth. I try to move to warm myself but my hands are secured with tight chains behind my back. There's something cold as ice on my face, some sort of metal mesh. I can't see anything; it's too dark for that. Then, as I attempt to move around, I realise the mesh is a body cage. My shoulders are just as tightly wrapped inside it as my legs. I don't know where I am, though I have a strong suspicion. I do know that I'm riding over a bumpy road, bouncing around in the back of an open cart. I wonder how I got here. If my suspicions are correct, it would have been interesting to have been conscious through the experience of tearing through a rift between the worlds, not just the time travel I'm used to.

The last thing I remember is the look on Isabel's face when that explosion hit, and the two of us were catapulted away from each other. The rest is blank. And now I find myself in a strange place, where even the air smells different, like rotting seaweed or stagnant marshland. I hope my stay here is temporary. I don't know how I would survive this eerie darkness if I had to live here indefinitely.

Two glowing torches up ahead stand out like beacons. One is held by an old man who leans on a stick to give him balance. I crane my head around to get a better view of the second one. This torch is also an open flame, held by a man much bigger, with stooped shoulders and a billowing cloak blowing behind him. He calls out something in a harsh and guttural voice that sounds vaguely familiar. For a moment, while trying to place it, I forget the severe cold.

The large man's arm reaches out to hit a smaller figure beside him. The force of the man's blow knocks the creature to the ground. The cloaked man then kicks out at this creature with a booted foot, while the old man looks on. The cart suddenly stops and three other creatures, similarly sized, run, or leap, to their fallen colleague. The younger man yells abuse at them. One of them squawks, then flaps cumbersome wings at its side, lifting slightly off the ground. Another approaches my cart, peering in with red glowing eyes. 'He's awake,' he calls out in a thick tone, as if his tongue is too large for his mouth.

The cloaked man bellows, 'Deal with him as I have commanded. We will arrive soon.'

At these words two of the creatures leap into the back of the cart with just a single flap of their wings. They tower over me, blocking the light from the torches. And while I can't distinguish their features in this blackness, I sense what they're about to do. I try to use my powers, to unbind myself from these chains. But nothing happens. The pair of creatures leap on me, and I kick out at them feebly with my chained legs. It has no effect, and soon the other two follow, hitting and kicking.

The beating continues. Instinctively I try to bring my feet to my chest to protect my internal organs as best I can, but the kicking at my back could be just as fatal. I finally realise what they're doing – beating me until I lose consciousness. They probably don't want me to remember the way. As if that were possible. I make my body go slack; I'm not far from unconsciousness anyway. They eventually leave, and soon the cart is moving again.

I try to breathe deeply and slowly to regain a mental balance. I need my powers to get out of this mess. If only I could use my wings. But if this place really is the underworld, then it would be pointless anyway, as only an immortal can force an opening. And while I might be able to move around within it, where would I go?

I try to loosen the chains and the mesh. But I'm tied securely. I try again to use my powers, but when I visualise what it would take to unbind me, I feel nothing. What strange capability do these creatures have? It feels as if I've been enslaved by some sort of enchantment. But magic? How can that be?

After several attempts to use the skills I've picked up over my lifetime, all unsuccessfully, I lie back and concentrate on soothing my aching body. While I can't heal myself, I can ease the pain of these bruises.

Eventually the cart stops, and I keep my eyes closed and my body as relaxed as I can for when the creatures make a return appearance. They lift me, two at my head, two at my feet. I gather from this that they're not all that strong. Their size must hold them back, about half that of an average man. And their wings appear to be more of a nuisance than any use to them.

We pass doors that squeak when they swing from their hinges, then another, heavier, I suspect made from iron. It slides across with a grating sound. Once through this door the creatures drop me. The old man is with them. He coughs and his chest whistles.

The man in the cloak enters. 'Release the chains,' he says, throwing them a key. And this time his words, spoken from a much closer distance, send a tremor of fear through my heart. He sounds very much like Marduke. But how can this be? That man is dead. Then I remember that he died whilst in the past. He should be in the middle realm, a wandering lost soul. Not here. Not unless … Lathenia went searching for him in that grey world and brought him back!

As the cage is removed, I roll on to my side and brace myself for the possibility of Marduke's rescue. My suspicions soon prove correct. The man towering over me is none other than Marduke himself, living and breathing. Yet the man before me is not the Marduke I remember. He is hardly a man at all. His time in the middle world has changed him considerably, with disastrous effect.

Somehow I have to warn the Guard. But how? And without my powers?

I swallow hard, wanting to form words, yet not knowing what to say. Marduke holds his torch up close to me. And now I see the old man, white-haired and wrinkly, and the four creatures that are part human, part bird and other animals combined. Their legs and arms are human, but their entire bodies are covered with animal fur, brittle and coarse.

One of them leans over me. 'Awake,' he manages to say through a mouth that juts forward in a square form, more like a pig's snout than a bird's beak, or a human jaw.

I look up at Marduke – or what he has now become – and see a similarity with the creatures or strange beasts he keeps as his soldiers in this world; and I wonder if these beasts were once men. The thought makes me quiver.

Marduke lowers his hood and I try hard not to look away. His one good eye has swollen to twice its size and now glows red. Where once he had a head of soft golden hair, snow-white bristles cover the entire top, and run down his face as far as a brow that juts forward.

'So, old friend, we meet again,' I finally say.

He snorts at my greeting and kicks me hard in the side, making me double over. I try again to strike up a conversation. 'The middle world has changed you … somewhat.'

He grunts and this time the sound is very much like that of a pig. The only thing missing is the pawing of the earth with a trotter.

'Where have you brought me?'

I don't think he's going to answer when his half-mouth drags down at its long end. 'You are in my world now.'

I look around at the stone walls and iron grate, the darkness overwhelming in its intensity. 'If this is your world, then you live in a very dull place, Marduke. Hardly an advancement, I would say, old friend.'

His boot connects with my stomach, hard, forcing bile into my throat, making me want to vomit. Another boot to the underside of my thigh sends muscles into tight spasms. Apparently this Marduke hasn't only changed physically, but has grown a lot more sensitive and intolerant of criticism. I'm sure Lathenia must be overjoyed! All the same, I'd better choose my words more carefully if I want to live.

'Strap him,' he says, turning his back on me to light several torches in brackets around the room, mumbling to the old man as he does so.

And now, as the rest of the room is revealed, I see exactly what he has planned. A rack stands ready to be used. And judging by the cobwebs, probably for the first time in hundreds of years. 'Your techniques are a little old fashioned,' I call out as the winged creatures reach for me. I kick at them and it takes all four in the end to secure me to this ancient mechanism of torture.

'The Medieval lords were experts in pain and confession,' Marduke says.

'You would know, Marduke.'

'Ah yes, I have suffered. In those days my powers were far less appreciated.'

'The Guard rescued you.'

Marduke snorts and his spittle stings my face. He points to his own half-missing face. 'Do you think I've not suffered because of the Guard?'

I could argue it was his own fault he got into that fight with Shaun, but I can see from his hard expression, he has moved beyond simple reasoning.

Vaporised air puffs out through snout-like nostrils. 'I will tell you this, Arkarian, your holding here is temporary. The Goddess seeks to stop you from meddling in her affairs. She also wants answers from you. She will be here before ...'

102

The old man coughs, I sense on purpose. But it soon turns into a chorus of whistling and wheezing.

Marduke waits until it is over. During this time he stares at me with his one eye narrowed. He seems to be assessing whether to give me the information or not. His hunched shoulders suddenly jerk forward as if he's come to a decision. 'Lathenia will be here before you are eliminated from your earthly world.'

His choice of wording is chilling. 'Eliminated? As if …?'

'You never existed.'

'But that would mean killing me at birth, or my mother before she bore me.'

'The portal to the time of your birth is opening as we speak. You have but hours before our soldiers succeed. Long enough to answer a few questions. You should feel honoured. Lathenia insists on questioning you herself. And then, *old friend*,' he mimics my own words, 'you will exist no more.'

I try not to let his words faze me. I'm not going to die in this miserable place! I yank my arms, testing the straps, but they're tight and cut into my wrists. A hissing sound snaps my head back to Marduke, only an instant before he slaps a whip across my chest. It rips my clothing right through to my skin. Blood oozes from the wound, staining my shirt with a dull red streak.

'Now,' Marduke says thickly, 'before my mistress appears, I have a question for you myself.'

'Ask away, for I will tell you nothing!'

The whip slashes the air once more, striking my chest at the exact same angle. He might as well use a butcher's knife; the damage would be the same.

'Stretch him,' Marduke orders, and his creatures – two together – turn the wheel.

Every limb and joint of my body burns like fire. Marduke's hand rises and the wheel stops. 'Where is my daughter being kept?'

I stare at him from the corner of my eye. This, of all questions, is the last I expect. Mostly because of its personal nature. 'Safe from you.'

His arm lowers and the stretching starts again. It's so hard not to scream out this time. But I don't. I would rather die. He raises his arm and the wheel holds still. 'Is it true she is *Named*?'

'Yes. As you were once.'

He must see something in my face, because he turns away with an expression that looks something like regret, then mutters, 'We shall be on opposite sides.'

'It doesn't have to be that way.'

He turns back to me. 'No, because you will tell me where she is.'

He goes to raise his hand again, but I jump in quickly before he gives his order. 'You may as well kill me, Marduke. Right now if you want. I'm not going to tell you where your daughter is. But before you finish me off, you'd better think about how you're going to tell Lathenia you killed me before she had a chance to ask *her* questions.'

'There is no need to concern yourself, my pet,' Lathenia's voice echoes around the room a second before she appears. 'For I am here now. And when I am finished, you can have your fun with him.'

Marduke nods and bows his head, stepping back from me.

She fully forms, dressed in a long white gown, belted

104

at the waist with a purple sash to match her lips. Alongside her, the mortal shape of a man forms. A young man. And for a second I think I recognise him, but he moves, and the moment is gone.

And while Lathenia stands before me, I take the moment to study her. The only other immortal I have been this close to is Lorian. I was his Apprentice for two hundred years and came to know him well. They are very different. Opposites in fact. Where Lorian is gentle (mostly), with translucent skin, eyes empowered with an energy that makes them difficult to withstand, Lathenia is more mortal in appearance. By anyone's standards she would be considered quite beautiful. There is irony in the fact that her soul-mate (for how else could she have rescued Marduke from the middle world?) would turn out to be so … disfigured.

She absorbs my thoughts, and even though my truthseeing power is contained, she lets me know hers. And now I understand her rage. Marduke may still be alive, but he is severely altered. And as there is only ever one soul-mate for each of us, hers has evolved into a different species. And this does not please her.

She turns her head around to the boy and gives him a withering look. Her mood is foul. The boy's eyes shift from Lathenia to Marduke, and his hands start to shake. She points to the wheel and the boy turns it easily.

Marduke looks impressed. 'It took two of the wren.' And to the boy he says, 'You grow stronger each time we meet.'

With praise lavished upon him the boy increases pressure on the wheel. The rack stretches my limbs beyond endurance. 'Hold it there,' Lathenia commands. 'Now, Arkarian, you will tell me everything you know.'

'I'll tell you nothing!'

'Is that so?' With needle-sharp nails, Lathenia scratches the side of my face from eye to jaw.

The pain, as my face slices open, goes through to the back of my eyes. I turn my head away. She grabs my jaw, yanking it back. 'Where is the opening to the ancient city?'

'I don't know.'

'You lie!' To the boy, she nods. He inches the wheel forward. I fight not to scream out. I will not show any weakness!

'The opening, Arkarian!'

Stubbornly I keep my lips closed.

Air hisses out from between her teeth. The boy tightens the wheel. Pain sears through every one of my limbs. 'Tell me where the weapons are kept!'

Continuing to keep my thoughts hidden from Lathenia grows harder with each turn of the wheel. Pain robs me of my ability to concentrate. To focus. Trying not to visualise is getting too hard. 'I don't know what you're talking about.'

'Are they locked in the vault in Veridian?'

'I know not!'

She turns away, giving me a precious moment to collect my senses. But when she returns she has a metal wand in her hand. I watch, as she takes the tip of the wand and heats it in one of the burning torches on the wall. She returns and holds it between my eyes. 'Tell me everything you know about the weapons. Everything!'

I think about what I know of the weapons, or what I have learned about them from Lorian. Thoughts of their power, their ability to slay the soul-less, skim across my brain. *No!* I stop myself quickly. *Don't think!* An image of the chest they are safely contained in, its intricate pattern of golden lace, forms before my eyes. *No! Stop!*

She realises what I'm doing and screams. 'Do you dare presume to withhold information from me?'

'Maybe I'm stronger than you think.'

Her silver eyes flare wide for a second and she steps back. My simple statement seems to have startled her. But why? Surely she doesn't really suspect I'm stronger than … what?

'Don't think yourself so clever, Arkarian. Give me what I want, or I will push this hot poker straight through your heart.'

I don't doubt for a second she would do it. But I get the feeling she didn't go to the trouble of bringing me to this other world to kill me at the first chance she got. At least not until she gets some useful information out of me. 'Go ahead.'

She raises her arm and holds the burning tip directly over the skin that covers my heart. 'Who has the key?'

Her question throws me. As far as I understand, Lorian thinks Lathenia has the key. I scramble my thoughts and attempt to play the innocent. 'What key? I don't know what you're talking about.'

But my game only serves to make her angrier. 'The key to the treasury of weapons! The key that cannot be handled by human hands!'

So neither side has the key, and neither side knows where it is! Unbelievable! When I get out of here, this information will be of great interest to the Tribunal. I stare at her with a puzzled frown. 'I honestly don't know.'

She slams the poker into the ground. It explodes, disintegrating into a shower of sparks and metal fragments. She keeps her face turned away, as if she needs time to contain her emotions. Then she says, 'For as long as your soul exists, you can still be of use to me.'

Her words sound like an ominous warning. 'How might that be?'

'It's a wonder you haven't worked it out, Arkarian.' She doesn't wait for me to reply. She just laughs mockingly and says, 'If for some reason my plan to destroy you at birth should fail, your friends will come for you. And while they might be able to get in, they won't get out. And won't the Guard be disadvantaged then? Hmm? Lorian will be eating out of my hand, kissing the ground I walk on. As it should be. As it should have been from the start.'

'They're not as foolish as you think. If they come, it'll be because they know how to get out again.'

She laughs outright. 'Only I know where the weakness in the rift is.'

'Only you? I doubt that.'

She stares at me, wondering at my certainty.

'You showed them yourself when you unleashed that storm on the mountain.'

'Ah, yes, the storm. Well, Arkarian, you're not as wise as your reputation would have us believe. Do you imagine I didn't plan that? If your loyal companions do get into this world of gloom, believe me, they will be trapped here. They will never find you, but live the rest of their lives walking these dark lands, searching. It wouldn't be long before they lost their sanity. Perhaps even their souls.'

I try to glean some information from her that might prove useful should the worst happen, and Ethan or Isabel, or any of the others, take it upon themselves to launch a rescue mission. 'Once they are in, what makes you think they wouldn't find that same location again to get out?'

'Don't think yourself so clever that I will simply tell you how to find the rift from the inside.' Her eyes narrow and a thin smile pulls at her purple mouth. 'But I will tell you this, the rift is impossible to find without light.' She waves her hand around. 'And as you can see, there's little of that around here.'

'One would think a coloured flash would be obvious in a black sky.'

'The rift flashes black on the inside.' She stops, and her teeth clench together.

But the reality is, a black flash would be impossible to find in a black sky. I find myself wishing desperately that Isabel and Ethan don't even attempt a rescue mission. It might be better if Lathenia's plan to kill me at birth does *not* fail. Far better for the Guard to lose one member, than all three of us.

The Goddess peers around as if looking for something, then speaks to her young soldier. 'Where have the wren gone? Fetch them.'

The boy glances at me with a look of wary concern, hesitating a moment before heading outside. Lathenia's eyes narrow. She's seen his hesitation too and is troubled by it.

The same four winged creatures, called wren, leap or trot into the room. Their eyes glow brighter red when they see me, their wings flap once or twice. Saliva drips on to their hair-covered torsos from slightly open, piggish snouts.

My eyes shift sideways to the Goddess. What in heaven's name does she plan to do with them? While holding my stare, she says to her young soldier, 'Release him. Have the wren beat him to within a breath of life, then take him to Obsidian Island. Secure him there. If they come, they will search in vain.'

Turning from me, Lathenia, with Marduke and the old man slightly behind her, disappears. But her young soldier remains, releasing me from the rack. I fall to the ground. Instantly the wren close in. When they begin to attack, the boy turns his eyes away.

Chapter Ten

Isabel

Mr Carter is co-ordinating our mission to save Arkarian from being killed at birth. We pass through the Citadel without any trouble. We're given new identities, though mine is the same as the last time I came to France. It turns out there was a purpose to Lathenia's mission, other than seeking revenge on Ethan. She also wanted to check out Arkarian's mother, even though she was only a child of six at the time. Now I understand the bond Arkarian and Charlotte shared.

So I'm back in France as Phillipa Monterey, with Ethan as my companion, Jean-Claude. Except now Charlotte is sixteen, and about to give birth.

'What the hell!' Ethan exclaims, unimpressed, as he dodges an English soldier's arrow.

Another arrow whips past my head, narrowly missing my ear!

'Get down!' Ethan calls out, yanking on my arm.

It appears that delivering us safely into France is something Mr Carter is having difficulty achieving.

'Watch out behind you!'

I spin around just in time to avoid the lunge of a

111

sword. Ethan dives at the soldier's feet, taking him down to the ground, disarming him at the same time. It appears Mr Carter has landed us directly in the midst of a raging battle between the French and English armies. A French soldier nearby notices us. 'Here, where did you two come from?'

Struggling to explain why I'm standing in the middle of a battlefield wearing a long green gown and soft brown slippers, I lift one shoulder and offer a pathetic helpless smile.

The soldier's gaze slides over us both from head to foot. 'You won't last long without armour.' He runs around for a minute gathering weapons from dead soldiers nearby, giving us each a sword and shield. When he hands me mine he points to the sword. 'Do you know how to use that, lady? If you stay close by my side, I will protect you.'

Ethan raises his eyebrows and rolls his eyes.

A mounted English soldier bears down on us. Ethan lunges for him. 'This is too dangerous,' he says. 'We also don't have the time. Not to mention the fact we could get killed, or kill someone in self-defence who's not supposed to die today.'

We struggle to make our way to the edge of the fighting. Eventually we see a chance to escape into some thick bushes. 'Come on,' Ethan urges.

I drop my sword and shield and run for protection into the nearby woods. Once deep inside, the sounds of battle diminish, and we stop to catch our breath and our bearings.

'Anything look familiar?' Ethan asks, knowing I was in this area not so long ago. 'Or has Carter stuffed that up too, landing us God-knows-where on this planet?'

'Mr Carter's doing his best.'

'Is he? Or did he land us directly in the middle of that battle on purpose?'

I shake my head. 'What have you got against that man?'

He makes a scoffing sound.

'I know he's harsh on you in the classroom. But maybe he's like that 'cause he's trying to bring out the best in you?'

His scoff this time turns into a fully-blown choking fit. I thump him on the back a few times. He motions me away. 'I'm OK.'

Finally, he gets his breath back. 'We never hit it off at school, that's for sure. But if you want to know the truth, what I've got against the man is … Now this is going to sound lame, but it's my gut instinct.'

It should be my turn to scoff. But he looks so serious. And well, Ethan has reliable instincts. 'Look, all I know is that bad mouthing Mr Carter won't help us save Arkarian's life.'

'You're right,' he concedes and glances around. 'Let's find our way out of here.'

It takes a while, but eventually we come to farmland that looks about right. A road up ahead leads into an area that looks similar to what we were earlier shown in the sphere.

Finally I see the castle, behind its outer walls and the small thatched cottages, just as imposing as it was ten years earlier. But that last time I was with Arkarian. Remembering brings a sharp pain to my chest, making my lungs feel as if they can't get enough air.

Ethan notices as he pulls open the wooden gate. 'He'll be all right, Isabel. We're going to make sure of it.'

Thankful for Ethan's optimism, I follow him through the gates. When we draw near the gate-house doors, Ethan makes me pull back behind a bush. 'We should check things out first.'

But my head says no. We lost enough time stuck in the middle of a battle, kilometres in the wrong direction. 'This is the day Charlotte is supposed to give birth. We could already be too late.'

'So what do you suggest, go straight up to the entrance?'

He thinks it's a joke, but I think his idea is spot on. 'Exactly. But I know we have to be cautious, so how about I go on my own?'

'What?'

'You can keep watch for anything unusual from here.'

He doesn't like my idea but eventually caves in. Before he changes his mind, I walk up to the front gate and bang on the iron door knocker a couple of times.

After a few minutes a woman servant answers the door. 'May I help you, miss?'

'Is Lady Charlotte at home, please?'

'And who might I say is calling?'

'Phillipa Monterey, an old friend of the Duke and his daughter.'

The maid's face forms into a suspicious frown. 'Miss Charlotte is not at home, and the Duke, God rest his soul, has been dead many years.'

'Oh.' This news is terrible. Poor Charlotte, how did she cope? But I can't let my thoughts on Charlotte delay me from finding her. 'Please, you must tell me where Charlotte is right away.'

The maid's frown only deepens.

I try to re-phrase so that my question doesn't sound so much like an order. 'I mean, could she be down by the river?' I point in the general direction I remember the river being.

The maid's frown softens, slightly. 'You do know Lady Charlotte is ...'

'With child? Yes. And far gone.'

The maid appears to relax her guard a bit. 'Well, she went out with a gentleman caller this morning.'

'What!' The maid's frown returns in full force. 'I mean, so near her time? Isn't that rather foolish?'

The maid's left shoulder lifts. 'The poor child was in sore need of a day's outing, what with the fighting being so near. The Duchess thought it would do the girl good.'

A sense of urgency fills me, giving a sudden release of adrenaline. 'Please, tell me where they were headed.'

But the maid's sense of protection kicks in. She becomes apprehensive. 'Why should I? I've never seen you before in my life. The gentleman seemed genuinely interested in Miss Charlotte's wellbeing.' Her voice lowers. 'He seemed particularly taken by Miss Charlotte these last few days.'

I'll bet. But I keep these thoughts to myself. Somehow I have to break through this woman's doubts of me. I start to panic. Time is passing while she tortures me by withholding the information I desperately need. 'Look, Lady Charlotte needs me. She's heavy with pregnancy, and without my help she will die.' My words are a mistake. Charlotte is going to die anyway – giving birth. That's how it happened all those years ago, and I can't change that fact today.

The maid, though, must sense something in my

115

impassioned plea. 'They took a basket of food to the falls by the picnic ground. Do you know where I mean? Just before the river bends.'

How could I forget? It was the place Arkarian kept Charlotte thoroughly entranced with stories about the great Gods of Ancient Greece. But it's a good long walk away. 'Yes, thank you. But we'll need horses.'

'We? Are there more of you? Where? Why don't you show yourselves? Who did you say you were?'

I could kick myself. No chance of any further help now. I'll just count myself lucky I got the information I need. I run back to Ethan, grabbing his arm. 'We have to hurry.'

We run all the way. It seems to take for ever to get there, but once we near the spot, Ethan, slightly ahead of me, pulls to a halt.

'What is it?' I ask breathlessly.

Then I hear it too. Screams. Long, ear-piercing screams of a woman in agony.

'Hell, he's beating her to death,' Ethan says, disgusted.

'Hang on, those are the screams of a woman in pain all right – childbirth pain.' A difficult one, I reflect quietly. 'We have to surprise this murdering soldier. At least we know Charlotte still lives, and by the sound of those screams, the baby's in a hurry to be born.'

But we have to be careful. There could be more than one soldier of the Order here. I remember one final warning. 'There might be a dog,' I tell Ethan. 'A big one. It might not be what it seems. So be cautious.'

We get close enough to hear the gentle sounds of a waterfall nearby, when Charlotte screams out, 'Something is wrong! You must take me home, sir. Please, take me home!'

Now I see her too. She's lying under a tree. Another contraction grips her and she arches her back, clawing at the blanket beneath her with both hands.

Two men stand by and watch. One fidgets restlessly, shifting his weight from one foot to the other, sometimes scratching at his head, sometimes looking away or up at the sky. 'Is there nothing we can do to ease her pain?'

The second man, taller, with red hair and a moustache, keeps his focus directly on the girl squirming before him. 'She's going to die anyway. I don't fancy killing a baby, no matter who it is, even though they are *Her* orders. Better the baby dies in the womb with its mother, and saves us the trouble.'

That's it! These words are all I need. The word 'caution' disappears from my vocabulary. Pulling a knife from my belt I charge out of our hiding place screaming. Both men have only a second to react, before I land fully on top of the one who callously wishes for the baby's death, while Charlotte endures more agony than she is supposed to.

'You coward,' I hiss in his ear, my blade near his throat.

Ethan, I notice out of the corner of my eye, has taken my lead. Not that he has much choice, but he seems to be holding up well against the other soldier.

The one beneath me pushes against my shoulders, rolling me on to my back. He grabs my wrist, shaking it hard. I refuse to let the knife go. He squeezes my wrist until it hurts like hell. 'I'm not giving in!' With these words I bring my knee up sharply between his legs.

His eyes water and his body goes still. For a second I

think I see something familiar in his eyes. As if he realises this, he jumps off me, and attempts to twist my hand behind my back. Grabbing his arm, I throw him over my shoulder. He grunts but gets up fast, then kicks me in the stomach, knocking the wind from my lungs. While I'm gasping for breath, he runs at me. I duck out of his way, and finding nothing but empty space, he falters and loses his balance. But he finds it again quickly and comes back for another round. This soldier is relentless.

In the meantime Ethan knocks his opponent to the ground, then comes over and gives me a hand. Spotting my knife, Ethan wills it to his palm while dragging the soldier off the top of me. Before long Ethan has the knife horizontal across the soldier's throat.

On the ground the other one is starting to come around. But Charlotte's agonising screams seize my attention, making my heart leap into my throat. I run over and put both hands on her stomach. I start working on easing her pain, softening and relaxing her muscles and making her womb open. There is a lot of blood now, and I fear for the baby's life, but under my hands the baby's heart beats strongly, only just a little too fast.

The soldier from the ground staggers to his feet, pointing at me. 'What are you doing?'

'Easing her pain, you pig.'

'You can't do that.' He tries to drag me away, but I claw my way back to Charlotte.

I try to think of something to say that will make him go away, if only it were that easy. But I have to try. 'The two of you are too late, you know.'

'What? What are you saying?'

'I'm a *Healer*! Can't you see?' I stare at him hard for a second. 'I've already done my work. The baby will be born alive. And if I have to, I will take this baby back with me for protection.'

His attitude changes immediately. He senses defeat. He glances at his partner. Ethan still holds the knife to his throat. 'Don't listen to her,' he manages to say. 'You know our fate should we fail this mission.'

Fear makes the first soldier's eyes widen, creating a look verging on hysteria. 'What do we do?' he practically hisses.

The one with the knife to his throat suddenly kicks back at Ethan's groin. Ethan doubles over and the soldier flicks the knife into the woods. Standing beside his partner, he says, 'You want to know what we do? We kill them all – except him.' He points to Ethan. 'I think he could be the one who stabbed our master.'

Ethan moves closer to where I kneel over Charlotte. We share a worried glance. Charlotte is exhausted, and the stress of being denied the safety of her bed and midwife is taking its toll. 'Think of something,' I hiss at Ethan. 'I have to help Charlotte. The baby is in trouble.'

Before Ethan has a chance to think, the air around us grows strangely hot. The tree giving Charlotte shade, and the bushes close by, make an eerie crackling sound. Their leaves begin to snap and shrivel up. I glance up and see the two soldiers concentrating fiercely. 'Ethan, we're in trouble. If it gets too hot—'

Before I finish my sentence, the bushes on either side, along with the tree over the top, suddenly ignite. And the temperature soars.

Ethan strips off his coat and starts beating back the

flames directly overhead. But it's so hot, the effort exhausts him.

'We need rain to put this fire out,' I tell him.

'I'm not sure I can make it rain. Not for real.'

I glance up at him briefly, 'Have you ever tried? I've seen you bring real live people into your illusions. I've walked on bridges you made solid simply with your mind.'

The air grows impossibly hot. Charlotte screams and tries to wipe her brow. Her head shakes from side to side as she mutters incoherently. She's becoming delirious.

Ethan looks up to the sky. 'Rain alone wouldn't solve our problem. It wouldn't get rid of those soldiers.'

He's right. What do we do now? Through the growing flames the two soldiers stand back with contented looks on their faces. One of them thumps the air with his fist. 'She's going to be so happy with us! She'll reward us like never before!' He points to Ethan. 'But I think you're right, you know. He could be the one who stabbed our master.'

The other replies, 'Yeah, so don't get too ecstatic. Remember, she wants the pleasure of killing that one herself.'

As they continue to watch, Ethan goes to work. 'Cover yourself and what you can of Charlotte. I have an idea.'

Doing as he says, I throw myself over Charlotte's upper body, covering her face with my arm. And from the corner of my eye I see Ethan close his eyes and inhale deeply. He holds his breath, then dives over the top of both me and Charlotte. As he does, an explosion thunders around us, and the Order's two soldiers let out a wild scream.

I peer up from beneath Ethan's body, and see the fire has exploded outwards. Huge flames wrap themselves around the two soldiers. They run around, continuing to scream, their bodies well alight. They run into the woods, both of them calling 'Bastian'. And with this name, the two of them disappear. No doubt they will return to their headquarters, where I assume they will spend time in their healing chambers.

Ethan runs around putting out the fires still burning in the nearby bushes. 'What do you think she's going to do with them now they've failed?'

I shake my head, returning my focus to Charlotte's heaving body. 'Who knows?'

'Well at least now they're gone, they can't come back to this exact time. And Arkarian can be born safely.'

Charlotte's hand grasps my arm. She lifts her head as far as she can to draw closer. 'Do I know you?'

I see no harm in telling her at this stage of her life. 'Do you remember a time when you had a dog? A large dog you fondly called Charlie?'

Her eyes go round and she gives a little smile, then she settles her head back on the ground as another contraction grips her strongly. Ethan takes off his vest, rolls it into a bundle, and slides it beneath her head.

'Phillipa,' Charlotte says, recalling my name. In her next breath she says passionately, 'Did you bring Gascon?'

Her remembering Arkarian so fondly makes me smile. 'He will be here soon.'

She sighs, feeling safe for probably the first time in hours. I feel the baby push down hard, eager to be born. I look around for Ethan. He finishes stomping on

121

some grass still burning and comes over. I tilt my head towards Charlotte's legs. 'You'd better get ready.'

His head jerks forward, eyes squinting at me. 'What? Do you want me to...'

'Uh-huh. And you'd better hurry. This baby is coming fast.' I turn my head to Charlotte. 'Not long now. Your pain will soon be over.'

She moans and grips the blanket in her fingers as a strong contraction takes hold of her once again. Ethan moves into position, pushing her skirts up over her knees. 'Oh God, I think I see it ... him ... it.'

His stammering brings a smile to my lips. I tell him what he has to do. For the next few minutes all three of us are busy, as first the baby's head pushes through, swiftly followed by the rest of his body.

Ethan looks at me with the baby's cord in his hand. I explain what to do. When he's finished he hands the baby to me. I give the baby a quick check, but can sense no problem within his small body, then gently place him in his mother's weakening arms.

Ethan indicates the enormous amount of blood gathering on the blanket without saying so out loud. 'Is there anything you can do?'

It pains me to think this beautiful young woman is going to die, and die soon, while I stand by and watch it happen. I have the means to heal her, but cannot. I have the power to give Arkarian the mother he never knew, but must not. How different would his life be if he grew up in the Duke's castle, with his loving mother to watch over him?

My eyes are drawn to mother and child, hers also filling with moisture. 'He is so beautiful,' she whispers, her lips brushing the baby's forehead ever so softly.

As if aware of his mother's words and gentle lips, the baby opens his eyes and looks directly at her face. She gasps softly and her mouth moves to form a smile. 'You're real. It was not a dream.'

Suddenly I hear the sound of hoof-beats and the running of a carriage over uneven ground. Horses soon appear; several riders jumping off as soon as they see us. The carriage also pulls up. The servants scurry over to attend to Charlotte, concern in their voices and actions, especially when they see the remains of the fire, and the gathering pool of blood.

Ethan and I step away from the scene, keeping enough distance not to be noticed. The Duchess climbs out of the carriage and turns her head away at the sight of the blood-stained blanket. 'Get her in the carriage,' she orders. Everyone scurries about to fulfil her command.

Ethan pulls gently on my arm. 'Come on, we're not needed any more.'

I swallow, as a lump the size of a rock forms in my throat. But healing Charlotte is out of my hands now. Her family and household will take care of her, though nothing will save her, not in Medieval France.

Ethan calls out Mr Carter's name, and the frantic scene before us begins to disappear.

Chapter Eleven

Isabel

I can't believe this! Mr Carter says we have to keep going to school. He says it would be dangerous to simply drop out. It would cause suspicion, be obvious to those that know – those of the Order he means.

OK, I get his point. Secrecy is so important to the Guard's survival, a word is enough to arouse suspicion.

I get off the bus with Matt right behind me to find Ethan waiting. He has a weird, troubled look on his face.

'What's wrong?'

He shrugs, his eyes scouring the school grounds laid out before us, as a couple of hundred students arrive, ready to begin morning classes. 'Apart from Mum not changing her mind about the sanatorium, I'm not really sure. It's just something about this place looks different today. *Feels* different.' And then he adds in a hushed whisper near my ear, 'Do you know that since Arkarian's been gone, the Guard has lost more missions than we've won? We were lucky last night. The Tribunal members are really worried about their sectors. Some of them have even lost soldiers. And now

Dad has to help Jimmy and will be away overnight.'

'Are you worried about your mum?'

'She hardly sleeps any more, and she's refusing to take her sedatives. It's really bad timing too. Mum needs constant watching.'

'Is there anything I can do to help?' It's a stupid question. With every day that passes, Laura gets closer to going to the sanatorium.

He shrugs. 'I'm trying to look after her. And Auntie Jenny's supposed to be coming today to spend the night. Dad arranged it before he left.'

We're quiet for a minute when Ethan's eyes drift to a boy wearing odd socks, neither of them part of the school uniform. He frowns deeply. 'Look at that.'

The socks sure look out of place. But then I spot a girl in Year 8 wearing chunky earrings that come almost down to her shoulders. 'Who relaxed the uniform code?'

'You know, with so many missions failing, Dad says we should expect changes. When too much of the past is altered, it affects the present.'

Ethan's friend, Dillon, sees us and comes over, putting an end to our conversation. His head follows a couple of girls as they come down the stairs into the quadrangle.

Matt joins us. 'Hey, what's that big grin for?'

Dillon raises his eyebrows, indicating the girls' short skirts by jerking his head at them.

They both stare at the girls until they disappear round the corner. It's a sight not normally seen at this school. At least, not since Principal Baker came to Angel Falls two years ago, and introduced a strict uniform code – long socks pulled up to our knees, school ties, blazers with white shirts tucked in, and navy skirts for girls right down to our knees. These girls, and others too now that I look around, have more leg showing above the knee than below it!

Ethan tries to pull me aside without anyone noticing. 'Do you know what I think is going on here?' He starts yanking at his tie. 'The changes are happening. You'd better shorten that skirt quickly or you're going to stand out.'

I turn the waist of my skirt over a couple of times. 'This is really weird, Ethan.'

Dillon and Matt come over. 'You two look stressed,' Dillon says. 'You need to go on a holiday or something.'

A great idea. If only I could.

'Speaking of holidays,' Dillon says pointedly to Matt. 'Is that what Rochelle's doing? Some of the guys are saying she left school. She's been gone for so long, they reckon she must have moved away. So where is she?'

Matt snorts loudly. 'Maybe you should be asking Ethan that question. If Rochelle was going to tell anyone where she was going, it would have to be him.'

Ethan looks speechless. I don't blame him. What is Matt going on about? And why is he drawing attention to Ethan? Linking him with Rochelle?

Finally Matt realises his cynical comment could be misread. 'Look, I don't keep tabs on Rochelle any more.'

Dillon's eyes shift from observing Matt to Ethan and back again. 'But you two were like … really together. What happened?'

Matt suddenly snaps. 'She was using me, and I'm over her. Now let's talk about something else!'

Dillon stops with the questions and starts scratching an itch behind his right ear, then makes a point of looking at his fingernails, while shifting his weight from foot to foot as if he has ants under his toes. 'Well, speaking of girlfriends …' he drifts off, inspiring sniggers and mock groans from Ethan and Matt.

'You'd better get it out before you burst,' Ethan says.

Dillon spins around, pinning us with a pair of deep green eyes. 'I've found my perfect woman.' Then to me he adds, 'Isabel, you gotta get me a date with her.'

'Me? I don't even know who you're talking about.'

His dreamy tone has everyone laughing. Matt whacks his shoulder. 'You meet the perfect woman every week.'

'I swear,' he says, covering his heart with a hand. 'This is the one. You gotta see this girl. She's hot! And she's sexy like you wouldn't believe.'

'So where is this perfect woman?' Ethan asks. 'Do we know her?'

'She's new and, well … I haven't actually met her yet.'

Ethan and Matt groan out loud, shaking their heads. Then Ethan catches sight of Mr Carter coming out of the front office doors. 'I really have to speak with him.'

'Yeah? What for? I thought you hated Carter?' Dillon is quick, considering a second ago he was in dreamland with some girl he hardly knows. Ethan hesitates, but only for a second. 'Ah, it's this history assignment. I'm running late.'

'What assignment? I'm in your history class. I didn't know we had an assignment due.'

Dillon's back with the questions, and I'm starting to get an uncomfortable feeling inside.

'It's one I did last year. I got an "A" for it, and Carter wanted to show it to one of his other classes. I was going to polish it up a bit before I gave it to him.'

'Sounds like it doesn't need any polish. Wish I could get an "A" in some—' He stops. Everyone's eyes follow his to see what has him looking so stunned. 'It's her!' Excited, he slaps Ethan's shoulder, knocking him forward.

'Hey!'

'Sorry. But look at her. That girl is all mine,' he adds dreamily.

Our eyes zoom in to where Mr Carter is coming out of the office with this new girl by his side. But it's not only Dillon who's reacting strangely at the sight of her. Even my own brother's mouth is hanging half-way open, his eyes glued to the girl as she and Mr Carter draw nearer.

I take a moment to look at this girl that's got both Dillon and Matt goggle-eyed. Well, she sure is beautiful, with wide oval-shaped doe eyes, flawless skin, dark hair surrounding a small heart-shaped face and cherry-red lips.

As they approach my heart starts thumping hard. This is no ordinary girl! I recognise her clearly. I've seen her before – she was the girl in Ethan's illusion last year. It was her image Ethan used to distract Marduke. This is Neriah – Marduke's daughter, though I'm pretty sure she doesn't know that fact, or anything about Marduke. Actually I'm pretty sure she knows nothing about the Guard, or who any of us are – yet.

Mr Carter and the girl come right up to where we're standing against the railing, where Mr Carter introduces her. Neriah exchanges a welcoming glance with me and instantly I get a sense of calmness about her. A feeling gathers inside that there's more to this girl than I first assumed, though I can't quite put my finger on it. Maybe she knows more than I have given her credit for. Even though we've only known each other a few fleeting moments she invokes a warm feeling of trust in me.

'Would you mind keeping an eye on Neriah for a couple of days, Isabel?' Mr Carter asks.

Before I can reply, Dillon jumps in. 'I'll do it, sir.'

Mr Carter snaps at him. 'I wasn't talking to you, Dillon.' Then, as if thinking twice about the tone he just used, says in a milder voice, 'Neriah happens to be in most of Isabel's classes. She's a Year 10 student, not a Year 11 like you boys, so it only makes sense that Isabel should show her around.'

Mr Carter stares silently for a second at Dillon's face, noticing his bulging eyes that can't seem to drag themselves off Neriah's downcast head, and adds softly, 'Settle down, Dillon. You're so transparent.'

While Ethan and Matt snigger at Dillon's mounting embarrassment, I smile at Neriah, catching her eye, and a friendship quickly begins to form. I let Mr Carter know I don't mind chaperoning Neriah for a few days.

'I knew I could rely on you, Isabel,' Mr Carter says. And without saying a word he lets me know that he is asking for more. I nod to show him that I understand. 'Good,' he says. 'Now you'd all better get to class.'

Right on time the morning buzzer sounds. We start to gather our bags.

'I left mine in the office,' Neriah remembers.

Both Dillon and Matt clamber over each other in a hurry to be the first to collect it for her.

Dillon spins around and thrusts his open palm against Matt's chest. 'I'll get it!'

Neriah looks uncomfortable, her mouth forming into a small embarrassed smile. She's obviously not used to this much attention. Dillon rushes off, almost knocking me over in his haste. When he passes, Neriah's eyes lift and lock with Matt's. They stay there, the two of them staring at each other. Ethan and I could be sinking in quicksand at their feet and neither of them would notice.

Slowly Neriah pulls her gaze away, focusing on her left foot, which has started moving around in funny little circles. Matt starts examining the distant hills as if he's never seen a horizon before, or at least none so breathtaking. What's got into him? Something about this girl has him reacting like a ten-year-old kid playing spin-the-bottle for the first time. And while his sudden interest in another girl should be a good thing, I'm not sure his interest in this one is the answer to his moving on.

Ethan snickers beside me, amused. But for some reason I suddenly feel chilled. It's then I realise this chill is being generated by my sixth sense.

Chapter Twelve

Isabel

The day doesn't pass fast enough as one lesson merges into another. My thoughts are with Arkarian, wherever he is. What are they doing to him? Who was that giant of a man in the crimson cloak who kidnapped him? Something about him prickles my senses. An image of Marduke comes to mind. But that's not possible. Is it? No. No one can come back from the dead.

Even having Neriah by my side all day doesn't help me focus. I do learn a little more about her though – she's smart, artistic, and shy because she's lived a reclusive life. Up until today she never attended a regular school. She's been home taught by her mother and a variety of private tutors. Security around her has been tight. It still is. She's driven to and from school, and whilst at school she will attend the same classes that I do. Mr Carter is also keeping a close eye on her.

One thing that didn't come up, and she didn't volunteer, was where she lived before she moved to Angel Falls. It probably has something to do with her past, or who her father is. My guess is Neriah and her mother have been living in hiding on some foreign land. But now the Tribunal have deemed it necessary for her to make an appearance and start fulfilling her role. She is one of the Named after all, and her part in the Prophecy will soon start unfolding.

At last the buzzer sounds for the end of last period. Even though I'm burning to get out of here, I walk Neriah to the school car park and prepare to wait for her driver to arrive. But her car is already there. Two large white dogs, apparently Neriah's pets, sit as if on guard beside the rear passenger door, while a uniformed chauffeur holds it open. When the dogs see Neriah their whole rear halves start wagging excitedly, but they don't change position until she calls them each by name.

The dogs follow her inside the back seat, and she waves goodbye through darkly tinted windows.

At last I'm free to do what I've been waiting all day for – work on rescuing Arkarian. Shrugging off the strangeness of this day, I go and look for Ethan, so we can make a start. But Matt finds me first, and worst luck, Dillon is right beside him.

'Was that Neriah?' Dillon asks, craning a look at the dark receding car. 'She comes to school in a chauffeur-driven Mercedes?'

'I have no idea what make of car it is, Dillon. Have you seen Ethan?'

Dragging his eyes away from Neriah's disappearing tail-lights, he finally looks at me. 'Oh yeah. He said for you to meet him at the back exit.'

Matt and I take off. Finally we can attend to the business needed. But Dillon tags along. I'm not sure if I'm imagining this, but today it feels as if Dillon is suffocating me. It's probably just my nerves stretched to breaking point.

But how do I get rid of him without being rude? An idea hits me. I try to sound casual, posing my question to Matt, but making sure Dillon can hear, 'Did you see Neriah's artwork today?'

Matt frowns at me. 'You know I don't do art. I don't go near those classrooms. What's up with you?'

I try to motion towards Dillon with my eyes, and mouth the words 'Shut up'.

'Oh well, that's a loss. What about you, Dillon?'

'Nah, I don't do art either.'

'She's so talented,' I ramble on. 'She did this drawing. It was an abstract of a forest, but it was so captivating, I swear, I couldn't stop staring at it. The whole class couldn't.'

'Yeah?' Dillon sounds impressed. 'Beautiful and talented.'

I smile as he takes the bait. 'Yeah, well, I only mentioned it 'cause I heard she's taking an after-school art class today.'

'Did you say this afternoon?'

Briefly I flick a look at my watch. 'In about twenty minutes. She said she was going to grab a cappuccino at the Falls Café before her lesson.'

He glances at his watch. 'I could get down there in five.'

Ethan finds us just as Dillon makes an about face. When he's out of ear shot Matt asks, 'What was that all about?'

'He just keeps hanging around.'

'That's because he's our friend,' Matt explains.

'I know that. I just needed to get rid of him. There are things I have to plan and I can't do them with

Dillon overhearing.'

Ethan stares after Dillon for a second. 'Well, it's just as well you did. Carter wants to meet us in Arkarian's chambers right away.'

Matt is quick. 'Let's go then.'

Ethan puts a hand out towards Matt's chest. 'Ah, he meant Isabel and me.'

Matt groans and looks up at the sky. 'And what am I supposed to do?'

'Train,' Ethan says. 'It's your physical skills that are going to get you by until...'

Matt's eyebrows lift accusingly. 'Yeah, I know. We all know. OK?'

'You're too hard on yourself. Just relax.'

'Well it's hard to relax when so much is expected of me.'

'Just concentrate on the physical aspect, the rest will follow.'

'But my Trainer's about to take off.'

Ethan has a quick think. 'Jimmy's back.'

'No way! I won't train with him.'

'That's a shame. You could learn a lot from Jimmy. He's a master trickster you know. He planted the booby traps in Veridian.'

Matt's head shifts up and down. 'That's another thing. If Veridian is so important to us, why haven't I been shown it?'

My patience finally erodes. 'Oh for pity's sake, Matt! Why don't you just shut up and stop whingeing. You never know, if you stop fighting yourself, your powers might finally emerge – all by themselves!'

Without another word, Matt takes off. Instantly I regret my outburst. I make to go after him, but Ethan pulls me back. 'He'll be all right.'

Nodding, I turn around, but from the corner of my eye I get a glimpse of someone staring at us from near the front gates. Spotting me, this figure slips behind a brick wall as if to conceal himself.

'What's up?' Ethan asks, dragging on my arm to make me hurry.

'Do you trust Dillon?'

Ethan studies me with a deep frown. 'What do you mean?'

I shrug. 'Oh I don't know. I just have a feeling.'

'Like what?'

'Does he ever ask you weird questions?'

'Dillon? Yeah, all the time. That's what he's like. Don't go getting paranoid. Dillon is like ... well, my best friend.'

I stare at him, slowly raising my eyebrows.

'After *you*, of course,' he corrects himself with a smile. 'Seriously, Isabel, you don't know Dillon like I do. He's OK.'

'Do me a favour, all right? Don't take your friendship for granted. Keep an eye on him.'

'You can't be serious! Dillon doesn't work for the Order!'

We move on through the back gate. 'Ethan, you can't know that for sure. Just like none of us knew Rochelle worked for the Order. What if he's a Truthseer, like her? He could be reading our minds and we wouldn't even know it.'

'All right,' he agrees softly. 'I'll be more careful around him.'

That settled for now, I try to put my suspicions aside. Hurrying up the mountainside, we soon arrive at

Arkarian's chambers. The secret door before us opens, allowing us entry. It feels strange walking down this corridor, expecting, yet knowing Arkarian will not be here. Passing many doors on both sides, I have to fight the urge not to look behind each one of them. Many of these doors lead to training rooms, others I know nothing about. But it would be a pointless exercise as Arkarian is not here.

We get to the main octagonal chamber and see Mr Carter. He's staring into the 3-D holographic sphere that monitors the past. His focus is so absolute, that when Ethan taps lightly on the wall, he jumps.

'What took you so long?' Moving away from the sphere Mr Carter directs us to some chairs he's brought in. But the sight of these chairs, nothing like the ancient stools Arkarian always provides, has tears hitting the backs of my eyes. I blink them away before anyone notices, and plonk myself down, trying to remember when I last slept.

Mr Carter doesn't quite make it into his chair before he issues us with new orders. 'The Tribunal has summoned your presence. Immediately.'

Ethan gets his exclamation out before me. 'What! In Athens?'

'But we don't have the time,' I explain, hoping Mr Carter is ready to back me on this, to the Tribunal if necessary. All day I've been thinking about tonight's rescue mission. Now I'm told I have to go to Athens instead. 'Arkarian is our first priority, then Ethan's ...' I decide not to say the word 'mother'. Her depression, while linked to past happenings, is not strictly a Guard issue, and really none of Mr Carter's business. Ethan wouldn't want me telling him, I'm sure.

136

But our arguments fall on deaf ears. Mr Carter is adamant. 'Look you two, you can't go off on a rescue mission without help from the Tribunal anyway, so whatever their reasons for summoning you, look upon it as your chance to get their assistance. Do you have any idea where Arkarian is being kept – exactly? Do you know where to go? How to get there? Or even where to start? Hmm?'

His questions make me think. He's bringing up some valid points. But to lose another night is almost too much to bear. And there's the added worry about Laura. The days to her possible suicide are counting down, and quite honestly I have no idea how to stop it happening. Arkarian said he would help. I believe him. I believe he has a solution, or a plan or something. Without him, in a thousand different ways, we are lost.

Ethan groans. 'You're right. We'll have to go to Athens.'

Well if we have to go, we'd better get everything out of it that we can. 'Who can we rely on to help us? Which of the royals should we approach?'

While Mr Carter thinks, Ethan comes up with a suggestion, 'Lord Penbarin. He helped me once before. I think he would do it again.'

For the first time Ethan and Mr Carter don't argue. After ironing out a few more details, Ethan and I make our way back down the mountain. It's dark now, but there's enough twilight to enhance my gift of light, making the path clear for me. Ethan follows, knowing my sight is a thousand times better than his in the dim light. But suddenly my head is hit with sharp pain. It makes me double over, and I wonder fleetingly if I'll ever get used to these things. I try to relax, to breathe deeply, but the pain is accompanied now by intense white light. I stumble, my head heavy and unbalanced.

Ethan takes me by the waist, helping me to the ground. I look up at him in a daze, my mind still recovering from that whirlwind flash. But Ethan is impatient to know what I saw. He has to be thinking of his mother. I know this. But while it wasn't his mother I saw this time, it was someone equally close to his heart.

'Are you OK? Was it another vision?'

Still overwhelmed, I try to form words. In my silence Ethan's fears leap. 'What is it? Did you see Mum again?'

I take a deep breath and try to explain, 'I was shown the past.'

'Yeah?'

'Arkarian said that might happen.'

'So what did you see?'

'I saw the woods where your sister was killed. And ... I saw Marduke kill her.'

He frowns at me, then lifts his eyebrows. 'Yeah well, so have I. A million times in my dreams.'

'But I saw something else, Ethan.' He waits for me to explain. 'I saw her *afterwards*.'

'What are you saying?'

'She was running through a field of unusual flowers that were growing under a deep red moon. And then I saw her inside a very tall building. It's her home, I think, but it's not where she's supposed to be.'

'Are you saying Sera is still alive somewhere?'

I think about this and the gaunt and waif-like figure I saw in my vision, then shake my head. 'I don't think so, Ethan. This Sera was ...' How can I put it? How do

138

I explain the transparency of her body, the lack of colour to her skin except for a faint luminescence, the haunted look to her eyes, or how she appeared to be running *through* the flowers themselves? I decide there's only one way, just come out with it. 'Ethan, your sister is a ghost.'

Chapter Thirteen

Arkarian

The beating doesn't last long. It doesn't have to. Within minutes of their kicking and punching at my limbs, back and head, it's obvious that much more of this would finish me off. And one thing I'm quickly learning in this place is that no one dares disobey the Goddess's wishes or commands. Lathenia doesn't want me dead – yet. And so the wren pull back.

I try to take a deep breath, but I think one or two of my ribs are broken. There is internal bleeding for sure. Blood surges into my mouth. I cough, which near kills me with pain alone. A fat globule of blood spills out on to the stone floor.

One of the wren steps back as the blood pools near his foot. He flaps his wings once and lifts into the air. 'Argh! He's going to die. It was your kick to his chest that did it!'

Two of them squabble for a minute, each one accusing the other of delivering the fatal blow. The boy yells at them to shut up and steps over for his first look. I can't see the expression on his face, as my sight is blurred, but I do hear his chest heave as he groans with a sound like repulsion, and oddly also like shame. Although this last thought is probably an exaggeration caused by that last hit to my head.

'Put him in the back of the cart. And be careful of his wounds. Do you hear me now? Be careful!'

His orders are heartening. And there's something in his voice, a trace of compassion if I'm not mistaken. But it's hard to tell if the boy has the possibility of becoming an ally.

The wren lift me and carry me outside. The short journey to the cart is agony as one wren lifts me higher than another, and one almost drops me. All thoughts fly from my head and I must lose consciousness, for when I wake, the cart is moving, and the wren are groaning and complaining amongst themselves how weary they are. With no sun, it's difficult to tell how long the journey is taking. It's impossible to measure when a new day has begun.

Many times I pass into a state of oblivion. Strange how in these half-wakeful moments, memories return to me. Memories I thought lay deeply buried, of other beatings at the hands of those charged with my protection, surrogate parents who treated me more like a slave than a son. And as always when these memories force themselves to my consciousness, so too does an element of anger. Why was I given into the service of others? After my mother died, why didn't my father come forward to claim me, instead of allowing me to become an orphan?

The cart stops, snapping me awake. And with the sudden stillness pain returns in just about every part of my body. I stretch out my legs, testing them for broken bones. The joints at my hips and ankles feel numb and dislocated, though the bones themselves I think are intact. One thing I know for sure: right now I would be incapable of escape, even if an opportunity confronted me. Where would I escape to anyway? To run heedlessly into this complete darkness would be pointless.

The wren carry me to a waiting boat, where they lower me to the floor. My body hits freezing metal. But only when all four wren are also inside does the boy release the rope and climb in. The boat sways as the wren find their places. They look nervous and try to keep their bodies near the centre.

'You two,' the boy orders. 'Pick up those oars and start rowing.'

Grumbling, two wren take up the metal oars. It's an effort and they heave and complain the whole time. A thump against the boat makes us sway dangerously. All four wren scream out in fear as a flash of fire lights the water for a brief moment. It's then I see the large chunks of ice all over the surface. The wren manoeuvre the boat between these great chunks, being careful to avoid them as best they can, screaming at each other when they draw too close. They scream even harder when a splash threatens to spill over into the boat.

I try to block out their obvious fear and attempt to change position as the touch of metal is icy cold against my skin. The boy notices, and, as if it affects him on some level, removes his cloak and wraps it around me. He then offers his water flask. I take a sip and thank him.

He makes an irritated sound in his throat. 'Don't get excited, I'm just a soldier doing my duty.'

Even in my beaten state I can't help but get excited –

by the fact that a soldier of Chaos appears to have a conscience. 'You …' I struggle to get my breath, 'are different.'

'I am as mortal as you.'

'And just as afraid.'

The boy takes offence. 'I'm not afraid, not of you.'

His hesitation speaks louder than any words. It gives me a surge of hope.

'Well, *I* am afraid.'

These roughly spoken words have me staring up in surprise. Especially as they come from the mouth of one of the wren. The other three snort and grunt a grudging agreement.

The boy thumps the wren's thick curved shoulder. 'Why are you afraid? You are kings in this land.'

The wren scoffs loudly. 'I tell you what I'm afraid of. I'm afraid of that.'

My eyes follow the direction of his outstretched hand. Though impossible to see through the dark, I gather the wren is pointing to our destination.

'I've heard some things about that island,' the boy says.

'It's not the island. There's a temple there.'

The other wren snort and nod their heads.

'I've seen this temple,' the boy says. 'It's big, I'll give you that, like nothing I've seen before. But hardly terrifying. It has a … a peaceful feel.'

The wren visibly shudder and hiss at his description.

'Tell me,' the boy asks. 'What is it about this temple that has you shaking in your boots?'

All four are quick to reply, their words falling over each other, making it hard to understand them.

'It's sacred ground,' one explains. 'Inhabited by one of *Them*.'

143

'Are you talking about the ghost that lives there?'

The wren mutter and curse amongst themselves.

One looks up at the boy. 'We'll not go there.'

Another one adds, 'Not one foot.'

The boy frowns. 'But we can't leave him on the beach!'

All four of them make hissing sounds and shake their heads. 'What's the difference where we leave him? He's still going to die, whether in the temple, or on the beach when the lake swells.'

'Listen, the Goddess doesn't want this man dead yet. I can't fail her again. She'll …' He hesitates, his eyes shifting over me, trying to decide whether he's said too much already. 'She has promised me a lot of things for my loyalty.'

The boat hits solid ground and the boy goes to jump off. One of the wren lunges out to grip his ankle. 'Beware the lake!'

The boy nods and secures the boat to a mooring. Soon I'm carried to the beach and dumped there. The moment my body hits the rocky surface, the wren clamber as fast as they can back into the boat.

The boy looks at me and how near I am to the water's edge, then at the wren. 'The tide is coming in and he is too weak to walk to the temple.'

'Forget him. We won't hesitate to leave without you. Get in! Quickly, the lake is swelling!'

The boy ignores the wren's threat, and taking his own initiative, helps me walk to higher ground. 'The temple is not far now and you are over the worst of the climb.' He turns from me, searching the ground around us. He comes back with an old broken branch, thrusting it into my hand. 'Here, lean on this and keep walking away from the lake.'

'You have a kind soul,' I tell him.

'I'm not doing this for you. My soul belongs to the Goddess,' he says, clearly annoyed, perhaps for having revealed so much of himself. He spins away.

'Wait,' I call out. 'I don't even know your name.'

For a second I feel the boy hesitate. 'She calls me Bastian.'

'Yes, but what is your real name?'

He looks over his shoulder at me, but doesn't answer. Then he says, 'I will tell you, if you answer me one question.'

'Anything.'

'Why didn't you select me to be one of the Named?'

His question is so unexpected I find myself speechless. He takes one look at my open mouth and turns from me to the waiting boat. I follow it until its torchlight becomes a pin-prick in the distance. Then it too is gone.

And now I am alone. I have to find shelter, even if it's with a 'ghost', or whatever it is that has the wren running scared. Something about the incoming tide is more dangerous than the below-freezing temperature. But my eyes are confronted with nothing but darkness. Even with the branch for support I stumble and fall several times, and the effort it takes to rise again exhausts me. My mind drifts near unconsciousness. But I haven't lived six hundred years to take my last breath on a desolate beach in total isolation. I try to keep my mind active, and recall that night in France when Isabel dozed with her head against my chest. That night I kissed the top of her head. Had she been awake, what would she have thought? Would she have turned her face up to mine? Her image brings an even sharper pain to my ribs than their fractures do. She has to be spending a lot of time with Ethan, probably working on a rescue plan. She loved Ethan not so long ago. Does she still? Thoughts of Isabel with Ethan have me sinking into the freezing rocks.

A soft light pierces the darkness. Am I awake, or have I drifted into some miserable delusional state? I blink to clear my vision. Someone – or something – approaches. As it draws nearer I see it's a girl coming. A young girl. She's wearing a white gown to mid-calf. But the strangest part about her is that her skin looks as if it's luminous. And stranger still, I think I can see straight through her!

She comes right up to me and tilts her head. 'You're Arkarian.'

It's not a question. This girl knows who I am. And now, looking upon her angelic face, framed by a head of black bouncing curls, softly illuminated by her white gown and gently glowing skin, I recognise her too. 'My dear little Sera, is it really you? What are you doing here in this nightmarish place?'

She giggles and squeezes her fists, shaking them in the air and jumping around in a circle. Eventually she calms down, a serious frown marring her innocent youthful features. 'You have to get up and come with me. The ice waters are swelling. And it's going to rain. Look!'

I glance up, but can't see a thing. 'Can you see in this darkness?'

'No. But I can tell.' She points to her head. 'My brain just tells me. So hurry, Arkarian. You have to get under cover.' She urges me upwards with her hands.

A thought hits me. 'Are you an angel?'

She laughs, doubling over. 'You won't find an angel in this horrible place.'

Using the branch I pull myself up, and Sera urges me to put one foot before the other. 'Where are you taking me?'

'To the temple of course. You silly thing. Where else?'

I have no idea, so I stay silent.

'The temple is safe. You'll be warm there, and I can take care of you.'

'Do you have soothing balms?'

'I have nothing!' she pouts sulkily. 'Except water that Bastian brings me.'

'Bastian looks after you?'

Her slender shoulders lift and she seems to lose concentration for a moment. 'Sometimes he visits. But never if Marduke is around. Oooh!' she cries in a shrill voice. 'How I hate him! And his ugly beasts!'

'The wren are afraid of you.'

She shivers. 'And I am afraid of them. But I know it's really the temple they fear. It protects me from them. A long time ago people lived here, you know. It's an old story.'

'Please tell me about it.'

'It was a beautiful world. The temple was a place of worship. A place where the people could speak to their god and he would visit with them. But then the dark came and covered all the land. They built the lake around the temple to protect themselves.'

'What happened to these people?'

She shrugs her thin shoulders. 'They needed their sun to exist. And when the darkness was complete, everything started to die. After a while they had no food to eat. They grew weak. Evil grew strong. Eventually they disappeared. After a long time without people, many more creatures came to live here.'

'The wren?'

'Yes, and others too. Then the flowers started to grow.'

'Flowers?'

'Black ones.' She points over her shoulder. But without light it's impossible to even estimate where she's pointing.

'How did you come by this story?'

'The flowers told me. They told me a lot of old stories.'

While the idea of flowers 'talking' sounds strange, who am I to doubt? I know nothing of this world's inhabitants, except for the wren; and they're certainly unusual.

'Have you been safe here, Sera?'

'I've been lonely, but I'd rather live alone than with those ugly beasts. As long as they think I'm a ghost, they let me be.'

Her words make me give a little laugh inside. I pay for it with pain from my broken ribs. 'Pardon me for saying, Sera, but … you *are* a ghost.' Her crestfallen face has me remembering that Sera was only a child of ten when Marduke murdered her. What does she remember of her other life? What has her time here done to her sanity? 'You do know that you died in the mortal world thirteen years ago?'

She sighs, the outer edges of her pursed lips sinking downwards. 'I know I died. But I didn't know it was so long ago! I'm so old now!'

I begin to understand Sera's problem. 'You're trapped here. Your soul can't move on.'

Suddenly she grins, and her eyes become as luminous as her skin for a brief moment. 'But now everything will be well!'

I stumble on a rock and almost fall, but somehow Sera helps me maintain my balance. How she does this is amazing. I can feel her touch me, yet her hands, her arms in fact, go partially through me. 'Thank you,' I say, then ask, 'But how can my coming to this island be good for you? I'm trapped too now.'

We start walking again, slowly. 'When they come to rescue you, they'll rescue me too.'

Her words make me go still. I don't want Isabel or Ethan, or anyone, to come. It could mean their death, or entrapment. But now here's Sera. She's been stuck in this place for a long time. Doesn't she deserve a chance of freedom?

At my hesitation she frowns, her eyes narrowing to the point of almost disappearing. 'They will come, Arkarian. My brother will come. And he will bring the girl.'

She skips ahead of me. I wish I could share her excitement. My mind's a battlefield right now. 'How can you be so certain Ethan and Isabel will come?'

She comes running back. 'Oh I've made sure of it. After all the years of trying, I've finally reached someone.'

'Who have you reached, Sera?'

'The girl. The girl with the psychic skills.'

'Do you mean Isabel?'

She shrugs her little shoulders. 'I tried to reach my brother, and my mother many, many times. But it

149

didn't work. Ethan would scream like I whipped him or something and block me out. And my mother would only cry. But the girl, the girl you call Isabel. The one that loves my brother. She will come. I have shown her. I have shown her the temple and ...'

Sera's words drone on, but my thoughts lock on to two things: now that a link has been made, Isabel will do anything she can to come here, the connection will strike her deeply; and, according to Sera, Isabel is still in love with Ethan.

Chapter Fourteen

Isabel

The last time I came to Athens, and stood in this peaceful golden courtyard, was the day of Ethan's trial, when he thought he was going to be ex-communicated, and ended up being awarded one of the Guard's highest honours – his wings. It was a day I will never forget for its tumultuous emotions. I have a feeling today will also be full of surprises, but not the kind one looks forward to. Neither Ethan nor I is on trial, yet I'm picking up an uneasy sense to this summons.

We wait for a sign to know where to go or who to see. The sign comes in the form of Lord Penbarin himself, the Lord of Samartyne. A giant of a man, today he wears a floor-length robe of shimmering red – not a good colour or fabric for a man his size. Hurriedly I switch my thoughts, remembering well how all the members of the Tribunal are Truthseers, and I'm not sure if it's possible to screen my thoughts from them.

'Welcome,' Lord Penbarin greets us. 'Come, good food is waiting.'

'We're not hungry,' I reply, without giving Ethan a chance to say a word. Food, right now, would only make me vomit. 'My lord, if you please, may we begin?'

'You're in such a hurry, my dear, I fear today you'll be disappointed. Lorian is in a mood fit to kill. Has been ever since ...' He pauses, then continues without finishing his thought, 'Come, at least partake of a drink while the Tribunal gather.'

Once inside the marble hallway, the temperature drops to something much more comfortable. Lord Penbarin leads us to a table laden with hot and cold food. I sip a glass of wine, but find it difficult to swallow. My heart is pounding with the anticipation I feel inside. I just want to get on with this ordeal.

Finally we're shown into the Tribunal Chambers. It's exactly as I remember – circular marble walls, with eight of the nine leaders of their Houses sitting in clock-like fashion. The first is Lady Devine of the House of Divinity. She sits left of the Immortal, while beside her sits Lord Meridian of Kavannah, and Queen Brystianne of the House of Averil in all her gold finery. Next in the circle is Sir Syford, Lady Elenna of Isle, Lord Alexandon of the House of Criers, and the delicate-looking Lady Arabella. Finally, and last to take his seat, is Lord Penbarin. But today there remains one vacant chair, laid out for Veridian's own King – Richard – who is apparently still recovering in the healing chambers, having been brought here through time, body and all.

Ethan and I are invited to sit side by side on stools provided. As we do, Lorian starts the proceedings, 'You have been brought here today for two purposes.'

I heave a sigh of relief. At last someone is ready to get to the point!

Lorian's skin flares for a moment and I remember to curb my thoughts. 'The first is to reveal the Tribunal's distress. As you know, Arkarian has been taken to the underworld, held there while Lathenia decides how best to use him now that her plans to eliminate him at birth have failed.' Lorian pauses, allowing us to absorb these words, or, the thought occurs to me with a shiver, prepare ourselves for what's to come.

Soon Lorian continues, 'The second is this: and I say these words clearly so that there will be no confusion, and you will understand my command. Arkarian is aware of his ... unfortunate situation, and he understands the Tribunal's dilemma.'

'What dilemma is that?' I ask, without quite making eye contact. The last time I did, the power of the Immortal's gaze sent me flying backwards with a jolt of blinding heat.

Lorian continues as if I didn't speak, 'Without Arkarian the Guard is severely disadvantaged.'

Well, this much I know.

Lorian pauses and stares at me. I gulp deeply, reminding myself to shut off my inner thoughts. After an uncomfortable silence Lorian continues, 'To risk a rescue mission would be to risk the lives of other members of the Guard, with the very probable consequence of losing them, disadvantaging the Guard to a point that may tip the balance of power in the Goddess's favour. Our very tenuous hold could slip. Remember, protecting the city of Veridian is vital to our success. It is the Named that are tasked with this guardianship. There are riches within the city walls that cannot be measured in terms of monetary wealth. If Lathenia should take control she will become infinitely more powerful. We cannot let this happen.'

The Immortal's words are starting to sink in, but I don't like what I'm hearing, or where I think they're heading. I swallow down my fear. 'What exactly are you saying, my lord?'

This time Lorian answers me directly. 'Any rescue mission planned for Arkarian will *not* go ahead.'

Ethan and I jump out of our seats. Ethan gets a word out first, 'But—' Except one withering look from Lorian has him freezing up fast.

For me it's clearer than black and white. 'How can you sit so calmly in your mighty chair and command Arkarian's death? You must know that's exactly what you're doing by denying us the chance to rescue him. If it's not already too late.'

My words have the effect of bringing a hushed stillness into the Chambers. Lorian stares down at me. I force myself not to connect with the Immortal's gaze. Right now it would probably burn holes in my head. 'Do you think this is an easy command I make?'

My head shakes a negative; words have disappeared. I feel, without having to look up, the intensity of Lorian's glare.

'Isabel, you have no concept of what it has taken me. What it has taken *from* me, to make this decision.'

Bone dry right to the bottom of my throat, I try to work moisture into my mouth so that I can form words again. 'Then I beg of you, tell me why.'

Lorian explains: 'Lathenia is on a rampage. She has escalated the war between us, unintentionally drawing a final confrontation nearer. It's as if she doesn't have a care or concern for her own armies. This is a new tactic. This is what we are up against now – a fearless enemy. An enemy willing to risk all – and I mean *all*!'

Lorian pauses a moment. 'I am not willing to risk all.'

And then, 'You have not thought this through. If you were to go into the underworld, you would not have your bodily disguises.'

'My lord,' I say my words quickly, before they dry up again beneath the Immortal's stare. 'Arkarian is without a disguise. So too is Lathenia. And I believe the Order are only moments away from discovering Ethan's identity anyway.'

'That may well be, but more is at risk than you think. Lathenia is making moves that will prove catastrophic to our world and hers too. She doesn't live in the underworld. It is a piteous place where men turn into beasts. It is a place for the soul-less.' Lorian inhales deeply, shoulders expanding and lifting beneath the silver cloak as power emanates from him.

I find the stool beneath my fingers and sit on it. Ethan follows, his breathing harsh and loud. If he were prone to asthma, I'd think he was having an attack.

Lorian continues in our silence, 'Have you noticed certain changes in your mortal world?'

This has us thinking, remembering that odd day at school, the slip in the uniform code.

'Have you noticed a hint of darkness in the wind that comes from the north?' These words have our heads shooting up. I struggle to keep my eyes from connecting with Lorian's, feeling an urge to search them for a clue. As for the darkness, I haven't noticed anything … yet.

'You will,' Lorian interrupts my thoughts, reminding me how careful I have to be. 'Members of the Tribunal are reporting failed missions under their control. Several have lost soldiers. It won't be long before our world changes beyond repair. The situation is so desperate the present is becoming a feeding ground for the advancing armies of Chaos. We cannot let this continue. We cannot risk losing a further two important members of our Guard. We are already reinstating your missing members. Rochelle will return immediately. Neriah, who is still to be initiated, is already in your care, Isabel. So hear my words.' Lorian's voice explodes into my brain, 'Until Lathenia's rage reduces, and we begin to gain back ground, Arkarian remains where he is. There is to be no rescue mission. I forbid it!'

To the Immortal it is clear this meeting is over. But my heart is crying out to be heard. The very thought of living another day without Arkarian makes me feel desperate inside. And so the words come: 'I can't follow your command, my lord.'

Ethan inhales a sharp breath and digs his fingers into my arm firmly. 'What the hell are you doing?'

I yank my arm out of his grasp and get to my feet. The stool beneath me shoots out and tumbles backwards, making a loud noise in the deathly silence. 'I can't obey you,' I repeat more forcefully. 'You see, for most of my life I've looked after myself. If there was a problem I fixed it – on my own. It's how I live. Perhaps in my small world these matters are innocent and unimportant, and I'm never in any real danger, but right now there is someone in trouble, someone I care for – we all care for – and I know in my heart that I *can* fix this. Thanks to Lady Arabella and her gift to me, I only need a drop of light to see. And most importantly, I ask for no assistance. In this way the risk to the

156

Guard will be minimal. If you will allow me to try, I will bring Arkarian back.'

Beside me Ethan groans and slowly gets to his feet. 'Um, well, I'm with her. And no offence to Isabel, but I think the two of us together have a better chance of rescuing Arkarian.'

I smile at him, and with a little more enthusiasm he says, 'Arkarian was my Trainer, and my mentor for nearly all my life. When I was a child, he stopped me from losing my sanity. I owe him as a brother and as a friend. Please reconsider your command, my lord.'

Lorian remains silent. Maybe the Immortal will relate to a more logical argument. I wave my arms around to include the Tribunal members, hoping to get some response, some support from them. 'Look, everything we do while the Goddess is on the warpath is more dangerous than anything we've done before. Arkarian is vital to Veridian. Everyone in this room is conscious of that fact. We need all our players to fulfil the Prophecy successfully, so we must take the risk to rescue Arkarian, or all will be lost anyway. Can't you see?'

Still the Chamber remains silent, and my frustration grows. 'Why don't you answer me? I thought you knew everything! How come you don't know how to get Arkarian back?'

Lorian stands, and the suddenness of it has everyone gasping and holding their breath. I have a fraction of a second to realise I over-stepped my mark.

Lorian's hands do a wide sweep of the room, and from them explodes a chilling flame of blue fire, hurling and unfolding straight at us with the speed of a rocket in full flight. Every person, Lord, Queen and

King alike, dives to the floor. This curtain of pulsing flame hovers threateningly over us for a few seconds, making us shiver with the sudden plunge in temperature. Power surges through our bodies, rocking us, and I understand this is a display meant for us to feel the Immortal's strength, and not just see it.

In a flash the flame retracts, and everyone breathes again, murmuring to each other. Lorian speaks inside our heads, as if speaking verbally is beyond the Immortal's own capability at the moment.

The room falls silent as each of us receives this message. None of us is left in doubt of the Immortal's command. *Arkarian remains in the underworld. I have spoken. Now everyone leave me. Everyone!*

Chapter Fifteen

Isabel

I wake in my bed with a wild jolt to my heart, the power of Lorian's rage still thundering through every cell of my body. I get another start when I see Matt sitting in my plastic lounge, reading. He notices I'm back and puts the book aside. 'What happened? You look like you just returned from the dead.'

It takes a minute to catch my breath, then I tell him about my visit to Athens, and how Lorian informed us of the precarious position the Guard has found itself in. 'Lorian forbade any attempt to rescue Arkarian, and …'

'And …?'

'I inadvertently provoked an immortal rage.'

'What!'

'Lorian swept the chamber with this incredible blue fire. It was like ice. It went right through me.' I hold up my hands. They're still shaking.

Matt stares at me. 'You idiot.'

'Well thanks, and here I was thinking you cared.'

'You made this … this superior being mad at you? Are you insane? What were you thinking?'

'OK, I hear you. Don't worry, I'm not going to do it again.'

'I'm glad to hear it, Isabel.'

His sarcastic comment ticks me off. 'Well, thanks. At least I get things done!'

He doesn't respond, and I feel like a heel for having the cheap stab at him. 'Sorry,' I mumble.

'Forget it.'

We're silent for a minute. 'Before the mad rage Lorian let us know that Rochelle is coming back. Are you going to be all right with that?'

He glances away to the door, then swings his gaze down to his bare feet and stares at his toes for what seems like ages. Finally he looks up at me, 'If it were up to me, and I wasn't involved in this Guard stuff, I'd try to win her back, with everything I have.'

His words make my stomach churn. 'But now?'

He gets up and stands looking out at a starry night sky. 'Unlike you, I'm not an idiot.'

'Jerk.'

He smiles briefly, his jaw sliding first left, then right. 'I don't like the fact that I was being used by Marduke, or anyone, but …' he sighs. 'Look, maybe Rochelle didn't have much choice.'

'Seems to me that she only had two: pretend to love you, or be tortured by Marduke. Maybe she wasn't strong enough to stand up to him. Maybe he held other things over her as well. Things you won't know about until she's released from her de-briefing and the two of you get a chance to talk.'

He nods.

'I'm sure her decisions were difficult to make.' Of course *not* becoming Marduke's spy in the first place

160

would have been her best one.

And yet there is another twist to Rochelle's tale. Ethan has feelings for her too. At least he did. When they first met, he swore there was a connection, a bond of some sort. But neither of them could act on that feeling, as their lives swung off in opposite directions.

Matt leaves, and I lie in bed awake for the rest of the night. By sunlight I'm a wreck. I would take the day off school, except I'm supposed to be looking out for Neriah, and acting normally. But how can I act as if nothing's wrong? There's just too much going on in my head.

Ethan, knowing I would be distraught this morning, rides over, and along with Matt, we get the bus together. And even though we know Rochelle is going to be returning soon, we're all thrown into shock when we see her at school already, sitting alone on one of the benches.

I grip Matt's arm. 'Do you want to get this over with?'

At first he doesn't answer, just keeps looking at Rochelle. 'I don't think so,' he finally says. 'Maybe another day.'

He takes off and now I notice Ethan looking at Rochelle. Does he still have feelings for her too? Love is one of those things that can't be turned on and off at will. I decide to bring the matter up to test his reaction. 'Ah, I wonder what you're thinking right now.'

'About what?'

'Well, since it's over between Matt and Rochelle … I thought maybe …'

His head swivels sideways and he stares at me without blinking. 'What are you on about? You know I

161

can't stand that girl.'

I whisper back, 'She's one of us now.'

'Yeah, but that doesn't mean I trust her.'

He's lying, right to my face. Maybe even to his own heart. 'You stood up for her once, before all the members of the Tribunal.'

He chooses to ignore me, which is probably a good thing, as Dillon, walking beside Neriah, makes an appearance. I recall I was supposed to meet Neriah in the car park. But I'm having trouble remembering everything I'm supposed to be doing these days. Somehow I have to get a grip.

Mr Carter comes out of the office and pulls Neriah to the side, pointing to some textbooks in his hand. Dillon spots me and comes over, and for the first time I notice just how vivid green his eyes are.

'Hey,' he says. 'I went to the Falls Café yesterday but Neriah wasn't there.'

'Oh?'

'Then I went to the art block, but the staff there told me that Neriah Gabriel isn't doing any after-school art class.'

'Well, she's new. Her name probably isn't registered yet.'

'When I couldn't find her, I went for a walk through the forest and stumbled across her house – or I should say fortress! Anyway, I got to talk to her after all and she's not going to any art classes. She doesn't know where you got that idea from.' For a minute I think he's mad at me. Most guys would be. But his scowl transforms into a teasing grin. 'I think you were trying to get rid of me yesterday.'

I lift my shoulders and offer a lame smile back. 'I'm

sorry, Dillon. Yesterday was one hell of a day.'

'Yeah, well, it was a weird day for me too. But look, I really like Neriah. I want a chance with her. I need you on my side, Isabel.'

Maybe Ethan's right when he says Dillon's a nice guy. Maybe I don't know him as well as Ethan does, or even Matt for that matter.

Neriah approaches, ending our conversation. And somehow, minute by minute, the day passes. But if anyone were to ask me what classes I had today, I wouldn't be able to tell them. Except for history, when Mr Carter found a moment to tell me a mission is planned for this evening.

When I get home I learn there are guests coming for dinner. But I don't mind really, 'cause it's just Ethan with his parents and his Auntie Jenny, who's going to be staying in Angel Falls for a while. This is a plan, apparently, to persuade Laura not to go to the sanatorium next week. But so far it's not working. At least tonight I'll have an opportunity to see how Laura's doing for myself.

But when I do see her, I get such a shock, it takes an effort not to be rude. I can't help staring. When did she get so thin? Her arms and legs are like billiard cues. And her eyes, normally so vivid and pretty, look over-sized in a grey and drawn face. Even Shaun looks gaunt. He must be so worried about his wife.

Ethan sits beside his mum at the dinner table; occasionally his hand whips out and squeezes her arm. On one occasion when he does this, tears spring to my eyes. Sensing something, he glances up and catches my compassionate look. I try to impart a supportive smile. I want to let him know I'm here for him, and that

163

somehow we'll find a way to make his mother better.

Mum serves dinner – roast chicken with four different vegetables. The plate is bright and colourful. The look of it makes my stomach roll. I can't remember when I last ate. I can't seem to think of food any more. But I try to force some down so Mum doesn't get worried. Beside me, Jimmy watches quietly. He knows how anxious I am, but we haven't had a chance to talk yet about all that happened while he was away. Mum comes over and rubs my shoulders. She catches sight of my plate and can't help staring at what is now a pile of unidentifiable mush. 'Did I cook that?' Her tone is light, but I know her well. It's a disguise for her concern. 'Not hungry, darling?'

I almost blurt out some lame excuse about having a tummy bug. Ethan makes a coughing sound, and I remember not to ever make a fuss before going to bed on the night of a mission. Mum would only come in and check on me. And while I'll appear as if I'm only sleeping, my body won't wake or even stir. And she'll get such a fright if she tries to wake me.

I force a couple of huge spoonfuls down my throat and try not to gag. 'It just tastes so much better this way.'

Jimmy and Ethan exchange amused glances. Under the table I swing a kick at Ethan's knee. But his leg is closer than I think and I end up hitting it hard. He jerks, and his knee hits the underside of the table. The plates and cutlery rattle. Mum, Laura and Jenny stare at him. Quickly Jimmy makes a wisecrack, and thankfully, everyone starts to laugh.

By the time Ethan and his family go home, I'm exhausted, and quickly go to bed. Within seconds of my head hitting the pillow, I feel myself drifting into sleep.

I drop into a room in the Citadel, the one filled with a strange multi-coloured mist. Not long after, Ethan arrives. He looks around, but as yet no doors are open. He walks through the mist towards me and shrugs.

A soft whooshing sound has us both look to the centre of the room. Rochelle appears within a cloud of sooty fog. It makes her cough and she tries to wave some of it away. I flick a brief worried look at Ethan. It looks as if Rochelle's first mission for the Guard (as opposed to the Order) is going to be with us. Well, that makes sense. I guess she can't exactly be trusted to work on her own yet.

She looks at us both, and her eyebrows lift. 'What do you think this means?'

'Huh?' I wonder what she's talking about.

'There's always a reason a room chooses you.'

Ethan's eyes lift to meet Rochelle's, and for a second it's as if a spark of recognition lights between them, a spark with the force of electricity. 'Fog usually means impaired vision. Perhaps this mist is meant as a warning.'

Rochelle's head flicks, her chin lifting. I get the feeling her nerves are kicking in, but really, I'm helpless to reassure her. It's not that Rochelle is new at this sort of thing. This is far from her first mission, but it is Rochelle's first for *our* side. And here she is working with the two of us – Ethan, the guy she dumped at Marduke's command, and me, her ex-boyfriend's sister. Then there's the added worry that the Goddess will be on the lookout for Rochelle's return.

'Has anyone been briefed?' I ask as an awkward

silence develops.

Neither of them have, apparently, and Ethan is quick to add his opinion, 'That'd be right. It looks like Carter's stuffing up again.'

Just as Ethan makes his complaint, Mr Carter appears in the room. He sighs and runs a hand through his hair. He looks stressed, and I feel a moment of empathy for him. He's filling in for Arkarian, as well as trying to continue in his own position, and teach at the school by day.

After giving Rochelle a long uneasy glance, he gets to the point, 'You're needed in Ancient Rome, during the late first century BC, when Octavius takes control of his empire.'

I've never been there, and the idea alone makes me gasp. 'Oh wow.' For a minute I experience that familiar buzz I get when about to embark on a journey into the past. But then thoughts of Arkarian, never more than fleeting seconds away, come thundering back, and I remember a time when Arkarian and I were about to head off to duel with Marduke and his soldiers. Arkarian handed me a specially made sword, given to him by King Arthur's knight, Gawain. He knew how worried I was about the upcoming duel and the slim chance we seemed to have of saving Matt's life, when suddenly he'd said to me, 'I would die for you.' At the time, I didn't reply. His words had taken me by surprise. But now, as I hear them unfold in my head again, a reply springs to mind, and I whisper, 'And I would die for you.'

I realise I've said these words out loud when everyone in the room stops still and looks at me. Rochelle rolls her eyes. Mr Carter looks at me sympathetically.

Ethan comes up behind me and rubs my arm. 'Are you OK?'

I look up at him and nod, my eyes blurred.

He checks again, 'Are you sure?'

'Yeah, I'm fine.'

Turning back to Mr Carter, Ethan asks him what our roles are. 'And make sure you get it right this time, and not land us smack bang in the middle of a raging battle.'

Mr Carter's eyes flare, but we're not in the classroom now, so his power over Ethan is slightly diminished. Ethan's mistrust of this man doesn't have much of a foundation. All the same, I would never dismiss Ethan's natural instinct.

Mr Carter takes a deep breath. 'I'm doing my best, Ethan. I'm not the one in this room whose trust should be in doubt.'

As he says these words his eyes travel sideways to Rochelle. It's no secret that Mr Carter has serious doubts about Rochelle's allegiance, but apparently the Tribunal think she's ready to join us, and Mr Carter's obvious disapproval won't make our mission any easier.

Rochelle groans, 'Let's just get on with it. I don't know what you lot were taught, but I was told that time isn't measured in this place.'

'Really? What else were you told?' Mr Carter asks. 'That could make an interesting conversation.'

Her chin does that little flick and lift again. 'I've briefed the Tribunal on everything I know, so I don't have to tell you anything.'

The air grows thick, even the mist has increased. It's as if the room itself can feel the tension. 'Shouldn't we get moving?' I suggest. 'Before we lose each other and all sense of what we're supposed to be doing in this fog?'

Mr Carter finally gets his thoughts together. He becomes the teacher once more, his demeanour one of authority and knowledge. 'The portal has opened during a time when Octavius, or I should say, Gaius Julius Caesar Octavius, is between battles with Mark Antony. He's relaxing for a few days at home, enjoying the company of his wife, Julia, and her two sons from an earlier marriage, Tiberius and Drusus. He is well into his campaign to attain the title of first Emperor of Rome, using his brilliant political cunning. But it appears that an attempt will be made on his life during these few days, by one or more of the Order. If they should succeed, you must all realise what effect this could have on life as we know it. Rome and Octavius, and all the events that followed, have enormous influences on the culture of the modern world. Do you understand what I'm saying?'

He doesn't have to be so explicit. Every mission is important, but we get it – this one is vital, especially as the balance of power between the Guard and the Order is very precarious right now.

'An opportunity has arisen to send you in under the guise of Roman doctors. Ethan will be in charge, with you two girls his assistants. In this way all of you will have access to the house without question to your citizenship, and, should you fail to stop Octavius from receiving a wound, you will be in the best position to heal him.'

Our instructions given, Mr Carter goes to leave, but stops as a doorway opens before him. 'Whatever the

Order plan, it's going to be big. Remember that.'

His voice is so serious it unnerves me.

'They're out to make a lot of damage,' he adds. 'That's why we're sending all three of you. Please, be careful.'

He leaves, and with nothing but silence and our own troubled thoughts for company, we go to a wardrobe room. It's here we're appropriately outfitted with new identities. All three of us become unrecognisable.

We end up wearing long under tunics, mine made of white satin, and covered mostly by a blue wool wrap. My hair has been changed to yellow gold and pulled back in rope coils to form a tight bun at the back. Rochelle's hair is a rich red-brown, also pulled tightly back, but the front third is now a mass of short and thick curls. She glances in the mirror, taking in her green tunic and salmon-coloured over dress.

Ethan's outfit is almost completely white, while his hair is black and cut short all over, except for a fringe pulled down over his forehead. A sprinkling of dust falls over us from the ceiling, and we are endowed with the knowledge we need to fulfil this mission. Specialist tools appear in my hands wrapped in cloth, and I understand that Ethan will be a doctor of professional standing, specialising in internal injuries and ailments.

Ethan turns and points to me. 'Claudia, my assistant.' And to Rochelle he says softly, 'Sempronia.'

Rochelle moves away from the mirror and dips her head in response. 'Petronius.'

The look they exchange is charged with electricity. They would both have to be numb not to feel it. Strangely they appear as if they're caught in a trance. I may as well not even be in the room! Ethan is first to

169

break contact. A scowl appears on his face as if he's annoyed with himself. Annoyed with his reaction. He hurries us out of the room. The stairwells take us up to a departure room. A door opens in the opposite wall and the three of us quickly leap.

Chapter Sixteen

Isabel

Rome is incredible. People are everywhere – hundreds of them, going about their business all in a rush. There's an open market, steaming with hot spicy food. The streets are cobbled and straight, the buildings two and three storeys high.

'Stop gawking,' Rochelle hisses at me. 'You're going to stand out. And ultimately that puts us all at risk.'

My gaze slides sideways. I wonder what's eating her? But when I think about it, I guess she's right. I probably am coming across as a typical tourist. Ethan gives a laugh under his breath. I stick him in the ribs with my elbow.

'Doesn't this just sweep you away?' I open my palms to indicate the multitude of people around us. To me, it's the men that stand out, in their white tunics or togas, slaves trailing behind like bodyguards to the rich and famous. 'It's just so alive!'

Rochelle turns sideways, making sure she doesn't brush up against a man pushing a cart of vegetables. 'You're such a romantic. One day your bubble's going to burst and you're going to end up with mud on your

171

face. Life isn't sweet. It stinks. Just smell it.' Her nose wrinkles up and I have to wonder where all this negativity is coming from. OK, she's been through some dramatic changes in the last twelve months, but this bitterness sounds as if it's specifically aimed – at me, or Ethan. She's probably just frustrated, unsure of Ethan's feelings.

'Can you believe that stench?'

Up until now I hadn't noticed, too caught up in the excitement of simply being here. But now that she mentions it …'Phew. What *is* that?'

'Garbage,' Ethan says. 'Sewage too.'

'And something burning, like a building that's been smouldering for days,' Rochelle adds.

We keep walking, a kilometre at least. 'Does anyone know where we're going?'

Ethan points up ahead to a white building of many columns. 'There, to the left of that temple. Octavius should be staying in a villa that's just a walk down that road.'

It ends up a long walk, but no one complains. And I'm not game to ask Rochelle what she thinks again.

At last we arrive at the front door of a villa Ethan thinks is the one. In a street of large houses, this one is by far the largest of all. At Ethan's knock the door is opened by a huge man, a slave apparently, wearing a white robe, a stark contrast to his dark African skin.

Ethan introduces himself.

'The doctor has arrived,' the slave announces in a strong voice with a bored tone to it. He ushers us into a cool atrium where the floor and sparse furnishings are made almost entirely of marble. As we wait, the slave examines us, a frown forming on his deep set brow. He notices the tools in my hands but doesn't say anything. After a minute he calls out again, 'It appears he has brought his entire entourage. Three in all.'

While the slave's tone is anything but warm, it's good to know that we're expected. At least Ethan is. Finally we're greeted by a woman who turns out to be Lady Livia herself – Octavius's wife. An attractive woman, she looks slender in a long dark gown with a sheer red wrap around her shoulders. She welcomes us warmly. Apparently their other doctor recently retired, and her eldest son, Tiberius, a ten-year-old who has lately come to live with them after the death of his father, has come down with some unexplained ailment.

My spine prickles, and I have to wonder if it's my sixth sense hinting foul play might be at work, or simply my healing instincts kicking into action. 'Can we see the boy?' She looks at me as if I've spoken out of turn. 'It wouldn't be good to delay, should he be afflicted with something serious, my lady,' I explain, my face heating up under her glare.

Livia's eyes slide down to the implements wrapped in cloth in my hands, then at Rochelle's empty ones. She's obviously got something on her mind, something bothering her. 'These women,' she says to Ethan, 'are they *both* your assistants?'

'This is Claudia,' he replies, pointing in my direction. He indicates Rochelle next, but before he has a chance to introduce her, the African slave moves in front of us.

'We were expecting two.' He crosses his muscular arms over his equally muscular chest. 'The doctor and his assistant only.'

It appears Mr Carter got it slightly wrong, putting

our credibility at risk. To my right Ethan's hand starts to curl into a fist. He has to come up with a plausible explanation for Rochelle's presence. It thankfully does-n't take him long, though I'm not sure Rochelle will be impressed with his brainwave. 'This is Sempronia. She is … my slave. She's very talented with her … with her hands.' He freezes. All three of us do. Other than truth-seeing, Rochelle's skill is her gift of touch. Her hands are capable of identifying just about everything, espe-cially substances like herbs, powders and chemicals. She doesn't need light or smell or any other sense to know exactly what's in her hands. Preparing poison is her speciality. Well, it used to be when she worked for Marduke.

A silence follows where all I can hear is Rochelle's breathing, which has suddenly grown noisy.

Livia speaks first. 'Very well, she'll sleep in the slave's quarters. Wanjala can set a bed up for her.'

Oh great. How do we get out of this? Isolating Rochelle from us would put her in a vulnerable posi-tion. If her identity were to be discovered, there's no doubt the Order would want her captured or destroyed.

Ethan's eyes spin to Rochelle's. Just identifying her as a slave has left her seriously powerless, let alone sin-gling out her hands as 'special'. She has to keep a low profile now, that's for sure. She especially can't go reacting indignantly. Keeping her eyes low and buried, they skitter across the floor from one end of the room to the other, while she waits for her awkward situation to be resolved.

Ethan's shoulders lift, and to Livia he says, 'If it pleases, my lady, I would like Sempronia to remain by my side. She is already trained in preparing medicinal formulations, and I have many uses for her.'

Livia glances from Ethan to Rochelle. Patting his arm, she looks at him with amusement. 'I'm sure you have, Petronius. It will be as you wish. The three of you shall lodge in the guest quarters.' And to her slave she says, 'See to it, Wanjala.'

The matter thankfully closed, Livia speaks to one of the female slaves that have gathered in the atrium, asking where her son can be found.

Cornelia, a small young woman, explains, 'Wanjala carried him to a bed in the courtyard, my lady, to give Julia some time to go to the market.'

The courtyard is located in the centre of the house. As we walk there Livia explains that Julia is the boy's nanny.

We find Tiberius sleeping in a shady corner, while his younger brother, Drusus, plays quietly around his couch. Without even feeling the boy, it's clear from his brightly flushed cheeks that he's running a temperature. But I have to be careful to maintain my disguise as Ethan's assistant. I've already spoken out of turn once. So I wait for Ethan to examine the boy first. His training helps him bluff his way through the examination. At last he calls me to assist, explaining how the boy's chest is internally inflamed and must be kept warm while he listens for the presence of damaging fluid. 'Lay your hands here,' he says to me, placing them directly over the boy's lungs.

Within seconds I have a clear picture in my head. The boy has pneumonia, his lungs struggling to inflate. One in particular is on the verge of collapsing. 'It might be easier on the boy if he were to sit up,' I suggest.

Ethan understands that I want to get my hands on the boy's back. As we move the child into position, and I begin working on healing the severe chest infection, Ethan tries to distract the household. 'We will need several medicinal herbs to prepare the boy's medication.'

Livia quickly comes to our aid. 'The household is well stocked, but if there's anything in particular you desire, I will send for it immediately.'

Ethan sends Rochelle to check the stores, giving her an opportunity to look for suspicious items. He then hands me a small vial of coloured liquid he has in his tunic. 'In the meantime this medicine will start the recovery process.'

As the slave, Cornelia, shows Rochelle where to go, I give the boy the coloured liquid to drink. It's a good idea, even though the 'medicine' is probably only water or syrup. Ethan knows it won't take me long to heal the child. All the same, it mustn't look as if he was healed by magic. And to heal him completely would be a mistake, as we're supposed to be doctors, not miracle workers. A real herbal mixture should be enough to return him to full health in a few days.

His temperature reduced, Tiberius feels better and grows restless. He wants to play with his brother, but Livia orders him to keep resting. While she is distracted by her suddenly energetic son, Ethan leans down to whisper in my ear, 'Was it poison?'

As soon as he asks a sinking feeling hits me deep in my stomach. Tiberius's illness *wasn't* foul play, but simply a chest infection. Glancing at the boy, I try to shrug off an eerie feeling I've done the wrong thing. How could healing a child of something he would eventually overcome anyway be wrong? Would my action be considered as tampering with the past? Suddenly I'm confused. I try to recall what Mr Carter's instructions were.

Soon a bustling sound from inside the house gets my attention. Slaves are running all over the place. Livia, in a wonderful mood now that her son is looking better, doesn't even realise it's her husband, Octavius, who has arrived home.

He walks into the courtyard. She sees him at last, and announces his presence using his full title of Gaius Julius Caesar Octavius. He stands still, strong eyebrows lifting. My eyes are drawn to him. His presence is very magnetic, standing there, not particularly tall, but seeming so in his white tunic and toga, his manner calm but purposeful, his hair fairer than I imagined. And there's something about his eyes that seem almost … divine, in the literal sense of the word, strange as that may sound.

Rochelle comes back holding a selection of herbs. She sees Octavius and gasps softly. He simply smiles, apparently used to this sort of reaction. Livia takes him by the arm, and brings him over to meet us. Introducing Ethan and me, she goes on to explain how much better Tiberius is feeling since Petronius's consultation.

From the corner of my eye I see Rochelle stare at the small boy jumping up and down on his bed.

Octavius claps his hands three times. 'Wonderful,' he says. 'For your excellent work, the two of you must join us this evening for a sumptuous meal.'

Rochelle is not invited, but as a slave, she wouldn't be, and there's not much Ethan can do about that. A quiet moment later I find myself alone with her in our room.

'So what was wrong with Tiberius?' Rochelle asks, unfolding a blanket.

'What do you mean?'

She smirks. 'You healed him, didn't you?'

Her tone is full of accusation. 'He had an infection. I helped clear it up. It won't make any difference, OK?'

The blanket in her hand drops to the bed. 'Yeah, right.'

Her attitude irritates. 'It just happened. Healing has become such a natural act lately.'

She picks up the blanket and spreads it over the bed. 'You'd best learn how to control your instincts. Sometimes the smallest mistakes have the largest impact.'

'Well thanks. I feel so much better now.'

She snorts and finishes making up the bed in silence. And I can't help thinking if Arkarian had co-ordinated this mission, I wouldn't have made that mistake with Tiberius, no matter how large or small it could prove to be. His instructions were always so clear. But I really haven't the right to blame Mr Carter either. I simply should have known. I just hope nothing will come of it, and that I'm worrying myself stupid for no reason.

I try to take my mind off Tiberius's sudden good health by asking Rochelle if she minds being on her own tonight, while Ethan and I attend the dinner with Octavius and his family.

She's quick to answer, snapping at me, 'I can handle myself.'

'I know that,' I tell her. 'It's just, I don't like any of us being separated. I've got this weird feeling we're being watched all the time.'

'Yeah, I know what you mean.'

'Do you recognise anyone?' I ask this doubtfully. To

178

recognise someone who doesn't belong in the past, she would have to look deeply into their eyes, which might put her own identity at risk.

She shakes her head. 'I'm not going to stare into anyone's face for more than a brief second.'

'Just be careful,' I warn her. 'My sixth sense has shot into overdrive at the moment. I'm getting one eerie vibe after another.'

The boy, Tiberius, suddenly runs into our room at full pelt, swinging around the two of us and dragging on our tunics. His cheeks are flushed again, but I get the feeling it's more from play than any lingering chest infection.

I pull him round to face me. 'What's going on? Didn't your mother tell you not to leave your bed?'

He looks to the door, his eyes laughing, his mouth an impish grin. 'But I'm feeling much better!'

Rochelle figures out his game. 'I bet your mother doesn't know where you are.'

'She sent Drusus and that demon woman to look for me.'

'What "demon" woman?' Rochelle asks.

He giggles as his younger brother shoots across the open doorway. 'I can't see him anywhere, Julia,' Drusus calls out to his nanny, who runs past in hot pursuit, looking very flustered.

Tiberius, spotting his nanny, quickly searches the room with his eyes. 'Hide me, please. That woman is a witch.'

Rochelle exchanges a look with me, then says, 'We'll hide you from your nanny, but only if you promise to go straight back to bed.'

He agrees and I point to a wicker basket meant to

hold our clothes. 'Here. Jump in.'

I lower the lid over him just as Drusus charges in, with Julia heaving behind him. 'Have you seen my charge?' she asks in a cold commanding voice. 'He's supposed to be taking a nap! If he's well enough to run around he should be doing chores, or working on his lessons.'

Rochelle and I exchange a secretive look. Drusus runs around the room looking beneath our beds and under clothes lying around. As he goes to lift the lid of the wicker basket, I grab the back of his tunic, stopping him just in time. 'You won't find your brother in this room.' I send him back to the heaving chest of his nanny.

She grabs the boy's arm in a firm grip, leading him to the door. 'If you see the little rascal, tell him if he doesn't get back to bed, his next lessons will be double in length.'

'Of course. I'll make sure he hears every word.'

She gives me a lingering look before taking off with her smallest charge. Tiberius peaks out from beneath the lid of the basket. 'Is it safe? Is the witch gone?'

I lift the lid. 'All's clear.'

He climbs out of the basket, a grin splitting his face from ear to ear. 'Oh thank you,' he says with great relief. 'If there is anything I can do for you in return …'

Rochelle motions for him to come closer. 'You can start repaying us right now by telling us why you think your nanny is a witch.'

His small body vibrates with a shiver that starts at his head and descends all the way to his bare toes. 'She makes things with herbs and other powders.'

He has our attention immediately. 'Sempronia makes things with herbs too, but they're good medicines. Why do you think Julia makes bad things?'

'Because she makes them in the middle of the night, with him, the big man.'

Rochelle and I exchange worried frowns over the top of Tiberius's head. 'Do you mean Wanjala?' Rochelle asks.

Tiberius's eyes grow wide. 'Uh-huh.'

'Have you spoken with your mother about them? Maybe you could ask her to have them dismissed.'

If these two are working for the Order, dismissing them could be one solution – a means to getting them out of the house until the portal to this time period closes.

'She thinks I don't like Julia because she's strict. I've had a lot of nannies.'

'Really?' I ask. 'So Julia hasn't been with the household for long?'

'She came only last week, the same day as Wanjala.'

Rochelle frowns. 'He has such an authoritative manner, I thought he must have been here for a long time.'

Tiberius looks back at us blankly. I pat his chest. 'Well, you'd better go now – straight back to bed. You don't want that fever coming back, do you?'

'Yes, my lady. I mean, no, my lady,' he says as he backs towards the door. 'And thank you again.' He bows dramatically, and when he lifts his head his eyes are sparkling, his grin huge.

I can't help smile at the boy as he runs from the room.

Rochelle, it seems, has the same feelings about him.

'The little charmer.'

Ethan walks in and we explain what we just learned about Wanjala and Julia.

'I wonder what they're brewing together,' he says.

'Well, whatever it is, we'll have to work fast at finding out, if we're going to have any chance of stopping them.'

'If they suspect us,' Rochelle says. 'And no doubt they do by now, they're going to speed up their plans. They're going to make sure they finish their job before we even work out what they're up to.' She looks at Ethan. 'Where have you been? Did you find out anything useful?'

His shoulders lift. 'I've been with Caesar, discussing his latest problems with Mark Antony. There was so much I could have told him, not least how successful he will ultimately be with this man.'

'That's not up to us,' Rochelle reminds him – unnecessarily. While it would be tempting, and so easy, to say or do something that could reassure Octavius about his future successes, an inappropriate word or action could have the effect of changing history, and ultimately the future. But Ethan, of all people, knows this.

'Remember we took an oath,' Rochelle says, adding to her insult.

He snaps. 'What do you think I am? An idiot? I'm not going to do anything that could jeopardise the future. I learned that lesson from my father's problems with Marduke.' Looking straight into Rochelle's eyes he adds, 'I don't cave in to temptation.'

I cough to clear the air, but it doesn't work. They keep staring at each other with daggers for eyes. 'Look you two, fighting is not going to get us anywhere.'

'Tell *her*,' Ethan says, crossing his arms over his chest.

Rochelle goes to the door, exhaling a long breath that sounds more like a mournful sigh. 'Why don't we split up?'

Ethan slips past her, and without looking at either of us, walks straight out the door, mumbling, 'Great idea.'

The afternoon passes quickly. Rochelle disappears to the kitchen, looking for evidence. Ethan sticks with Octavius, closer than a bodyguard, while I try to keep a general eye out for anything suspicious. But nothing unusual or extraordinary happens. Drusus gets some free time and chats with me in the courtyard while his brother looks on with amusement from his bed. It eventually grows dark, and the slaves of the house rush around preparing the sumptuous meal Octavius promised. Finally we go inside.

The children lead me to a large room, where three long couches on high legs, and a long table, sit in the form of a square. The couches are covered in cushions. Ethan and I are shown to a couch opposite Tiberius and his step-father, Octavius. Livia and her younger son, Drusus, share the other. Slaves soon bustle about bringing food to the table, some carry platters, which they offer to each of us.

It feels strange eating food in this manner – lying on a couch! But I try to look comfortable, as if I've done this all my life. Rochelle, in her role as slave, has offered to help with the food.

As I sit and listen to the conversation passing from Livia to her husband, and Ethan by my side, my thoughts turn to the brew Tiberius has seen Wanjala and Julia mixing. It has me wondering what on earth they could be making. Mr Carter's words come back to haunt me as I recall him saying it will be something big.

Rochelle leans over my shoulder with a tray of bread, olives and fish and whispers, 'He's been working like crazy on an unusual centrepiece – a pig's head. It's stuffed with a strange-smelling mixture that's supposed to be herb bread and mixed grains. He's going to present it to Caesar. My first thought was poison.' She screws up her nose. 'But it doesn't have the right smell. I wish I could get my hands on it without either of them seeing me.'

'That would be too risky,' I mutter. 'You'd give yourself away.'

She nods. 'Whatever it is, don't let Caesar, or anyone for that matter, eat the pig.'

Her words have the same effect as ice water poured down my spine. Poison is Rochelle's speciality. If the Order suspect she may be here, they could have devised a way to disguise the smell. Passing this information quickly to Ethan, I warn him about the pig's head.

I hardly get a second to think when Wanjala makes a grand entrance with a silver tray in his hand, a silver dome lid over the top. 'For our master, Gaius Julius Caesar Octavius,' he announces flamboyantly. 'And his special guests.'

Laying the platter down on the table, Wanjala steps back to the wall. It occurs to me that this action is quite strange. One would think a man of such pride as Wanjala would be only too keen to display his handiwork himself. Mr Carter's words, 'It will be big', come back and taunt me.

Tiberius jumps up, just as Octavius reaches across to the domed lid. 'Let me do it,' the boy asks in his familiar, charming voice.

Octavius smiles down at him, then says, 'Your arm must grow another whole length before it will reach the table.'

'Watch me,' Tiberius says, stretching as hard as he can for the lid. 'I can do it.'

At the very moment both Octavius and Tiberius reach for the domed lid, it hits me. It's not a poisoned pig's head under that lid. But something much more deadly.

Their fingers grip the handle just as I scream out, 'No! Don't lift it!'

But they do. And as the lid lifts Octavius looks at me with an amused frown. For a second it appears as if he's about to ask me something, but he doesn't get his words out before the tray, with everything on it, explodes.

The force of the erupting bomb catapults Octavius and Tiberius into the air. The table bursts into shards of splinters and food flies everywhere. Livia screams and runs to her husband and child, both unconscious and sprawled against the wall.

Amid a scurry of slaves running everywhere, Ethan and I scramble off the upturned couch. Out of the corner of my eye I see Wanjala and Julia take a look, and seeing the destruction and gathering pool of blood beneath the soon-to-be Emperor, start to back away.

'It's done,' Wanjala says in a voice devoid of all his earlier bravado. 'He'll be dead in a few minutes. Let's get out of here.'

'No wait,' Julia replies. 'Let's make sure.'

185

Rochelle hears the woman and sees red. She grabs a splintered piece of timber from the floor and goes to stab her. But Wanjala intercepts her. Pulling a dagger from his tunic, he holds it beneath Rochelle's ribs. 'Don't try it. I won't hesitate to kill you.'

Ethan takes one look at Rochelle in trouble and uses his skill to animate objects. Cushions, broken bits of furniture, platters, and even food, start whirling towards Wanjala's head. Using this distraction, Ethan pushes Julia roughly out of the way, then drags Rochelle out from Wanjala's grasp. 'You're not going to die here in the past! Do you understand?'

As the debris starts to settle, and slaves stop screaming, I finish assessing Octavius and Tiberius's wounds. Both of them are critically ill, having received massive injuries. Suddenly Wanjala towers over the back of me. I look up, expecting to see him wearing a look of smug satisfaction. But he's not. He stares at the man and child sprawled below him, his mouth drifting open as his eyes rest on the boy. He sees me looking at him and pulls away. Without saying a word, he takes Julia's hand, and the Order's two soldiers run from the room.

Rochelle, still caught tight in Ethan's hold, snarls and hisses in frustration. 'Let me go!'

'No. You're needed here. Help stem this blood flow.'

Livia looks from her husband to her son and moans hysterically. She must think she's about to lose them both.

But the decision of who lives and who dies right now is unbelievably up to me. I have the power to heal, but only one at a time. And looking at Tiberius my heart skitters uncontrollably. The only reason this child is lying here on the verge of death is because of me. If I hadn't healed him of his chest infection this morning, he would still have been in bed. He wouldn't have opened the lid not meant to be touched by his hand. With these thoughts thundering through my brain, I bend over him, running my fingers over his blood-stained head, searching for internal injuries, and looking for a point to begin healing.

But Ethan grabs my arm and drags me backwards. 'No!'

I look up, hardly seeing him through my rapidly blurring vision. I know what he's saying, but I can't accept it. 'I have to heal the boy! He's dying,' I whisper.

He swallows deeply. 'You have to save Caesar first. He's dying too. That's what we came for.'

'But the boy,' I try to tell him, even though I know he knows. 'He will be an Emperor too.'

'Gaius Julius Caesar Octavius will be the first, the famous Augustus Caesar and his changes will be the ones that will shape our modern world. You have to heal *him* first. And you have to hurry. He's losing a lot of blood.'

Livia wails, pulling her son into her arms. Meanwhile Rochelle tries to stop the blood flowing from a deep wound to the base of Octavius's skull. 'Hurry!' she calls.

I move to Octavius. He's in a bad way. Other than the head wound, he has severe internal injuries and a badly damaged arm. I work at stopping the rapid blood loss, repairing burst blood vessels and scarred and damaged organs. Then I work on repairing torn ligaments, muscles and bone.

I'm hardly finished when Livia screams a woeful sound, a sound that lets us know we have lost the child. My heart clenches, my breathing tightening unbearably. What have I done?

I force myself not to look, to keep working on Octavius, but can't help one brief glance. What I see will remain with me for the rest of my life – a grieving mother rocking her lifeless son in her arms.

Once healed, Octavius sits up, stunned at the massive destruction around him. 'What happened here?' He crawls over to where his wife grieves, the dead child in her arms.

'Is there nothing you can do?' Rochelle asks softly.

'I can't bring back the dead. His injuries were too severe. He wouldn't have recovered without immediate healing.'

Ethan grabs our arms, yanking us both up. 'We have to get out of here. Caesar is going to want answers. And we can't give them to him.'

Understanding this, the three of us back out of the room. Finding an isolated corner, Ethan calls Mr Carter's name. In seconds I feel the imminent pull of transportation taking hold. I can't stop thinking how miserably we failed. How miserably *I* failed. Then an image comes to me. The image of Wanjala's face as he stared at the destruction of human life before him. A flash of recognition hits my senses, and I wonder, what's a dark-skinned African doing with such deep green eyes?

Chapter Seventeen

Arkarian

The temple is a pyramid-shaped structure, with an enormous base, the centre point reaching far into the darkness and the disappearing sky beyond. It is, so Sera informs me as we enter through an open doorway, made entirely of crystal, glass bricks and marble sheets. The glass is apparently constructed from elements able to withstand freezing temperatures and incredible heat. Inside, the walls are shaped in a design that forms a perfect octagon, a design that can also be found in a room within the Citadel. A smaller, inner octagon forms the base for this high slanted roof. Each panel of this roof is a myriad of etched, coloured patterns. Not that I can see all the way to the top. There's only the light coming from a single fireplace built into one distant wall, which hasn't a chance of heating this entire building. But somehow the cold takes second place in here. There's another more dominant sensation – more a feeling really. Of solace. It helps me control my pain.

I make my way to the fireplace, and it's obvious the temple hasn't been used for a long time, centuries or maybe even millennia. It has the look and sound of hollowness. Dust lies thickly on the sparse furniture – a chair, a footstool, a bed, a simple stone bench, a table and a rug before the fire.

Sera leads me to the chair near the fire, where I sit gratefully. She says she will bring me a drink of water, but first helps me remove the cloak. Taking the cloak she looks at it with a frown, then buries her face in it. 'It smells of Bastian.'

'That's right. He was wearing it. Tell me, Sera, how do you know him?'

'He visits me sometimes.' Her face scrunches up with a frown and a smile at the same time. 'He confuses me.'

'I think perhaps Bastian confuses himself.'

'He brought me here after a long time of wandering through Marduke's gardens. They were so beautiful I could have lived amongst those fragrant petals for ever.' She sighs like someone who misses something she once loved, then shrugs her slender shoulders. 'I don't know why Bastian dragged me from them. They're here, you know. On the other side of this island. But Bastian won't let me go there any more.'

She leaves me with these bizarre thoughts of Marduke having a garden, a beautiful one at that, to fetch me a cup of water. In all his years in the Guard, I never knew of Marduke's love of flowers, though he did appreciate beauty in those days. It was his love of a beautiful woman that played a large part in his turning traitor in the end.

Sera soon returns with the cup of water. I sip it slowly, rinsing my mouth of the taste of blood. We sit and stare at the soothing fire, and in these quiet moments I bring my thoughts into focus to try and manage my pain. Still without my powers, the most I end up accomplishing is to take the sting out. I'm not a healer anyway, and so my ribs stay broken, while some of my joints remain bruised or even dislocated. But of these injuries, the worst is to my kidneys. I fear they may both be bleeding.

Suddenly a thunderous noise has me bolting from my seat. Pain seers through my lungs and every joint with the effort.

Sera giggles, covering her face with her hands. She has taken a place on the corner of the rug right before the fire. 'I told you it was going to rain.'

I have never heard rain as heavy as this before, then realise that it's actually thick clumps of ice hitting the ceiling and everywhere around us. Neither have I felt anything so cold. I'm suddenly very grateful to be inside, rather than still out on that rocky beach getting pounded into the ground.

Sera seems oblivious to the noise and chilling air. Now that she's stopped laughing, she sits hugging her knees and staring wistfully into the fire. Eventually the hail eases, and Sera turns her eyes to me. 'Tell me about my parents, Arkarian. What happened to them after Marduke murdered me?'

I tell her how her father withdrew from the Guard, and life itself, for a while, afraid Marduke would take more revenge on the rest of his family. And I tell her how her brother became indentured as my Apprentice when only four years old, and how superbly his skills have developed. 'He has an amazing talent – the ability to bring real things to a scene created from his mind.'

'But he has no psychic skill. I spent years trying to reach him.'

'Through his dreams. Yes, I see that was you now. Ethan had no idea. He blocked out your murder, believed what the doctors told him, that you died of a medical condition.'

She sighs, 'And my mother? What of her, Arkarian?'

I'm not sure how much I should tell her. She appears to be the same ten-year-old girl I last saw the day before she was murdered, the day I told her about the Guard and how she was to play a part in it all. But that moment was such a long time ago. How has thirteen years in this place affected her?

'I tried to reach her too,' she says in my silence. 'Sometimes I thought she heard me, or felt me at least. I heard her cry out my name lots and lots of times in her sleep. And sometimes even when she was awake.' She looks down at her clasped hands. 'I cried with her.' She turns to look at me with enormous, piercing eyes, 'Do you think when Ethan rescues me, I will be able to see my mother once more before I go?'

'I don't know,' I tell her honestly.

But my answer is not enough. She stands up and stomps around the room. 'Ethan *will* come! I know this! I have finally broken through to the girl Isabel. You called her that. She knows to come. She will bring my brother. I will finally be free!'

She speaks of rescue and freedom as if it is a certainty. And part of me wishes it were true. A large part! But the risks to attain this freedom are so high. Yet, what right do I have to dampen Sera's spirits? She finally has hope for release from this morbid prison. At least now I understand what's wrong with Laura. The least I can do is get Sera to stop sending her mother messages. 'Listen to me, your mother is … having problems.'

192

'What? Tell me how? You make it sound like it's my fault.'

I try to make her understand, 'She hears you, Sera. And she feels you too. But she's not like us. She's a normal human being with no powers. Your distress is torturing her. You have to stop, so your mother can heal and move on with living.'

'But I can't move on!'

She doesn't understand, and I don't want to upset her. It might even be too late to help Laura anyway. She's probably so attuned to sensing her daughter's entrapment, and feeling her daughter's pain, that even if Sera stopped sending these messages, Laura might still look for a means to escape. Probably the only way to save Laura will be to save her daughter first. Freeing Sera's soul, allowing it to move on to its destiny, might be what it will take to free Laura's mind.

That's it! That's the answer to saving Laura's life!

But even if a rescue is accomplished, and Sera's soul is freed, would it be in time? I honestly can't say. Yet there's one thing that I can do right now, and that's to make Sera understand. 'You have to stop sending these messages to your mother, Sera. You're in touch with Isabel now, and as you say, trying to reach Ethan is a waste of time. But each time you connect with your mother she grows more disturbed. Do you understand what I'm saying? You have to stop, Sera. You have to stop now.'

Chapter Eighteen

Isabel

For twenty-four hours I can't sleep. Ethan, though, is wonderful. All afternoon we talk about what happened in Rome, and he reminds me of the time he botched a mission and the woman he was supposed to protect unfortunately died. 'The Tribunal aren't blaming you. You didn't put the bomb under that silver dome, Isabel,' he tells me over and over. 'Just remember that.'

It grows late and he leaves, worried about his mother. She's worse than usual, and no one can understand why. I regret burdening him with my problems when he has so many of his own. I go up to my room and flop down on my bed. Eventually I start to doze.

I dream of Arkarian. His face, his gentle eyes and vivid blue hair, as always, bring me comfort. I feel myself shift into a kind of oblivion, a semi-awareness, as if I'm neither awake nor asleep. He's exactly as I remember him, tall and slender, calm and strong, poised and in control. His eyes draw me to him, and instantly I'm lost in them. But it's a sweet feeling of warmth, trust and security that I lose myself in. He steps up to me and smiles. I run my fingers through his hair, marvelling not just at the unusual colour, but at the feeling of silk in my hand. And for the first time in a long day I feel myself unwind.

But the dream changes, and my old enemy Marduke appears. Yet here is a man who is nothing like I remember. He's changed, taken on the look of a strange beast, almost entirely covered in a bristly fur. It crawls down his forehead and the sides of his face, making me shudder with repulsion.

Arkarian and I are thrown apart at Marduke's appearance. My head swims with a foul odour that I recognise as the evil that has resided in this man since he chose to serve the Goddess. Marduke holds Arkarian back with just the point of his finger and a wild green energy that radiates from it. He grins, and his half-mouth, and one blazing eye, seem to laugh louder than any words.

As sure as my next breath, my heart knows what's going to happen; and the fear that grips me makes me curl into a ball, knees tucked tightly to my chest. I try to wake, try to make a sound. Matt is sleeping in the room next to mine, and our walls are thin. Jimmy is across the hall with Mum. But the only sounds being made are the ones playing out in my dream. Horrifying sounds of Arkarian being tortured. Now I see him, in a dark room lit by burning torches, strapped to a medieval rack. I stretch my hands out to him. 'Arkarian!' But the distance between us only seems to grow further.

Marduke laughs. I hear it both in my heart and in my head. And then I see why. Those same four creatures who abducted Arkarian from the Citadel make an appearance. One turns and looks up at me, staring with glowing red eyes. It flaps awkward wings, lifts into the air, then snorts with the contentment of a pig.

Marduke barks a command, and two of these creatures make the rack stretch Arkarian's bones to breaking point. 'No!' I scream and thrash about in my bed. I have to wake from this nightmare, which I feel in the pit of my stomach is not a dream at all, but a glimpse from another world. 'Let him go!'

Marduke speaks, his words slurred as if his tongue is out of proportion with his mouth. But I understand his meaning all right. And it makes me scream even harder, while my hands and feet try to hit out at him.

Someone starts shaking me. It helps drag me from my nightmare. I open my eyes to find Jimmy holding my shoulders, with Matt yelling in my face to wake up. Mum is looking worried, grasping her pyjama shirt top together between tightly held fists. 'Heavens, what's wrong with her? She's having so many nightmares lately.'

I try to calm down so Mum doesn't suspect anything weird about me. She doesn't know about my double life. That's how it has to be for her own protection. But my heart is still in overdrive as I try to figure out what just happened. This same person reached me through my dream once before.

I have to tell Jimmy and Matt, but especially Jimmy. He'll know what to do. Who to tell. Thank God he's back. His light joking manner is a blessing in a crisis.

But first I have to reassure Mum. Straightening, I pull out of Jimmy's hold. 'It's all right everyone. I'm fine now. It was just a bad dream, that's all.' With my eyes I try to tell Jimmy we have to talk.

To Mum he suggests, 'What about a mug of hot

chocolate, love? Always good for a sleepless night. What'd'ya say, darl'?'

Mum looks at me, a hand to her throat. 'Would you like that, honey? Some hot chocolate?'

'Oh yeah, that would be great, Mum.'

Reluctant to leave, she touches Matt's arm. 'You go, Matt. Make some for all of us.'

But I need to talk to Jimmy, and I can't wait until Mum goes to bed. 'But Mum, he doesn't know how to make it like you. Matt will make it in the microwave.' I can't believe what I'm saying. I sound like a spoilt brat. 'Please, Mum?'

She relents. And as soon as she walks out the door I spin around and grab Jimmy's shirt front. 'He's not dead!'

'Who's not?' Matt asks. 'What are you talking about?'

I have to hiss the word. Speaking it out loud scares me half to death. *'Marduke.'*

'But, Isabel, we all saw him die. You were just dreaming, darl'.'

'It happened while I slept, but it was no dream, Jimmy. He's alive I tell you. As alive as you and me.' But then I think about this. 'Well, not quite as you and me. He's changed. It's as if he's become part monster. An animal.' I'm starting to sound more hysterical than believable. 'Look, last year he did the same thing. He reached me through my dreams.' My head shakes. 'I don't know how he does it. Maybe it's one of his powers. But I recognised him straightaway. He wanted to tell me something.'

Matt's eyes squint as worry lines crease his forehead. 'What did he say? Are you in any sort of danger?'

Suddenly it becomes clear, but I have to hurry. I can

hear Mum downstairs switching off lights already. She's made the fastest hot chocolates in her life. 'I think it was an invitation.'

Jimmy catches on. 'He's inviting you to the under-world.'

Matt comes to his own decision. 'It's a trap! Lorian is right not to risk lives to bring Arkarian back.'

I turn on Matt as if I'm a snake and my words are venom. 'Lorian is not right about this!' Mum's foot-steps are near, but we're not finished yet. Jimmy spins his head to the door just as Mum gets to the top of the stairs. The door slams shut.

'Hurry, Isabel. I won't keep a door shut in your mother's face for longer than absolutely necessary. What do you want me to do?'

'You have to get me into that world, Jimmy.'

'No way!' Matt cries out.

I ignore him, keeping my eyes fixed on Jimmy, but all he does is shake his head. 'I haven't got the power, Isabel. It takes an immortal.'

But his answer is not what I want to hear. I grab his shirt front once again, and bring his face down to mine. 'Don't feed me that crap, Jimmy. I've seen your work in the ancient city. You have power.'

'We all have powers, Isabel. That's why we're in the Guard.'

Matt scoffs at this; both Jimmy and I ignore it. He's just impatient, and I'm impatient for Jimmy's help. Anyone's help.

Jimmy unwinds my fingers from his shirt. 'I don't have the powers you need.'

Mum bangs at the door with her foot. 'Honey? Matt? Someone open this door.'

Matt gets up. 'Coming, Mum.' He walks over slowly.

I stare at Jimmy one last time. 'Then find me someone who will help me get through the rift.'

'And induce the wrath of Lorian?'

'Well yes, if that's what it takes!'

His eyes narrow as he thinks about my request. Arkarian is his long-trusted friend, someone Jimmy totally respects. He too must be hurting over Lorian's decision not to approve a rescue mission. Matt opens the door and Mum comes in with a tray and four mugs of steaming hot chocolate drinks. While she puts the tray on my dresser, Jimmy whispers near my ear, 'The one you need is Lord Penbarin. I'll see if I can arrange a meeting. But you have to understand the consequences of your act. What you plan to do is treason – disobedience of a direct command. Isabel, you could die for this.'

For the first time since Arkarian's abduction I feel a surge of hope. Action has always been the way I work. And now I have a plan that I know is right. When this is all over, I'll accept whatever fate I'm dealt. But for now, no one is going to stop me.

Mum comes over and hands me a mug of hot chocolate. She looks so concerned. She probably thinks I'm coming down with something. I take the mug and feel a sharp stab of pain. I sure as hell don't want to die, never to see my family again. Or put my mother through any sort of grief. But how can I leave Arkarian in that place, in the hands of a madman, without even trying to help? The answer is simple – I can't. If death is a risk, then I'm willing to take it. For him. Only for him.

I look across at Mum as she takes a seat at the foot of

my bed, and force a reassuring smile to my face. But the smile develops a tremor as a wave of uncertainty almost overwhelms me. I force it aside. Now is not the time for doubts. Turning my head to the side where Jimmy waits, I whisper in the softest voice, 'If that's how it has be, Jimmy … then so be it.'

Chapter Nineteen

Isabel

Ethan wants to go with me. We're standing outside the secret door to Arkarian's chambers. Arguing. But I don't see why Ethan has to risk his life too. Suddenly the stakes have risen. If only Lorian hadn't given us a direct command, but the Immortal did this on purpose, knowing we'd plan a rescue.

'Look at you,' Ethan says, staring down at me.

I don't follow his sudden change in tactic. I glance down at my clothes – nothing unusual, just my old black jeans and a grey jumper. Unconsciously I run my hand through my hair. 'Yeah? What?'

'I know Lord Penbarin. He's helped me before. Your solo attitude right now would really tick him off. We're supposed to be a team, Isabel. The Tribunal put us together. They know we click. But you've never recognised it. You always complain that you don't get to do the missions on your own. And now you're obsessed with finding Arkarian without anyone's help. You're out of control.'

I would argue, but this time Ethan's right. I've been out of control since Arkarian's abduction. It's like there's a churning hurricane inside me that just won't blow away. I feel all twisted inside. And I'm not really sure why. All I know is that a world without Arkarian is a world I don't want to live in.

My head feels heavy all of a sudden. There's so much to think about, especially this rescue attempt. It carries enormous risks. That's why I want to do it alone. 'Look, Ethan, it's enough one of us has to risk her life, don't you think?'

He looks me straight in the eyes, gripping my shoulders. 'Tell me this: if it has to be only one of us, why should it be you?'

'Because I …'

'Love him?'

My head lifts slightly, and I shrug out of his hold, finding myself unable to meet his gaze.

'Isabel, I love him too. He's like a father, a brother, a friend, everything to me.'

The thought that maybe I just don't trust anyone else to succeed in bringing Arkarian back crosses my mind, but I push it away. I would trust Ethan with my life. But where Ethan has more skills than me, more effective powers, I'm the one with the gift of sight. This has to be a huge advantage in this underworld. 'It's not a matter of who's got the right, Ethan. I just think I can do this alone.'

'What is it with you?' he snaps at me. 'Why do you feel compelled to do everything on your own? You only make things harder for yourself you know. You've got nothing to prove, Isabel. Nothing you haven't already proved to everyone you've ever known a thousand times over.'

'What are you talking about? I'm not trying to prove

202

anything to anyone.'

'You're lying!'

'That's rubbish!'

'You're lying to yourself, Isabel. Think about it.' He turns his back and goes in through the secret door.

Alone for a minute I think about Ethan's accusation. Am I really always trying to prove myself? Is that how he sees me? But prove what exactly? My strength? That I can cope on my own?

A sudden stab of pain and bright light hits me, making me drop to my knees. I try to relax, to allow my breathing to slow. At last the light softens and an image forms more clearly. I realise straightaway that I'm seeing my past. It's my father. His face is crystal clear. And while I've never seen a photograph of him (Mum took scissors to every one she had the night he walked out), I know this is him. I feel it.

It's then I see myself in this vision too. I can't be more than three or four years old, running down a flight of wooden stairs, strands of white-blonde hair clinging to my face – which is wet and red and puffy. Inside my chest, my heart pounds like a heavy drum. Dad has a suitcase in one hand, and is heading for a blue station wagon. He hears me and turns, drops the suitcase and holds his arms out to me. 'My little Isa, come here.' His voice sounds broken. 'I'm not going anywhere until I've said goodbye to my favourite girl in the whole world.' I fly into his arms, wrapping my legs around his waist, and feel his wet face against my neck.

'Daddy, you're crying too!'

He tries to lower me to the ground as if in a desperate hurry, but I cling to him tightly. He glances at Mum to help him remove me, but she raises her head and turns it away. She doesn't want him to go either, and I feel this with every part of me, making me hold on even tighter. Mum goes inside, sobbing now, and Matt runs after her. Dad tries hard to break my hold. I slip, sliding to the ground, where I attach myself to his leg.

'I have to go, sweetheart,' he says. 'I can't live with this deceit any more. You don't understand. I tried to explain it to you last week at our picnic, but you're so young, my words don't mean anything. They probably never will, even if one day you do remember them.'

'Daddy, what's wrong?'

He lifts me up and holds me at eye level. 'Do the best, Isabel. Always do the best that you can. Promise me?'

As quickly as the image hits me, it disappears, leaving me crouched to the ground and breathless. Ethan comes up behind me. 'Hey, are you all right? I turned around and you weren't following. What are you doing?'

I get up, but the look on my face must give him a fright. He drags me into his arms, rubbing my back with his hand. 'You've had another vision.' It's not a question. 'What did you see?'

I push my open palms at his chest, giving myself a little space. The vision of my father has shaken me. I can hardly form words. What was that all about? What was the deceit he couldn't live with?

But Ethan is worried, and I try to collect myself. 'It was nothing. Nothing to do with Arkarian, or your mum, or anything like that.'

He steps back and just looks at me, his head at a slight angle, but doesn't say anything. He simply waits.

'All right,' I tell him. 'We'll do this thing together.'

Chapter Twenty

Isabel

Mr Carter makes us promise not to incriminate him in any way, should Lord Penbarin, or any member of the Tribunal, ask who helped us get to the palace in Athens. Though it seems obvious to me; transportation through time is not something either Ethan or I can manage on our own. We're not trained, and we don't have that kind of authority. Not many do. The Tribunal members and Arkarian would. And of course Mr Carter. Ethan exchanges an amused look with me before making an easy promise. We also have to promise we'll be back in the courtyard by midnight, so that Mr Carter can return us safely before going off and doing the many extra things he has to do these days.

Mr Carter delivers us into the palace's golden court-yard, except it's hardly golden right now. It's obviously late, shrouded in darkness, except for lanterns strategically placed to enhance a garden bed or stone bench.

'Do they live here?' I suddenly wonder. 'I mean, all nine members of the Tribunal? And Lorian too?'

'Apparently. It's a safe haven. Arkarian told me once this palace is kind of between places. It can't be infiltrated or even detected.'

'He thought the Citadel was safe too, but look what happened there. Maybe nowhere is safe.'

Ethan takes my hand and starts to pull me across the courtyard. 'Come on. And walk lightly,' he whispers. 'We don't want Lorian finding out we're here.'

I think Ethan is being naive. Lorian is probably already aware of our presence. I don't think much gets past that immortal. But my hunch is Lorian will watch first, then act. If Ethan and I are to be accused of treason, the Tribunal will gather its evidence against us first. And just being here, in this palace, doesn't prove anything. Yet.

Ethan leads the way into a spacious foyer. 'It's down here,' he says. 'And remember, Mr Carter wants us back in the courtyard by midnight.'

I follow Ethan, and with every step marvel at the surrounding grandeur. There are white marble stairwells that lead to hallways lined with intricately designed carpets. Paintings, in gold frames, hang over the top of sculptures, thousands of years old.

Finally we stand before a set of carved double doors. I want to push the doors in, announce our reason for being here, and hurry up and get Lord Penbarin's overwhelming support. But my stomach has decided it doesn't want to reside under my rib cage any more. It starts jumping and twitching erratically. Any second it's going to leap right out through my mouth.

'Are you all right?' Ethan asks from beside me.

'Uh-huh. I mean, I think so. Why don't you go ahead and knock?'

He gives me a funny look. 'What happened to wanting to do this all by yourself?'

'Well, you may as well make yourself useful.'

He sniggers, which helps ease the tension inside me. But before he even gets a chance to raise his hand to the doors, they swing soundlessly open, and a man in a white baggy suit stands before us. We tell him our names and that we wish to see Lord Penbarin. The man nods and motions us in.

On seeing us, Lord Penbarin groans – loudly. Several women – six after counting heads – surround him at a large dining table spread out with a feast of mouth-watering dishes. 'I didn't think it would take long before you sought me out,' he mutters, wiping the corner of his mouth with a gold silk napkin. Putting the napkin down with a smirk, he sweeps his hand wide, dismissing the women. 'Get rid of the food too,' he says to the man who answered the door. 'I was hungry, but the sight of these two has depleted my appetite.'

Both Ethan and I stand still and silent, unwilling to say anything in response to Lord Penbarin's apparent unhappiness to see us. He ushers us over to a sofa that overlooks a series of differently shaped swimming pools, and invites us to sit. 'I know what you want. You seek me out to open the rift that allows a union between the worlds. Well you've come for nothing, for I will not help you. In fact, I doubt I could anyway. It would take three times my power to even stand a chance.'

His words, his callous brush off, irritate me so quickly I forget my nervousness. Ethan hits me, picking up on my leaping mood, making sure his one quick slap to my arm gets his message across loud and clear. 'Let me handle this,' he whispers, to make sure I thoroughly understand. He turns to Lord Penbarin. 'You're Arkarian's only chance of survival. How many times in your lifetime has he helped you?'

Lord Penbarin looks away to the swimming pools beyond. A young woman wearing a sheer blue gown enters the pool area, diving gracefully into the pool furthest from us. With her gown drifting around her, she floats languorously around the pool. Lord Penbarin drags his eyes from the woman reluctantly. Ethan has made a point, but will it be enough?

'There's no doubt as to Arkarian's worth. It can't be measured in mortal or immortal terms if you ask me. That is not the issue here. What you ask – even if I were able to twist the minds of two Tribunal members to help us – is treason.'

'You've risked Lorian's anger before to help me,' Ethan reminds him.

'Hmm, that was rather different. The risks now are far greater. Have you two any idea what could happen if the joining between the worlds is left open a few seconds too long?' He doesn't wait for us to answer. 'Should even one of those underworld creatures find its way into our mortal world, everything we have, and everything we've worked so hard to maintain, could be destroyed. Do you want that responsibility hanging over your heads?'

'But if we're careful—' I start to say.

He brushes my protest away with a wave of his hand. 'How careful can one be when working with the unknown?'

'If you pardon my asking, my lord, have you seen this world yourself? Has anyone? How do you know what creatures live there, and what risk they pose to our world? I guess I'm asking what proof do you have?'

His black eyes flare at me, then close to slits. 'My dear, in some cases proof is not necessary. Have you learnt nothing in your time with the Guard?'

His put-down is to the point. I feel my face burn from the neck up, but I'm determined not to leave this palace without help from someone. 'Are you saying you won't help us?'

His head shakes a definite negative. 'That's right. I will not.'

I get up, disgusted in him. 'And you're a leader of a house? With soldiers that answer to your command and a whole sector of the earth to watch over? I think you earned your title by default.'

'Isabel, what are you doing?' Ethan tries tugging me down.

I ignore him. I'm just too riled up. 'Well, my lord, I think you're little more than a coward!'

'Isabel!' Ethan stands right in front of me, blocking me completely from Lord Penbarin's view. He turns with his hands open wide, trying to ensure not one part of my body is showing. 'We were just leaving.'

I decide he's right, and that we may as well leave. Penbarin is useless anyway. I start making for the door, when he calls us back. We turn around and he says, 'Find me two other Tribunal members who agree to help you with their powers, *and*,' he adds smugly, 'find the exact co-ordinates of this rift in our earthly sky. If you can do this, I will be there tomorrow morning at first light, your time.'

He thinks we can't, and that's why he's smiling at us in his lordly superior way. He doesn't know us very well. 'Do we have your word on that, my lord?'

'Do you doubt me?'

My mouth goes dry very quickly at his sudden look of outrage. 'Of course not, it's just—'

'You have my word,' he snaps, dismissing us.

Outside his rooms, Ethan and I turn to each other wondering who else might help us. We decide to go knocking door to door.

The first royal we approach is Lady Arabella. But it turns out she's away overlooking her lands and her staff can't say when she's expected to return. We move on to Lord Alexandon, but his reply is an adamant no. We end up spending the next few hours walking corridors, approaching all the Lords, Kings and Queens we can find. But no one, it appears, no matter what arguments we come up with, is willing to go against Lorian and help us. Completely dejected and exhausted we go and sit in the courtyard to re-think our strategy.

Ethan's shoulders sag as his elbows slide to his knees. 'I'm starting to think it's hopeless.'

I can't believe he's doing this. Giving in! I glare at him. 'Don't say that. We'll find a way.'

He moans softly. 'We have ten minutes before it's midnight, and we've seen every Lord, Lady, King and Queen, that's here right now. No one will help us. Lord Penbarin's challenge is proving impossible. And you know what? He knew we would fail. No one is willing to go against Lorian. I'm starting to think neither should we.'

Without wanting to admit it, a part of my brain registers the thought that maybe Ethan's right, maybe it is impossible to get anyone to agree to help us. But my mind refuses to believe we're going to fail before we even get started. 'There must be someone who will help us. Think, Ethan. Who haven't we seen?'

'I believe you've been looking for me?'

We both turn at the sound of Lady Arabella's voice. She's back! But is she willing to help?

As delicate and beautiful as I remember her, Lady Arabella comes over to stand right in front of us, her translucent skin revealing an intricate pattern of blue veins beneath.

She takes my hand and covers it with Ethan's, then her own. I look up into her blue eyes, lashes encrusted with fine shards of ice, and words leave me. She lifts a finger to her lips. 'You don't have to say anything. I will help you with whatever you need.'

Ethan squeezes my hand. 'We're still one short, my lady. You see, Lord Penbarin said we need—'

Lady Arabella just smiles. 'I will persuade another to help us. Don't worry. Now come quickly. We have an appointment with my good Lord Penbarin.'

When we get to Lord Penbarin's suite, he's sleeping, but Lady Arabella walks straight past the man in the baggy suit. 'Wake your master, Elsepth. I assure you he will be only too pleased to see us.'

Her over-confidence and the fact that we are here again, in Lord Penbarin's rooms, one step closer to rescuing Arkarian, makes me giddy with relief. I have to physically stop myself from bursting out in hysterical little giggles.

Lord Penbarin comes out of his bedroom, grumbling as he slips his arms into a shimmering red dressing gown. 'What have we here? Oh no, not you, my lady.'

'It appears you have struck a deal with these two good people that you must now fulfil, my lord.'

'But who is the third?'

'Leave that to me. There will be a third by morning.'

Grudgingly he accepts her word that she'll find someone else to help, then looks at me and Ethan, 'As I recall, you two must tell me the exact location of the rift before my part in this fiasco is cemented. Hmm?' He waits, his mouth forming into a smug line. He thinks he has us beat. How could we mere mortals possibly know where this rift is?

But Lord Penbarin wasn't there on that open field on the mountain when the Goddess sent that storm – from the underworld. I take a deep breath and recite the co-ordinates that Ethan and I earlier worked out, hoping that, if they're not exact, they will be near enough. 'Thirty-six degrees south of the equator, one hundred and forty-eight degrees east of the prime meridian.'

Lord Penbarin's mouth drops open. He's impressed, yet unimpressed at the same time. But one thing is certain, he made a deal. And there's no way, as Lord of Samartyne, he's going to back down now.

Chapter Twenty-one

Isabel

We meet at dawn, on the field above Arkarian's chambers. Matt is with us, and for a second, while Ethan is busy double-checking the supplies in our backpacks, I'm tempted to ask if he knows anything about why our father walked out all those years ago. My recent vision of him still plays in my head. Dad said he couldn't live with the deceit any more, and it's eating at me not knowing what that deceit was, or who caused it.

But Ethan's checking doesn't take very long. He comes over, and I drop all thoughts of Dad for now.

'You're too inexperienced,' Ethan tells Matt. Lost in thought, I miss the first part of their conversation. But it's easy to pick up. Matt, it seems, is adamant he's coming with us.

'How can I learn anything if you protect me from any form of possible danger?' My brother points to me. 'Isabel has no fighting powers. And while I know she's … well, really good at everything, I can manage these trips too. I know I can.'

'This isn't going to be an "ordinary trip",' Ethan argues back.

'I know, it's just ... well, I have to look out for Isabel.'

'What!' I can't help squeal at this. 'You just admitted I'm "really good at everything", don't pull the big brother act on me now.'

'I'm not going to apologise for wanting to look out for you. It's just something I've always done, you know that. I promised ...'

He doesn't finish. An awkward silence follows. 'What are you on about?'

'Nothing.'

'Matt?'

'Nothing!'

Ethan's patience snaps. His hands jerk into the air. 'Look, Matt, amongst other things, Isabel is a healer, and healing is one of the most significant powers a Guard can have. We don't know what condition Arkarian is going to be in, or what dangers we're going to face, but Isabel's skills could make the difference between life and death.'

Matt keeps arguing, rationalising why he thinks he should come with us. 'You don't even know if any of your skills will work in this world.'

'Maybe not, but I can't stop Isabel from going, even if I tied her arms and legs together with chains.'

Ethan's words spark an image of Arkarian's abduction, his hands and feet chained within that gilded cage. Tears spring to my eyes and I glance away before either of these two see them. Especially Matt. He already feels he has to 'protect me'. I don't want to give him ammunition to feed his cause. So I make a point of peering around as if looking for signs of Lord Penbarin, Lady Arabella and the third Tribunal member

Lady Arabella promised to bring. Hopefully they'll be here soon. It's almost sunrise. There's plenty of light starting already.

'I *can* stop you, Matt. Like it or not, I'm your superior.' Pulling rank has got to be Ethan's last resort. 'As my Apprentice you're my responsibility. And I'm not going to stop protecting you just because *you* think you're ready.'

'I've been your Apprentice for a whole year already!' Matt practically yells. 'Don't tell me I'm not ready!'

'Arkarian was Lorian's Apprentice for two hundred years,' I say softly.

Both heads turn and stare at me.

Ethan looks at Matt as if to say, 'Well, there!' But when he speaks his tone is much more gentle. 'Look, it's enough I'm risking my own future doing this. If you're worried about Isabel, well, for what it's worth, I'll be there. I'll look after her.'

Ethan's words make me groan. 'Spare me please.'

Exasperated with their over-inflated egos, I glance at my watch. There's so much light now, I'm afraid the royals aren't going to show. What if Lady Arabella can't convince anyone to help? 'Where are they?' I ask no-one in particular, looking around the vast field.

Matt and Ethan look around too, but it's Matt, the tallest of the pair, that spots something first. 'I don't believe this!'

I stand on my toes to see what he's looking at. Ethan hisses air out between clenched teeth. 'Oh great.' He gives Matt a hard stare. 'Did you invite her to come with us? This isn't a picnic you know. She could get hurt.'

'It wasn't me. I swear!'

At last I see what's got them so agitated. It's Rochelle, running up the hill, a bag on her back. She sees we've spotted her and gives a little wave. Before long she comes right up.

'What are you doing here?' Ethan snaps.

For a second it's as if his strong tone takes her breath away. Her deep green eyes skim the distant ridges where ice rests on some of the higher peaks already. Finally she says, 'Don't sound so happy. I'm coming with you.'

Everyone has the same instant reaction.

'Nah-huh.'

'No way.'

'Forget it. You're not coming.'

She persists, her hands sliding to her hips. 'You could use my skills.'

She's not wrong there as her skills of truthseeing and touch are fully developed, but it changes nothing. 'We can't put more members at risk. Lorian is going to ex-communicate us as it is,' I explain.

'Oh, so you think I haven't taken risks before? What do you reckon it took to turn traitor on the Order? It wasn't easy, you know. Now I've got Marduke and Lathenia after me. Without Arkarian's help I wouldn't have done it. He believed in me. He trusted me. And didn't I prove my loyalty in Rome recently?'

She thinks we don't want her to come because we don't trust her. Maybe she's part right. How do you fully trust a former spy? Sure, I was there in Rome, and while Rochelle's loyalty on that mission couldn't be faulted, how do we know it wasn't all an act?

For a second I forget that she can read my thoughts, just as I forget to screen them. 'Come on, Isabel. How weak is your faith? How short is your memory?'

She's probably reminding me of when she saved Matt from being burnt at the stake last year. I haven't forgotten, but trust – or our lack of it – isn't the main issue here. 'Look, this isn't solely about trust, Rochelle. Matt wants to come too—'

She glares at him, her eyes open wide. 'What! Don't be a fool, Matt. You haven't any—'

It's Matt's turn to interrupt. 'I'm not useless just because I don't have any powers.'

For a moment all four of us are quiet. The silence is broken by Rochelle's earnest plea. 'You don't understand. I have to do this.'

'Why?' Ethan asks.

'Of all of you, he's the only one who believes in me without doubt. If we lose Arkarian, I have no future. Without him, I … I would have trouble believing in myself.'

Everybody shuts up, completely wordless. Rochelle always seems so confident. It's a shock to discover otherwise. She glances away, blinking rapidly. She's close to tears. Ethan goes to say something, but she brushes him away. He persists, grabbing her arm. 'There's something else you have to understand.'

She looks up at him, and he says, 'We're going into this world undisguised. If we should meet up with anyone from the Order who can recognise you …' His head shakes. 'It's too big a risk.'

She seems to chew on these words, absorbing their full impact. For Rochelle to have no disguise could prove fatal. 'All right. But you don't have to make it so obvious you don't want me. What will it take to get you lot to accept me?'

With these words she storms off, and we're left looking at each other in an uncomfortable silence. But something about her brief visit has the hairs prickling at the back of my neck.

Ethan is the first to speak. 'Well, that was enlightening.'

'I'll say,' Matt says.

'So how do you suppose she knew what we were doing, and exactly where to find us?'

Matt is quick to defend himself for a second time. His hands fly into the air. 'Don't look at me. I haven't gone near Rochelle since she's been back.'

'So how did Rochelle find out?'

'Maybe one of you inadvertently let her read your thoughts.'

I take offence at Matt's accusation. 'One of *us*?'

He shrugs. 'Didn't you two just go on a mission with her?'

Ethan shares a puzzled look with me. Just how careful are we when in Rochelle's company? We all know, mistakes happen.

And then there's the possibility that Rochelle is telling the truth about Arkarian's belief in her. If this is true, then I should trust her too. In fact, so should everyone.

Any more thoughts of Rochelle fly from my head as a soft whooshing sound gets my heart beating fast. All three of us move back at the sound as Lord Penbarin and Lady Arabella materialise in front of us. And they have Queen Brystianne with them! I can't help grinning and jumping on the spot like a hyperactive two-year-old. At last the royals are here – all three – and we can begin.

The instant Lord Penbarin's body completely forms he looks up to the sky. A zigzag of brilliantly coloured light appears above us for a fraction of a second. If we weren't looking in exactly the right direction, none of us would have noticed. 'Well, well, it appears I may have underestimated you two.' He looks at Matt, lifts one finely arched eyebrow, then, as if recognising him, or something about him, bows his head just slightly. 'I don't believe we've been introduced.'

Ethan introduces him. 'May I present my Apprentice, Matt Becket.'

Lord Penbarin can't seem to drag his eyes off Matt. Finally, he says to Ethan, 'Not for long, I'm sure.'

It's a strange thing to say. Ethan looks at me with a frown. I shrug my shoulders lightly.

Lady Arabella approaches, and catching sight of Matt, gives a little breathy gasp. She then does the most amazing thing. Grabbing her wide skirt in both hands, she curtsies, low and deep. When her head lifts, her ice-tipped eyelashes are fluttering against her pale cheeks. 'It's a pleasure to meet you.'

Queen Brystianne is next. She takes one of Matt's hands and stares at him for a little longer than seems polite, then her shoulders lift and she exhales a long breath. This action floors me. She's so nervous I think she's having trouble breathing! Finally she lowers Matt's hand, giving him a coy smile.

I can't believe this. The woman is blushing!

The royals' strange reactions to my brother has me wondering. What's going on? But I can't very well ask them; I'd feel like an idiot. And Lord Penbarin, now that he's here, has developed a sudden urgency. 'We'd better get a move on before somebody discovers what we're doing.'

His words worry me, but I'm as ready as ever. 'Where do you want us to stand?'

He explains, 'Well, my dear, much like you, I've been busy doing my research on how best to make this happen. With the help of Lady Arabella, I have searched thousands of ancient texts through the night.'

'How will this passing through the worlds be accomplished?' Matt asks.

I may just be imagining this, but at Matt's words, Lord Penbarin's shoulders square off as if he's just been singled out for a best lord-of-the-land award. 'We're going to use the gods' own power generator.'

At our blank stares he continues, 'We're going to form a pyramid with our bodies within an octagon base. It's a vehicle of ancient power.'

'Do we have to be a part of this design?' I ask, not quite understanding yet.

Lord Penbarin explains, 'You and Ethan will stand within the pyramid formed by our bodies.'

'But how can you create this shape when there are only three of you?'

Lady Arabella holds up her hand. Instantly a lengthy white plaited cord appears. 'We shall use this to make the eight-sided base. We will then stand within this octagon and use our bodies to form the pyramid.'

'The idea is,' Lord Penbarin goes on to explain – to *Matt*, as if he's the only one going on this journey, when in fact, he's the one *not* going – 'using the three of our powers combined, we will endeavour to force a small opening in a rift that is like a doorway that leads from one world to the other.'

Lady Arabella takes over in her gentle voice, explaining the rest to Ethan and me. 'The two of you will be propelled into a temporary vortex. What happens then, none of us really knows. We believe that nature and gravity will deposit you into the underworld. These same gravitational forces should seal the rip behind you.'

'The problem is,' Lord Penbarin sounds even more hurried now. 'As we have never combined our powers to attempt something of this magnitude before, we can't guarantee what will happen. Should the rift open for longer than anticipated, the possibility arises that a creature from the underworld could make the leap into earth.'

'Why would that be so bad?' I ask.

It's as if all three royals take a simultaneous deep breath.

'Because, my dear,' Lord Penbarin explains, 'it's not the way of things. The order of life. The progression of souls. Eternity.'

'I don't understand.'

Lady Arabella tries to explain, 'What my lord is trying to say is that the creatures that now inhabit the underworld would upset the balance of our natural environment.'

Lord Penbarin waves his hand in the air. 'Huh! They had their chance!'

'Their presence … their appearance – so unearthly – would cause panic and disorder the like this world has never seen before.'

Again, all three royals shudder.

'Well what about us?' Ethan asks. 'Will our presence upset the balance of *their* natural environment?'

Lady Arabella's shoulders shrug almost imperceptibly.

'We don't know what effect your visit will have, but as their world is already governed by chaos, we think any effect would be minimal.'

The enormity of what we're doing – at my instigating – suddenly hits me, leaving me wordless for a moment. I mean, not only are there risks to my own world, but to this other one as well. I feel the stirrings of panic inside.

An image of Arkarian's gentle face forms before my eyes, helping me pull myself together. 'The risks appear almost too high, but I feel I must at least try to bring Arkarian back. I just hope you don't get in trouble for helping us today.'

Lady Arabella takes one of my hands. 'My dear child, no one forces us to do anything. Not even my good Lord Penbarin,' she adds with a giggle. 'Each of us has been touched by Arkarian's presence in some form or another. Any risks we undertake in his name are our own, and come from our hearts.'

I appreciate her words, yet still can't help feeling a tinge of guilt. Surely two humans passing through a rift in the sky are going to attract attention, and would hardly go unnoticed by an immortal. But, so far, there's no sign of Lorian. I just hope we can get through this procedure before Lorian appears. As yet, we haven't done anything against the Guard – except perhaps to plot treachery! And if someone should see us right now, we could simply say we're watching the sun come up. Only after we enter this other world can we be charged with treason. But once there, even Lorian will be unable to stop us from going ahead with the rescue. There'll be time enough when we return to face any serious charges.

As I think these thoughts Lady Arabella arranges the cord into the shape of an octagon, and gives us some last-minute advice, 'We will watch this area for a sign, but it won't be easy to return you. You will probably have to find your own way out. Hopefully Arkarian will have some idea on how to accomplish this.'

Finished with the cord, she looks across at Ethan, who starts double-checking our supplies (again). He goes through the backpacks, softly mouthing the names of each item: torch, batteries, food (mostly dried), water, matches, ropes ... Lady Arabella goes over and gives him what appear to be two long, fur-lined cloaks, and two pairs of black leather gloves. 'Where you're going you'll need these. Put them in your packs. They look bulky, but they won't take up any room. Trust me.'

She glances briefly at Lord Penbarin and Queen Brystianne as if trying to make her mind up about something. Lord Penbarin gives a slight nod, and she says, 'We don't know what challenges you will find yourselves facing, and well, we can't help you from here, should you get into difficulty, but we can give you some advice. Listen carefully.'

She has our full attention. 'Have courage, have faith, and be true to your heart.'

Ethan and I exchange puzzled glances. What is Lady Arabella talking about? She moves away quickly and the subject closes. Ethan holds my gaze for a moment longer, then shrugs lightly. 'Help me get these cloaks in, so we can get going.'

I help Ethan shove the cloaks into one of the packs. Once inside, they take up no room at all, squashing down to almost nothing.

With the packs loaded on our backs, Ethan and I go and stand in the centre of the octagon. Lord Penbarin and Queen Brystianne come over and join Lady Arabella, placing their feet oddly within the white cord. They then link their hands high above our heads, forming the slightly obscure shape of a human-pyramid. As I peer outside their arms I see Matt staring at the pyramid centre, and the thought suddenly hits me that we didn't say goodbye to each other.

A sizzle overhead gets louder and the power of the three royals begins to take effect. Heat from their combined hands spreads over me. I look up and see their fingers glowing orange and white, streaks of energy sizzling and crackling between one set and the next. Their heads remain still and upright, their eyes closed, breathing slow and steady. Inside the pyramid, the atmosphere starts to change.

Two things happen almost simultaneously. The first is an explosion that jolts through the centre. It covers the two of us in a brilliant light, and my body tingles as if charged with electricity. The other is my brother, who leaps through the arms of Lady Arabella and Queen Brystianne, to lodge himself firmly between Ethan and me. He places himself in the direct centre of the force of power.

Ethan yells and tries to shove him out, but Matt is holding on to both of us tightly. The light and energy within the pyramid rapidly escalates, and a strange sucking sensation sets in, as if my body is being pulled in myriad directions. It becomes hard even to think.

The next thing I know all three of us are moving, hurled with a force that we have no power over, into space. My own hand, held in front of me, appears distorted. Our backpacks become dislodged and start spinning around in the air. All three of us get caught up in a strange whirlpool. The air grows darker, but not black exactly, just as if it is endless.

The whirlpool picks up power, and the three of us end up spinning towards a narrow peak. As we rise into this peak, the forces keeping us there increase. None of us can hear the other call, though Ethan's mouth is moving. There appears to be no gravity, and our bodies spin around in different directions. It grows even darker as a wind kicks up and quickly increases to a deafening roar. Now I can only see shadows.

I start to wonder if I can take much more of this. The pull on my limbs has become unbearable. But suddenly we begin to drop. The fall is fast and feels as if it is a great distance. To compound this, the depth of darkness has become total. I can't see the others at all, not even my backpack! But I sense we're about to hit solid ground. And I don't need any sixth sense to know that we're going to hit it hard.

Chapter Twenty-two

Arkarian

Sera is ecstatic, jumping up and down with child-like excitement, squealing, 'They're here! They're here! I'm going to be free, free, free!' She spins and skips in a wide circle round and round the large room until she gets dizzy and falls in a heap near my feet. Sitting up, she holds her head until the dizziness eases, then grins up at me, simply euphoric.

I wish I could feel the same enthusiasm. But their journey is not going to be easy. For starters, I've seen some of the creatures that live here – the part-human, part-bird, part-animal called wren. I've seen how loyal they are to Marduke. And if Ethan and Isabel do get as far as the lake that surrounds Obsidian Island, how will they cross it? Not to mention how severely disadvantaged the Guard is in their absence. Lathenia's probably rubbing her hands together just at the thought of Veridian in a weakened state. I don't want to imagine what chaos she's planning.

I drag myself out of my chair, and stoke the fire to try and rid this place of some of its miserable freezing air. But even this small effort has cost me. I drop back into my chair with a heaving cough. Blood surges into my mouth along with bile. I spit the mixture into the clay bowl Sera provided me with for this same purpose. It's now three quarters full.

Sera puts her hand partly through my knee. 'Not long now, and she will heal you.'

But I think I could already be too far gone, even for Isabel to heal. My kidneys have ceased working altogether, and fluid is gathering in every one of my cells. I have limited time left before I die of blood poisoning. There's a very real possibility I will never see Isabel or Ethan again. If only there were some way I could guide or protect them. I try feeling their presence as Sera can, but I'm left with nothing but emptiness. I'm still powerless, something I haven't experienced since my days as a youth in France. I feel like only half a person – less. Anger surges through me. I have to do something!

'Look there!' Sera calls from the doorway. She can't see anything, she's just so excited at the idea that at last her dreams are coming true, that she can't keep still.

Turning from the door she returns with a bowl of green mush and a cup of water. 'It's snowing outside. Do you think they thought to bring proper clothing? I don't want my brother to die of exposure before he finds me.'

I stir the mush, wondering what on earth it could be. Taking a mouthful I have to wash it down with the cupful of water. For a second it takes my breath away. I hand the bowl back, thanking her. 'Is it possible for you to go and find Ethan yourself, and bring him here? It's not like you're chained to this place.'

'But I can't fly. That's the only way off this island.'

'No, it can't be.'

'This island is my prison.'

'But how? I was brought here, why wouldn't you or I be able to leave the same way?'

'You were brought here in a steel-bottomed boat.'

She's right. I remember the icy feel of that steel on my skin. 'What's wrong with the water, Sera?'

'It's not water, Arkarian. That's the whole problem. That lake is acid.'

Acid? Oh no! How are Ethan and Isabel going to get across a lake of acid? And what other difficulties will they have to deal with to get to this point? 'Sera, they're in so much danger here. Tell them to go back. Maybe they still have a chance before the rift closes and they lose sight of its position. Tell them, Sera. Tell your brother to go back.'

Sera stands up and stomps both feet. 'No. I will not! They will all be here soon!'

Her mentioning the word 'all' stops any other thoughts. It sets my heart thumping hard. Surely no more than *two* of them are here? 'Tell me, Sera, how many have come through?'

She thinks for a second. 'There are three.'

'Three! No! Why three?'

I'm not really asking Sera. I just can't believe three of them are out there risking their lives. She doesn't reply anyway, just lifts her small shoulders.

'Do you know who they are? Can you see them?'

'Well, there's my brother. And there's the girl who loves him.'

Her persistence on this point rattles me like an irritating stone stuck in my boot. 'How do you know Isabel is in love with Ethan?'

228

Her head tilts towards her right shoulder while her eyes, in fact her whole face, acquires a dream-like state. 'I have a strong sense of it when I connect with the girl. They have a special bond.'

'Friendship can be a special bond.'

'It's more than that,' she says, irritating me no end.

'Affection can appear like love, while it's really nothing more than a deep friendship.'

'It's definitely love I feel between them.'

An anger rushes through me that will not go away. 'This love you're sensing, you're mistaking it for the love someone feels for a sibling.'

'I may not know much about love,' she admits in a soft voice. 'But I remember how my father loved my mother, and how she loved him back. And I remember how my brother used to follow me everywhere, even though we fought all the time. That was love too, but different.'

Her words have the effect of dissolving the aggression inside me. How much of life has she missed? Not just the love of her brother, and parents, but also as a member of the Guard? As I look at her, sitting and staring into the fireplace, the glow against her pale skin making her look almost mortal, I feel nothing but compassion for what could have been. While death has kept her imprisoned in a child's body and mind, the force of her strong character can't help but break through. She would have been one of the Guard's great ones.

As I sit and contemplate what can never be, the identity of this third person gnaws at my brain. Just who could it be? Shaun? Or Jimmy maybe? It wouldn't be Marcus Carter; more than likely he would be the one to replace me. 'You said there were three of them. Ethan and Isabel are two. Who is this third?'

Resting her chin on her knees she appears to meditate. 'I don't know,' she finally replies. 'I can't feel anything when I search for a connection. It's as if his brain is sleeping.'

'But you can reach Ethan and Isabel.'

'Yes, but Ethan is vague and I get nothing out of it. The girl's much more receptive.'

'Can you connect with Isabel and find out through her who this third traveller is?'

She shrugs. 'I don't think so. We can't talk to each other like we're having a conversation.'

I think about this talent Sera has, a skill she's worked hard at developing. She's done well considering she's had no formal training. It makes me wonder how Isabel is doing in developing *her* skill. I doubt she understands the potential for what it could become just yet. I wish I could be the one to teach her. But any level of psychic connection right now could be a tremendous advantage to the travelling trio. With Sera's help, perhaps some dangers could be avoided. And maybe Sera's dreams of release will finally come true. 'Sera, tell me everything you see and feel when you connect with Isabel.'

'Why?' she asks in her child-like innocence.

I take her hand, telling her exactly what she needs to hear to make her want to work with me. 'So that we can guide your brother straight to us.'

Chapter Twenty-three

Isabel

I hit the ground hard, my feet going out from under me. I pull myself to a sitting position on frozen dirt and take in a deep breath to settle my nerves. But a sudden sharp hissing sound makes the hairs on the back of my neck stand on end. For a second I think someone – or something – is touching my shoulder. I jerk away, spinning around on the spot. 'Who's there?'

Silence, except for the biting wind pushing through trees somewhere nearby. I breathe again and quickly do some self-healing. Luckily there are no broken bones, just some nasty grazes on the arm and thigh that took most of the fall.

The healing complete I rummage around on all fours to find my backpack. I can't believe I stupidly left my torch in it. This darkness is hard to take. I get to my feet feeling completely disoriented. Where can Ethan be? And of course Matt too? He surprised us both with his burst into the pyramid at the exact moment of projection.

A cold hand circles my leg and I scream.

'Shhh, you're going to wake the dead,' Ethan says

from the ground. I spin around so fast I lose my balance. Ethan tries to catch me before I fall on top of him. 'Hey, watch my leg. I think it's broken.'

I squat down beside him and try to stop shaking. He guides my hand to his leg, but misunderstands the reason for my shivering. 'Cold, isn't it?'

I feel his injured leg, assessing his injuries. 'I sure could do with Lady Arabella's cloak. But you know what? It's not the cold chilling my bones.'

A mournful shriek overhead rends the air. It has the two of us gripping each other's arms.

'I know what you mean,' Ethan hisses.

'What do you suppose that was?'

'Probably your brother,' he says jokingly, aware of my terror. But his attempt at humour does nothing for me.

At my silence he says, 'Hurry up and heal me, Isabel. I'll feel better with two legs working.'

I have to work hard to concentrate; my heart is thumping like crazy with no natural rhythm. 'Where do you think our packs ended up? Can you believe I left my torch in one of them?'

'Well, yeah, so did I,' he mutters.

Suddenly a torch lights up, revealing a vast rocky field covered in snow patches. I see Matt pointing the torch light down as he clambers over slippery boulders.

He reaches us and shines the torch on Ethan. 'Hey, what happened to you?'

'The fall broke his leg. Can you see our packs?'

He holds the torch directly over Ethan's injury. 'When you're finished fixing him up, I'll take a look around.'

I wave the torch away. 'I don't need that much light. But we do need some warmer clothing. See if you can spot our packs with that thing.'

'*He* shouldn't be spotting anything,' Ethan says in a tight voice that's difficult to distinguish between pain and anger. He looks up into Matt's face. 'You shouldn't be here. Do you know what you've done?' He doesn't wait for an answer. 'You risked your own life and put us into deeper trouble when we get back.'

'No one's going to blame you. I'm responsible for my own decisions.'

'Not in the Guard. We take responsibility for each other. And now we've got you to look after. You're going to be a pain in the neck.'

Oh no, they're at it again. And while I know Matt's actions were questionable, I think Ethan's words are a little harsh. He's here now and we can't do much about it. I point to Matt's torch. 'We'd have a hard time finding our packs without that. We'd probably die of exposure first. So I reckon he's already made himself useful.'

Ethan says nothing, just makes a kind of scoffing sound.

Matt announces he can see where one of our packs ended up. 'Over there. Look. I'll go and get it.'

Ethan yells at him. 'Stay where you are! When Isabel is finished with my leg, we'll go together, OK? We're not separating in this place, not for a second. We could lose each other in this absolute darkness, just like that.' He clicks his fingers, making a snapping sound. 'Since you're here now, you're not to make one move without clearing it with Isabel or me first. You got that?'

'Yeah, OK. I don't want to go off by myself anyway.'

He shudders as he peers into the darkness.

Ethan stands up, trying out his leg. 'It's great. Thanks, Isabel. At least now we know our powers still work.'

'What about your wings?' This skill could be the handiest of all. If Ethan could use his wings to check this place out, we might have a chance of finding Arkarian more quickly.

He looks around, but his sight is restricted to the distance of Matt's torch light. 'I'd have to visualise my path. It only takes a second or two, but I can't see what this landscape looks like. It would be too easy to get lost here. Besides,' he adds, 'I haven't perfected them yet. I could end up anywhere.'

So it's agreed Ethan shouldn't even attempt to use his power of flight. If he were to inadvertently end up alone, whether near or far, he could be lost for ever. A horrifying thought.

We locate both backpacks and, since Matt brought his own, we decide to conserve one of the torches.

The darkness here is more than I imagined, but as the light produced from Matt and Ethan's torches lights up a large enough area for me to see where I'm going, I'm happy to leave my torch tucked safely in my pack. We don't know how long this journey will take, but without light we would be in a hell of a lot of trouble.

Ethan dives into his pack for Lady Arabella's cloaks and gloves. He pulls out the first cloak, which unfolds to exactly my size from head to foot, then hands me one of the sets of gloves. Looking up at Matt he says, 'Lady Arabella didn't give us a spare set for hangers on.'

It's a cutting thing to say. I haven't seen Ethan this angry before. He's really upset with Matt tricking us. I

234

bite down on my tongue; these two are going to have to sort out their own issues. I have enough of my own right now. And I'd offer my cloak to Matt, but I know he wouldn't take it. It would be pointless even to try. His protectiveness of me wouldn't allow it. So I put it on, deep hood and all, and revel momentarily. It's just so warm. The gloves too are a perfect fit.

Ethan makes a sudden noise deep in his throat. 'Huh? What's this?'

'What?' I ask.

'Look!' He pulls out two more cloak and glove sets. 'How did I end up with *three*? I swear Lady Arabella handed me *two* cloaks and *two* sets of gloves. Where did this third one come from? You were there, Isabel. You helped me shove the cloaks inside this bag.'

'Yeah, I know. But Lady Arabella must have …' I search my brother's face for a clue. 'Do you know anything?'

He gives me a smirk, rubbing his arms to warm up. 'Do I look like I know anything? Maybe it's for Arkarian. For when you find him.'

Ethan doesn't buy it. 'Then why didn't Lady Arabella say so?'

'Maybe she did and you just weren't listening.'

'Oh really?'

'Yeah, she probably said: "And this third cloak is for Arkarian".'

If they keep this up much longer I'm going to scream. I jump in before Ethan retaliates and this stupid argument grows even more out of proportion. 'Look you two, I don't get it either, but I do know one thing, this wind's getting colder. And we should hurry.'

Glaring, Ethan throws the third cloak set to Matt,

who quickly puts them on, gloves and all.

Direction is our first big decision, and probably our most vital. After an awkward moment of silence we start discussing where to go and how to make sure we don't end up going round in circles.

'We should leave a mark of some sort,' Ethan suggests.

But the ground is mostly rock, and snow is starting to fall. Ethan pulls out a compass wrapped in a red silk handkerchief. Earlier we decided to stick to a northerly direction, but his exclamation has Matt and me craning to see what's wrong.

'Wow.'

The dials of the compass are spinning madly, not just in one direction either, but clockwise and anti-clockwise with no visible pattern.

'Maybe we're standing on magnetic rock.'

Ethan slides the compass into his trouser pocket and wedges the handkerchief between two rocks on a large boulder, giving it a strong tug to make sure it's in good and tight. 'Maybe,' he says without much enthusiasm. 'We'll try it again later. But right now we have to decide which way we're going to call north, and stick to it.'

Another mournful shriek slices the darkness. All three of us stare at each other with wide-open eyes.

'Does anybody have any idea what that sound is?' Matt asks.

While it's hard to tell which direction it's coming from, I have a sense of it being at my back. I point in the direction to the front of me, 'I have no idea, but I reckon thataway's north.'

We head off without any real idea of where we're going. Without a compass, without a sun, stars or a moon, we're seriously disadvantaged.

After a while we realise we're not walking on rock any more. The terrain is changing, becoming more fertile, if that's possible in this sunless place. But it's soon evident that we're walking into some sort of valley. A type of grass squishes under our feet. It could be wet from dissolved snow, or recent rain, or an underground water table. We have no way of knowing. There are trees here and there, barren looking with few or no leaves. We come to an area that's even more swampy, with string-like trees, dripping with moss, their roots and lower branches buried beneath patches of ice and smelly stagnant water. It's lucky we're all wearing ankle high boots.

Matt lifts one leg off the ground. Murky water drops from beneath it. 'This is disgusting. Can you smell that?'

But it's not the smell that gets my attention. A sound in the distance has me searching as far as I can see.

'What is it?' Ethan asks.

Before I get a chance to answer, all three of us hear it. But it's nothing like that shriek we thankfully left behind. This sound is more of a hiss. It dims slightly, then surges again, this time louder.

'What do you reckon?' Ethan asks again.

'I don't know. Insects maybe?'

'In this temperature?'

But Matt has his own idea, his own idea on this world altogether apparently. 'Who says they have to be alive?'

Ethan and I look at him, wondering if he's going to elaborate, but he only lifts his eyebrows and shrugs at us.

The hissing sound turns into buzzing and grows overwhelmingly louder. It becomes difficult to hear each other speak. Ethan manages to mouth a warning, 'We'd better find cover.'

Too late. From the dark boundaries a coloured glow forms. Within seconds we're covered by what could only be millions of buzzing insects, individually coloured red, blue, violet, even pink. They're fireflies! Some are painted colours I haven't seen before.

We throw our arms over our faces in self-protection, keeping well within our cloaks. Still, some get in between my fingers, and flutter noisily against my face. They don't stay long, and soon the dazzling display of fireflies lifts over our heads, they swarm around us for a few more seconds, then fly off.

We watch, mesmerised, as they disappear. It's their beauty that has us in awe. It's as if the fireflies themselves have found a way to bring splendour into their lives.

Matt shakes his head and fireflies swarm out of his hood. He looks dazed, and Ethan offers his water flask. I reach for my own, but I'm not too thirsty yet, so I decide to conserve. While there's evidence of plenty of water here, I'm reluctant to drink any of it, especially the swamp water with the foul odour.

But apparently Matt has his own flask too. He tugs it out from the front of his trousers. So that's where he must have hidden the torch! If only Ethan or I had seen it earlier, Matt wouldn't be here right now. Not that I'm in the habit of looking at the front of my brother's trousers! 'What else do you have stashed down there?'

Matt's eyebrows lift, giving me one of his smirk-like

grins. He earns a thump from my fist for his sick humour.

Ethan can't help a snigger. 'Personally, I'd rather not know.'

The tension between them reduces, and we push on into the valley. But right from the start I sense something very different about this part of the landscape. At first it's hard to put a finger on, 'cause it's not so much a physical strangeness, more like a feeling generating inside. But then I hear a sound, a voice if I'm not mistaken.

'Did you hear that?' I spin around, unable to work out where the voice is coming from.

Coward!

'There!' Ethan hisses, turning so fast he almost falls over. I reach out to help him find his balance. He brushes his own shoulder as if trying to rid himself of something there. 'Who said that?'

Failure!

Ethan's eyes hold mine; breathing hard. 'What's happening?'

'I don't know. Let's just keep walking.'

My eyes can't stop shifting from left to right and back again, looking for the owner of that eerie voice. A whooshing sound grows louder. Something's coming. And if my senses are right, it's coming straight for us. I look for a hiding place. But where? And from what? The whooshing sound grows unbearably close, and a shadow appears directly in front. Something cold and wet folds over us like a clingy skin. I can't help but scream out. We all squirm around, bumping into each other, as we try to get this sticky thing off. But fighting makes no difference. The cold wet sensation passes right through me. And with a whoosh, the shadow, with all its stickiness, disappears behind us.

I fall to the ground, shaking. Ethan doubles over, while Matt heaves as he tries to catch his breath.

'What was that?' Ethan says.

Murderer!

It's back. That eerie voice. And for some reason it affects Ethan the most. He jumps at the sound, reaching for his left ear. 'Go away! I know you're talking to me. Now get lost!'

I stare at Ethan, wondering what he's talking about.

'It was my fault,' he says.

I don't like where his thoughts have taken him, and I curse this miserable voice for putting the idea in his head.

'I stood by and watched her die. I could have stopped it, but I didn't.'

'You were a child, Ethan. There was nothing you could do. Marduke would have killed you too.'

His face scrunches up and folds under the pressure of his guilt. 'I loved her. She was everything I wanted to be. But I was jealous, Isabel. Maybe part of me wanted her to die.'

'No! That's not true! Push that thought from your mind. You loved Sera. And you love her still.'

Worthless!

'What?' Matt calls out, peering over his shoulder. Oh no, the voice is tormenting Matt now.

Imposter!

'I'm not an imposter!'

I yank on his arm. 'Ignore it! Keep moving, one foot after the other. OK?'

Coward! Imposter!

Now there are several voices, surrounding us. I keep pulling on Ethan and Matt to keep walking. But with each step, the voices multiply. Soon there are hundreds of accusations coming from every direction.

Abandoned! A voice shrieks into my ear. I spin around, but nobody's there. 'What do you want from us?'

Beside me Matt's hands flail in the air surrounding him. 'Who are you?' he cries out. 'Why are you doing this?'

'It's the valley,' I try to explain, looking ahead to see how much more of this wretched place we have to cover. 'There's something in the air here, or the ground. Whatever, only your inner strength can stop the intrusion into your mind.'

'It's impossible to stop,' Ethan says. 'The voices are everywhere. I couldn't stop my sister from dying. I may not be able to stop my mother either.'

'Work harder, Ethan. Force a block.'

'It's no good, Isabel,' Matt whispers hoarsely from between us. 'Listen to them!'

Loser!

'That's what you should be trying *not* to do!'

Piercing through the voices, a scurrying sound makes all the nerves in my spine tingle. Ethan and Matt both glance at me, then each other. The scurrying sound grows into a furious rumble. Suddenly hundreds of animals, small like rats, come into view. Like a wave, they roll across the landscape towards us.

Ethan grabs my arm. 'Quickly!' He pulls Matt over, making us huddle together on the ground in the shape of a ball, our cloaks wedged tightly around us.

Beneath our feet the ground vibrates. In seconds the

animals are on us, clambering over our backs with sharp claws and scrambling down the other side. Several force their way under our cloaks. They nip at our boots. One scurries up my arm. I scream, and it tries to claw into my hood. The look of its over-sized front teeth makes my blood curdle. Frantically we push them out. Finally they pass over, disappearing into the dark.

And with their passing, the voices come back in force, making my skin crawl with their eerie accusations. It's as if someone's been inside our heads and dug up our deepest feelings of doubt and guilt. Slowly we trudge forward, but every step gets harder. 'How much more can we take of this, Ethan?' My pace slows to a crawl.

Matt's arm comes around my waist, but he's hardly able to hold up his own weight. He shakes his head as if trying to clear it. But the voices don't go away.

Ethan stops. 'I have an idea.'

He closes his eyes and concentrates. He's trying to create an illusion. How hard will it be to focus through this incessant screaming?

But somehow he does, creating an illusion of a beautiful forest just up ahead. Ethan lifts his torch, and the forest glistens as if a warm sun is shining on its moist leaves. The illusion is like a rope we cling to, pulling ourselves closer to safety with each step.

And suddenly we find ourselves standing at the edge of a fast-flowing river, the voices fading behind us.

But we have to step back quickly not to fall in. If we did, we'd die for sure. And quickly. This river doesn't flow like any other that I know. It has many currents, all pulling it in different directions, forming several whirlpools, frightening rips and lengthy rapids. It also looks deep. And while I can just see over to the other shore, it's quite a distance. The thought of having to cross it scares the life out of me. I fall back on to my heels with a feeling of despair. There must be another way, but which way is the correct one? Maybe we should never have crossed that valley. Maybe we should have headed in the opposite direction in the first place.

I glance up at Ethan and Matt. They look weary but relieved, slowly regaining their composure.

'What's wrong?' Ethan squats down to ask me.

But all I can think is that if I don't know the way, how can I find Arkarian? How can we survive in this place? I don't want to ever hear those voices again. This place is harsh. It works on two levels – physical and emotional. I throw my head back and stare up at blank nothingness. 'Oh where are you, Arkarian?'

Not expecting a reply, it's a shock when my head fills with a blinding light and sharp stabbing pain.

'Isabel?' Ethan calls. But the pain in my head is too much right now and I ignore him.

'Flow with it,' he whispers close to my ear, understanding that I'm experiencing another vision, and that only by relaxing the tension, will the pain ease and the images come clearly.

I know he's right, but accepting pain, accepting the blinding light, is a difficult task when in the midst of it. Eventually the pain and light reduces, revealing an image of a beautiful child. Her face is pale, but softly glowing, framed by a mass of black bouncing curls. It's Sera! Ethan's dead sister. She's here, in this strange cold world, calling to me. My urge to fight the vision disappears as I understand that here is the help we desperately need. So I open my mind and embrace the images as they unfold for my viewing. As I do this, a surge of power thunders through me, making my whole body shudder.

'Isabel?' I hear my brother's concerned voice call. 'Are you all right? Talk to me.'

I hold my hand up to stop his intrusion. He goes quiet and I open myself to the vision again. Immediately I'm lifted upwards, so that I can see the river for kilometres, winding between mountains and valleys for great distances. Then I'm brought back to my body and we take off again. This time it's as if I'm in a fast train — a supersonic fast train, that passes straight across the river, through a barren landscape, to a mountain of black ice, and onwards to an island surrounded by an icy lake on which a single, yet incredible structure stands. As the vision disappears, I understand that I have just been shown the way.

I open my eyes and slowly bring Ethan and Matt back into focus. They're both squatting before me. 'What did you see?' Ethan asks.

'We're being guided,' I start to explain. 'But it's a long and treacherous journey.'

'Did you see Arkarian?' Matt asks.

I shake my head. 'No, but there's a building. It looks like an elongated pyramid. It glistens like a shimmering beacon with all the colours of the universe.'

'It's the temple,' Matt says. 'It's sacred.'

Both Ethan and I stare at him. Ethan asks, 'How do you know this?'

A blank expression fills Matt's eyes, a deep frown forming, and he shrugs.

Dragging his eyes off Matt, Ethan drills me further about my vision and I explain what I remember, 'This … *temple*, is on an island. That's where they're keeping Arkarian.'

'Well, if it wasn't Arkarian who sent you the vision,' Ethan says, 'then who's guiding us? Did you see a face?'

I take his hand, knowing my words are going to shock. 'Our guide is your sister.'

Chapter Twenty-four

Isabel

We stare at the river for ages, studying it from various angles. And still no one has any idea how to cross it.

'Well,' Matt says. 'One thing's for sure, we can't swim it.'

Ethan and I both nod in agreement. This river is just too wild. The speed it's travelling is staggering. And it's also icy cold. We wouldn't live long if we fell into it. Great chunks of ice pass us by. The sound of one hitting the river bank, and exploding into several smaller chunks, echoes like an ear-shattering roll of thunder.

'We can't go round it,' I explain, working moisture into my mouth. 'This is where we're meant to cross.'

'You didn't see any bridges in that vision of yours, did you?' Matt asks hopefully.

'No. But a bridge would be nice. What do you say, Ethan? Can you build one? You know, like you did for me in the ancient city last year?'

He aims his torch across the water. 'I can't see the other side. It would be too risky.'

'Oh well. Now what?'

Suddenly Ethan claps his hands together as if struck

by a brilliant idea. 'Well, that settles it. If I can't build a bridge, we'll just have to row.'

Matt flicks his torch around the river bank. 'And the boat is ... where?'

I'm inclined to agree with Matt. Not because I don't have faith in Ethan's illusions. I've seen the reality Ethan can create with his mind. It's just, I'm reluctant to get in *any* boat to cross *this* river. 'It's too fast for a boat. We'll end up way down river. Or up river. Or ...'

'Somewhere down the bottom,' Matt finishes for me.

'It will have oars,' Ethan says by way of explanation. 'Good strong oars.'

The thought of crossing this river in a rowing boat has my stomach churning into knots. I take a deep breath to control my composure, at least outwardly for Matt's sake. But right now Ethan's idea is the best option we have – in fact, the only option. 'Give it everything you can, Ethan. I don't like this river. It's as if it thinks on its own, but can't make up its mind on which direction to go. It has a hungry look about it.'

'I'll give it a rudder too, one that will work with a rowing boat and help us steer it.'

Matt's head is shaking as he turns his back to the river to stand in front of Ethan and me. 'In case you two haven't noticed, there is no boat. None. Zero. And even if there were, you wouldn't get me in it, not in these waters.' His head keeps shaking. 'You two are crazy.'

Ethan's tolerance snaps. 'Do you have a better idea? I mean, you're supposed to be our leader, aren't you? Everyone knows it. Why even the Prophecy says so. How does it go now? Oh yeah, *"Not before a leader pure of heart awakens"*.'

'Ethan, that's enough!'

He waves a hand to shut me up. 'But what are you doing instead? Putting doubts in our minds. We don't need that. If you believe with your soul, this illusion will work. Remember Lady Arabella said to have courage and faith. Besides, the boat will be as real as you or me. It will stay solid for the duration of the illusion. I can do that, Matt. Trust me. You know, this will be a good test for you. See if you've got what it takes to be a—'

Another hair-raising shriek pierces the darkness nearby. All three of us peer around and over our shoulders.

After a moment of complete and eerie silence, Ethan turns his attention back to Matt. 'Of course, you could stay here, with that thing screeching at you until we get back.'

Ethan spins away and Matt and I are left alone. 'You know, Ethan didn't mean that you're not good enough to be our ...' My sentence falls away as Matt turns and stares at the thrashing water. With his back to me, I watch his shoulders lift as he sucks in a calming breath. Ethan's words have dug deeply. I know my brother, he takes life, and his responsibilities, very seriously. It was probably his feelings of inadequacy that made him leap into that pyramid and force his way into the underworld with us. Matt has a lot to prove, and now he's faced with a different challenge, to use his faith to believe in what he can't see, and to trust another with his life. It's what we do in the Guard all the time. And I know from personal experience it's not easy. But Matt's having a real struggle.

Ethan comes back. 'It's ready.'

My first thought is that it should be larger – like ten times the size of this very ordinary-looking boat!

'Oh hell!' Matt comes up beside me. 'So that's it? I thought you were supposed to be gifted!'

Taking a swig from my flask to moisten my mouth, I attempt to distract Ethan from reacting to Matt's comment, 'Are you sure it will hold up in this river, Ethan?'

Ethan nods. 'It'll hold.' And to Matt he says, 'You can wait here if you want. Alone. You'll have your torch and we'll leave you some of *our* food. Did you bring any spare batteries? The torches will need changing soon. Oh, don't worry, we'll come back for you – if we can. That is, providing there isn't a back door out of this place. Don't know how long that'll be though – hours, days, weeks!' His shoulders lift in a light shrug. 'Then again, you could do what you came here to do – learn what it is to be a Guardian of Time.'

I get in the boat, taking a position at the stern with one set of oars. I wonder for a second if I'm doing the right thing, trusting my life to this illusion. The boat feels solid beneath me, the oars fit snugly in my hands, and yet I know they're only real as long as Ethan can maintain the illusion. I recall the first time I saw Ethan's creation of a bridge, and how difficult it had been to put my trust in him, even though I could smell the flowers he'd created around it. I shift sideways on the bench and call out to Matt, 'Don't think about it, Matt. Just get in. Your strength is really going to be needed here.'

Curling his fists into balls he tentatively steps into the boat. Feeling its solidity for himself, he drops down beside me, shoving me over. 'All right then, but I'll row.'

Relinquishing the oars, I move to the opposite bench and take up the other set. Ethan gets in and takes the oars from my hands. 'I'm rowing too.'

I open my mouth to argue, but Ethan, as usual, is faster with his words. 'Don't go getting all snotty, Isabel. You have to let us row. We'll last longer than you. And don't take offence. It's a matter of stamina, not an anti-feminist insult.'

'I'm as strong as both of you! How many times have I proved it in training?'

'Will you sit down?' Ethan snaps at me. 'I don't know how long this illusion's going to last. And besides, we need you to steer. At least you can see where we're going. That's why I put a rudder in this thing. You're the only one who can see the other side!' His voice softens, sounding weary. 'Look, just take us straight across. If we end up drifting down river, this illusion could dissolve, and then where would we be?'

Matt's eyes flare wide, but he doesn't say anything. He must be wound up like a tight spring. I think all of us are. Not wanting to inflame the situation, or make Matt feel worse, I shut my mouth and take up a position at the stern, controlling the rudder.

Ethan and Matt start rowing, quickly getting their rhythm in sync, and amazingly, the boat takes off in a straight line, slicing through the current. We go over some rapids and lose momentum for a few minutes, swinging dangerously down river, but the guys row faster and harder, and soon we straighten up again, heading towards the distant shore.

But rowing turns out to be a hard slog. Even in this freezing cold, perspiration makes their faces shine. One of the torches flickers and goes off. Luckily the other seems OK. Matt pushes his fur-lined hood back, while Ethan starts slipping his cloak right off, trying to keep the rhythm going as he does so.

Watching them work so hard makes me feel slightly guilty. I like to think I could help, but there's no way I could last as long as either of these two. It's only because of their steady pace that we've come so far this quickly.

'How much further, Isabel?' Matt asks in a strained voice. 'Can you see?'

'Not far at all. Maybe ten minutes, I swear.' The remaining torchlight flickers, but holds, though at a much reduced strength. 'As long as this light holds I'll be able to steer us straight.'

'Don't trust it,' Ethan says, and kicks over my pack. 'Change the batteries on Matt's torch.'

While trying to keep the rudder in position, I fish around in my pack and locate one set of the six sets of spare batteries we brought with us. While undoing the wrapping, a clump of ice hits us, tilting the boat dangerously, before veering away and allowing us to right ourselves.

The torchlight flickers again. It's obvious now it hasn't much energy left to give. 'Hurry, Isabel,' Ethan says with a tight edge to his voice. 'You have to keep us straight. Matt and I can't hold this pace much longer.'

Matt picks up on Ethan's concern and finds an inner source of courage. 'I'm not going to stop! Not unless my arms drop off. Your boat is ... unbelievable. I know it doesn't really exist, and yet I can feel it. I'm sitting in it! If you can do this, Ethan, maybe it's possible, just maybe—'

A sharp jolt against the side of our boat sends the

batteries flying out of my hand and over the side. 'Oh great!'

'Forget them,' Ethan calls out. 'Get another set out.'

'Here.' Matt pushes my pack up close to my leg with one of his feet.

I lunge down to get it, but as I do, another chunk of ice crashes into us, sending the boat careering into a set of rapids and spinning us off course.

'It's OK,' Ethan says, trying to maintain a level of calm. 'Just keep rowing, Matt. Forget the batteries for a second, Isabel. Keep us straight until we get out of this mess.'

But this mess is harder to break free of than anything else we've had to deal with so far. The rapids are fuelled by a maze of mixing currents, tossing us in different directions. And while the torchlight grows dimmer with each passing second, there's enough light for me to see we're heading for more trouble. Straight ahead is a whirlpool. We're going to have to swing around it, or be sucked in for sure.

'Faster,' I tell Matt and Ethan. 'You have to row harder and faster. Pick up the pace. This is crucial.'

Ethan peers over the edge of the boat. 'What can you see that we can't?'

'Trouble,' I tell him. 'Just keep rowing and let me do the steering.'

Just as I think this crossing can't get any worse, the torchlight flickers once more, then goes out. For a second, as the darkness consumes us totally, everyone is silent, except for the guys' heavy breathing and grunting with every motion of their arms. I wonder fleetingly how we're going to get out of this now. First things first, I tell myself, and concentrate on steering the boat around the approaching whirlpool. The boat lifts suddenly. We've caught the edge. Holding the rudder steady becomes difficult as the pressure of the whirlpool increases. Finally we're free and glide into smoother water.

'Yes, we cleared it!' Quickly, I reach into my bag for the batteries. I find another packet and rip it open. But in my haste to get the batteries into the torch, I drop one into the bottom of the boat.

'What did we clear, Isabel?' Matt asks in a slow voice, as if, while most of him wants to hear what we just missed, his heart doesn't.

'You don't want to know, Matt.'

He contents himself with this, then rolls something to the rear of the boat with his foot.

It's the other battery, and now I have the two again. Fumbling in the dark, while still trying to maintain a steady rudder, I manage to get the fresh batteries into the torch. I flick it on and it lights up the whole area for me. 'Yes!' But the better news is, though we're way down river from where we entered, the other side is fast approaching. We make it across, get dragged a further twenty or so metres by the swift current there, when finally Ethan finds a place to jump off and secure the rope.

As soon as we get ourselves and our packs off, the boat begins to disappear. Matt and Ethan collapse on the sandy bank, panting and dragging in deep breaths. Matt gives his arms a shake, then sags again, spreading out on the sand.

A feeling of euphoria begins to take shape inside me. We crossed the river and made it, so this part of our journey is now behind us, bringing us that much closer to finding Arkarian. But before I get a moment to savour this feeling, and share it with Ethan and Matt, I'm overwhelmed by a prickly sensation.

I shake Matt, then Ethan, who collapsed on my other side. 'Hey, get up! Quickly!'

'Huh?' Matt moans, rolling over, exhausted.

Ethan drags himself up. 'What is it?'

Around us the trees are thick. I peer into them as best I can. 'I can't shake this feeling.'

'What feeling?' Matt asks in a tight voice, suddenly sitting up beside me too.

'A feeling that we're not alone.'

Chapter Twenty-five

Isabel

At first there is the sound of hissing, squealing, and pounding in the near distance. I think there might be wolves in the bushes, but Ethan shakes his head. 'Wolves aren't that heavy on their feet.'

Suddenly red lights appear out of the darkness, like lasers, except in pairs.

'What on earth?' Matt hisses.

I soon realise what we're staring at. 'They're eyes. I've seen these creatures in my vision.'

The second my words are out they come at us from all directions, snorting and hissing with their beady glowing eyes. They appear bigger in the flesh. I wonder fleetingly if maybe they're just short humans. They have feet, and arms with human hands. But their bodies are no way human in form. They have bulky curved shoulders, and, stranger still, wings attached to their backs. Though they seem to prefer using their feet.

Ethan quickly flicks a dagger from each of his boots, throwing one to Matt. 'Isabel, see if you can get a fire going.'

They attack, a dozen or more, screaming a shrill kind of war-cry. It makes me wonder if they can talk; their faces have a creepy human-like quality. One of them leaps into the air with the help of its wings, then spins around, placing himself between Matt and me. He surprises us again by attacking his own kind!

Matt sends me a startled look, but neither of us has time to analyse what on earth is going on.

'Watch your back,' Matt yells. 'It could be a trick.'

From a short distance away, Ethan reminds me to get that fire organised as soon as I get a spare second. But the creatures are determined and fierce. One latches on to Ethan's leg and takes a bite out of him. Matt tries kicking furiously to help Ethan dislodge it. Ethan sticks his dagger into its back, finishing it off. While his leg drips blood, he reminds me again about that fire.

In the end, gathering enough dry wood and tinder proves to be the hardest part to getting the fire started. But suddenly, the creature that has chosen to fight on our side runs over with his arms full of bark. It's perfect, and I take the tinder from his arms. 'Hey thanks.'

Matt stares at me hard for a second. 'What are you doing?'

'Huh?'

'He's the enemy, for crying out loud!'

Ethan brings down four more creatures with his dagger as if they were dominoes, while Matt uses his fists to knock one particularly stubborn one to the ground.

The creature who handed me the firewood gives a snort, then helps Ethan, who's limping badly now, blood oozing from his leg wound.

Without giving us a second to recover our strength,

the half-dozen creatures knocked unconscious start coming round, including the stabbed ones! They must be invincible!

'We have to turn this around, Isabel,' Ethan calls. 'We need to attack with fire.'

While Matt and Ethan watch my back for a few minutes, I work furiously at getting it started. After what feels like for ever, a flame ignites, and it's not long before I hand Ethan and Matt two sticks each, burning at one end. And with two of my own, we scream and yell at the top of our voices, charging the flames right into the creatures' faces. Beside me, their traitor makes his own weapons and joins us.

Just as Ethan suspects, the creatures turn and run off in different directions. Exhausted, we stand and watch for their return. But after a few minutes it's clear they're gone, leaving us in silence, except for the sound of our own breathing, and the crackling fire.

We set the torches up in a circle around us, collapsing on the sandy shore.

As we allow ourselves a moment to catch our breath, Ethan's eyes drift to the traitor. 'What do you think you're doing here?'

The creature speaks, his words thick but perfectly understandable, 'I believe I'm sitting by your fire.'

It's a shock. Other than screaming, these are the first sounds we've heard these creatures make. And for those sounds to be proper words, stuns us to the point of losing our own ability to talk.

Ethan is first to recover. 'Who are you?'

The creature stares into the fire, lifting his rounded shoulders, his wings flapping once. 'Well, the truth is, I don't know.'

'You don't know who you are?' I ask, while working on healing the bite on Ethan's leg. It's deep, and takes a few minutes.

The creature smacks his forehead with an open palm. 'My memory isn't what it used to be.'

Ethan's head does this roll, almost right around, like he can't believe what's happening, that we're even having this conversation. 'I saw you fighting your own kind and helping Isabel get the fire started. Why did you do those things? Why did you turn on your own kind like that?'

'Because my kind are morons. They don't know how to think for themselves.'

'Uh-huh, and what, you do?' The creature doesn't reply and Ethan stares at it. 'Why aren't you afraid of fire like your friends?'

'Fire is something none of us is afraid of. Now water, that's a different matter.'

'Then why did your kind turn tail and run when we charged at them?'

'When you turned the fire into weapons, you surprised them. They may be morons, but they're not entirely stupid. They know all about fire, especially the fact that it burns.' He scrunches up his forehead, making deep creases in his brow, and sighs, a very human-like sound. It has me thinking, but no way, this creature can't have evolved from human form. Surely.

'Do you have a name?' I ask.

His frown deepens and his red eyes seem to glow brighter. 'I think it once was John.'

For some reason his telling us his name is 'John' shocks us all over again. It just sounds too … human.

'Your name is *John*?' Matt has to be sure he's hearing

258

right. 'What are your people called?'

'Ah, now that I do know, for the master calls us his wren.'

'*Wren?*' Ethan rolls the word on his tongue. 'Hmm, so what are your plans now, John Wren? I don't think your friends are going to want you back.'

He doesn't hesitate. 'To come with you.'

Silence is our reply to this. Just how much does he know about us? Ultimately Matt asks, 'Where do you think we're going?'

He shrugs. 'Since you're wearing travelling clothes, I assume you're on a journey. And well, I know this place thoroughly. I can guide and protect you. With me in your party the wren will leave you alone. And there are many facets to these lands that you could not possibly understand.'

'Like what?'

'The challenges.'

Matt and Ethan make scoffing sounds of agreement, recalling the two 'challenges' we just passed. And suddenly I recall Lady Arabella using the same term earlier when giving us advice. 'We have a mountain to cross yet.'

John Wren's wings flap twice but he doesn't move. Eventually he says, 'What sort of mountain?'

'A black one. Made entirely of ice.'

He snorts a real piggish sound. Spittle sprays over his bulky chest. 'This is not good.'

'Why?' Ethan and I say simultaneously.

'It's the most difficult challenge of all the lands.'

'How so?' Matt asks. 'What will we have to do?'

'Face your inner demons.'

The wren is right when he says we've found ourselves in a strange land. And he seems to know a lot about it. He would probably make a useful guide. But why would this creature turn traitor to help three strangers? I just don't get it. 'So what's in this for you?'

John Wren looks at each of us in turn, then stares off past the torches to the darkness beyond. 'I haven't always lived here. That much I can still remember. The three of you trigger a memory of something I can't quite put a finger on. Perhaps the more I keep your company ...' He shrugs. 'Who knows?'

'Do you think you'll get your memory back just by hanging around us?' Matt asks.

He makes a shrugging motion with his wings. 'Perhaps we can be of use to each other.'

'Well,' Ethan says. 'I guess we could do with a guide. But it has to be all right with Isabel and Matt. And one foot out of line, and you're gone.'

Ethan glances at Matt. 'I don't know. I guess it's all right.'

'Isabel?'

I can't help but hesitate; trust doesn't come as easily to me as Ethan. I've seen these wren before. They're the ones who helped abduct Arkarian. I also saw them in the dream Marduke sent me. They were beating Arkarian in his cell. And didn't I just heal Ethan from a deep wound caused by the teeth of one of them? 'Your kind are dangerous. Why should I trust you?'

'Begging your pardon, miss,' John Wren says. 'Trust has to start somewhere. And so far, *I* haven't done anything to prove I'm unworthy of it. Have I?'

I don't answer immediately and he goes on, 'I do believe you're judging me by the deeds of others.' He continues to hold my gaze for a few moments. I pick up the sense that he's telling the truth, and more importantly, that he has nothing to hide.

'All right. But I want you in my sight at all times. And you're never on guard duty by yourself.'

'Well,' Ethan says. 'Since that's settled, do you know anything about the island we're headed for?'

At the mention of the word 'island', John Wren goes strangely still. 'What island – specifically – do you mean?'

'It's surrounded by a lake,' I tell him, a shiver running through me at his nervous attitude. 'On the other side of the mountain.'

'There are several islands in this place,' he says, as if in denial. 'And many more mountains.'

Matt looks up and says, 'It's the island with the temple.'

John Wren draws in a sharp breath. 'I knew it! Are you crazy? You can't go there you know.'

'And why not?' I snap at him, concern growing quickly to panic, because if anyone knows anything about the island that keeps Arkarian prisoner, it would be a creature who has lived here so long he has no memory of any other life.

He says, 'It's called Obsidian Island. You can't go there because ... Well, to put it bluntly, it's haunted.'

Chapter Twenty-six

Isabel

It takes a couple of days to get to black-ice mountain, though it's hard to tell without a sun or even a moon. And our watches don't work here, nor our torches any more. The batteries, only lasting a few hours, ran out long ago. John, as we call him now, has shown us how to make long-lasting torches by burning an element dug out of the ground. I try not to think what it's made from. The foul smell is enough of a clue.

I've learned a lot about this place, thanks to John, who's full of information, though he can't remember how long he's lived here, or where he lived before. As we pass through different landscapes, one thing that doesn't change is the harsh weather. It makes me wonder if there are seasons here and maybe we were just unlucky enough to be making this journey in winter.

'The cold is something I don't feel and have no memory of,' he explains. 'But to answer your question, sometimes all but the most lush of valleys are covered in ice.'

The thought of lush valleys makes me wonder about

the many different trees and grasses we see. 'How do plants grow here without light or warmth?'

'Where there is a will to survive, a need, a desire . . .' he shrugs, and I recall the thousands of brilliantly coloured fireflies we saw soon after our arrival.

'But there is a moon,' he goes on to explain, surprising me. 'Over there.' He points into the distant sky ahead. 'Once a month, for a matter of minutes, it rises high enough to bathe the land in a rich red glow, directly over the master's garden.'

I glance in the direction he points, but the mountain is too high, and the darkness absolute, reminding me of our vulnerability.

'Can you see it, Isabel?' Ethan asks from beside me.

I shake my head. Weariness is starting to get to me. And the lack of food doesn't help. We're down to only a small ration of dried fruit now. 'I can't see over the mountain.'

'What about you, John?'

'My eyesight is very poor. Living here in the dark, what use is it?'

And yet it's in this darkness we've seen so much, sights that I know will live with me for the rest of my life, some that will give me many sleepless nights. Like the hundreds of different types of creatures, those with human features such as eyes and hands, or whole bodies, though skeletal in appearance. Others with wings (that actually work) or tails or leathery skin. Attracted to our flaming torches, they come in droves to see who these strange travellers are. Some even follow us for a kilometre or two. Luckily, with John by our side, for the most part, they leave us unharmed. The one creature we haven't spotted yet is the one making that mournful shrieking sound. John tells us it's a bird, with long talons, beaks to match, and eyes like ours. I still shiver every time I hear it, and try hard not to visualise its eyes.

Hours later we finally stand before the mountain; and from this close the mere sight of it makes my chest tighten. It's not as if I haven't climbed a mountain before. But never in such consuming darkness, and never a mountain made completely of ice. Where on earth will we find footholds? This ice is too smooth, with incredible sheer drops. 'Impossible,' I whisper, feeling humble and small in the face of such power and force. 'We can't climb this.'

'Well what do we do now?' Matt asks.

No one appears to have any idea.

'What about my sister?' Ethan asks. 'She helped us before.'

Right now Sera is our only hope, but so far *she's* been the one to initiate contact, and I haven't heard from her for some time now. This psychic skill is still new to me. I don't know its potential. I hardly understand how it works. 'I'll try to make contact,' I say tentatively, not promising anything that I'm not sure I can do.

Unwilling to venture far on my own, I take my torch and stay within visual distance of our makeshift camp. I sit cross-legged, wrapping Lady Arabella's warm cloak around me like a blanket. The air here is vastly colder than anywhere we've travelled so far, the ground frozen beneath us.

Closing my eyes, I take several deep breaths, releasing as much tension as I can. Not really knowing what to do, I use instinct to guide me. I visualise the rest of our journey the way Sera first showed it to me, zooming past the mountain, crossing the lake, taking myself right up to the white pyramid-shaped temple as if standing at the front door. *'Sera, can you hear me? It's Isabel. I need your help. I need you to show me how to cross this mountain.'*

Not really expecting my simple request to work, or to work so quickly, I'm way not prepared for her screaming reply. The vision she sends me thunders into my brain. When she's done, I get up and stagger, unbalanced, for a few seconds.

Matt and Ethan run over. 'Are you OK?' Matt asks quickly.

'Yeah, I'm fine.' I look into his face, then Ethan's. How do I tell them about this test, and what happens if we don't pass it?

But Ethan reads my expression. 'Just come out with it. We've come this far, we're not going to turn tail and run now.'

I tell them about a secret path. 'It cuts straight through the ice. Apparently all we have to do is walk along this path until we get to the other side.'

'That's too easy,' Ethan says. 'What's the catch?'

'Well, according to Sera, we'll be confronted with our hidden truths. As long as we keep focused and don't stray from the path, we'll be OK.'

Ethan isn't buying my watered-down version. 'What happens if we don't pass the test?'

'Well … the mountain will make us permanent fixtures in its corridors of ice.'

'Permanent?' Matt asks, his voice strained. 'As in …?'

'Eternity.' That said, I try to distract them. Dwelling on what's ahead will only make us nervous and prone to error. 'According to Sera we have to hurry.'

'What did she say?' Ethan asks.

'She didn't speak to me exactly. There was just this urgency in our connection. It was very strong.'

Ethan starts collecting our things, but Matt's thoughts are still on the challenge ahead. 'How do I stay focused? Do we know what form our "hidden truths" will take, or even what they are?'

Ethan hands Matt one of the backpacks. 'Just try to keep your mind clear of all negative emotions.'

'Oh yeah, that should be a piece of cake,' he replies sarcastically.

Ethan thinks for a second. 'What do you feel when you think of Rochelle?'

Matt gives him a sharp look, like he wants to thump him. I don't think he's going to reply, but then he mutters, 'Anger, mostly.'

'And when you think of being a Guard?' My brother's head shakes negatively. 'I think the Tribunal made a mistake and that I'm not Named at all.'

He's so full of doubt! How on earth will he get through this challenge? An idea hits me, as I recall his reaction to meeting someone at school recently. 'What do you feel when you think of the girl Neriah?'

Ethan's eyebrows lift at this suggestion, but he gives a little nod. He's seen Matt look absolutely besotted by this girl too. A dreamlike expression makes his eyes look glazed. 'Hold that thought,' he tells Matt. 'Forget your problems. Forget everything. Draw on the image of Neriah, and fill your head with only positive thoughts. OK?'

We take off in the direction Sera showed me, to a point that looks like one ice wall, that in fact is actually several walls slightly overlapping. Between these zigzag walls is a path.

Before we begin, Ethan pulls me to the side. 'You should take the lead.'

My instinct is to argue. But he knows what I'm thinking. He knows I'll be worried about Matt.

'Let me look out for Matt. If I sense he's getting into trouble, I'll pull him back and stay with him on this side. You keep going with John and rescue Arkarian.'

It's a selfless act. But it doesn't surprise me. I give him a hug, and he holds me close. His reassurance makes me feel as if everything is going to be all right.

When we pull apart he says, 'You'll be fine. And so will Matt. He's just so full of doubt right now, it's stopping him from being his true self.'

Matt comes over, probably wondering what's taking us so long. I force a smile to my face I don't really feel. The last thing I want is to fill Matt's head with more doubt.

So the four of us make our way along the zigzag path, with me in the lead, then John, Matt, and Ethan at the end. Not knowing when exactly the test will begin, I start screening my thoughts and clearing all negative ones straightaway. I tell myself, no matter what comes at me, don't turn around. If the others should see my face, and read fear or something else just as off-putting, it could affect their concentration. Carrying one of the lighted torches, and with a pack on my back, I force one foot before the other. Meanwhile, I try to keep my breathing slow, and my mind clear of doubts.

The path is actually a tunnel, right through the ice! I'm not sure when it starts to change, or when I feel the pressure building. But soon the tunnel opens up and a valley spreads out before me. I'm not expecting to see anything quite so breathtaking; it takes me by surprise. But quickly the valley changes, and the path turns into a bridge over a trickling stream that leads into a lake. Along its borders sit barbecue tables and playground equipment. Where am I? I get a distinct feeling I've been here before. I try to place the memory.

But up ahead, someone is standing on the bridge, directly in my path. It's a man, leaning on his elbows, overlooking the stream that flows briskly beneath him.

The impulse to turn and check on the others is strong. Especially as right now I'd like to see Matt's reaction. I think this man is our father.

As I draw nearer, the man turns his head, and I see that it really is our father. My heart slows to a heavy beat. What is he doing here? And why does this bridge and everything around it seem so familiar? I've been here before; the feeling is strong.

Suddenly I'm overwhelmed by a compulsion to ask the question that's been gnawing at my brain ever since that vision I recently had of him. But I don't want to get distracted. The danger is too real. And I mustn't stray from the path!

Despite all this, when I get close enough, I still can't stop myself. 'On the last day we were together you told me you were leaving because you were deceived. Who was it that deceived you?'

His head tilts to one side, while his mouth forms into a small smile of regret. I blink away a tear and try to keep focused. I have to remember not to pause too long. But my feet won't budge until I have his answer.

'Your mother,' he says simply.

'How?' My voice sounds odd, like it's coming from

deep inside, or far away.

He sighs. 'How I wish I didn't have to go. And you, my sweetheart, must move on with your life. Forget this conversation. It's the last time we'll speak of it.'

I grab his arm. 'Daddy! What is it?'

For a second I stop breathing. Was that my voice? But it was the voice of a child! What's going on?

Around me the temperature drops. A cold wind whips across my face. 'Please, Daddy! What's wrong?'

His hand reaches out to touch my face. He tugs a lock of hair blowing across my eyes, and tucks it behind my ear. 'When I married your mother she was already pregnant.' He lays both hands on my shoulders. 'I love your mother, Isa. I love you all. But this deceit is hard for me. Do you know what a secret is?'

I nod, unable to speak, my mouth is trembling too much.

'Your mother keeps secrets from me. Secrets I can't live with any more.' And then he says, 'Matt is not my son.'

A gust of wind blows fiercely, pulling at my cloak, distracting me. When I look up my father is gone. I spin around, searching for him, but there's only darkness behind. A shadow passes overhead and I look up. There's a wall of ice lowering on top of me! The wind turns into a chilling gale and my torch blows out. I'm plunged in total darkness. The air turns so cold I find it hard to breath.

'What's happening!'

I reach up and my hand hits solid ice. The walls are shifting and now I hear voices. People are screaming and they're very close. I slide down with the pressure of a mountain closing around me. Flat to the floor I find an opening, but it's disappearing fast! I crawl on my stomach, but my pack gets stuck. I yank it off as fast as I can. The screams grow louder. Blindly, I keep crawling. At last a blast of sleet hits my face and I realise I'm out.

I stagger to my feet and run. *Matt is not my father's son!* I keep running until I can hardly breathe. *What does this mean?* Every step becomes more painful as I suck in huge gulps of freezing air. *How could I not know? If my father told me all those years ago, could he have told Matt too? Did Matt bury this knowledge into the pit of his very being as I did?*

With nothing but darkness around me I stop. What the hell am I doing?

I turn right around, slowly, making sure I'm now facing the exact direction from which I came. And with one foot carefully placed before the other, I walk until I feel a wall of ice with my own hands.

Depleted, I sit on the ground and wait. It's not long before I see John's torch come out of the path, making the whole area light up for me. He looks strained and scared and I go over to him.

He sinks to his knees, his short legs jerking nervous-ly under him; and I wonder what truths – or memories – or demons, confronted him on the path.

'Are you OK?' I ask with real concern, burying my own experience for now. There'll be time to think soon enough.

Looking at John heaving with exhaustion, I can't help wonder how friendships, made over a brief period of time, can have the potency of one made over many years. And to think at first I couldn't trust him.

'The truth is, Isabel, I saw a lot of things. Things that

reminded me of another time, another world, a long time ago. And yes, I'm fine … now. I think I'm really fine.'

His words, the relief he obviously feels, make me inquisitive. 'What did you see, John?'

'Well, I think that's private,' he begins, but goes on to explain anyway. 'I saw a woman. A beautiful woman. She was my wife.' He waves a hand briefly in the air. 'I loved this woman very much. She was my wife you know.' He looks up at me. 'Did I tell you this woman was my wife?'

I nod and smile, hoping to encourage him to go on. Obviously his experience has touched him deeply; he's practically stuttering over every phrase. But when he does continue, his words shock. 'She was so lovely. Even in death, she was lovely. I wanted her so much, I couldn't let *him* have her.'

I moisten my mouth and try to form the question bursting to be asked, 'How did your wife die?'

While looking straight ahead he says, 'I murdered her. I killed her. I put a knife in her stomach.' His arm moves and makes the killing motion several times. 'I stabbed her seven times. And then I took this knife and I put it here.' He thumps his chest with a closed fist. Silently, a tear falls.

As I sit shuddering inside my cloak, I wonder what sort of place this is. The last place you want to get trapped in, the thought occurs. Suddenly the urge to get out of here overwhelms me and I feel dizzy. And then Ethan comes staggering out, holding his head with both hands.

I run over to him and he sags in my arms. 'We can't go back that way.' His head rocks from side to side.

'There has to be another way. OK?'

'Do you want to talk about it?'

He doesn't answer, so I prod a little, thinking it might help to relieve him of the trauma. 'Did you see your sister's murder?'

'No.'

'Was it something about your mother?'

His stillness and refusal to explain is unnerving. But it's his decision, so I rub his arm gently to let him know that he has a friend, right here next to him, just as he does for me all the time. He puts his arm around my shoulders, and over the top of my head his words pass, 'I saw Rochelle. I saw her face in the wall. Did you see those walls? They were full of people. I think they were dead, but hell, Isabel, they were screaming!'

I stay silent and he goes on in a softer tone, 'Rochelle was one of those people, screaming for me to save her.' He looks down at me. 'What do you think it means?'

Honestly, I have no idea. 'My experience was a memory, so I really don't know.'

'I have to know, Isabel. I have to find out, or how will I ever be able to sleep again? Does it mean Rochelle is in trouble? How can this be a hidden truth? And what was it John said about this challenge? That we'd be facing our inner demons?'

'Maybe it was a reflection of your concern for her.'

He looks at me strangely, and I elaborate, 'I think you're in love with her, Ethan.'

He pulls away. 'You don't know what you're talking about!'

He could be right, and maybe I don't, but I see the way he looks at her. And he's the first to jump to her aid, and when needed, even her defence. But Ethan's not ready to admit it, not ready to accept the truth. Maybe that's the reason he saw Rochelle in the ice. She loves *him*. Well, that's what I think. And without his love in return, she will always be lost to him.

He remains silent. And it's in this silence I feel an odd sensation, like a part of my arm, or my lung, or something, has gone missing. It dawns on Ethan the second our eyes connect. 'Oh no! Where's Matt? He should be out by now. He went through *before* me. But I didn't see him. Once the path turned ugly I didn't think of Matt any more. I didn't think of any one of you.'

'We have to go back and look for him. What if he's been enclosed in that wall?' And then I recall, 'My pack's still in there! What will we do for tools?'

'We'll find a way,' Ethan says. He sees John huddled on the ground nearby and starts to call him, but notices something from the corner of his eye. 'Look!'

It's Matt, coming out of the mountain. He's strolling down the path, whistling, as if he hasn't a care in the world.

'Matt?' I stop just short from giving him a great big hug. Something about him makes me freeze. And it's not because of what I just learned about him. We may not have the same father, but we're still brother and sister. I try to put my finger on what's different. It's the look he's wearing. Slightly glazed around the eyes, as if he's overwhelmed by something, something that's taken his breath away. 'Are you OK?'

He looks down at me and smiles. 'Oh yeah. Wasn't that the greatest?'

'Huh?' Ethan and I exclaim together.

He glances over his shoulder. 'In there. Wasn't it just

so beautiful? And what about those waterfalls? Magnificent. And the flowers. I've never seen anything like them before. And those butterflies ... weren't they the most amazing colours?'

Ethan's head simply shakes. 'Well I wouldn't know. I didn't see any butterflies.'

'You're kidding,' Matt sounds amazed, then opens his palms and releases twenty or more butterflies into the air, all shapes, all sizes, all brilliant colours. They flutter around us briefly, as if reluctant to leave. Finally, after a last circle around Matt's shoulders and head, as if sharing a secret goodbye, they take off. With their wings flapping they create the most amazing range of colours. Some I can't put a name to.

Ethan looks at me with questions struggling to form. He's shocked at Matt's strange euphoric experience, so unlike his own. Unlike mine or John's as well.

I have many questions too, but a sudden surge of energy hits me, along with a flash of blinding light. It's a vision again. Straightaway I know it's from Sera, but it lacks the clarity of her other contacts. This one is strained and, if I'm not mistaken, fuelled by something powerful – fear or anxiety.

When it's over I look up at Matt and Ethan, knowing that my questions are going to have to wait. 'Something's wrong. We have to hurry.'

'What did you see?' Ethan asks, his voice filled with concern.

'I didn't see anything really. I only felt.'

Matt's eyes start focusing clearly again. 'What did you feel?'

'Fear mostly. Sera's. She was shaking with it.'

Chapter Twenty-seven

Arkarian

Lathenia is furious. She comes to the temple, surrounded by seven frolicking Great Danes. She rolls her eyes to the ceiling as if half expecting something to come flying down at her. She takes a few steps and finds herself within the inner octagonal base. A shudder passes through her as if someone is walking on her grave. But this is a ridiculous thought. Lathenia is eternal. The hounds, I notice, remain outside the octagon, several whine for her return, as if she is separated from them by some invisible force.

She has others with her, and they follow. The first is Marduke. He grins at me with his half-mouth. The four wren, who put me in this state, remain cowering by the door. Marduke bellows at them and they move forward, only to retreat again when his back is turned. There is also the boy Bastian, who keeps his eyes averted. And lastly, an old man.

It's the old man who intrigues me. His long white hair and beard, grey eyes and stooped and frail physique, reveal his age. He stands in the background, and I sense that's how he likes it. Only once do I catch his eye, but it's enough to see his aura. He's a Magician. A very powerful one. With talents different from anyone in the Guard, except possibly for one – Dartemis. The stories of Dartemis are only a legend, but seeing this old man makes me suspect there could be some truth in the ancient tale.

It's clear now why my powers aren't working. This Magician has thrown an enchantment over me. A strong magical spell. So why is he here now? Does Lathenia suspect the enchantment needs renewing?

She sweeps her hand in a wide arc. Sparks, in the form of a shower of electric detonations, spray from her fingertips, making me blink. 'It seems I have underestimated your friends.'

I smile. It's too hard not to. Not only are they alive, but they're nearby and close enough to be a threat.

'Allow me the pleasure of wiping that smile from his face, Mistress,' Marduke utters by her side, his one blazing red eye staring straight at me.

She produces a whip and tosses it to Bastian. 'I want Bastian to do it.'

Bastian looks at the whip, flicking a brief glance at me, then back to his mistress. 'You want me to … to …?'

'What's wrong, Bastian?' she asks in a mocking tone. 'What weakness has generated inside you of late? What demons are you battling with?' Her eyes flash brilliant blue as they flare in his direction. 'I am your mistress! Don't ever doubt it! I took care of you when nobody else would. Nobody! What is this doubt I see in your eyes?'

'I don't doubt you, Highness. I am nothing but your loyal servant.'

She looks at him with narrowed eyes. 'Perhaps a night in the pit amongst real demons will help chase away the demons in your head.'

Bastian's eyes flick around the room, colour draining from his face. He holds his hands out and steps backwards. 'No, Mistress. Oh please no!' He looks at me and the fear I see in his eyes makes me shiver. 'I … I'll do it,' he hisses. 'I'll do anything.' As if to prove his loyalty, he cracks the whip in my direction. It snakes at my feet, but doesn't connect.

Lathenia stares at him with her eyes unblinking. She's searching the boy's mind, reading his inner thoughts. I find myself urging Bastian to conceal any doubts he might have with every ounce of strength he can find. Suddenly Lathenia inhales sharply, her eyes flashing fire. 'Into the pit!'

Bastian screams out, 'No! Don't do this!'

'I will release you in one hour. And you will be so grateful for my mercy, you will truly be my humble servant. For your destiny is always in my hands, Bastian. Think about that when you are running in those tunnels.'

With these words she waves both hands towards the pleading boy. He starts to disappear, but for seconds after he is gone his piteous screams reverberate in the room.

Marduke walks over and picks up the whip, keeping his one eye on me. 'Shall I, Mistress?'

Lathenia pats Marduke's hand as if she were petting one of her many hounds. 'You will have your chance to deal with him soon, my pet. But before I have this mortal permanently exterminated, I have one more question for him.'

'Don't waste your breath. I won't tell you anything.'

She comes over to stand before my chair. 'Get up!'

'That if I could,' I mutter, but force myself to do just that, leaning heavily on the branch Bastian earlier gave me.

Her head lifts while she waits for me to regain my breath. 'Answer me one last question, Arkarian, and I will ensure you live long enough to see your friends arrive.'

'How generous of you.'

She ignores my sarcasm. 'It's a simple question, requiring a simple answer. Do so, and while you will not live long, you will see your colleagues one more time.'

Her offer is tempting. I would love to see Isabel and Ethan again, even for just one brief moment. But she is hardly trustworthy. 'How do I know you'll live up to your end of the bargain?'

'It's a risk. But ultimately the choice is yours. Death now,' she pauses, glancing at the cowering wren half in, half out of the doorway, 'or after you've said your final goodbyes.'

'I'll decide once I have your question.'

Her pale skin flares luminous as she tries to control her temper. 'You will tell me the name of the man who fathered you!'

Her question both surprises and confuses me. Why is the knowledge of who fathered me of any significance? At least this time I don't have to struggle with keeping my thoughts from her. 'You know this is a question I can't answer. I don't know who either of my parents were. My mother—'

She cuts me off. 'You know your mother. You met

her recently.'

For a second she throws me. An image of the child, Charlotte, flashes before my eyes. And in my heart I realise the truth. 'Why didn't you kill her when you had the chance?'

'I wanted to see who your father was.'

'Of course, through your sphere. That would have been easy for you. You control the opening of the time portals. So why ask me the question? Why not just look for yourself?'

'Why? Because the act of your conception was shrouded in a blanket of invisibility!'

This news stuns me so much that I find myself falling into the chair for support. To create a shroud of invisibility would have taken the powers of a Magician. So the legend of Dartemis must be true! He does exist, at least on some level, in some place, to have performed this enchantment to conceal the identity of my father. But why was this secrecy necessary? If my father was someone of importance, why was I abandoned after my mother's death to be raised by peasants and soldiers?

'Tell me, Arkarian, everything you know.'

I look up at Lathenia, lifting my hands. 'I know nothing. I was raised by strangers, sent from one house to another.'

'Surely someone from those houses told you something!'

'Who would tell me anything? I was a foundling. I had no status.'

Her rage increases with every second she realises I can't give her the information she wants. Of course the question arises, if I did know who my father was, would I tell her anyway? Even if this information was of no significance to anyone, I would die first.

Hearing my rebellious thoughts, Lathenia lashes out, striking me across the face with the back of her hand. The force of her simple slap sends me careering backwards.

From my position on the floor I catch sight of Sera, huddling beneath the table, head buried deeply in her hands. It's the sight of this tortured innocence that forces a surge of anger through me, so powerful that for a second I feel it break through the confining bonds of the enchantment. Quickly, glancing up at Lathenia, I raise my hands and force as much energy in her direction that I can, considering my weakened physical state.

The room ignites with a flash of power that hits Lathenia front on, surprising her. She falls sideways, screaming. Staggering quickly to her feet she yells at her Magician. 'Quickly, Keziah! Your magic has expired.'

I can't let this opportunity pass. To try to fight them all is pointless; they would destroy me in an instant. But what if I use my wings? I might end up anywhere in this underworld, but surely anywhere would be better than certain death here, except perhaps for that 'pit' Lathenia sent Bastian to!

If I use my wings I'll be leaving Sera, yet, what use am I to her in this state? It would be better to escape now with my powers, and return for her when the danger is passed.

I close my eyes and visualise the rocky escarpment by the side of the lake, and the path from here to there. The Goddess's screams penetrate, stalling me. 'Hurry,

Marduke! He's escaping!'

Marduke raises his arms. And from the doorway the sound of squawking breaks my concentration. Dozens of birds swarm in and head straight for me. I freeze at the sight. Their strange human-like eyes seem to devour me, and their bone-piercing shrieks slice into my consciousness.

Any chance of using my wings disappears as the focus I need to concentrate shatters beneath the onslaught of these strange birds as they attack me. I try to use my powers, emitting a burst of energy, and they scatter, hovering over my head. Some of them squeal and fly off. But Marduke sends them back to me, and Keziah begins to chant.

As I try to fight Keziah's spell, my skin forms tiny bubbles, as if singed with hot oil. But my concentration keeps breaking as the birds attack, pecking at my flesh, and, where none is exposed, they dig away at my clothing until they find some. I try to beat them off, but there are just too many. They overpower me quickly and I fall to the floor.

Through all the noise of the screeching birds and Keziah's chanting, I catch a glimpse of Sera, still hiding under the table, curled up in a tight ball, shivering violently. I would call to her, to give her comfort, but I don't want to attract attention to her position. For now, at least, Lathenia's main interest is me.

Keziah's chanting finally stops, and the old man withdraws to the back of the room. After a series of rasping coughs he says, 'He is contained, Highness.'

She motions to Marduke, who calls his flock of birds off me and sends them out of the door. As blood oozes from the fresh wounds all over my body, and I sense death can't be far now, I find the strength to glare at Marduke one last time. There was good in this man once. He was a brilliant Guard – strong, sensitive and fiercely loyal. 'Your skills have altered,' I manage to gasp.

He laughs. 'Would you like to see more?' He points at me; instinctively I turn my face away. He makes a satisfied sound deep in his throat, then glances at Lathenia. 'My Goddess has bestowed me with many talents, Arkarian. Some that you would never dream of.'

'Why not put them to good use?'

'And give up all of this?' He flicks his fingers and a wave of green power distorts the air between us. It sizzles and crackles. He picks up one of the injured birds and throws it into the field of energy he has created. With an agonising shriek the bird explodes into dust.

'I have something the Guard would never give me – as much power as I want.' He turns his head and stares at the four accompanying wren, who haven't stopped cowering and trembling since entering this place.

Marduke looks back at me. 'See? The wren are scared of me.'

I try to get up, but find I have to hold on to the chair. 'You gloat over the taming of the mindless?'

My taunt has him seething, but Lathenia puts a staying hand on his arm. 'He has served his purpose, and soon his friends will find their journey was in vain. There is still much to do, including the torture of the treacherous wren that accompanies them. And if my suspicions are correct, we will get our revenge on the one who sought to take your life, my pet.'

'Why not let them be?' I call out. 'Why not satisfy yourself only in my death. You don't want the whole of

Lorian's rage on you. Kill one of us, not all four.'

Lathenia stares at me, and I think for a second she's actually thinking about my idea. But then she says, 'You mistake your self-worth, Arkarian. It seems I need to remind you of my goal. One day I will control it all, including the minds of mortals, wandering souls, creatures of the light, all the living, and the dead that inhabit the dark.'

'Do you think the Tribunal will hand you all these worlds on a platter?'

She walks away, then slowly turns and gives a little laugh, one eyebrow lifting. 'The Tribunal are having enough trouble overseeing the mortal world right now.' She glances at her fingertips. 'The Prophecy changes as we speak. And the tragic loss to the Guard of four of The Named will be sweet justice. A blow straight to the heart of the Tribunal, I'm sure you agree.' She glances at me. I hold her stare – and my tongue. She's right, and we both know this. But I won't acknowledge how damaging the loss of four of The Named could prove. We are, after all, supposed to be the nine that protect Veridian, the nine that will go up against Lathenia in a battle that will end all battles once and for all.

'My armies are growing stronger by the second. Can you say the same for yours?'

With these sickening thoughts she turns to Marduke. 'Remember your promise to the wren.' She glances at them, huddling together just inside the door. 'Miserable cowards. It is *I* you should cower from and not a wretched spirit!'

Marduke's eyes stay with the Goddess until she disappears, taking Keziah and the hounds with her. When he turns, a look of adoration lingers on his face, and I recall the last time I saw it – well before his face was sliced in half, the day his daughter was born, when he gazed upon her mother.

'I am as I should be, Arkarian. Nothing you say or do now will change anything. The clock is ticking.'

'It doesn't have to be like this. You have the power to change. Don't you see, you're as trapped here as all the lost and damned souls that inhabit this world.'

His one eye flares brilliant red. 'I am free!'

'No, Marduke, listen to me—'

At my plea he throws his head back, arms stretched high, and gives an ear-shattering roar. When he finishes, he orders his wren to come and stand before him. They trot and leap over obediently, constantly peering around as they do. Once standing before their master, Marduke lays his hands over the tops of their heads, and they look up at him. 'By entering this temple you have conquered your fears. Didn't I tell you it could be done?'

They nod, almost too vigorously.

'Am I not your master who knows all?'

Again they nod.

'For your loyalty you shall be richly rewarded.' He smiles at them, and with two simple words, puts my life into their hands. 'Finish him.'

Chapter Twenty-eight

Isabel

Standing at the edge of what is supposed to be a lake, we stare out at nothing but ice. By my side John nods and flaps his wings.

'What's got you so excited?' Ethan asks.

'I think you might be in luck.'

'How do you mean?'

'It's the lake,' John explains. 'It's iced over.'

It doesn't feel like we're in luck. Across the lake we hear the sound of a familiar ear-shattering roar.

Ethan grabs my arm. 'You were right! He's alive!'

'And he's over there, in the temple with Arkarian.'

'Who's with Arkarian?' Matt asks, coming up beside us.

'He's going to murder him.'

'Who!' Matt yells.

John tugs on Matt's cloak. 'The master.'

Matt looks at me, then Ethan. 'Marduke? That one-eyed freak who dragged me into the past and tried to burn me at the stake?'

We both nod.

'But he's dead, isn't he? You killed him.'

John gasps and stares at Ethan. 'That was you!'

'But he's not dead,' I say.

John shakes his head with deep concern. 'No, but he's uglier than ever. The mistress is not pleased.'

Ethan doesn't get it. 'OK, so she's not pleased. But he's alive, so why does she still want to kill me?'

I've seen what Marduke has become. For me, the answer is obvious. 'He's more monster now than man and the Goddess can do nothing about it.'

'Oh,' Ethan says.

'Yeah, well. Forget about her right now. Sera's last connection wanted us to hurry.' I pick up my pack and head straight for the lake.

John leaps after me, dragging me back only seconds before my feet connect with the ice. I turn on him, irritated that anyone or anything should try to stop me now. 'What!' I yell louder than I should. So far John has proved himself a trusted friend. Except ... how does one trust a murderer from another lifetime, or a traitor from this one?

'No, miss,' he says in a frantic tone. 'The ice is unstable. It's not like any you would be used to. You must prepare by adding protection – anything – to your feet.'

Ethan pulls on John's shoulder. 'What's wrong with the lake? Is the ice too thin? We can tie ropes to each other. In case one of us should drop through, we can pull them out.'

'There would be no point,' he says. 'If you fall through this ice, you'll die a horrible death.' He holds his hands up high to stop our questions. 'Let me explain. The lake is not made of water, it is made of acid.'

'Acid?' Ethan stares at the ice, the light from his

torch adding a gentle glow. 'Frozen acid?'

John nods. 'Actually, the top layer is a mixture. Some of it is water – snow, some recent rains, but mostly acid. It's a strange composition. Very unstable.'

'Can we walk on it in this state?'

'I can't be sure. You will have to protect your feet and be careful not to rest in one spot for more than a second.'

Matt still struggles with the concept of unstable ice. 'But our feet are already protected by our boots.'

John explains patiently, 'The ice is called crystal ice. As soon as something solid hits it, it will ignite. The more protection, the safer your feet.'

John's warning has my stomach twisting into knots. How can we cross this lake when every step will turn ice into fire? To get this far and fail is too horrible to think about.

Ethan gets down on his haunches, his long cloak fanning out across the snow. He starts digging into our packs. He finds a thick pair of socks and hands them to Matt. He hands me a jumper. I rip off the sleeves, tying them around my boots, then give Ethan the front and back parts. He secures one each around his own boots, then tears up his spare jacket, offering two pieces to John.

But John steps backwards, his eyes blazing. 'Oh no. Your offer is generous. But this is as far as I come.'

'Why won't you cross the lake with us?' Matt asks.

John flicks a nervous glance across the ice. '*They* used to live there before they disappeared. And now there is another.'

While I don't know who '*they*' are, I strongly suspect the one that John says has returned is probably Ethan's sister. I try to make him understand that his fears are unfounded, and that the ghost he earlier referred to is the same person who's been guiding us all along.

He remains adamant. 'I won't go there. You're on your own now.'

I groan loudly and kick the snow-packed ground. I really don't feel like spending one more moment trying to convince John that his fears are unfounded. My heart tells me Arkarian is in serious trouble and in need of healing right away. 'OK, have it your way, John. But when you're here – alone – and the master calls to make you pay for your treachery, don't expect us to turn around and come running back for you. We won't, even when we hear you scream. We'll be too busy rescuing Arkarian. That's what we came here for. Got it?'

Taking a deep breath I start to cross the lake. The instant my feet step on the ice a flame ignites under them. And even though I know this is going to happen, seeing the flame, watching it lick up the side and back of my foot, startles me.

'Don't stop! Don't look back. I'll be right behind you.'

I recognise the voice without looking all the way round. It's John's. Relief sweeps through me, giving me an added push.

We almost make it across without incident, when a familiar, unnerving shriek pierces the air, quickly followed by another, and another, the sound becoming unbearable.

'Keep moving,' John calls out, just as the flapping of many wings flying together comes into view.

They're the birds John told us about, large as eagles,

but far less graceful. They fly into us, flapping their wings to knock us over, attacking us with their sharp needle-like beaks, shrieking wildly. We fight them off as best we can, while trying to keep moving and yet maintain our balance. Fire licks at our feet, and other exposed parts when we fall.

'Keep moving,' John squeals, using his wings to leap up and draw the birds away.

But ultimately it's fire that gets rid of them, from our torches and burning pieces of cloth. They take flight, and, while the birds are momentarily gone, we finish the crossing.

Releasing a sigh of relief that the ice held and we made it across with mostly minor injuries, I turn around for the first time. Matt, Ethan and John turn with me. All of us gasp at the sight. The lake is alight with hundreds of tiny fires at the places our feet touched its icy surface. And, while otherwise immersed in darkness, it is truly an amazing sight.

'If I were an artist, this is what I would paint as my vision of hell.'

The others simply nod.

Chapter Twenty-nine

Isabel

On the beach my sixth sense goes crazy with fear. There's the temple up ahead, but it's quiet. Too quiet. We start making our way towards it. As we near the front I see that the temple is indeed enormous, reaching hundreds of metres up towards a single point. It must have been used for worship once, and probably protection too. In its day it could easily have contained a thousand people.

My legs feel drained of energy. I push them to keep moving. My stomach feels as if someone stretched out my intestine and tied it in a thousand little knots before shoving it back in.

Ethan runs up beside me. 'Are you OK?'

I nod, finding myself overwhelmed suddenly with a strange feeling that after everything, I'm going to be too late.

'Slow down, Isabel. We're nearly there.'

'I can't, Ethan. I'm scared.'

'I know. I am too. But wrecking yourself now is not going to help Arkarian. He's going to need you … your skills, you know?'

I glare at him. He doesn't get it. I'm nervous enough already. 'What if my skills aren't good enough? What if it's too late and he's already—' I have to stop suddenly to get my breath and regain some composure.

Ethan grips my shoulders. 'It's going to be all right.'

Matt catches up to us. 'What's wrong?'

Brotherly concern is the last thing I need. It snaps me out of my anxious state. 'Nothing, come on.' Urging everyone to hurry, I break into a run.

There are a series of stairs made of smoothly polished stonework that lead up to the front doors of the temple. I jump them three at a time, and before I know it I'm standing on a platform staring into a vast hollow interior that, at first glance, appears completely deserted.

Looking up, a soft breath escapes at the sight of the ceiling, where panels of etched glass in vivid colours extend to a high single point. A moment of déjà vu passes through me, disorienting me for a second. I've seen this ceiling before, in the Citadel, the day Arkarian was kidnapped.

Matt comes up beside me, wearing the strangest look on his face. 'Déjà vu,' he whispers.

I don't know why he's getting the same feeling. As far as I know he's never been to the Citadel, at least not that part. He walks past me in a daze, right to the centre of the room, and starts looking up, down, everywhere. His hands reach out as if to touch an invisible structure before him. His strange actions give me the creeps.

Looking away, I angle the torch around the outer walls searching for signs of Arkarian, but I see nothing except columns and vast emptiness.

Where is he?

A draught of icy wind pushes aside my cloak and a chill rips through me. Then I spot him. 'Oh no!'

He's lying in front of a dying fire across the room, completely still. Shock paralyses me.

Ethan catches up. 'Where is he? And where is ...?' He catches sight of Matt. 'What's *he* doing?'

'Over there. I don't know. And your guess is as good as mine.' I hand him the torch, assuming his second question refers to the whereabouts of his sister. 'Will you hold this?'

The strangest feeling hits me as I cross the shiny marble flooring and approach Arkarian, the sound of every footstep echoing loudly in my ear. It's as if I'm walking on a platform of air, a platform that leads to my own death. Forcing this scary sensation aside, I search for signs of movement. Anything to let me know Arkarian still lives. And while his back is to me, shouldn't I still be able to see his chest rise and fall with each breath? But I can't. He's completely still. Emotion swells within me, choking me, blurring my vision. 'Don't let me be too late.'

Up close it becomes obvious Arkarian has been severely beaten. There is a lot of blood, bruising, an open wound across his chest, weeping scratch marks down one side of his face, and if I'm not mistaken, bite marks too, covering almost every exposed part of his body. Even his clothes are shredded in places. I drop down to my knees, swipe moisture from my face, blinking hard to clear my vision. I lay my hands on his arm, and with gentle pressure, roll him on to his back. His eyes flick open in an unblinking stare, and for a second I think he is dead. But then he inhales a short gasp, and his eyes – glazed and bloodshot – move to find mine. *'Isabel.'* It's just a whisper from cracked and dried lips, but it's enough to bring a flood of tears to my eyes. I fight to keep them away. 'Save yourselves. It's too late for me. Lathenia is after you. And there's something you must know. Mar—'

I put my finger to his lips. 'No, don't speak. You have to conserve your energy. I'm not leaving without you, Arkarian.'

'You must be careful …'

I realise what he's trying so hard to say. It floors me that he's using his remaining meagre strength to make sure we're aware of this danger. 'We know, Arkarian. We know that Marduke has somehow returned from the dead.'

He sucks in a painful short breath and allows himself to pass out. How long has he been in this state? Hardly able to breathe? How long has his body been struggling to get oxygen to damaged organs and cells?

Ethan drops down on Arkarian's other side and gently strokes his blue hair. Without saying anything Ethan gulps deeply, and catches my eye. I don't need to be a Truthseer to read his mind or scan his thoughts, or whatever it is Truthseers do. Ethan's concern is there on his face, etched as if in stone. 'Can you help him, Isabel?'

With trembling hands, I lay them on Arkarian's chest. His lungs will have to come first. With my vision blurring again, adrenaline thumping through me, I find myself unable to hold thoughts still long enough to find a stable meditative thought.

Ethan picks up that something's wrong. 'Are you OK?'

With Arkarian's eyes closed it's easy to think I've lost him. I feel his heart beating slowly beneath my hands, but how much longer does he have? His severest injuries are the ones I can't see on the surface. I need my healing skills – but something's wrong! They don't seem to be working. I try again to visualise Arkarian's internal injuries, but nothing happens. How can this be? Healing is second nature to me now.

I experience a moment of sheer panic. The room spins away from me and everything takes on a strange sense of unreality. My hands fly up to either side of my face. 'What's wrong with me?'

Ethan takes my trembling hands in both of his. 'You need to get a grip. You're losing control.'

'I can't seem to focus.'

'Yes you can.'

A single tear runs down my face. 'I'm so scared, Ethan.'

John comes over, with Matt trailing behind him. His boots make loud noises on the shiny floor. The sound is almost too much for my strained nerves; while their presence just increases the pressure. I spin half my body around and scream at them with words that echo with an hysterical note around the hollow room. 'Go away! Get out of here! Can everybody leave me alone!'

They stop still at my screams, probably thinking I've gone and lost it completely now when I'm needed most.

Matt assumes the worst. 'Is he gone?' he whispers to Ethan.

Ethan shakes his head. 'She needs to compose herself before her healing skills will work.'

Matt lays his hand gently on my shoulder. 'You can

do it, Isabel. You healed Ethan's leg from that bite wound. Look at it, there's not even a mark now.'

Ethan reminds me of another time. 'You healed my father after Marduke stabbed him through his heart. And you did this under the threat of your brother's imminent death.'

But their words fall flat because here, right now, while precious seconds pass that could mean the difference between Arkarian living or dying, my healing power has disappeared. 'Why can't I heal him, Ethan?'

'You have to step back. Gain perspective. Take control of your emotions. Isabel, you love him.'

Matt jerks his hand away as if stung by a poisonous insect. 'You love *Arkarian*? But he's … he's not like us.'

Ethan scowls at Matt before purposefully drawing my attention back to him. 'Isabel, you've been trained for this very thing. Shut everything out. Don't let your emotions cause a block.'

I take a deep breath and exhale slowly, and, closing my eyes, lay my hands back on Arkarian's chest. This time an image of torn ligaments, dislocated joints and broken ribs appears before me. One rib pierces through a lung.

Somehow I manage to keep control and visualise the healing that must take place. First I disengage the broken rib, join it with its other half, seal the lung, then inflate it once again.

My reward comes in the form of Arkarian taking a strong deep breath. But I have a long way to go before he's completely healed. At least now that I've started, surely it's only a matter of time.

Returning my hands to his chest, I repair his flesh wounds, then his damaged joints and ligaments. Yet there is still much more to be done. He has a lot of blood and fluid pooled in dangerous places, drowning cells and vital organs. I start working at re-directing the blood back to appropriate tissue, while channelling the excess fluid through Arkarian's kidneys. But it's here I find a serious problem, as these vital organs have ceased working altogether, probably caused by their severe bruising and swelling. Their repair could take precious time.

I am vaguely aware of noises around me, but my concentration is deep now, and they remain distant enough not to disturb me.

'You have to hurry, Isabel,' Ethan says, returning from wherever he disappeared to. 'The temple is surrounded by dogs. Huge ones. And they sound hungry.'

Still it takes me a long time to reduce the bruising and swelling of Arkarian's kidneys. So long, that at times I think it's hopeless, that these badly beaten cells will not – cannot – repair.

Ethan comes back a second time. 'Isabel, seven hounds are circling the temple.'

My concentration is so deep, for a second his words don't penetrate at all. I finally have a hold on Arkarian's kidneys, somehow healing them enough to get them working again. With the worst of Arkarian's internal injuries restored to health, his recovery should only be moments away. I sense this with every fibre of my being, though as yet Arkarian hasn't regained consciousness. I stare across at Ethan as I realise he's still here, waiting for my response to something. 'What did you say?'

'The hounds, Isabel. Lathenia won't be far behind them. Either that, or she's playing with us.'

For a second I wonder what he expects from me. I'm exhausted, and have more healing yet before Arkarian is well enough to come back with us. 'You deal with it,' I snap at him. 'I'm fine with whatever you choose to do. OK? We're a team, aren't we?'

He looks surprised for a second as if in shock, but walks away looking pleased with himself. I hardly give his strange reaction a second thought and get back to healing Arkarian.

Only a few moments later an angry lion's roar penetrates my senses. I jump at the sound and look up. The room is filled with hungry-looking lions! At least a dozen of them. One spots me looking at it and roars in my direction. Goose bumps erupt, making every soft hair on my body stand on end. What on earth is going on?

My glance finds Ethan's and I realise the lions are his creation. Outside Lathenia's hounds snarl. They're very close now and that's why Ethan has created the illusion of lions.

Ethan cracks a whip sharply and the lions give a wild roar. Another crack and the lions leap, charging out the door, chasing the hounds away from the temple.

I can't help but give a soft gasp of admiration. Ethan hears and gives me a nod.

Matt and John come over and get down on their knees. 'How's the healing going?' Matt asks.

'I'm nearly—'

But I don't finish this thought as a pair of warm hands cover mine. I look down to see Arkarian moving into a sitting position, my hands now firmly gripped in his. With violet eyes beginning to re-focus, he smiles at me. 'You are amazing.'

Seeing him like this, not only recovered, but just ... seeing him alive and knowing he's going to be all right, overwhelms me for an instant. Tears hit the back of my eyes that I struggle to contain. I'm not going to fall apart now!

Sitting up, he pulls me to him fiercely. 'I thought I'd lost you.'

Out of the corner of my eye I see Matt frown. I try not to analyse my brother's look; it's not unusual for him to over-react where I'm concerned. At least Arkarian is well again. He's not going to die! And as long as we get out of this place in one piece – there is a chance for us.

After holding me tightly he looks into my face. With the tips of his fingers he wipes away my tears. Then he leans his forehead against mine and slowly kisses me. At first it is a gentle meeting of our lips. Then the pressure increases, and the kiss becomes a mixture of sweetness and passion.

I don't ever want it to stop.

Chapter Thirty

Arkarian

Ethan almost knocks me over with his greeting. I grip his shoulder with one hand while hanging on to Isabel's with the other. I'm finding it impossible to let her go, even for a second. And she hasn't tried to pull away.

'I thought I was never going to see your ugly face again,' Ethan says.

'It probably would have been better if you hadn't,' I tell him as we pull apart. 'Lathenia will be back for you.'

'Don't say things like that,' Isabel mumbles softly.

I turn to her and see Matt for the first time. *Matt!* So Matt is the third person on their journey. Oh no! This has got to mean trouble. I wonder why Sera couldn't identify him? And how did they get Matt's inclusion past Lorian? A sickening thought takes hold at the growing look of discomfort on all three of their faces. 'I can't imagine Lorian agreeing to Matt coming along.'

'Well,' Ethan says, looking at the floor, 'Lorian didn't exactly.'

Just what is he saying? Something isn't right. He

looks too uncomfortable. 'Which one of you is in charge?'

No one answers, but it's not difficult to guess what they're trying to conceal. 'The Tribunal didn't sanction a rescue attempt, did it?'

Ethan says softly, 'No, but I'm sure they would have. It was Lorian who gave the direct command against it.'

Sadly this action I understand. 'All three of you risked too much for me.' No one meets my eye, and I tell them what I think will happen. 'Lorian won't punish you all. Not during a time of such crisis. But one will have to be made an example of. Who will be held responsible?'

They remain silent as their eyes skim around each other. Finally Isabel says, 'I guess that'll be me.'

My hand squeezes hers tighter. 'You went against a direct order?'

'Yes, and I would do it again!'

Her courage is breathtaking, but it will be her downfall. 'Isabel, we humans can't presume what's in the minds of those who are above us. They know more, they understand on a higher level.'

Stubbornly, as only Isabel can be, she pushes her argument, 'This time Lorian was wrong!'

'You did this for me?'

She nods and I pull her closer to me. Would I do the same had it been Isabel taken to this world? I don't even need a second to think. I would fight the devil itself to get to her.

In an attempt to lighten the tension, Ethan introduces me to their 'friend' John Wren. My first instinct is wariness. But it's clear by just looking in his eyes, that this wren is unlike Marduke's disciples. He grips my hand in a firm shake.

The second he releases it, I take Isabel's again, just to make sure she stays close.

Matt's keeping his distance and I'm getting an inkling of why. I catch his eye and we nod our heads by way of a greeting. Then his eyes drift downwards to where my hand is linked with his sister's. It's as if this sight disturbs him. He moves to my other side. 'Look, I don't know you like Ethan and my sister do. And, as I'm not one to believe in rumours or take notice of hearsay, tell me in your own words. Is it true that you're six hundred years old, and that your body will never age?'

I see where he's heading, it has me squeezing Isabel's hand tighter again. Her eyes fly up to my face, then fasten on her brother's. I hear her sharp intake of breath when I give Matt the answer to his question. 'Everything you heard is true.'

His eyes bore into mine. 'Then where can this possibly lead?'

I whisper back, 'All my life I've been empty inside. When I'm with Isabel I am whole.'

'But you don't live in our normal world. It's impossible!' He glances at my blue hair as if to make a point. 'What sort of life would Isabel have in your world, growing old and watching you stay young? Listen to me, Arkarian, you have to stop this now before my sister's heart is broken. I've never seen her look so lovesick or so driven, not even when she had that crush on Ethan. This is serious. It can't continue!'

The reality in his words explode through me.

While Matt's words stem from brotherly love and his strong sense of protection, what he says is true. But seeing Isabel beside me, *feeling* her, it's just too hard to let her go.

She peers at us both carefully. 'Stop whispering! I want to know what you two are talking about. What the hell are you saying, Matt?'

I raise my hand to the side of her head. She leans her face into my palm. I want so much for her, to love her with an open heart. And it's because of this love that I can ... I *must* do what Matt bluntly points out.

So, after one final caress, I force an impersonal tone into my voice. 'Matt is concerned that too much time is passing.' The sound of lions roaring outside proves timely. 'And he's right. We have to hurry and find our way out of here.'

Without giving her a chance to say anything in return, I spin away, pretending to look for something. I don't want Isabel to see through my façade. Right now I'm nothing but a fraud. It's then I see Sera, still hiding under the table, still trembling.

I hold my hands up to the others. 'Wait here, don't move.' Bending down, I try to coax Sera out.

She twists her head sideways. From her position on the floor she would only be able to see their legs, but it's Ethan's legs her eyes are glued to. 'Come on, Sera, how long have you waited for this moment?'

Taking my offered hand she comes out and totters on unbalanced feet to stand before the others. She lifts her eyes and catches sight of the wren that accompanies them and starts screaming and gripping me so hard her hands go almost all the way through my arm. John screams too, leaping towards the door. Matt grabs him before he makes an exit, dragging him back.

Seeing Sera, Isabel gasps softly in surprise. Ethan

simply stares. With eyes fixed on his sister's spiritual presence, he comes right up close. 'Sera?'

Calming down a little, but keeping a watchful eye on the wren, Sera peels herself off me. Turning to her brother, she flings herself into his arms.

Ethan embraces her back, but stares up at me alarmed when his arms go slightly through her, and her body comes to rest slightly through his. I smile and give an encouraging shrug. 'It seems to be the way.'

She stands on tip-toes and he lowers his head to the top of hers. Now it appears as if their bodies are melded as one.

Isabel looks at them with tears in her eyes. She too knows how much Ethan has suffered. 'Will we be able to help her, Arkarian? Release her from this prison?'

'If we can get her out of this world with us, then her spirit should be free to go wherever it was meant.'

A distant lion's roar and the sounds of yelping remind us exactly where we are. 'Do you think you could lead us back to the rift that brought you into this world?' I ask hopefully.

Isabel and Matt share a strained look, while Ethan gives his head a thorough shake. 'No way. I'm not going through that mountain again.'

'Why not the mountain?' Matt asks.

It's the wren, John, who decides it for them. Peering suspiciously at Sera, he leaps over with a flap of his wings. 'There's another rift that joins with your world. Unfortunately, I don't know where it is.'

Sera's eyes grow huge and she grips her brother's arm tightly again at the sight of the wren so close. 'It's all right, Sera,' Ethan explains. 'John is our friend.'

Sera looks at John sceptically, and Ethan says, 'Trust

me. For this once, you can rely on me.'

With a tremor in her voice she asks, 'What does this rift look like?'

'A black flash in the sky,' I tell her.

She thinks for a moment, her forehead creasing deeply. 'I've seen this rift when the blood moon rises.'

The hounds draw nearer. Ethan's illusion must be breaking up. We have to hurry and get out of here.

'Can you lead us to this other rift?' Ethan asks.

Sera nods excitedly. 'I know exactly where to go. It's right in the middle of—'

Her words are interrupted by a loud bang near the door. Someone is there, half hanging on to the doorway. I take a closer look. It's Bastian, battered and bleeding, his clothes torn to shreds. I run over just as he slides to the ground. 'Isabel! Quickly, you're needed here.'

Before the others arrive, Bastian holds his hands up. 'No,' he heaves. 'It's too late. But ...' He tries to take a breath. 'The other rift ... you can't. It's over Marduke's garden.'

Ethan and Matt arrive and recognise him instantly. 'Dillon!'

'Ethan? Matt!'

Matt gets down on his knees. 'What happened to you?'

Ethan, on his other side, is more cautious. 'What are you doing here?'

Isabel pushes both Ethan and her brother to the side. 'Don't ask him any more questions until I've finished.'

It takes her a few minutes, but eventually Bastian – no, his real name is Dillon – is healed. He gets up, still looking shaken, and grips Isabel's hands. 'How can I thank you?'

She tugs her hands out. 'Are you one of them?'

'Yes,' he says. He flicks a look quickly over his shoulder. 'Lathenia will be back soon. I have to get out of here. But I just had to tell you, the rift over Marduke's garden is inaccessible.'

'Why?' I ask.

'It's drugged. You can't go near it. It will numb your mind and you won't be able to think for yourselves.'

'Hell,' Ethan exclaims. 'Then how—'

John Wren runs in from outside, making a high-pitched squeal. 'Hurry. The master is coming!'

Dillon looks around frantically. Seeing nowhere safe, he closes his eyes, preparing to use his wings. I grab his arm before he takes off. 'Where will you go?'

His head shakes. 'I have no idea. But I can't stay here. She'll kill me.'

'You will come with us,' I tell him.

He gives me a wary look. 'Why? So the Guard can kill me too?'

'You have my promise you will not be hurt.'

'Will I be interrogated?'

'Yes. Thoroughly. But you will also be protected.'

The hounds come bounding in, scattering us from the doorway. As before, they remain just outside the inner octagon. The rest of us take sancturary within it. Marduke walks in close behind them. He sees Dillon and stops. 'So this is where you are! Lathenia has been running through the tunnels herself looking for you! What are you doing with *them*?' His eyes shift to John. 'It seems we have a room full of traitors! And look at you, *old friend*.' He attempts to mock me. 'Your healer has troubled herself in vain. But my mistress will be pleased. For you are all together now. And this temple will soon become your tomb.'

Chapter Thirty-one

Isabel

Lathenia appears before our eyes, along with the old man with the silver beard who helped kidnap Arkarian. She sees Dillon immediately. 'You stand with them!'

Dillon stiffens by my side.

'Stay with us,' I whisper. 'We're your only chance, you know.'

He nods so vigorously I think his head's going to drop off. Not that Matt would notice. He hasn't even realised Lathenia is here yet. He's distracted again, standing in the direct centre of the octagon, sometimes staring at the high central point, but mostly down at his feet. I'm starting to worry the strain is too much and he's losing his mind. I have to get his attention. 'What are you doing? Lathenia is here!'

His head shakes. 'I feel something pulling me to this spot. I keep coming back to it.' He starts tapping his foot on the marble flooring.

'We're all about to die, and you can think of nothing except tap dancing?'

He gets down on his knees and starts running his hands around the floor, drilling his fingers.

'Leave him,' Ethan says. 'There must be something we can do to get out of here. Maybe I could try another illusion.'

Arkarian moves to stand in front of us, touching Ethan's shoulder as he passes. 'I feel my powers resurging. Stand behind me, all of you.'

'No,' I tell him. 'We'll stand *beside* you.'

Ethan stands on Arkarian's other side, with Sera clinging to his arm. Dillon takes a position beside Ethan. Even John steps forward. But Matt is now on all fours, his ear to the flooring.

Lathenia smiles, but it's a smile that reeks evil. 'Did you think I would simply let you go? I am more powerful than all of you combined!' She looks directly at Dillon. 'How did you get out?'

'You forget my power is strength.'

'I forget nothing! But it seems you have. How can you forsake me after all that I have done for you? What about our cause? It's your cause too!'

Dillon remains silent and Lathenia's eyes flare. 'Haven't I shown you the riches that will be yours? I can give you everything you dream of!'

Dillon's voice drops to a mere whisper. 'Whatever I do now, you will kill me. If only to set an example to your soldiers.'

'You give me no choice!' Lathenia's whole body flashes a brilliant luminescent hue. Even her eyes glow. It's difficult not to cower and run at the sight. 'You have brought this on yourself with your foolish doubts, and your fear of becoming like him!' She points towards Marduke, then hisses like a snake. Marduke grunts.

'You have chosen death,' she says. 'You shall die with them.'

Lathenia raises her hands. The seven Great Danes snarl viciously and start to drool. They look as if they haven't eaten for a year.

Focusing on the hounds, Arkarian makes eye contact with each of them, seizing and holding their attention. Suddenly they shake their heads, give a painful whimper, and run out the temple door as fast as they can.

Lathenia practically growls. 'Quickly, Keziah, his powers are back!'

It looks as if the old man could be a magician. That's how she must be securing Arkarian's powers. Strange how she sounds hurried, desperate even. I have to wonder why. Sure, she's had first-hand experience of Arkarian's powers, but my sixth sense is telling me there's another reason, one much more relevant to her very existence. One that has to do with our getting out of this world.

Lathenia's head turns in my direction. She perceives my thoughts, and she's not happy with my reasoning. Her eyes flash. I don't get an instant to react. Her hand lifts, long fingers pointing at me. The power of her hit sends me skittering backwards. For a moment the room and everything in it goes white. Matt drags me into the very centre of the octagon and starts talking rapidly.

'Slow down,' I tell him. 'My head's fuzzy and I can't understand you.'

He takes a deep breath and whispers, 'I think we can get out through this temple.'

'What! How?'

'Well, I'm not sure. But see this?' He looks to his feet. He's found a loose slab of marble. He puts firm pressure on one particular spot and it tilts to reveal a crystal, about the size of a small hand, in the shape of an eight-sided octagon. I go to touch it, but when my hand draws near, the crystal starts to glow. It startles me and I take my hand back.

'I think it's a dial or something,' Matt says, then looks up. 'I reckon the ceiling wasn't built that way for nothing. It's going somewhere. Didn't John say the people that lived here simply disappeared?'

'Are you thinking they didn't disappear at all, but *escaped*?'

Ethan comes running over. 'What are you doing over here? Arkarian can't hold them off much longer. He needs everyone's help.'

Lathenia's voice sings out, 'Now, Keziah! Hurry! Marduke, hold him still so Keziah can do his work.'

I drag Arkarian back to the centre, just as Marduke raises his hands. Green light, like a wave, pulses towards us. We hit the ground hard and the green light continues on, exploding two pillars of marble. I dig my fingers into Arkarian's arm, rushing my words out before Lathenia and Marduke have time to work out what we're doing. 'Listen, you can get us out of here.'

His head shakes. 'Only an immortal can open a rift. But I think I can hold them while you get the others out. Dillon is helping.'

I give him a strong shake. 'Listen to me: immortal or not, Lathenia thinks you can do it.'

'But how?'

Dillon, apparently, agrees. 'It's true. That's why she's so paranoid about containing your powers.'

'She knows something that you don't,' I tell Arkarian. 'Now is the time for you to believe in yourself. Look at the power that comes from your hands.'

Lathenia screams, a sound of frustration. I look across and see her eyes blazing, hands outstretched. 'Watch out!' I scream. Beams of vibrant energy shoot from her fingertips. They hit us full on, scattering us in all directions.

Stunned, I crawl over to Arkarian. I have to make him understand. 'You have the power we need.'

He struggles to get his breath back. 'But Isabel, I was trained to make the power you speak of. It wasn't one of my skills.'

'Whatever, Arkarian, I believe you can propel us out of here. And I think Lathenia knows this too.'

Lathenia lifts her hands, preparing to send another blast of energy our way. But just as it starts to generate, Ethan rams her, knocking her to the ground, and her fingertips flash in Marduke's direction instead. He doubles over in pain, groaning.

I tug Arkarian back to the centre where Matt is still fiddling with the crystal he's discovered. 'Trust and believe,' I whisper. 'Isn't that what we're trained to do?'

'Yes, but, Isabel, there's no rift here.'

Marduke is up again with a wild look in his eye. He descends on Dillon, while Ethan tries to keep Lathenia on the ground. She screams, and suddenly Ethan is flung backwards. I call him over, then look frantically at Arkarian. 'Just concentrate on creating that power.'

Hurrying now before Marduke and Lathenia strike again, I yank on Dillon's arm and get everyone to form a circle around Arkarian and Matt.

'What are you doing?' Ethan asks me.

'We have to protect Arkarian from Keziah's magic. And Matt has an idea to get us out of here, so we have to protect him too.'

'*Matt?*'

'Yes, Matt.' I cross my fingers behind my back. 'I just hope he's right.'

Suddenly an explosion shatters the air. The ground vibrates below us, the marble cracking in several places. We stumble and fall over each other. When I find my balance, I see it's Marduke's work, and I wonder fleetingly what magnitude of power he possesses these days. Power I don't want to know about. He raises his hands, attempting to strike at us again.

'They're protecting him!' Lathenia screams out. She catches my eye and her own blaze brilliant blue, then deeper blue again; and from her fingertips shoot sparks of sizzling electricity, exploding around and over us. We try not to lose our positions, protecting Matt and Arkarian our first priority.

'Nothing's happening,' Matt says behind me.

Lathenia screams out, 'Keep trying, Keziah!' And to Marduke, she says, 'We finish this now!'

Turning my head slightly, I see Marduke and Lathenia separate and stand at right angles from us. Both of them – their entire bodies – begin to glow. There's a power building between them, and I get the sense that it's going to be something special. It becomes clearer as they hold out their hands towards each other. Electric currents sizzle and crackle as their energy reaches out across the space between them and meets in mid air, where a luminous ball of blue and red and purple light begins to generate. It doesn't take long to work out what's about to happen. The Goddess and Marduke are creating something huge, a powerful explosion of energy. It will bring the temple down.

This is how she plans to entomb us.

'It's going to be big, Isabel,' Ethan whispers in awe as their bodies continue to glow brighter. He glances over his shoulder. Dillon's eyes follow. Matt is still on his knees on the floor. Arkarian sees the crystal and his body freezes, distracting his concentration. 'You found it!'

'Hurry, Arkarian,' I whisper.

'But, Isabel, you don't understand.'

'We're running out of time! Keep trying!'

He nods and closes his eyes again.

'Whatever they're doing, I'm afraid it's going to be too late,' Dillon says.

It's in this moment that despair touches my soul. Within the cover of our arms and bodies Matt is still trying to work out what to do with the crystal, while Arkarian still searches within him for the power he needs.

Ethan looks at Lathenia and Marduke's glowing bodies, which now fill the temple with dazzling light. 'Lorian knew this would happen, knew there was no way the Goddess would let us escape.'

The entire temple starts to vibrate. Without the need for words, we all come to the understanding that it's only a matter of seconds before we're eliminated – for ever.

My mother's face flashes before me, bringing tears to my eyes.

Beneath my feet vibrations begin to shift the marble flooring. The Goddess and Marduke's combined powers swell to scorching point and the marble shatters. Between them they have created a shimmering orb of pulsing energy. It sparks a flash, and the entire temple fills with intense white light. We have to shut our eyes and bury our heads to avoid blindness.

It's at this precise moment Matt screams out, 'Yes! I've got it!'

Arkarian calls back, 'Bring it with you!'

'I can't. It won't budge.'

Arkarian's voice takes on a panicked tone. 'You must! If we leave it here, Lathenia will find—'

Arkarian abandons this thought as the room, and everything in it, ignites. 'Too late,' he says, then throws his hands up into the air. *Now!*

The panelled ceiling flickers to life. It starts spinning, picking up speed quickly. Light pours down and all seven of us are propelled into the high central peak, swirling ever upwards. Then there is nothing but darkness.

Chapter Thirty-two

Isabel

We drop a long way into a room in the Citadel. The same room I stumbled across when running from Arkarian's abduction. Looking around, it seems everyone is here, including Dillon, Sera and John, sprawled out across the floor.

Getting up, I notice others gathering around us. Strange-looking people of different shapes, sizes, colour and species, though all appear to resemble human beings.

Arkarian comes towards me, each slow step making my heart slam against my ribs. Raising his eyes, they lock with mine, and my mouth goes tinder dry. He stops in front me, so close that it would only take one small movement for his hand to skim the side of my face. 'Are you all right?'

How can I be? My thoughts can't help but scream out. *When you don't want me!* I make sure this last part is thoroughly scrambled.

We hold eye contact but the effort is costing him. 'Isabel,' he whispers in a tone of regret. The effect is crushing and I turn away.

Nearby Matt groans, but seems fine. He helps Dillon to his feet. Sera starts getting up too, as does John beside her. But as our eyes drift to the wren, we notice something strange happening. He appears to be growing taller, his shape lengthening right before our eyes. Sera notices too and starts backing away. 'What's happening, Ethan?'

Ethan shrugs his shoulders, flicking Arkarian a worried look. We brought John through with us, but did we have a choice?

John continues to change shape. The transformation only takes a few moments, but once complete, has us all look on in amazement. Even the growing crowd surrounding us give a collective sigh.

John is no longer part bird, part human or mostly beast, but a man of about thirty years of age, with soft blue eyes, dark brown hair, and skin that slightly glows. Just like Sera's. In fact, he has the same ethereal look about him.

He gazes down at himself. 'I … I think I'm free.' He pauses as moisture floods his eyes unashamedly. 'I don't know how to thank you.'

Sera's hand comes up to cover her mouth, her head shaking. 'Does this mean we'll be leaving together?'

'I believe it does, miss.'

Sera gives a little nod, her eyes glistening. 'I guess we'd better say good-bye then, before whatever happens, happens.'

Arkarian and I turn unconsciously to look at Ethan. His eyes flick to ours and back again to his sister in uncertainty. 'I can't believe that after all these years we're only going to have a few moments together. There's so much I want to say to you.'

Before our eyes Sera begins to fade, as does John; and Ethan starts to panic. 'No, you can't leave yet!'

Arkarian goes over to John and shakes his hand, then gives Sera a hug, which she fiercely returns. He motions to Ethan to hurry. 'A few moments is all you're going to have, Ethan. Go straight to what's in your heart.'

Sera fades a little more and Ethan runs over and drags her fast-disappearing body roughly into his arms. 'I'm so sorry. I should have protected you from Marduke. I should have remembered his name. I should have sought justice for your death. And I should have listened to you through my dreams. You wouldn't have suffered all these years.'

She pulls back to stare up at him with disbelieving eyes. It's obvious she wants to tell him none of what happened was his fault, that there is nothing for him to feel guilty over. But it's clear that a simple denial will not be enough, especially with so little time left. And so she raises her small hand to his face, and says, 'I forgive you.'

With these words Sera and John completely disappear.

It takes several seconds for us to collect our thoughts and take in what just happened. But a whooshing sound behind us gets our attention quickly. We turn to find Lord Penbarin and Lady Arabella.

Lord Penbarin is first to speak. 'You're to accompany us straight to Athens. Your hearing has been set.'

Though all of us have questions to ask, Ethan's concern for his mother has him pushing roughly to the front. 'I have to go home first. Take me home, Lord Penbarin. Take me home now.'

Lady Arabella holds her hands up. 'I'm afraid that's impossible, Ethan.'

'You don't understand.'

'It's you who doesn't understand. All will be explained at the hearing.'

Ethan can't believe it. His head rolls backwards as he glares at the vivid panels overhead. How long has he carried the weight of his mother's depression on his shoulders? And now he has to wait even longer. 'Well tell me this much, what day is it?'

Lady Arabella appears puzzled. 'In your time?'

Frustration and concern adds a hard edge to Ethan's voice. 'Yes, in my time!'

'Why, I believe it is Thursday the tenth.'

Ethan looks at me, but I've figured it out already. We spent ten whole days in the underworld. Before we left, there were still five days before his mother was due to go to the sanatorium. She was to stay there for a further five, which means ...

'I'm too late. She could already have ...' He glares from Lady Arabella to Lord Penbarin. 'My mother ... Do you know anything ...?'

A soft smile comes to Lady Arabella's lips. 'She is perfectly well, Ethan.'

'What?'

'She has spent the last ten days waiting by the phone for any word on your disappearance. She had no thought for anything but your safe return.'

Disappearance? When I planned this rescue I never thought that our mortal bodies would just seem to have disappeared. 'What about my mother?' I flick a brief look at Matt.

'She's been fraught with worry. Shaun and Jimmy

released the story that the three of you went missing while hiking in the woods. They've been trying to keep everyone calm, and convince your mothers that you will make a safe return.' And to Ethan she says pointedly, 'Your mother hasn't spared one thought on herself these past ten days.'

'So she didn't go to the sanatorium?'

'No.'

'And she didn't … attempt … anything stupid?'

'No, Ethan.'

Ethan turns to me with a huge grin, blue eyes shimmering as he sheds his greatest fear.

'And now that Sera's soul is free,' Arkarian says, 'Laura won't be traumatised any more.'

Arkarian is right. I try not to think about what trauma I put my own mother through these past ten days. After the hearing will be soon enough.

Arkarian grips Ethan's shoulder, giving it a generous squeeze, but he has more concerns on his mind. He turns to Lady Arabella, 'Tell me, you're not planning to take our mortal bodies to Athens?'

He's brought up a good point. Everybody knows that to take our body and soul out of our own time is harmful and could prove fatal.

Lady Arabella replies in her trusting voice, 'In your absence much has changed. There's an urgency now in everything we do. Isabel's hearing will be brief, not long enough to do your bodies damage.'

'*Isabel's* hearing?' Arkarian repeats in a tight voice.

Lady Arabella's head bows in an almost apologetic nod. 'Lorian is holding Isabel accountable for the direct breach of a superior command.'

Ethan tries to argue, but Lord Penbarin shuts him up

fast. 'Save your arguments for the trial. But be warned, Lorian is in no mood to listen to anyone.'

Arkarian steps right up to Lord Penbarin's face. 'Lorian will listen to me.'

I've never heard him sound so defiant.

'We'll go with you,' he continues. 'But I want a private visit with Lorian before Isabel's hearing. And I want a safe room set up immediately.' He pulls Dillon over and introduces him. 'I'm sure you will find the information Dillon brings to the Guard very useful.'

Lord Penbarin and Lady Arabella agree to organise a safe room. Safe, that is, for the Guard as well. Changing sides is a serious matter. Very few do it. There are a lot of risks. Dillon will be briefed thoroughly and under constant surveillance for a long time.

'But as for your meeting with Lorian,' Lady Arabella explains. 'We can only do what we can.'

Arkarian nods, accepting, and Lord Penbarin puts an arm around his shoulder. 'It's good to have you back.'

Lady Arabella smiles, and a trickle of tears slides down each side of her face.

The surrounding crowd, which has now surged to more than a hundred, start to cheer, with whistles and wild clapping.

I can't help but ask, 'Who are those people?'

Lady Arabella shares a look with Lord Penbarin, who shrugs almost imperceptibly, and she says, 'They are the survivors – charged with the protection of the living.'

Chapter Thirty-three

Arkarian

In my entire six centuries of existence, I have never felt this way – compelled to strangle an immortal! But if Lorian were here, right now, in this room in the Citadel, I would take my mortal hands and put them to this superior being's neck and squeeze. That Lorian could hold Isabel entirely responsible for disobeying a direct order fills me with absolute rage. Part of me knew it would happen. Part of me even understands why. But now that I'm faced with the reality – the prospect of losing Isabel – I can't even accept the thought.

'You'd better calm yourself,' Lord Penbarin warns me as he wraps each of us in a silver protective cloak. Instantly we're transported to Athens to the year 200 BC.

Once in the palace courtyard I flick my cloak off. 'Thanks for the advice, my lord, but I would rather you spent your breath organising my meeting with Lorian.'

He tips his forehead to me. 'As you wish.'

As Lord Penbarin disappears, Lady Arabella collects our cloaks and explains that Dillon has been taken elsewhere and that his protection is secure. 'Now come and partake of some food and drink. You must be hungry.' She looks at me and pauses, her eyes drifting shut for the briefest of moments as if she's holding her breath. The moment passes and she smiles gently. 'Lorian will meet with you now. In Chambers. You are allocated five minutes only, then the hearing will begin. Good luck.'

Without looking around and giving Isabel, Ethan or Matt a chance to say anything, I use my wings and disappear, materialising in the Tribunal Chambers before Lorian, sitting alone at the Circle's head. All other nine chairs remain empty, but not for long. And as I have only five minutes, I try to make the most of each second. So I get right down to the purpose of this meeting. 'You mustn't punish Isabel.'

Lorian looks up, and for a second, I think I see a small smile, a glimpse of relief. 'Welcome back, Arkarian. I thought I was never ... I must say, you are looking well.'

I shift the conversation straight back to the point. 'Because of Isabel, yes. She's a gifted healer, the best the Guard has ever seen. She has so much potential now that her second sight is developing. The possibilities are endless. I want to work with her, to develop these skills. It's possible she may one day be able to heal through her psyche. Do you understand what enormous benefit she brings to us at this needy time?'

'I know everything, Arkarian. I know why Isabel breached my direct command. There are many issues to be dealt with here today, and very little time in which to do it. And while I don't doubt Isabel's extraordinary talent and benefit to our cause, my decision on her future is final. No amount of discussion will sway me. You waste your breath and everyone's time, Arkarian. The subject of Isabel's punishment is closed. Now,' Lorian pauses, giving me a chance to catch up and absorb these words. 'Do you have anything else to discuss?'

Lorian's finality on Isabel's future has me reeling and I find words hard to form. 'I … I have so many questions.'

'There is much that you are unaware of. Remember what I taught you when you were my Apprentice: put your trust in me as I will only ever make decisions for the greater good.'

'My head is full of doubts right now, Lorian. I fear that you are sacrificing Isabel for this "greater good".'

Lorian's head lifts suddenly as if insulted. 'The subject of Isabel's breach of my command will only be discussed at her hearing!'

'All right! But this subject is only closed – *temporarily*.'

Lorian appears amused that I dare to make a demand. But what I'm about to relate will remove every remaining fibre of humour. 'Lathenia doesn't have the key.'

The Immortal goes still. But a look of anticipation soon starts to grow. 'Explain.'

'It was hidden beneath a secret panel in the temple floor.'

'What!'

'Matt found it.'

Lorian stares at me. Quickly I add, 'Unfortunately, we had to leave it there.'

'Do not tell me that! Surely, Arkarian, you, of all people, know its importance!'

'We had no time. And as it seems Matt is the only one who can touch it without losing his life, I couldn't help him dislodge it.'

Lorian sighs. 'So it remains in the temple, probably exposed, just waiting for Lathenia to find it.'

'It may not be that easy to find. As we left, the temple was being destroyed.'

Lorian sits in silent contemplation. And then, 'Is there anything else to report?'

'No. But I do have a question.'

'Go on.'

'Who is my father?'

Lorian's eyebrows lift and for a second I think the Immortal isn't going to reply. 'I am your father, Arkarian.'

It's a shock. But a fraction of a part of my brain suspected it might be true. Still, how is this possible? All my life I have understood that Lorian is of no fixed sex.

Lorian absorbs my thoughts with ease. 'I was born male. Having no fixed sex was a decision I made. To be a good leader I wanted to be impartial and fair, and I felt I could only do that if I was of no sexual persuasion and desired none. But there came the need to create another immortal. For this purpose I chose to resume the male form. To have become female would have meant living as a mortal for too long, neglecting my duties here. Impossible! So I chose a young woman, whom you have recently met, to be your mother. Unfortunately she passed away. It was decided you were to come here to live and be raised in the palace. But all did not go as planned.'

Slowly the mystery of my birth starts to unravel.

'Because I wasn't born an immortal. How you must have been disappointed.'

Lorian's eyes drift downwards and stay closed for a moment. 'Only by the fact that your life-span would be limited.'

Now I understand. 'So you gave me the ability to stop ageing.'

Lorian's – my father – head tilts slightly in silent acknowledgement. 'Other than all the Tribunal members, I have only given this power to two people. And one of those people I very much regret.'

'Marduke.'

'Yes. A difficult decision at the time, but our healer had died and without this gift, Marduke would have too. And at the time he was a brilliant Guard – young with strong developing powers and unlimited potential. It seemed a fitting reward.'

A thought occurs: if my father has the power to give this gift, then it must be possible to take it away. Lorian misreads my thoughts, assuming that I'm thinking of Marduke. 'Even an immortal has limitations, Arkarian. I could not strip Marduke of his power without his knowledge, especially now while Lathenia watches him carefully. I hardly think he will walk in here and give me his permission.'

I look my father straight in the eye, holding his gaze firm. 'But you have mine.'

For a second my father simply stares at me, understanding what I'm saying, but reluctant to accept that this is my wish. 'You want me to strip you of your power to stop ageing?'

'Yes.'

'Explain yourself, Arkarian.'

324

'Isabel is my soul-mate.'

'I'm aware of that.'

'She can't live in my world, so I want to live in hers.'

The chair falls away as Lorian rises and approaches me, wearing a look of complete disbelief. 'You would sacrifice the closest thing to immortality for this girl?'

My answer is instantaneous, 'For the chance to be with her. Yes.'

The stare is hard to take. Finally my father says, 'Then it is just as well I am the supreme being around here, and not you, my son.'

Chapter Thirty-four

Isabel

The exact second I enter the Tribunal Chambers a hush descends. I stand in the open doorway on legs unable to move. My hands are sweating. I run them up and down the side of the long white tunic they put me in. The room itself appears as it did the last time it was used for the purposes of a trial. But now I am the one who is being judged, not Ethan, and my breach is far more severe.

As before, the nine Tribunal members have taken their seats in the Circle. And to my surprise, though he still doesn't look very well, King Richard II sits to Lord Penbarin's right. And I have to wonder why they brought him to the Circle when he's not completely cured. He's going to be Veridian's representative on the Tribunal, making all the sectors of the earth complete. King Richard wouldn't be here at all if it wasn't for Ethan, taking the risk to rescue him last year. Apparently Lorian thinks him well enough to sit and watch the proceedings.

Lorian motions for me to enter and sit on the stool provided. Sucking in a deep breath I walk on wobbly legs to the centre of the Circle and gratefully sit. The moment I do, a warmth and sense of calm fills me, and I know straightaway that I'm sitting on one of Arkarian's ancient hand-carved stools. He must have provided it for me himself. I flick a look around the room in search of him. He appears directly in my vision, his violet eyes reaching out to me, and I feel somehow stronger, calmer, ready to face whatever judgement is handed down.

With this inner calm residing in me, I risk a quick look at the Immortal's face, being careful not to connect with Lorian's eyes. In my previous experience I've found this difficult to do. But what I see surprises me. Lorian is wearing a look of contemplation, a creased and frowning brow, with eyes that remain downcast. For a second I wish I was a Truthseer and could read Lorian's thoughts. But then the Immortal stands, raises both hands, and says, 'The punishment for disobeying a direct order is death.'

The room erupts around me. Arkarian, Ethan and Matt have to be physically restrained. And while I hear the sentence, a part of me becomes detached, as if this whole scene is not happening to me. It's as if I'm watching from behind a screen.

Lorian turns sideways and an image – a three-D holograph of my school – appears before me. The image zooms in closer and now I see the classroom and students mucking around inside. Once more the image increases, so now it's as if we're in the classroom with them, Mr Carter standing in front of the whiteboard.

The first thing I notice is the lack of school uniform. Students are wearing whatever they like – short skirts, dresses, brief tops, all-black outfits, some with chains and body piercing in every conceivable location, others with heads shaved or hair that looks as if it hasn't seen a comb in a month. A couple of students are wearing jeans with rips at their knees and thighs and just about everywhere.

The second thing is the noise. Craig Johnson stands up and flings something across the room. I duck as this projectile feels as if it's headed straight for me. It's only a pen, but it strikes Zoe Fielders on the back of her head. She screams out a string of vile swear words while half climbing over her desk. Mr Carter thumps the board with a ruler and yells at the class to settle down. He is then abused with more vile language and has a book – the history textbook we're working on in class at the moment – thrown at him. He catches it and sets it down with a loud thump on the desk in front of him, the look on his face one of pure devastation.

'What's going on?' I ask out loud.

Lorian's head moves just slightly and the image switches to the town mall, where the Angel Fall's Café is being robbed by an armed man, the patrons terrorised with the threat of a gun. The proprietor, Mr McGowan, hands over money from his till in a grey bag with shaking hands. The robber strikes him with the butt of his gun, before racing outside to a waiting car. And the worst part about this scene is the fact that I recognise this thief. He lives in my neighbourhood, someone I thought to be a loving family man, struggling to raise his young family.

Again I have to ask, 'What's happening? How can this be? I know these people.'

'This is your world now.'

'What? But how can it change so quickly? We were only gone ten days.'

'The war has escalated. The situation is serious. The Prophecy has changed, predicting a disastrous outcome. We are at the brink of losing complete control and any chance of attaining peace for all the worlds.'

The image of my home town disappears and Lorian comes to stand before me. I can't help but think this is all my fault. By leaving Veridian vulnerable for ten whole days, the Goddess has taken the advantage and stepped up her campaign. And obviously she's winning. Tears hit the back of my eyes, which I'm helpless to do anything about. They begin streaming down my face.

With fingers longer than normal, Lorian touches the underside of my chin, urging me to look up. I'm reluctant to do so, as the power that emanates from the single touch of these fingers makes me want to run. But the pressure of Lorian's hand intensifies and I understand this is not a request, but a command. I've broken one of those already, so I take a deep breath and lift my head.

Intense violet eyes stare back at me, holding me in position. Lorian's stare is harsh, and it pains me to maintain it. 'Do you think I make decisions lightly, Isabel?'

My head shakes a no, then slowly I work moisture into my mouth and reply verbally, 'No, of course not.'

'Do you have anything you wish to say?'

'Yes, I do.' And somehow I try to explain, 'I'm really sorry. In rescuing Arkarian I never meant to cause such devastation. But ...'

'But?'

I take a deep breath. 'I'd do it all again, taking more risks if I had to, to bring Arkarian back.'

The whole room goes deathly silent. Then Lorian says, 'Isabel, who do you think opened the rift?'

What does Lorian mean? As far as I know the rift was opened by … But I don't want to even think these names in case it incriminates one or all three of the royals.

But screening my thoughts is useless, as Lorian is aware of every one of them. 'Only an Immortal can open the rift, Isabel, or a descendant with immortal powers.'

'*Arkarian!*' I whisper, knowing in my heart all along, Arkarian must be Lorian's son! But does this mean Lorian *wanted* me to rescue Arkarian?

Lorian answers without my having to voice this question out loud. 'Isabel, understand this – Arkarian is *vital* to our survival and success against the forces of chaos. There was never any doubt about launching a rescue. It was always going to happen. The only question was who was strong enough to undergo the challenges of the underworld. So I devised a test, which you passed, brilliantly. And I was comforted that Ethan planned to go with you. What did surprise me though,' and here Lorian glances to the side to Matt, 'was your brother's intention to join you both. That was the only glitch to the plan, although Lady Arabella realised at the very end, but was helpless to do anything except provide him with warmth.'

The Immortal's words render me speechless. It wasn't true that Lorian didn't want to rescue Arkarian! It was all a test to find the strongest person. Someone with enough determination to get through the challenges and hardships Lorian knew would have to be overcome in that place.

I grip the stool to keep from falling backwards.

'Therefore,' Lorian continues, stepping slightly backwards and giving me some much-needed breathing space, 'you are exonerated of breaching my command. In fact, you are to be commended for your success and unfailing courage.'

The room explodes in cheering. My eyes search for Arkarian, and a bitter-sweet joy fills me. I'm going to be free, yet what is this freedom if Arkarian doesn't want to be in my life? To see him only when he has to explain a mission will be torture.

'There is just one more issue that must be dealt with here today, before you are returned to your homes,' Lorian says, then looks across the room to Arkarian. 'Come and stand within the Circle, Arkarian.'

As he does, Lorian explains to the entire room, 'Earlier Arkarian came to see me with two requests. The first – which I wouldn't discuss with him – was to plea for Isabel's freedom. But the second, the second not only surprised me, but shook me deeply. So deeply that I feel compelled to act on it.'

Murmurs erupt around the room. Beside me Arkarian slips his hand in mine, but otherwise remains motionless before his father.

Lorian says, 'So that he could live in the same world as the girl that he loves, Arkarian asked me to strip him of his power to stop ageing.'

The murmurs reach loud proportions. But I don't take in any of this. My entire body is shaking with Lorian's revelation. Arkarian wants his power to stop ageing stripped. And he wants to do this so he can be with me. Unable to stop myself from trembling, I look up at him. 'You would do this for me?'

'And more,' he says simply.

Now I understand why Arkarian has been keeping himself at arm's length from me. His ability to stop ageing puts us in different worlds. And while I respect that Arkarian can make his own decisions, this one is just too much to make on his own. 'Arkarian, I can't let you do this. It wouldn't be right.'

Lorian raises both hands, and the Tribunal and surrounding crowd go quiet. Lorian stares down at the two of us standing side by side. 'Isabel, I agree with you.'

'But—'

Lorian dismisses Arkarian's argument before it even has a chance to get started. 'And so I have decided to empower Isabel with this same skill.'

'What!' I can't help call out.

Lorian asks, 'Is this what you wish, Isabel? Answer carefully.'

My eyes skim around the room. To become ageless? That would be a dream! But to watch my friends and family grow old and die, how would I cope with that? Arkarian shifts into my vision, his violet eyes shimmering and reflecting their love; and I know that I could handle anything as long as we're together. I search for Ethan and Matt. Ethan has a frown between his brows, while Matt's mouth is hanging open.

Lorian holds his hand out towards them. 'Go and talk to them.'

Leaving Arkarian in the Circle I go to where Ethan and Matt are standing. For a minute we don't say anything. Finally Ethan starts nodding. 'I think you should do it. It's too amazing to pass up.'

'But I will miss you so much.'

'I still think it's the right thing. If it were me, I would do it.'

Ethan's words are heartening. I turn slowly to Matt. He has trouble meeting my eyes. Finally he says, 'Do you love him?'

'Yes.'

He starts to nod. 'Then you should do it.'

'Are you sure?'

He hesitates, but then his answer is decisive. 'I'm sure.'

I give them both a hug and return to the centre of the circle. Arkarian reaches for my hand and I give it a firm squeeze, then look up at Lorian. 'My lord, I accept your generous offer.'

And with these words Lorian lowers both hands to my head. Light surges from them, covering me like a warm liquid cloak. For several moments I am blinded, my entire body shuddering and jerking with the power of the Immortal's gift driving through me. When it is over, and Lorian's hands withdraw, I fall backwards to the stool.

'Are you all right?' Arkarian asks me.

'Perfectly,' I reply, though I don't feel any different really.

'It takes time,' he says. 'You have two years to get used to the idea. It won't begin to take effect until you turn eighteen.'

Lorian picks up on Arkarian's mention of the word time and gives it a different meaning. With hands spread wide, silence descends, and to everyone assembled in the Chamber the Immortal says, 'Go now and fulfil your duties to the Guard. Time is of the essence. Our most difficult challenges are about to unfold. Remember always that a traitor walks amongst us. And do not despair when my sister unleashes unspeakable horrors on our earthly world.'

Book Three in THE GUARDIANS OF TIME TRILOGY

the Key

An ancient evil. A battle for all time.

Marianne
Curley

The battle between the Guardians of Time
and the Order of Chaos sweeps toward its
thrilling conclusion in . . . THE KEY

Prologue

They agree to meet in an abandoned monastery at the top of an ancient monolith of rock and cliff in Athos. Lathenia, known as the Goddess of Chaos since her quest for domination began, is first to arrive. She is accompanied by her loyal soldier Marduke and trusted magician Keziah. The rules are simple: bring no arms and only two allies. Instigated by Lorian, this meeting is for peace, for brother and sister to come to an agreement and stop the prophesied final battle from destroying life as it is known on the earth.

The night is black. A blizzard roars through the gorges. Lorian appears at the foot of the monolith, trailed by Tribunal members Lord Penbarin and Lady Arabella, and a third figure.

Swathed in thick warm cloaks the Immortal and his party trudge up the two hundred and seventy-two slippery steps of icy rock, one after another.

Lord Penbarin steps hurriedly but carefully to catch up with Lorian. 'I can't help but suspect, my liege, that there is more to this meeting with your sister than you have allowed us to believe.' His eyes shift purposefully to the third member of their party.

Lorian halts. All three behind him stop and look up.

'And you, Lord Penbarin, are far too cynical as usual.'

Lord Penbarin scoffs, though gently, for he knows Lorian speaks the truth.

As the wind drives the shifting snow even harder, Lorian's eyes momentarily drift past Lord Penbarin's shoulder to the third member of his party. He gives an acknowledging nod and a wry smile.

'Will the meeting take long, my lord?' Lady Arabella asks.

Lorian's gaze shifts sideways to the lady, and even while her face remains almost completely concealed beneath the shadow of her deep hood, the Immortal finds it difficult to drag his eyes from her. She lifts her head to meet his gaze and Lorian wonders for the millionth time in a thousand years how he has the strength to maintain his determination to remain genderless. He is tiring of the task; he has made many sacrifices for the sake of unbiased and unprejudiced rule.

Finally they stand before the monastery door. Made of cypress wood, centuries of neglect have seen it reduce to a few dark and rotting boards. It creaks open. A flurry of servants, hired especially for the occasion, usher the esteemed party within. Once inside, warm air washes over them. Only Lorian, unaffected by either cold or heat, seems indifferent to the change.

To their left a sweeping staircase of stone bricks raises their eyes to the upper level. It is there Lathenia stands watching. Lorian nods in her direction. Their minds meet and clash, and a rough greeting of sorts follows. She descends, her white gown trailing on the steps behind her, the purple sash at her waist defining her narrow figure, while long fingers slide elegantly down the banister railing.

Behind her Marduke and Keziah keep a suitable distance. Their Mistress is the focus, the reason for this meeting. They are, after all, only her humble servants, as she is apt to remind them.

'Brother,' she says as she comes and stands before Lorian. 'Or … being neither male nor female, is there another term by which I should call you?' With these words she glances briefly at Lady Arabella, but the action is so swift and fleeting none in the room perceives it.

Sounding irritated and slightly bored, Lorian lifts a hand in a brief dismissive gesture. 'As you so obviously have difficulty grasping the concept of impartiality due to gender, you may refer to me in the masculine as I have allowed others to do for their own comfort.'

'What a pity,' she sniggers. 'I could have enjoyed calling you … *It*.'

Lorian stares deeply into her eyes. Lathenia is first to glance away, her gaze coming to rest first on Lord Penbarin and then briefly on Lady Arabella. Although it's impossible not to notice her brother has brought a third party, she ignores the uninvited guest's presence – for now. 'It has been a while, my lord and lady.'

'How unfortunate that we have to meet at all,' Lord Penbarin says in a mocking tone.

Lathenia's shoulders lift, the only indication that the insult penetrated. Her face remains a stoic mask of indifference. She allows her gaze purposefully to single out her brother's third supporter. As if commanded, the cloaked figure steps forward. Piercing blue eyes are the first things she notices. A shiver begins at the tip of her spine and slithers along every vertebrae as she inhales a sense of the importance of the man standing before her. A Tribunal member for sure. But not one she recognises. She pins her cold gaze on her brother, trying hard to conceal her surprise and interest, but fails.

'We agreed on only two allies! Who is this *intruder*?'

Lorian acknowledges his sister's reaction, keeping his sense of gratification well hidden. It is exactly as he hoped. He motions the cloaked figure forward. 'Allow me to introduce the former King Richard II of England.' Lorian waits while his sister absorbs this much first. Then, 'He is now the new King Richard … of *Veridian*.'

She moves backwards. 'Veridian has a *king*?' A slender hand lifts to hover above her breastbone.

Lorian doesn't say a word. He doesn't need to. All those present understand that now Veridian has its King, the Tribunal will be complete, and the power of the Guard will be stronger than ever before.

'My lady.' King Richard bows deeply before the stricken goddess. 'I am … *intrigued* to meet you. I look forward to further acquaintance.'

Their eyes hold for indefinable seconds while Lathenia takes a moment to regather her thoughts. King Richard has affected her on many levels. Lorian gloats inwardly, while Marduke, fully aware of his Mistress's sudden interest in this stranger, makes a snorting, grunting sound through nostrils that resemble a pig's snout. Physically altered from his earlier experience in the middle realm, Marduke has fallen out of favour with Lathenia.

The sound of Marduke's displeasure is enough to jolt Lathenia's senses, though it is with an effort that she drags her emotions away from sudden public scrutiny. She sighs, appearing disinterested. 'We shall see, my lord.' Abruptly she lifts her gaze and stalks off towards an open doorway, leaving behind a tense, suffocating atmosphere.

The servants show the Tribunal members to a large room of stone bricks lit with hundreds of glowing candles. In the centre stands a table made entirely of crystal with seven matching stools brought here from Lathenia's own palace especially for the occasion.

Lorian notices the seven stools but says nothing. Surely she couldn't have known about King Richard! But then nothing his sister does should surprise him now.

All seven sit around the table, Lathenia and Lorian opposite each other. For a long moment there is silence and King Richard, being a recent addition to the Tribunal, wonders whether they are communicating without his knowledge, something he understands to be quite possible. He rather hopes they aren't. It would be enormously arrogant on their part. After all, what else are the rest of them doing here if not bearing witness to these proceedings?

Lorian glares in his direction. Instantly King Richard regrets his outspoken thoughts. But Lorian's stare soon softens and he gives an almost imperceptible nod. 'You are quite right, my lord.'

King Richard grunts a soft acknowledgement, vowing to keep his thoughts under a tighter rein from now on. He still has much to learn.

'What I was thinking,' Lorian continues to address King Richard, 'is what my parents would say if they were alive today.'

'Bah!' Lathenia waves a hand into the air. 'While I was thinking how my brother has grown so melancholy lately. A sign of weakness I find amusing.'

'The fact is, Lathenia, an immortal can only be killed by another immortal.'

Lathenia's silver eyes flash the colour of obsidian while her long fingers slam down on the table top. 'Are you threatening me, brother?'

Lorian appears amused at the dramatic leap his sister makes. Their parents loved and fought so fiercely that they ended by killing each other in a moment of inflamed passion. 'You think I find the deaths of our parents amusing?'

Lathenia remains silent, but something in her silence alerts Lorian's senses. 'What more do you know about our parents' death than I?'

'Nothing. You were there.'

'Yes. I saw each holding a blade at the other's throat. But while I walked in after the deed, you were there before me.'

'I walked in only a second before you.'

'A lot can happen in a second of immortal time,' he says accusingly.

Lathenia takes the defensive and quickly changes the subject. 'Listen to *you*. When it is *I* who should be asking questions. Questions about our brother. You are more devious than you would have your supporters think.' She stares at each of the Tribunal members in turn. 'You don't really know him. He's not the honourable Lorian you trust. He murdered our own brother!' She turns her gaze to Lorian. 'Dartemis was no threat to you. *I* was the threat! So why did you destroy an innocent child?'

Lorian recalls how Dartemis was never an 'innocent child', but the youngest and most powerful of the three siblings. He'd had to take his brother to another world for the boy's own safety. A world where he remains very much alive today. A world where even his greedy sister cannot detect life. And it is there he will remain, continuing to harness his powers – a lord, a magician and much more.

Lorian remembers the day he saw his brother working magic – such powerful and unusual magic. He knew then that with Dartemis's talents at her fingertips, Lathenia would become too strong.

But for now there are other matters more pressing – the resolution of this conflict, without war.

Allowing this last thought to penetrate all minds in the room, everyone's attention is quickly refocused. Lathenia scoffs at the thought. 'What is happening to you? You are more melancholy than I thought. If I didn't know better, I'd say you have allowed yourself to fall in love.'

Her words anger him. 'I am not so foolish as to allow the very notion of love to interfere with my judgement!'

A quiet descends, where Lathenia finds she has to struggle with the urge to look upon Lady Arabella's face.

Stirring emotions circle the room. Lady Arabella dares not lift her eyes and takes to scrutinising the ice-blue veins that reveal themselves beneath the pale skin of her hands, while Lord Penbarin stares across the table as if seeing his fellow Tribunal member for the first time.

It is Marduke's rough, guttural voice that penetrates and dispels the atmosphere. 'This meeting is a waste of time. Nothing will be resolved here. Nothing is ever resolved without war. It is the way of the universe.'

Lorian asks, 'Does Marduke speak the truth, sister? Is there no hope for peace between us?'

Lathenia stares pointedly at her brother. 'There can

only be peace when there is justice, for you rule by default.'

'Need I remind you that of the three of us, I was born first.'

'So you claim,' Lathenia argues. 'But it should have been me!'

With eyes as fiery as coals Lathenia leaps from her stool, her body upright and rigid with rage. 'Marduke is right. This meeting is pointless. Only force will give me justice. Control of all the realms should be mine, and I will have it!'

Calmly, Lorian replies, 'Sister, neither of us controls the realms. The humans govern themselves. They have free will and choose their own destiny. For as long as they are mortal we are only their caretakers.'

'That will change.'

Lorian's shoulders stiffen and he too rises. Around the room all eyes move from one angry god to the other.

'You cannot change what must be,' Lorian hisses. 'Marduke speaks of the way of the universe, but I speak of the way of life.'

'It is my ambition to combine the realms,' Lathenia explains. 'And I will succeed.'

'But that would be disastrous.' Lorian is aghast. 'The humans would … alter. Their very existence would be in danger of domination from the soulless. The inconceivable will become reality, and over time the line between mortality and death will blur.'

It is in her silence that Lorian understands the depth of his sister's determination. And for the first time in his long life the makings of real fear flutter within. It quickly turns to anger. In a whisper-soft voice that has the hairs prickle on the back of Lord Penbarin's neck, Lorian says, 'You cannot do this.'

'Don't lecture me, Lorian.' Lathenia raises her hand, pointing one long finger directly at the narrow opening in the ceiling. 'This is what I think of your peacemaking.'

The ceiling begins to peel away. Great chunks of rock and brick jettison into the sky. With another wave of her hand the ceiling completely disappears into the raging blizzard.

'What are you doing?' Lorian asks, his violet eyes flashing with concern.

Lathenia doesn't answer. Instead she angles her face up towards the blizzard. In a flash of lightning and resounding thunder, the thick clouds swirl and begin to scatter. In seconds the blizzard blows away, revealing a night sky sparkling with clarity and millions of stars.

But Lathenia is hardly finished, and Lorian knows it. His eyes remain riveted to the brilliant night sky. An explosion of light, followed by a hiss, quickly grows into an ear-piercing whistle. It has the mortals diving to the floor a second before the descending chunk of rock explodes above their heads.

Lady Arabella screams and joins King Richard further beneath the table.

Lorian doesn't move, but the power radiating from him is tangible in what's left of the exposed room at the top of the cliff. His eyes shift upwards, centring on a blue star vivid in the distant sky.

'Uh-oh,' Lord Penbarin remarks. 'Keep down and out of the way. This could get interes—'

Before he finishes, a blazing light starts hurtling towards them, accompanied by a high-pitched whining sound that near deafens the Tribunal members. The star shatters in the atmosphere, showering the room in heat and light and burning debris.

Servants pour out of the monastery, covering their ears and whimpering about the heavens falling. Like ants they run from the cliff as fast and as far away as possible.

Within minutes the earth is showered with the most brilliant meteor display ever witnessed by human eyes. One explodes so close that the entire monolith shakes and the walls of the monastery crumble on one side. Lorian stares at his sister in disgust. 'Do you respect no life but your own?'

She shrugs.

Another meteor careers almost horizontally across the sky to crash into some far distant land.

'That was Angel Falls!' Lorian glares at his sister.

'Really? Are you scared of losing a few soldiers?'

'Have you no thought for your own soldiers who live there?'

'I can risk a few to see the death of your elite.'

Lorian stares at her in silence for a moment. Disgusted. 'You go too far.'

'Know this, brother, I will always go one further than you.'

He pauses, and all those cowering beneath the table emerge just enough to see what he plans next. Without moving, Lorian closes his eyes. Lady Arabella peers across the table to Lord Penbarin. She has never seen her liege look so focused, or so angry. Lord Penbarin gives a light shrug, then watches as his Lord and Master begins to glow from the inside out, then slowly starts to shake.

Lathenia's eyes shift to Keziah, her aged but trusted Magician. Even Keziah, who has lived a long time, has never seen anything like this before. He shakes his head. 'I know not, Your Highness.'

'Brother?' she says. 'What are you up to?'

Finally the light from Lorian's body begins to dull, his shaking slows and he sags. It becomes obvious that whatever he was doing, is over. Some look to the sky, but Lord Penbarin keeps his eyes firmly on his Lord. Slowly Lorian becomes aware of where he is. He opens his eyes and finds those of Lord Penbarin. Through his mind he shows him what he has done and Lord Penbarin lunges for breath. He wonders fleetingly what it has cost his liege, but it is done now – there are only the consequences to follow.

Lady Arabella looks to Lord Penbarin for answers. In fear the Goddess will hear him, he sends her only a single thread of thought ... *The Named.*

Marianne Curley

was born in Windsor, New South Wales, Australia. When her family moved to a small farm on the outskirts of Sydney, with no close neighbors, Marianne soon discovered her love of books—and became a school librarian at the age of nine.

Marianne has three teenage children, whose conversations and experiences inspire her writing.

Read the Guardians of Time trilogy
from the beginning

What if you could protect the future
by traveling into the past?

Ethan and his apprentice, Isabel, live secret lives as two of the Named. The only defense against the evil Order of Chaos, they travel through time to prevent the Order from altering history and gaining power over the world. As the threat from the Order intensifies, secrets of the past are revealed and villains and heroes exposed. But who will win the ultimate battle between good and evil?

"Swashbuckling time-travel plus soap-opera relationships make for a page-turning start to a promised trilogy. . . . An ongoing guilty pleasure." —*Kirkus Reviews*

"Magic blooms in Angel Falls, the setting of this promising launch to Curley's time travel trilogy." —*Publishers Weekly*